# STARSHIP FOR RENT 3

## STARSHIP FOR RENT
### BOOK 3

## M.R. FORBES

sly under his breath. Then again, what
ve to worry? He wasn't the fish out of
sticking with us wasn't totally magnani-
get free room and board out of the deal,
ing more quark down the road.

al way to look at the engineer who had
rescue Nyree, escape Cacitrum, and block
Head Case's Primary Control Systems,
im out of the location of his forgotten star-
gone from the highs of surviving the arena
ving control of our fate once more torn out
is new imposition felt like another nail in
ing our hopes of escape from Warexia.

learly intended to delay our exploration of
us space station and the disabled Warden-
e for as long as possible. We couldn't wait
s to follow that slim lead. Not with Ben's
eping through his system and with every
rying Alyssa and Tyler further from their

ismay, some small part of me understood
otivations and accepted them, at least in
here for his exclusive use and amusement,
oiled child unwilling to share his favorite
n't have us, then no one could. Allowing us
t assigning us a new task to keep us under
atened his ego and gave us control he
quish. After all, why would he let us go
ess of getting home when he could send us
harder tasks to make certain that our only
his self-centered purposes?

going to let us go, is he?" Tyler asked,
king the same thing.
lied with certainty. "But that doesn't mean
e."

# CHAPTER 1

"How many credits for this Warden plush?" Alyssa asked
the bored Hemid behind the Asterock Arena's Treasure
Room counter. She was clutching a lifesize plush of the
Warexia System's…leader? Protector? God? Nearly two
months in, I still had no idea what kind of entity the
Warden thought of himself as being. Probably all of the
above.

We'd found the large plush at the treasure room's
entrance, standing at the front of several rows of identical
stuffed toys, each row decreasing in size. While all the other
plushes were marked with how many credits or quark were
needed to take one home, the big boy clutched in Ally's
arms lacked a tag.

"Nine hundred fifty thousand quark," the checkout girl
replied. Seeing an ILF rather than a bot handling the
register had been a pleasant surprise.

"We'll take it," Lantz said before rattling off each of our
Arena identifiers for payment. The cashier entered everything too slowly, leaving me fidgeting while we waited to
get out of there and back to Head Case with our news.

"Hey, check this out," Tyler said, holding up one of the

impulse items. It looked like a Warden bottle opener.

"Is there anything in here that doesn't have the Warden on it?" I asked, surveying the rest of the treasure room. The large space felt cramped with all the cheap crap stuffed onto every available shelf.

"There's some Arena branded stuff in the back," the cashier replied. "If I were you, I would save my credits for mods. But that's just me."

"It's tempting," I admitted. "But we might never have a chance to cash out or use the mods."

"We'll take this too," Tee said, passing her the bottle opener.

"What do you want that for?" Ally asked. "Asshole can make you a bottle opener that doesn't have an asshole on it."

"It's a souvenir. To remind me of all this once we get home."

"You want to be reminded? Of this...?" Her opinion of the Warden was evident in her derogatory expression.

"I probably will one day."

Finishing the checkout, the woman turned the plush onto its side and disintegrated the security tag on the bottom with a laser device. "A million credits," she said. "How long did it take you to get that many?"

"One match," Tyler replied with an arrogant grin.

Her face registered surprise. "You four earned a million credits in one match?"

"Why is that so hard to believe?" Ally asked.

"It's not easy for anyone to score that high. Plus, there's no history for you in the treasure room database, so this must have been your first match."

"Our one and only match," I confirmed with a shrug. "Beginner's luck...maybe."

"Like hell," Tee complained, raising and shaking his flesh and blood rocket fist.

She handed
Enjoy."

Ally stole
will," she replie

We hurried
tion I'd felt only
anger. It churn
unwelcome intr
morphed into jo
purchased effig
return to Head
task the Warde
delayed our chan

The crowds a
tered as we retra
oid's transit hu
endlessly analyz
next tram bound
Claiming seats ne
short trip betwee
window, my gaze
folding beyond t
failed to inspire t
upon our arrival.

Tyler slumped
braced on his kne
with the cashier i
posture. I knew h
silent fury over o
aimlessly at the ba
lips compressed in
in her arms in a wa
like a hug, but to n
the hell out of the th

As usual, Lantz

whistling tuneles
reason did he ha
water here. And
mous. He would
plus a shot at ear

It was a cyni
helped us almost
the Warden from
thereby locking h
ship. I'd quickly
to the lows of ha
of our hands. Th
the coffin contain

The Warden
Levain's mysteri
ship docked the
weeks or month
cancer again cre
passing day ca
loved ones.

Despite my
the Warden's n
part. Wanting u
he was like a s
toys. If he could
to depart witho
his thumb thr
refused to reli
about our busin
on harder and
outcome served

"He's neve
apparently thin

"No," I rep
we won't escap

"I wish I shared your optimistic view, man."

"We all need to hold onto our belief that we will get home. It's the only chance we have of beating the Warden at his own game."

"Seems like our puppet master has managed to light a fire under your tail," he grinned.

"He may be your puppet master," I answered. "He's not mine."

Tee held up his fist. "Yeah. I'm not so sure this is worth the cost anymore."

"Not so sure? You should be pretty damn convinced, one way or the other."

"I know but…it's just so cool."

I sighed, unable to hide a laugh as Tee chuckled beside me. Ally glanced over, and I pantomimed her grip on the plush, pretending I was the Warden being asphyxiated. That got a smile from her, too.

The tram eased into central docking, and we shuffled out with the other departing passengers, pushing through the incoming traffic to get back to Head Case. Once clear, we ran into Goloron's engineer, Manat, pushing a hover cart stacked with crates in Head Case's general direction.

"Hey, Manat," Lantz said as we caught up to him. "What do you have in the boxes?"

"Replacement comms equipment," he replied. "Crystals, power converters, the new antenna array. You know, both Twama and Meg were upset with your departure, since you have the most experience working with both software stacks."

"Only when Meg translates for me," Lantz replied. "I don't speak English."

It felt weird to hear him say he didn't speak English and hear it in perfect English. The amusement in Tee's expression told me he felt the same. Not everything the Warden did sucked. Even his task didn't really suck. It just forced us to do something he could easily do himself to further his own selfish goals.

"Anyway," Lantz continued, "It's going to cost you. I didn't plan to stay on Head Case for much longer." He cast me a side-eyed wink. Manat didn't know Lantz had already decided to stay on board and help us or that it wasn't our quark he aimed to earn on this one but Goloran's.

"You'll have to take that up with Twama."

"You can be sure I will."

"We'll see you onboard," I said, eager to pick up the pace.

We hurried the rest of the way back to Head Case to share the Warden's latest request with Ben and Matt. After leaving the Warden plush in the hangar, we burst onto the flight deck. My gaze immediately switched to the hole Twama and her crew had created where our original comms station had been only a couple of hours earlier. Wires and fiber optic lines spilled everywhere, and consoles were dismantled and pushed aside to make room for the installation of workstations.

Twana and Koti glanced up, nonplussed by our abrupt entrance before returning attention to their tasks. Ben and Matt conversed with Leo in the stadium seating over-looking the front of the flight deck. Shaq rested on the arm of the chair behind them.

"Ben, Matt!" I shouted to get their attention.

Concern creased Ben's brow as he looked back over his shoulder. "What's wrong, Noah?" he asked, noticing some-thing hinting at trouble in my expression.

"We need to talk. Right away."

"You all look like you've seen a ghost," Rising slowly, Ben motioned us to the last row of seats against the compartment's rear bulkhead.

"It's worse than seeing a ghost," I said as we all gathered in a seated huddle. "And you're not going to like it."

# CHAPTER 2

In a hushed tone, I quickly recounted everything about our bizarre encounter with the Warden, including his insistence that we eliminate Markan and dismantle the smuggler's organization.

Ben's expression darkened with the more details I shared, his jaw visibly tightening. "That son of a bitch!" he finally spat. "Does he really expect us to just roll over and do whatever he demands every time we turn around ?"

"Pretty much," Ally murmured. "He threatened to hurt us if we don't comply."

"Yeah, no kidding!" Tyler snorted. "Fried me good with that freaky shock collar!" He rubbed reflexively at the fading electrical burns circling his neck. "Word of advice. If you ever try out the arena, *do not* go with Level Five."

"What are you talking about, Tee?" Matt asked.

"Don't forget the part where he admitted he orchestrated the deaths of everyone who knew how to travel back to Earth and used us to do it," I added before Tyler could answer Matt's question. "He's enjoying this way too much."

Ben put a hand to his head, mulling over everything we

had just revealed. "Lantz, you may not know the answer, but hypothetically, do you think it would be possible to remove the Warden's pill from our bodies?"

"I'm sure the Warden's considered that angle," Matt said.

"Hypothetically," Ben repeated.

Lantz shrugged. "I don't see why not. Unless…"

"Unless what?" Leo pressed.

"Well, from what I understand the pill's served multiple purposes since the Warden forced you to swallow it. Not only alteration, like Tyler's hand, but also automation and mental manipulation, like Ally's sharpshooter aim. I guess you could count the whole boon thing in there too, whatever else he…*rewards* you with. Then there's your ability to speak, understand, and to a lesser extent read Wardenian, Hemidian, Gothorian, and I'm sure any other language in the galaxy."

"Not to mention the Warden's ability to use the pill to prod us like cattle," Tyler added. "Wardenian is seriously a language?"

"I'm sure it's the most common language in Warexia," Ally said.

"That's right," Lantz confirmed.

"Or the Warden's ability to poison us," Matt said. "Unless that falls under genetic mutation. If he can make Tee's fist turn to metal and detach from his wrist, I'm sure he can make our bodies poison themselves."

"That's so messed up," Leo said. "Unless what?"

"There's a chance the pill isn't just sitting in your body with nanowires and electrodes poking into your nerve endings," Lantz continued. "If it contained nanites, it's likely embedded into every part of your nervous system."

"Nanites?" I asked. "You mean nanobots? Molecular machines?"

"Exactly."

"You have that here?" The technology impressed me. The Warden's use of it, not so much.

"It's still experimental. Or rather, to anyone not the Warden it's still experimental. He might already possess the finished tech. Emphasis on *might*."

"Is there a way to tell?" Ben asked.

"If you have an advanced enough scanner to see if the pill is there, then yes. If you can find the pill, then you don't have nanites. If you can't..." He trailed off.

"Let's say we do," Tyler said. "How would we get rid of them?"

"We can't," I said. "They're probably attached to individual cells. Killing the nanite would kill the cell. To kill enough nanites to make a difference would probably kill you."

"Oh," Tyler replied, face falling. "Damn. On the bright side, does that make us cyborgs?"

"Technically, I guess it does," I answered. "But you were already a cyborg with your rocket fist."

"I never thought about it that way."

"I know what you were thinking, Captain," Lantz said. "It's not a bad idea, but it's impractical, bordering on impossible."

"Well, we're pretty desperate," Ben replied.

"And getting more desperate by the day," I added, aware that Lantz didn't know about Ben's cancer.

"I hate to say it, but I think your best bet is to do what the Warden wants. Take down Markan, then go to Levain's station."

"Come on, Lantzy," Leo said. "We all know that if we manage to complete the task, he'll give us another one the moment we go for the station again."

"On the contrary," Lantz said. "He'll try. But he needs to be able to contact you to do it."

"That's right," I agreed. "Lantz's upgrades to system

security blocked him out of Head Case, at least for now. If we keep away from anything he can use to push a signal through, then he can't give us a new assignment."

"He won't like that," Ally said.

"Actually, I think he'll appreciate it if we can pull it off," I countered.

"What about this?" Tyler asked, closing the middle fingers of his right hand to make the 'call me' gesture.

"What's that?" Matt asked.

"The Warden gave us an enhancement," I said, copying the gesture and thinking of Matt.

"What the…?" he said, muscles quivering as he tried to stop himself from repeating the gesture.

"Hey, Matt," I said into my pinkie.

"You have to be kidding me," Matt replied, his voice audible both from his lips and through my thumb.

"Bye, Matt," I added, lowering my hand. He yanked his into a fist as soon as he was able.

"If he can do that, how can we cut him off from contacting us?" Leo asked.

"We have no proof that he can eavesdrop on those weird comms," Lantz said.

"We have no proof that he can't, either," Ben pointed out.

"We have time," Lantz said. "If we can isolate the signal, we might be able to prove the transmission one way or another, and even if the comms signals are transmitting out, if we can see them, then we can block them."

Ben considered before nodding. "It's the only idea we have so far, so I'll take it." He paused, sighing. "I guess this means we need to bite the bullet on this one and do what the Warden wants."

"Hopefully for the second and last time," I said.

"Okay," Ben agreed, rising to his feet. "I need to let

# CHAPTER 1

"How many credits for this Warden plush?" Alyssa asked the bored Hemid behind the Asterock Arena's Treasure Room counter. She was clutching a lifesize plush of the Warexia System's...leader? Protector? God? Nearly two months in, I still had no idea what kind of entity the Warden thought of himself as being. Probably all of the above.

We'd found the large plush at the treasure room's entrance, standing at the front of several rows of identical stuffed toys, each row decreasing in size. While all the other plushes were marked with how many credits or quark were needed to take one home, the big boy clutched in Ally's arms lacked a tag.

"Nine hundred fifty thousand quark," the checkout girl replied. Seeing an ILF rather than a bot handling the register had been a pleasant surprise.

"We'll take it," Lantz said before rattling off each of our Arena identifiers for payment. The cashier entered everything too slowly, leaving me fidgeting while we waited to get out of there and back to Head Case with our news.

"Hey, check this out," Tyler said, holding up one of the

impulse items. It looked like a Warden bottle opener.

"Is there anything in here that doesn't have the Warden on it?" I asked, surveying the rest of the treasure room. The large space felt cramped with all the cheap crap stuffed onto every available shelf.

"There's some Arena branded stuff in the back," the cashier replied. "If I were you, I would save my credits for mods. But that's just me."

"It's tempting," I admitted. "But we might never have a chance to cash out or use the mods."

"We'll take this too," Tee said, passing her the bottle opener.

"What do you want that for?" Ally asked. "Asshole can make you a bottle opener that doesn't have an asshole on it."

"It's a souvenir. To remind me of all this once we get home."

"You want to be reminded? Of this...?" Her opinion of the Warden was evident in her derogatory expression.

"I probably will one day."

Finishing the checkout, the woman turned the plush onto its side and disintegrated the security tag on the bottom with a laser device. "A million credits," she said. "How long did it take you to get that many?"

"One match," Tyler replied with an arrogant grin.

Her face registered surprise. "You four earned a million credits in one match?"

"Why is that so hard to believe?" Ally asked.

"It's not easy for anyone to score that high. Plus, there's no history for you in the treasure room database, so this must have been your first match."

"Our one and only match," I confirmed with a shrug. "Beginner's luck...maybe."

"Like hell," Tee complained, raising and shaking his flesh and blood rocket fist.

She handed the plush back to Alyssa. "It's all yours. Enjoy."

Ally stole Tee's more common devilish grin. "Oh, we will," she replied, grinning broadly.

We hurried out of the arena, the wonder and exhilaration I'd felt only minutes before replaced by frustration and anger. It churned in my stomach over the Warden's latest unwelcome intrusion into our lives. Those feelings quickly morphed into joy over the thought of lighting up our newly purchased effigy with blaster fire. But first, we needed to return to Head Case and inform the others about the new task the Warden had bestowed upon us. Again, he'd delayed our chance of finding a way home.

The crowds and garish lights of Asterock barely registered as we retraced our steps to the entertainment asteroid's transit hub. My thoughts spun in restless circles, endlessly analyzing our predicament as we boarded the next tram bound for the station's central docking point. Claiming seats near the rear, we spoke very little during the short trip between asteroids. I leaned wearily against my window, my gaze locked on the spectacle of ships and scaffolding beyond the transparent tube. Somehow, the view failed to inspire the same sense of awe in me now as it had upon our arrival.

Tyler slumped on the padded bench beside me, elbows braced on his knees while he brooded. For all his bravado with the cashier in the arena, tension radiated from his posture. I knew him well enough by now to guess at his silent fury over our situation. Meanwhile, Alyssa stared aimlessly at the back of the seat directly in front of her, her lips compressed into a rail-thin line. She hugged the plush in her arms in a way that, to a casual onlooker, might seem like a hug, but to my knowing eyes mimicked her choking the hell out of the thing.

As usual, Lantz seemed the least concerned among us,

whistling tunelessly under his breath. Then again, what reason did he have to worry? He wasn't the fish out of water here. And sticking with us wasn't totally magnanimous. He would get free room and board out of the deal, plus a shot at earning more quark down the road.

It was a cynical way to look at the engineer who had helped us almost rescue Nyree, escape Cacitrum, and block the Warden from Head Case's Primary Control Systems, thereby locking him out of the location of his forgotten starship. I'd quickly gone from the highs of surviving the arena to the lows of having control of our fate once more torn out of our hands. This new imposition felt like another nail in the coffin containing our hopes of escape from Warexia.

The Warden clearly intended to delay our exploration of Levain's mysterious space station and the disabled Wardenship docked there for as long as possible. We couldn't wait weeks or months to follow that slim lead. Not with Ben's cancer again creeping through his system and with every passing day carrying Alyssa and Tyler further from their loved ones.

Despite my dismay, some small part of me understood the Warden's motivations and accepted them, at least in part. Wanting us here for his exclusive use and amusement, he was like a spoiled child unwilling to share his favorite toys. If he couldn't have us, then no one could. Allowing us to depart without assigning us a new task to keep us under his thumb threatened his ego and gave us control he refused to relinquish. After all, why would he let us go about our business of getting home when he could send us on harder and harder tasks to make certain that our only outcome served his self-centered purposes?

"He's never going to let us go, is he?" Tyler asked, apparently thinking the same thing.

"No," I replied with certainty. "But that doesn't mean we won't escape."

"I wish I shared your optimistic view, man."

"We all need to hold onto our belief that we will get home. It's the only chance we have of beating the Warden at his own game."

"Seems like our puppet master has managed to light a fire under your tail," he grinned.

"He may be your puppet master," I answered. "He's not mine."

Tee held up his fist. "Yeah. I'm not so sure this is worth the cost anymore."

"Not so sure? You should be pretty damn convinced, one way or the other."

"I know but…it's just so cool."

I sighed, unable to hide a laugh as Tee chuckled beside me. Ally glanced over, and I pantomimed her grip on the plush, pretending I was the Warden being asphyxiated. That got a smile from her, too.

The tram eased into central docking, and we shuffled out with the other departing passengers, pushing through the incoming traffic to get back to Head Case. Once clear, we ran into Goloron's engineer, Manat, pushing a hover cart stacked with crates in Head Case's general direction.

"Hey, Manat," Lantz said as we caught up to him. "What do you have in the boxes?"

"Replacement comms equipment," he replied. "Crystals, power converters, the new antenna array. You know, both Twama and Meg were upset with your departure, since you have the most experience working with both software stacks."

"Only when Meg translates for me," Lantz replied. "I don't speak English."

It felt weird to hear him say he didn't speak English and hear it in perfect English. The amusement in Tee's expression told me he felt the same. Not everything the Warden did sucked. Even his task didn't really suck. It just forced us to do something he could easily do himself to further his own selfish goals.

"Anyway," Lantz continued, "It's going to cost you. I didn't plan to stay on Head Case for much longer." He cast me a side-eyed wink. Manat didn't know Lantz had already decided to stay on board and help us or that it wasn't our quark he aimed to earn on this one but Goloran's.

"You'll have to take that up with Twama."

"You can be sure I will."

"We'll see you onboard," I said, eager to pick up the pace.

We hurried the rest of the way back to Head Case to share the Warden's latest request with Ben and Matt. After leaving the Warden plush in the hangar, we burst onto the flight deck. My gaze immediately switched to the hole Twama and her crew had created where our original comms station had been only a couple of hours earlier. Wires and fiber optic lines spilled everywhere, and consoles were dismantled and pushed aside to make room for the installation of workstations.

Twana and Koti glanced up, nonplussed by our abrupt entrance before returning attention to their tasks. Ben and Matt conversed with Leo in the stadium seating over-looking the front of the flight deck. Shaq rested on the arm of the chair behind them.

"Ben, Matt!" I shouted to get their attention.

Concern creased Ben's brow as he looked back over his shoulder. "What's wrong, Noah?" he asked, noticing something hinting at trouble in my expression.

"We need to talk. Right away."

"You all look like you've seen a ghost," Rising slowly, Ben motioned us to the last row of seats against the compartment's rear bulkhead.

"It's worse than seeing a ghost," I said as we all gathered in a seated huddle. "And you're not going to like it."

# CHAPTER 2

In a hushed tone, I quickly recounted everything about our bizarre encounter with the Warden, including his insistence that we eliminate Markan and dismantle the smuggler's organization.

Ben's expression darkened with the more details I shared, his jaw visibly tightening. "That son of a bitch!" he finally spat. "Does he really expect us to just roll over and do whatever he demands every time we turn around ?"

"Pretty much," Ally murmured. "He threatened to hurt us if we don't comply."

"Yeah, no kidding!" Tyler snorted. "Fried me good with that freaky shock collar!" He rubbed reflexively at the fading electrical burns circling his neck. "Word of advice. If you ever try out the arena, *do not* go with Level Five."

"What are you talking about, Tee?" Matt asked.

"Don't forget the part where he admitted he orchestrated the deaths of everyone who knew how to travel back to Earth and used us to do it," I added before Tyler could answer Matt's question. "He's enjoying this way too much."

Ben put a hand to his head, mulling over everything we

had just revealed. "Lantz, you may not know the answer, but hypothetically, do you think it would be possible to remove the Warden's pill from our bodies?"

"I'm sure the Warden's considered that angle," Matt said.

"Hypothetically," Ben repeated.

Lantz shrugged. "I don't see why not. Unless…"

"Unless what?" Leo pressed.

"Well, from what I understand the pill's served multiple purposes since the Warden forced you to swallow it. Not only alteration, like Tyler's hand, but also automation and mental manipulation, like Ally's sharpshooter aim. I guess you could count the whole boon thing in there too, whatever else he…*rewards* you with. Then there's your ability to speak, understand, and to a lesser extent read Wardenian, Hemidian, Gothorian, and I'm sure any other language in the galaxy."

"Not to mention the Warden's ability to use the pill to prod us like cattle," Tyler added. "Wardenian is seriously a language?"

"I'm sure it's the most common language in Warexia," Ally said.

"That's right," Lantz confirmed.

"Or the Warden's ability to poison us," Matt said. "Unless that falls under genetic mutation. If he can make Tee's fist turn to metal and detach from his wrist, I'm sure he can make our bodies poison themselves."

"That's so messed up," Leo said. "Unless what?"

"There's a chance the pill isn't just sitting in your body with nanowires and electrodes poking into your nerve endings," Lantz continued. "If it contained nanites, it's likely embedded into every part of your nervous system."

"Nanites?" I asked. "You mean nanobots? Molecular machines?"

"Exactly."

"You have that here?" The technology impressed me. The Warden's use of it, not so much.

"It's still experimental. Or rather, to anyone not the Warden it's still experimental. He might already possess the finished tech. Emphasis on *might*."

"Is there a way to tell?" Ben asked.

"If you have an advanced enough scanner to see if the pill is there, then yes. If you can find the pill, then you don't have nanites. If you can't…" He trailed off.

"Let's say we do," Tyler said. "How would we get rid of them?"

"We can't," I said. "They're probably attached to individual cells. Killing the nanite would kill the cell. To kill enough nanites to make a difference would probably kill you."

"Oh," Tyler replied, face falling. "Damn. On the bright side, does that make us cyborgs?"

"Technically, I guess it does," I answered. "But you were already a cyborg with your rocket fist."

"I never thought about it that way."

"I know what you were thinking, Captain," Lantz said. "It's not a bad idea, but it's impractical, bordering on impossible."

"Well, we're pretty desperate," Ben replied.

"And getting more desperate by the day," I added, aware that Lantz didn't know about Ben's cancer.

"I hate to say it, but I think your best bet is to do what the Warden wants. Take down Markan, then go to Levain's station."

"Come on, Lantzy," Leo said. "We all know that if we manage to complete the task, he'll give us another one the moment we go for the station again."

"On the contrary," Lantz said. "He'll try. But he needs to be able to contact you to do it."

"That's right," I agreed. "Lantz's upgrades to system

security blocked him out of Head Case, at least for now. If we keep away from anything he can use to push a signal through, then he can't give us a new assignment."

"He won't like that," Ally said.

"Actually, I think he'll appreciate it if we can pull it off," I countered.

"What about this?" Tyler asked, closing the middle fingers of his right hand to make the 'call me' gesture.

"What's that?" Matt asked.

"The Warden gave us an enhancement," I said, copying the gesture and thinking of Matt.

"What the…?" he said, muscles quivering as he tried to stop himself from repeating the gesture.

"Hey, Matt," I said into my pinkie.

"You have to be kidding me," Matt replied, his voice audible both from his lips and through my thumb.

"Bye, Matt," I added, lowering my hand. He yanked his into a fist as soon as he was able.

"If he can do that, how can we cut him off from contacting us?" Leo asked.

"We have no proof that he can eavesdrop on those weird comms," Lantz said.

"We have no proof that he can't, either," Ben pointed out.

"We have time," Lantz said. "If we can isolate the signal, we might be able to prove the transmission one way or another, and even if the comms signals are transmitting out, if we can see them, then we can block them."

Ben considered before nodding. "It's the only idea we have so far, so I'll take it." He paused, sighing. "I guess this means we need to bite the bullet on this one and do what the Warden wants."

"Hopefully for the second and last time," I said.

"Okay," Ben agreed, rising to his feet. "I need to let

Goloran know that our trip to Levain's station has been delayed. She's not going to be happy."

"Especially once I tell her how much my retainer rate is," Lantz said.

Ben returned to the command station, dropping into his seat with a hesitant sigh. "Twama, are the communications still online?"

She looked up from the tangle of wires where the comms station had been. "No, Captain. My apologies. You said you wouldn't need them for a while."

"I need to speak to her highness," he explained.

Twama stood and crossed to him, digging into a pocket of her uniform to retrieve her personal comms device, a thin square of glass that floated a holographic projection just over its face. "You may use this."

"Thank you," Ben said, accepting the device. "Princess Goloran, this is Captain Murdock. Do you copy?"

Her cultured voice emerged promptly through the glass. "Captain. I didn't expect to hear from you again so soon. I trust Twama and her team are satisfactory?"

"They're doing a great job so far," Ben said. "This isn't about them. I have some news to share."

Ben offered a concise recap of our plight. The other end of the comms remained silent for nearly a minute after he finished. He opened his mouth to check on the princess when she finally replied.

"This is very unfortunate. And not completely unexpected. I'm sure you've also come to the conclusion that the Warden's reluctance to allow you to reach his ship provides damning evidence that we will find something of value on board."

"Yeah, we were thinking along the same lines."

"If the Warden won't allow you to split your party, I think the solution is rather obvious. While Twama and her team are expert engineers, they aren't cut out for those mission parameters. I can arrange to have a Gothorian Ranger unit at my position within a few days."

"You're suggesting we give you the coordinates to the station and let you see what's inside," Ben said.

"Of course. We've forged a partnership, have we not? We both have a vested interest in the Wardenship's secrets."

"Secrets that you'd have a chance to filter before passing on to us," Matt said from our spot in the cheap seats.

"I have no reason to withhold anything related to your desire to return to your galaxy," she replied.

"That's not the same thing as saying you wouldn't withhold anything from us," Ben pointed out.

"Of course I wouldn't," Goloran insisted unconvincingly.

"My apologies, your highness. But we went through too much to get these coordinates to hand them over to you. We have a plan to visit the station once we've completed our task."

"If you complete your task," Goloran snapped, becoming angry. "While I've never personally heard of a Poto named Markan, I'm confident that if he's managed to slip the Warden, he'll be no easy mark for you."

"We scored a million credits in the arena," Tyler said, "We're not pushovers."

"That may be, but what if you fail in your task? I've already invested a considerable sum of quark into this venture. I have no intention of coming away empty-handed."

"Once your engineers finish the comms upgrade, we'll be able to send you messages from across Warexia, right?" Ben asked.

"Yes."

"If we run into trouble we don't think we can handle, I'll instruct Levi to transmit the exact coordinates to you. I promise you won't come out of this with no return on your investment."

A weighty pause ensued before she replied, a dangerous edge sharpening her words. "I'm becoming increasingly unhappy with this arrangement, Captain."

Ben hesitated, carefully considering his next words.

"Your frustration is completely understandable. Believe me, we feel it too. How about this? I'll have one of my crew provide regular encrypted updates regarding our status as an act of good faith. We'll keep you in the loop on everything we do."

He waited expectantly while the princess mulled over his offer. The silence stretched agonizingly before she finally let loose an irritated huff.

"Very well, Captain. I don't see that I have much of a choice. I can't force the coordinates out of you, and I can't harm you without bringing down the Warden's direct wrath. I have no choice but to sit back and wait." She angrily disconnected the comms.

Beside me, Ally released a shaky breath. "That woman terrifies me."

Tyler grunted. "No joke! Good play getting her majesty to back down, Cap."

Ben exhaled in much the same way that Ally had. "I'm glad that's done."

"What do we do next?" Matt asked.

"The Warden suggested Markan has agents on Asterock," I said. "We need to locate them and find out what they know or perhaps follow them to see where they go and who they contact."

"Princess Goloran said she's never even heard of Markan," Matt replied. "If he does exist and isn't just a time-wasting figment of the Warden's imagination, that means his crew isn't openly advertising their affiliation. How are we supposed to locate them?"

"I have an idea," Lantz remarked. All eyes turned his way expectantly.

"Don't say Hzzt, don't say Hzzt, don't say Hzzt," Ally murmured under her breath.

"For the right price, I'm sure Hzzt can get us pointed in the right direction," he finished.

"Damn it," Ally groaned.

# CHAPTER 3

It didn't take long for Lantz to get in contact with the big-eyed alien. Within the hour, we were seated around a table with Hzzt in what had to be Asterock's cheapest pub. Located deep beneath the station's primary housing planetoid's surface, its smell of tobacco smoke, spilled alcohol and body odor reached us long before we laid eyes on it.

I shifted uncomfortably on a rickety stool, still wrinkling my nose against the place's stale smell. Raucous shouts carried from the bar, where a mix of ILFs slugged back vibrantly colored drinks and placed bets on races and combat bouts flashing across screens overhead.

I flicked uneasy glances between the establishment's questionable patrons and Hzzt, who occupied the seat opposite me. Ever the opportunist, his earlier desire to return to his family vanished quickly once Matt had promised him more quark for his aid. He leaned expectantly forward, waiting for us to explain what we needed.

Clearing his throat against the smoky atmosphere, Ben met his oversized gaze. "We need intel on someone named Markan. Apparently, he runs a smuggling network that's grown too big for the Warden's liking. Ideally, we need to locate potential connections here on Asterock so we can make initial contact, but any information you can dig up will help."

I glanced over at Ben. The ease with which he'd laid out our needs suggested that he'd done this sort of thing before. Probably more than once. Then again, why else would a ship like Head Case need an entire armory full of weapons and armor?

Hzzt's bulbous eyes narrowed. "You don't ask for much, do you, Captain?"

"After your achievements on Cacitrum, I figured you'd handle this kind of task without difficulty."

"You figured incorrectly. It will be no easy task for me to track down the type of individuals you've described. The cost will be…significant."

I managed to avoid visibly cringing. Of course, money was the primary motivator for his cooperation.

Ben seemed nonplussed, ready for that particular response. "I thought you'd say that. As I'm sure you're aware, our funds are running dry."

"Yes, I am very aware. I only agreed to meet you here because Lantz promised me free drinks."

Ally snorted derisively. Both Ben and Hzzt ignored her.

"I was hoping you would consider an IOU," Ben continued. "As you're also aware, we're working with Princess Goloran of Gothor on this. I would rather not hit her up for more quark right now when I can do that later with better results."

"I'm sorry, Captain," Hzzt replied. "I don't offer credit lines or loans. Quark only. Up front."

"Come on, Hzzt," Lantz said. "I'll vouch for them. They're good for the payment. You know that."

"A difficult promise to make, considering the danger involved, both to the payer and the payee. I am sorry, but it is not possible, and nothing will change my mind."

"Thanks for nothing, you slimy little worm," Ally barked in frustration.

Ben glanced over at me, keeping a clean poker face as he spoke. "Noah, do that thing the Warden told you to do if we need to get in touch with him. I'm sure he'd like to know who was responsible for preventing our progress in carrying out his task."

I knew hesitation would destroy the ruse, so I immediately nodded, shifting my hand into the call-me gesture as I slid off my seat and turned my back on Hzzt.

"W...wait!" Hzzt cried. "Give me a moment, please."

I glanced at Ben, who nodded. I lowered my hand and returned to the table.

"I'm certain we can work something out." He tapped spindly fingers against his narrow chin, working through potential options. Finally, his gaze shifted to Lantz. "You received quite a large sum of quark from Princess Goloran for your work breaching Lariv's network. I propose that you forward payment to me and take on the burden of debt yourself."

Lantz's face flushed, eyes dancing from Hzzt to Ben and me. He didn't want to part with his quark any more than Hzzt wanted to go without his upfront payment.

"You said yourself that Ben and Noah are good for the payment," Hzzt added when Lantz hesitated. "Do you not believe this to be true?"

Lantz glared at the wily alien. "You offal of a Nagathi."

"Do not be sore, my friend. You walked right into this counteroffer with your eyes open." He bared his thin teeth in a chittering laugh. "That is my proposal. Either accept it or make another offer."

All eyes turned to Lantz. For a second, I thought he might jump out of his seat and bolt, never to be seen again. Finally, he lowered his head and sighed in resignation. "How much do you want?"

"One hundred thousand now. One hundred thousand when I deliver."

"Two hundred?" Lantz spat, nearly falling out of his chair. "That's almost everything I've got, and I risked a whole lot more than you will to earn it. My best friend died."

"And you collected Tarvik's paystick from his corpse," Hzzt replied. "You think I didn't see it, but I did."

"Is that so?" Matt asked, unsure how he could have managed that with all the plasma bolts landing around us at the time.

Lantz frowned sheepishly. "He was my friend."

"I thought you wanted to help us, man," Tyler said, piling on the guilt.

"You're all Nagathi offal," Lantz cursed, reaching into his pocket and dropping a paystick on the table. "Here. I hope you choke on it, Hzzt."

Hzzt's eyes lit up as he snatched the paystick and made the transfer. His extortion complete, he tossed the paystick back to Lantz and bolted for the exit, nearly bowling over a server in his haste.

"That went well," Tyler quipped. "Thanks for covering us, Lantzy."

"Yeah, thank you, Lantz," Ally added.

We finished the round of thank you's with Lantz glowering the entire time. Finally, he exhaled loudly. "Easy come, easy go, I guess."

"We'll pay you back," Ben said.

"Assuming we survive," Matt amended.

"Look on the bright side," Tyler said. "If we die, you'll probably die too, so it won't matter much."

Lantz chuckled. "I suppose you're right. I probably won't have much chance to spend it for a while, anyway."

"I'm surprised he left in such a rush," Ally said. "I

thought he might stick around to down a few more free bottles of whatever he was drinking before he took off."

"Two hundred thousand quark beats a few cheap free smoothies any day," Lantz answered. "Even for Hzzt, I guess."

We lingered only a few minutes longer at our greasy table, finishing our drinks and paying the tab. After that, we left the pub behind without hesitation, the noise and smell already fading from memory by the time we navigated through twisting station corridors to re-board a waiting tram bound for central docking.

My thoughts wandered as we zoomed among the asteroids, absently watching Lantz point out various sights and attractions to an enthralled Ally. My focus kept circling back to our conversation with the Warden, conscious and subconscious, working together to assemble the puzzle pieces of intel we'd picked up along the way. Some of it probably didn't fit, but certainly some did.

Remembering the way the Warden reacted to my mention of Zariv's interest in chaos energy, there had to be a link between the Warden, Levain's reasoning for sending Jaffie to Earth, the Sigiltech bracelet the two-timing bodyguard had retrieved for Zariv, and our role in snuffing out both crime bosses. I threw my parents' deaths, along with Nyree's, and the dearth of chaos energy in Warexia into the mix as well, since it all seemed at least tangentially relevant. Then I focused on logic to put the pieces together.

I still believed the car crash was an accident, but the more my mind lingered on the data points I'd assembled, the more sharply my mind brought the moments before the impact into focus with meaning. Had Jaffie tried and failed to activate the bracelet, using our car as a test to see if he could erect an invisible shield ahead of his SUV? Had their deaths really boiled down to having been in the wrong place at the wrong time?

The odds that Jaffie and I would reconnect billions of light-years from Earth seemed so minute as to be impossible. Was I here for another reason?

The last question seemed the most ridiculous of all the considerations swirling like an angry maelstrom through my mind. This was no fairytale driven by destiny and fate. I was nothing special. Just a kid from Cedar Rapids with no especially outstanding talents. I was both physically and intellectually average.

Still…there had to be a reason beyond fate that had killed my parents and put me here. I just needed to figure out what it was.

"How long should we give Hzzt to get back to us?" I asked, more to get myself out of my head than anything else.

Lantz shrugged, unworried. "No clue on the timing, but don't worry. The promise of collecting the second half of my quark will motivate him to work as hard and fast as he can."

"I'm surprised he hasn't pinged your comms already," Tee told Lantz. "I can't be the only one here who thinks he's fleecing us. He either already knows Markan's agents or is a couple of well-placed shoutouts away from the answers."

"Of course, he's fleecing us," Lantz replied. "But I don't think it will be as easy for him as you think. He's been to Asterock before, just like I have. This isn't Cacitrum, but he'll come through. It may just take a few days."

"In that case, I don't suppose you want to go another round in the Arena."

Lantz shrugged and smiled. "You know, I just might."

# CHAPTER 4

Almost a week later we still hadn't heard from Hzzt. I'd tried not to worry too much, occupying my time with arena matches and training sessions in the ship's gym. But despite the entertainment distraction doubling as combat experience and welcome muscle gain, I was running out of patience, and I knew I couldn't be the only one. The slippery alien should have made contact about locating Markan's agents by now. His extended silence left me increasingly certain he'd skipped town with the quark. I could only hope Lantz knew where the big-eyed bastard lived.

I found Tyler in his usual spot, the galley, happily snacking on one of his eclectic burger concoctions. Today he'd opted for cheese, bacon, jalapeño peppers, and some purple alien goop I couldn't believe Asshole had in its database that smelled like sour milk and peanut butter. I wrinkled my nose at the mingled scents, my own appetite fading.

Tyler glanced up, blinking in surprise around an enormous mouthful. Clearly I'd interrupted a transcendent culinary moment. Grimacing apologetically, he made a production out of chewing and swallowing before he trusted himself to speak.

"Hey, Noah-san. You're just in time to bask in the glory of my genius! Have you ever tried jurscht?" Grinning, he took another huge bite and chewed with exaggerated relish.

"Is that the stinky purple stuff?" I asked.

"Mmmhmm," he answered with his mouth full.

I rolled my eyes in mock disgust. "As tempting as that sounds, I'm going to pass." I dropped into the seat opposite him. "I can't stop thinking about Hzzt. He should have checked in by now."

Tyler shrugged, unbothered. "Yeah, probably. But you know Hzzt. Tarsier-face would sell his own mother for the right price. And he did score a small fortune off Lantz. I bet he's dragging his feet hoping we'll pony up even more quark." Another giant bite disappeared. Around the mouthful, he mumbled, "Fleecin' fffleefers gonn fleece."

I wrinkled my nose against the unappealing display of half-chewed burger. "My point exactly. What if he took the money and ran?"

"Not the first time you thought that, and he came through in the end," Tyler pointed out before taking another huge bite.

"You're probably right. But I'd feel better if we at least touched base with Lantz again. See if he's heard anything."

"Fffine wiff me." Tyler shoved the last bite home and stood, licking stray grease from his fingers. I followed him from the galley up to Deck Four and off toward the flight deck.

My first glimpse of the area brought me up short. Where our communications array had once perched now rose a sleek bank of Warexian technology. The gracefully curved station reminded me of something from a sci-fi movie—all holograms, touch screens, and interfaces—more complex than anything I'd worked with before. Goloran's engineers had called Head Case's tech antiquated on more than one occasion, and the end result of their work made that fact starkly clear.

Deep in conversation with Ben near the command chair, Twama gestured animatedly toward the ultra-modern hardware. The new comms were like a glimpse of the starship Head Case might have been, instead of the starship she was.

We stepped onto the flight deck proper and Ben glanced over with a welcoming grin.

"Gentlemen! Perfect timing. Twama and her team just finished buttoning things up." Rising from the seat, he crossed over to join us by the entrance.

Tyler let loose an appreciative whistle, openly gawking. "Dang! Look at all that slick new gear! Lantz wasn't kidding when he said they brought the latest tech." Still staring, he angled closer, trying to get a better look.

Twama finished checking a final panel on the console's underside and straightened gracefully. Stepping around the station's curved edge, she paused before us with an easy smile. "Advanced compared to your current systems, yes. But to us, it's commonplace."

"We really appreciate everything you and your team have done for us, Twama," Ben told her sincerely. "I know it hasn't been easy."

"Installing new systems is never easy, but your engineers were quite helpful. And educational! You certainly have a unique ship here, Captain."

"You can say that again!" Tyler laughed.

"She has a lot of heart," Ben replied evenly. If her unintentionally disparaging remarks bothered him, nothing in his relaxed posture betrayed it. "Did you and your team test comms functionality before packing up?"

"Of course." Twama angled back to the curving console,

gracefully inputting a command via the holographic controls. The large display behind the station shimmered, emitting a musical chime before resolving into a sharply defined interstellar map. Various comm frequencies and relays blinked alongside colored trajectory lines linking hundreds of points across an impressive range.

"As you can see, your communications are now linked into the Warexian Commweb," Twama explained, her dark eyes sparkling with subdued excitement. As an engineer, she clearly couldn't resist showing off her handiwork despite her earlier disclaimer about it being common tech. "The relay integrates crystalline waveform oscillation and quantum entanglement modulation, utilizing microscale..."

I listened intently while Twama dove eagerly into a highly technical explanation of how the upgraded equipment functioned. Most of it swiftly outpaced my grasp of the topic, but I still enjoyed the sound of her voice as she deftly described advanced science that Earth remained at least a century from conceptualizing. Her obvious enthusiasm and pride were infectious enough that we all smiled and nodded, pretending rapt comprehension.

Fortunately, our blank stares eventually seemed to penetrate Twama's engineering zeal. "Ah, my apologies. I sometimes get lost in the details." She tapped the console again, and the display reverted to standby mode. Behind it on the rear bulkhead, a separate screen lit, parsing an incoming transmission before highlighting the source coordinates. "Suffice to say you now have faster-than-light communications across the breadth and width of Warexia."

"Outstanding!" Tyler's eyes lit up. "Think we could call Earth with that thing?" He raised the pitch of his voice, holding up his index finger. "E.T. phone home!"

Twama smiled gently, uncertain how to react to his antics. "I'm afraid not. Earth's technology isn't advanced enough to send or receive transmissions via the Commweb." She turned to Ben. "Is there anything else you need, Captain?"

"I assume Meg and Leo are fully trained on the system?" Ben asked.

"Yes, Captain. They understand both the interface and the underlying mechanics, and we've left behind enough replacement parts that there should be no cause for concern."

"And what about our antiquated systems? Do we still have access to those?"

"Of course. That was the primary source of our lengthy stay. Integrating your tech with ours proved to be quite an exciting challenge!"

"I'm glad you enjoyed it so much. Please make sure to thank Her Highness for me. And tell her we'll send a report as soon as we have something to share."

"Yes, Captain," Twama said. She paused, suddenly hesitant.

"Is there a problem?" Ben asked.

"It is no problem, Captain. Only, Her Royal Highness charged me with remaining aboard Head Case, with your permission of course, until you have completed your examination of the Wardenship." Her face tightened, expecting a strong rebuke.

Ben's grin faded. His hand ran absently through his hair as he considered the request. "That wasn't part of our agreement," he said softly.

"Yes, I agree with you on that, Captain. However, Her Royal Highness suggested you could use someone with my experience during your travels."

"We already have someone like that," Tyler said. "No offense. I personally don't mind if you stay."

"Yes, I agree with you on that, too," Twama said. "This

request comes from Her Royal Highness, not me. I would prefer to return to my post."

"Then please tell Princess Goloran that I refused your assistance."

Twama swallowed nervously. "I…I would strongly prefer not to relay that message, Captain."

Ben sighed. "I take it Her Highness doesn't take no for an answer very well."

"She will lay the failure on me, Captain. I will be removed from my post, stripped of my rank, and relegated to…" Her face twisted in disgust. "…office work."

"That is horrible," Tyler agreed.

"Are Manat and Koti also supposed to remain?" Ben asked.

"No, Captain. Only me."

He threw up his hands. "Fine. But you're restricted to Deck Three unless Meg or Leo need you for a specific task." He tapped on his comm badge, refusing to use the Warden's enhancement unless absolutely necessary. "Matt, you there?"

"What's up?" Matt replied.

"I hate to do this, but I need you to swap rooms with Meg."

"What? The Captain's Suite is mine. It's part of our agreement."

"I know, but we have a new temporary crew member. Twama is remaining on board to assist Meg and Leo."

"Seriously? How many engineers do we need on this ship?"

"About two fewer than we have now," Ben answered. "Anyway, Meg's room isn't big enough for three women. The suite is."

"If you and Meg hadn't broken up—"

"Don't start that again," Ben said. "Please."

Matt growled before responding. "Fine. Only because you're my BFF."

"Hearts," Ben replied jokingly. "Thanks for understanding."

"Yeah, as long as it's temporary."

Ben disconnected from Matt, tapping on the badge a second time. "Meg, Ally, do you copy?"

"Aye Captain," Meg answered.

"Hi Ben," Ally responded a moment later.

"Twama will be staying with us for a while, which means we need to play a little musical-quarters. You two will shift to the Captain's Suite with Twama. Matt will take your quarters. Is that okay with you, Meg?"

"Okay?" Meg answered. "That's awesome!" She cheered over the comms, drawing laughs from Ally.

"I assume that means the suite is nice," Twama said.

"Nice?" Meg responded. "It's the nicest compartment on the ship, and Matt's been hogging it for the last four years. This is the best news I've heard in a while."

"Okay, okay," Ben said. "Don't rub it in too much. Matt's already sulking about it."

"Sucker!" Meg laughed.

"Ally, are you on Three?" Ben asked.

"Yup. Just playing chess with Archie."

"I thought he was asleep under his blankets," I said. "He plays chess now?"

"Yeah, and he's freaking good. I won the first two matches, and haven't won since."

"Smart little booger," Tyler commented.

"Twama, head down to Three. Ally will meet you there."

"As you command, Captain," Twama replied. She stiffened before snapping her head down in a sharp bow.

She nearly collided with Lantz as she left the flight deck. The other engineer burst through the doors, looking highly agitated. Normally pretty slow unless a killer robot chased him, he practically sprinted to where we were standing.

"Lantz, what's wrong?" Ben asked, his face suddenly tightening with concern.

"It's Hzzt," he panted, shaking his head. "I think he's in trouble."

# CHAPTER 5

"What kind of trouble?" Ben asked.

"Yeah, how do you know he didn't just ghost you?" Tyler asked.

"I've tried contacting him nearly two dozen times over the last three days and ten more times today. His automated service keeps picking up." Lantz raked frustrated fingers through his hair. "I haven't received a response to my messages, and when I tried remote hacking his pad, my system couldn't complete the handshake protocol!"

"Whoa." Tyler blinked. "Uh...that sounds bad?"

Lantz shot him a withering glare. "Yes. It means he isn't simply ignoring me, which I might expect him to do. His pad is offline."

"Maybe he dropped it in the toilet."

"Most personal access devices are waterproof and impact proof," Lantz countered. "It would take a bullet or plasma bolt to compromise the shell."

"We shouldn't just automatically assume the worst," Ben said. "There could be a dozen other reasons why Hzzt's device might be offline."

"Name one," Lantz replied.

Ben stared at the engineer, clamping his teeth down. "Okay, but that doesn't mean something bad happened to him."

"We paid him to dig up dirt on informants connected to a crime lord the Warden is struggling to rein in," I said. "I don't want to think the worst either, but the facts are the facts."

"My feelings exactly," Lantz agreed. "I've known Hzzt for a while. He wouldn't leave his pad offline unless he had no other choice. Unless someone made him turn it off."

"Maybe he found the henchmen he was looking for," Tyler said. "And they did what henchmen do."

"That's what I'm afraid of."

"We need to find him," Ben decided, glancing at Lantz. "Any ideas where to start looking?"

The engineer retrieved his pad from a pocket and activated the floating screen. "When I started getting worried, I took the liberty of logging into the admin controls for the nearest commweb relay." He turned the face of the device so we could all see a list of numbers and alien characters that reminded me of IP and MAC addresses besides what I assumed was the identifier for Hzzt's pad. "According to the access logs, his last ping came from the entertainment asteroid."

"The same place we've been almost every day?" Tyler asked.

"Yeah," Lantz confirmed. "Hzzt is nothing if not predictable. The network identifier is for the Blazing Star Casino. We should start our search there."

"So, he took your quark and used it to gamble?" I asked.

"It was either that or drink himself into a stupor," Lantz replied.

"We have no idea if he was there to blow his windfall or meet someone about Markan," Ben said.

"Or both," Lantz said. "But I get your point. We can't assume he wasn't on the job when he vanished."

"Maybe he was drowned in cement," Tyler said.

"I don't follow," Lantz replied.

"Never mind."

"I want to head over to the casino," Lantz said. "I don't really want to go alone, which is why I came to you, Captain."

"Understood," Ben replied. "Matt and Ally are busy swapping rooms. Noah, Tyler, do you feel like taking a field trip?"

"I'm game," Tyler answered excitedly.

"It could be dangerous," Ben reminded him. "If Markan's responsible for Hzzt's disappearance, it's possible more goons are waiting for whoever comes looking for him."

"We aren't going to finish this task without any danger. I'm still game."

"Me, too," I said. "Are you coming with us, Ben?"

He nodded. "I'm not going to send you anywhere I won't go myself. Noah, why don't you bring Archie along, too? He might come in handy."

"Sure," I replied, glad he'd included the Aleal.

"Let's make sure we keep a low profile, and don't draw too much attention. As far as anyone else is concerned, we're in the casino to gamble, just like everyone else. But make sure you wear your underlays and grab a sidearm you can conceal, just in case."

"Thank you, Captain," Lantz said.

"I know you're worried about your friend."

"Friend? He's hardly that. What I am worried about is the quark, and the intel we sent Hzzt to fetch. I know six months seems like a long time, but it can sneak up on you quickly if you aren't paying attention."

"Agreed," Ben said. "I'll let Matt know we're leaving and meet you in the hangar in ten minutes."

"Aye aye, Captain!" Tyler replied.

The three of us headed for the lift, pausing on Deck Three to prepare for the recon mission. Ally was in the hallway when Tee and I arrived, a bunch of clothes on hangers draped over both shoulders. I knew they were Matt's by the size and style.

"Hey, Red," I said, waving to her from the far end.

"Hey, Noah. What's got you all giddy, Tee?" she asked as we closed on one another.

"We're going James Bond on this place," Tyler replied.

"Is that supposed to mean something?"

"It means we're heading out to a casino to look for Hzzt," I explained. "Lantz thinks he might be in trouble."

"Oh. And I wasn't invited?"

"You look busy," Tyler answered.

"Are you kidding? Matt can move his own clothes. I swear, he has more outfits than Lady Gaga."

"It's a man-date," Tyler said past his laughter. "And you don't want to be a fifth female wheel, do you?"

Ally rolled her eyes. "If there's trouble, you could use me."

"Ben said you had enough to do," I told her. "With the comms upgrades done, he'll want to ship out as soon as we have a lead."

"Nice try, Noah."

"Captain's orders?" I offered.

"We're the renters, we can overrule him with a vote." Tee and I looked at one another. Ally growled. "Seriously? Who on board has the kill shot boon?"

"We're not looking to get into a fight with anyone," I said. "So we shouldn't need your boon. And if you want to go home as soon as possible, slowing things down by tagging along instead of swapping quarters won't help."

She sighed. "Yeah, you're probably right about that. I

don't like gambling anyway. Just be careful out there, okay?"

"We will," I replied, accepting a quick side hug.

"Don't I get any love?" Tyler asked when Ally turned to enter her former quarters.

"No," she replied simply with a grin before disappearing inside.

"What did I do?" Tyler asked.

"Fifth female wheel?" I questioned.

"I was trying to let her down easy."

We went into our quarters and quickly changed into our underlays and the fanciest clothes we had already made. For me, this consisted of black pants and a black, collared shirt with a long, navy duster over it, perfect for concealing my blaster. Tee emerged in more garish colors but with a similar overall style.

Before heading down to meet Lantz and Ben, my last act was to find Archie beneath its blankets in the corner and gently shake it awake. The Aleal stirred slowly, tendrils waggling lazily in the air. Its overall lethargy amused me since it had been playing chess not ten minutes earlier.

"Sorry to wake you up, bud, but we're going out to look for Hzzt, and Ben thought you might be useful. Want to come along?"

Archie responded by swiftly flowing up my leg to take his usual position inside a pants pocket. His increasing bulk left a bulge large enough that it wouldn't escape notice.

"I think you're getting too big for pockets, Arch," I said. "Maybe you can flatten out on my back or something?"

Archie climbed from the pocket and up to my collar, tickling my neck as he vanished beneath my shirt. Glancing back, I noticed a single, hair-width tendril rising up over my shoulder like a periscope.

Chuckling at the Aleal's eagerness, I rejoined Tyler in

the lounge, and we hurried to the hangar, where Ben and Lantz already waited.

"Nice look," Lantz complimented our outfits. He had also changed. While he always kept his face shaved and hair neat, he normally wore clothes that looked like they'd spent a week being trampled on the floor before he decided to wear them. Now, he wore a neatly pressed, pinstriped suit beneath a long, leathery overcoat.

"You look totally gangster," Tyler commented. "You need to have Asshole make me something like that."

"When we get back," Lantz promised.

I noticed Ben remained in his typical Han Solo-esque away attire, shunning the concept of dressing up for the casino. I figured Lantz knew the dress code better than we did, but he would fail to meet it. He rarely seemed to care what he wore.

"No Shaq?" I asked.

Ben patted his sleeve, where the Jagger had tucked in tight to avoid detection. "Archie with you?"

My neck tickled when it lifted a few more tendrils to wave at Ben.

"Then we're all set. Let's roll."

# CHAPTER 6

A short tram ride took us to the garishly lit entertainment asteroid we were already familiar with. That familiarity helped me avoid distraction from the active concourse, where raucous alien shouts echoed from the drinking establishments and gaudy holographic signs flashed by. My focus remained fixed and alert. The situation had changed the surrounding atmosphere from vacay to an arena match.

"The Blazing Star is on Sub Level Ten," Lantz told us as we navigated through the crowds. "We'll hop on a conveyor to descend." He pointed to a bright, round station squatting a short distance ahead.

Since our prior field trips had mostly centered on the Asterock Arena, we'd yet to descend into the depths of the carved entertainment planetoid that Tyler had taken to calling the Big E. Even so, I'd seen the conveyors in action. Large round discs, they rose to the station and slid slowly enough across the floor to step on without risk before arcing downward through clear tubes that made it impossible to fall or jump off them. As Lantz had explained, they would slow to a crawl when they reached openings for the sub-levels, allowing easy transfer to each floor.

We got off on our floor and followed the engineer into the station, where he quickly used his quark to pay for a day pass for each of us. We held our hands under a machine that printed an invisible code before passing through a scanner that verified payment, finally stepping onto the next platform that passed.

"Do they have anything like this in the Spiral?" I asked Ben while we descended through meters of solid rock.

"Not like this," he replied. "This is incredible."

"Totally," Tyler agreed.

The platform's slow descent meant a ten-minute ride down. After that, we stepped out into the station and, from there, into a surprisingly large and open concourse similar to the one on the surface, only more subdued. This level appeared to be for serious, discerning customers looking for a specific kind of entertainment.

Namely, losing their quark to the House.

Lantz led us unerringly toward a brightly lit area tucked into one side of the concourse. Garish red and gold-framed double glass doors emblazoned with a name that didn't translate to English led into the establishment before us. I didn't need to read the name on the door or hear the telltale sounds of games in progress to know this was Blazing Star Casino.

Lantz drew us into a shadowed doorway across from the establishment. His worried gaze remained locked on the casino's doors, opening and closing with the comings and goings of both excited and disappointed patrons.

"Noah, Tyler, why don't you go inside with Lantz?" Ben suggested. "I'll wait out here and keep an eye on the entrance. I assume since we're underground, there aren't many back doors anyone can slip in or out through."

"A pretty safe assumption," Lantz agreed.

"You know how to get us if you need us," Tyler said, making the call-me gesture.

"Just keep one hand free," Ben replied. "I don't want to inadvertently make you drop anything."

"Oh man, I hadn't thought of that," Tee replied, glancing mischievously at me.

"Be careful, all of you," Ben added.

Tyler and I followed Lantz through the casino's entrance. A huge rock-man bouncer waited there, bringing us to a quick stop before we reached the two revolving glass doors behind him.

"Paystick," he requested in a gravelly voice.

"There's a cover charge?" Lantz asked.

"No. Just to verify you have funds. We don't have space for spectators in the Blazing Star. You want to watch, head up to the arena."

"Hey," Tyler said. "We know you, don't we? We played a few matches with you."

The rock-man eyed him for a moment. "Rock on," he said before laughing. "I still don't know what that means. How are you, soft skin?"

"We're good, man. I didn't know you worked the BS."

"It won't get you in if you don't have any quark."

"No problem," Lantz said, passing over his paystick. The rock man scanned it before grumbling in awe.

"High roller?" he asked.

"No. Business has been good lately."

Rock-man moved aside. "Enjoy the games."

"See you around," Tee said as he moved past. "Rock on!"

We slipped through one of the revolving doors, pausing again to survey the main floor. After the relative dimness of the entrance, I blinked against a sensory assault of sights, sounds, and smells. The rock man hadn't been misstating it when he'd said the casino had no room for onlookers. The place was crowded, particularly around the multitude of game tables. Most of the action was purely holographic and too alien for me to understand at a glance. Occasionally, a thrilled winner's jubilant shout accompanied by the ringing of bells could be heard above the more numerous groans of dismay over losing outcomes. Free-flowing alcohol fueled both outcomes, but no immediate sign of trouble presented itself.

While Tyler and I gawked, Lantz flagged down one of the many servers expertly navigating the maze of tables with trays full of drinks. He leaned close, speaking urgently near her ear, gesturing first toward a nearby bank of gambling machines and then across the room toward door-ways likely leading further into the casino's back areas. The server blinked once before responding with obvious confusion and a denying head shake. Lantz tried again more insistently. This time, the server responded with clear annoyance. She shook her head again and bustled off, multiple arms balancing a heavily laden tray. Lantz scowled after her briefly before moving to intercept another worker. This one reacted much the same: denial accompa-nied by dismissal.

Frowning, Lantz rejoined us. "No luck so far. The servers claim they haven't seen Hzzt."

"Maybe they've confused him with a different stick-thin, grey-skinned, big-eyed drunk," Tyler suggested.

"Not likely. Broothurs aren't commonplace around here."

"Is it possible your data is corrupted?" I asked.

"The commweb access logs? No."

"Maybe someone stole Hzzt's pad and brought it down here. Maybe he never actually made an appearance here."

"That's possible," Lantz admitted. "But we need more information. Maybe I just asked the wrong staff."

"So we keep asking around until we find someone who knows something," Tyler said.

"The only problem with poking around with questions is that you're poking around with questions," I said. "What if we draw the wrong kind of attention?"

"I don't see any other option," Lantz said. "We can section the place off and split up to canvas the bartender and servers pretty quickly. With six servers per section, it should net us a reasonably high probability that if they all respond in the negative then we can assume Hzzt was probably never here."

"Spoken like a true geek," Tyler said. "You and Katsuo are like peas in a pod." He pointed to the bar in the back corner. "I'll start over there."

"I'll start with the bartender," Lantz countered. "He'll have the highest probability of having seen Hzzt if he was here."

"Fine, I'll take that section," Tyler said, leaving me with the most raucous playing area.

As we split up, I reached back toward Archie's tendril, collecting a reassuring squeeze on my finger—silent confirmation that the Aleal would alert me if anything seemed amiss.

We fanned out, threading gradually deeper through the maze of tables, machines and milling patrons. No one I approached, whether patron or employee, admitted remembering Hzzt. If body language meant the same thing across species, most seemed actively annoyed by my questions, quickly dismissing me. I endured outright hostility in one corner where a multi-limbed creature crouched alone over shifting holographic diagrams. It didn't appreciate the interruption, spitting what I took as a curse before pointedly ignoring me. Unfortunately, I got the uneasy impression the staff might be subtly complicit in perhaps hiding what might have happened to our friend.

After fifteen frustrating minutes, I met back up with Tyler and Lantz. "Any luck?" I asked them, even though both wore equally grim expressions. Their headshakes confirmed they hadn't found any leads on Hzzt either. "I guess we need to assume he never made it here. Someone probably stole his pad."

"Then whoever that was would have been the last person to see him alive," Lantz said. "If we find him, we can make him talk."

"It's a dead end," I countered. "We'd have zero ways to identify the perpetrator."

"I think we should check the employee's only areas in the back," Lantz suggested. "Maybe his pad is still back there, disabled."

"Or maybe our rock-man friend will smash us to grape juice if we get caught snooping around back there," Tyler argued.

Lantz deflated, making it obvious that he cared more about Hzzt than he'd let on. "Yeah. Give me a minute to think."

While he deliberated, we took up positions at the back of a group of patrons playing a game involving squares of colors and a ball dropped from overhead, which bounced wildly around an enclosure before coming to rest in one of the slots. Observing for a few minutes, I gathered that players who won guessed the right color and won even more if they guessed the right space.

"I bet it's called Wardenian Roulette," Tyler called it, elbowing me gently in the ribs. "Better than Russian."

A firm hand abruptly clamped down on my shoulder. My heart lurched, and I whirled, grabbing for my concealed blaster before I registered the worried face hovering just behind me.

"Whoa, take it easy!" Lantz whispered sharply. Beside him, Tyler frowned in confusion.

I dropped my fingers away from my weapon. "What is it?" I asked as Archie squirmed with a warning against my back, responding to my anxiety.

Lantz leaned closer, dropping his voice. "I think they're onto us. We're being watched."

# CHAPTER 7

"Don't look around!" Lantz continued. "I noticed from the corner of my eye. That first server I talked to is tracking us from the corner. She ducked back there right after making an odd hand gesture I'm guessing triggered some kind of alert."

"I told you asking questions was risky," I whispered.

"Yeah. But why would they care unless they knew something?"

"That won't help us if we're dead."

"Just follow my lead."

I nodded, letting Lantz steer us closer to the entrance. It took considerable effort not to scan our surroundings for threats or do anything that made us look more suspicious. My neck prickled, sensing hostile gazes clinging to our backs.

"So what now?" Tyler kept his tone light despite the dangerous undercurrent. "Grab that server for a friendly chat?"

Lantz shook his head. "I have another idea. We'll split up again and head toward the rear access points like we planned. I'm betting whoever is watching us won't react openly unless we seem intent on going where we shouldn't. Noah, you watch close for anyone moving to intercept you. I'll do the same from another angle. Tee, stick by the main entrance and cover the outside. Be ready in case ownership decides to get proactive about kicking us out."

I didn't love the notion of solitary recon with potentially hostile surveillance, but I couldn't argue the logic. With luck, one of us would manage to slip past casino security's awareness, find proof Hzzt had been here, and maybe even pick up a solid lead on his whereabouts. "Got it. See you guys on the other side."

Tyler clapped my shoulder encouragingly, if a bit forcefully. "Watch yourself, Katsuo."

"You too."

I turned away, striding with renewed purpose toward the rear, doing my best not to look like I knew I was being watched. Finding a sign for the restrooms made it easier, and I redirected that way, pausing at one of the tables to observe the outcome of one of the games before continuing.

My ad hoc subterfuge seemed to do the trick. The subtle weight of observation faded away. Apparently, I no longer registered as a priority threat. Perfect. With most attention likely still clinging to Lantz, I figured I could manage a little clandestine snooping. A server bustled past, and I made eye contact, requesting directions to the restroom despite having already locked on the destination. He pointed toward the arched doorway ahead without slowing.

I headed for one of the tables, doing my best to scan the entire casino floor subtly. The server Lantz had pointed out was gone from her prior position, back amongst the patrons serving drinks. I caught sight of Lantz at the far end of the place, also watching one of the games. My heart quickened when a pair of stooges in dark suits moved up behind him, their appearance close enough to human I had no idea where they belonged in my ILF compendium. Sweeping the room, I noticed Tee had reached one of the swinging employees-only doors at the opposite end of the floor. He looked like he was about to try to duck in when the door opened, and another pair of goons stepped out and took guard positions nearby, forcing him to shy away.

If anyone would sneak into the back, I knew it had to be me. Not because my actions had been so impressively sneaky. More because I was so nondescript as to go unnoticed or so unthreatening as to be ignored. In this case, it worked in my favor.

Breaking away from the group of onlookers, I angled toward the restroom, diverting at the last few feet toward another restricted door. The servers coming and going made it harder to time the entry, but I managed to slip in the door unnoticed as one of them came out. A nondescript corridor led back toward the casino's inner workings, and I hurried to the nearest closed portal to get out of the hallway before another server arrived. I pushed through the unmarked side door and discovered a maintenance section filled with neatly organized bins, racks of cleaning materials, and humming climate and air filtration controls. The room also contained a pair of one-size-fits-all janitor's uniforms made of a flimsy, chemical and waterproof material that felt like latex. I slipped it on without a second thought, trying to ignore the ammonia smells it had absorbed after multiple rounds of sanitation work. The hazmat suit easily swallowed my duster, held fast only by the clasp at my neck.

"Dad, if you could see me now," I whispered, picturing how much I must look like a clown in the way-too-big coveralls. Still, he would have been impressed with my reason for donning the ridiculous disguise.

Tempted to use the Warden's enhancement to contact Tee, I decided against it. I didn't want to draw attention to him when his hand snapped up to his face. Instead, I grabbed what I assumed to be an electronic mop from the corner and stepped out of the room, nearly colliding with a server.

"Watch out!" she cried, turning away from me just in time to almost save her entire laden tray of drinks. One of them rocked and toppled, crashing to the floor. It didn't shatter but spilled its contents. "That's coming out of your paycheck," she growled, shaking her head as she bent from the knees to scoop up the empty container.

"Sorry," I replied. "Got a bad spill in the back."

"I don't care," she replied, moving on without giving me a second thought.

I scurried down the hallway, passing the kitchen on the right, where a mix of organics and bots assembled cocktails and hors d'oeuvres with skilled precision. Continuing past, I made my way to a second door leading to a t-junction with a row of closed doors in both directions. The fanciest door sat at the end on my left, likely the owner's office. Having seen movies featuring organized crime, I figured that if Markan's goons had done anything to Hzzt, they wouldn't have made a mess of the office, so I took the right fork. Reaching the first door, I tapped the control panel on the wall, revealing an empty office. Good thing because I hadn't prepared a reasonable excuse to give someone. I had one ready when I reached the second door, but didn't need it. It was also empty.

Talking from behind the third door stopped me from opening it. I continued on to the next, opening the door to find a Hemid woman in a dark, trousered suit occupied it.

"Can I help you?" she asked, sharp eyes latching onto my coveralls.

"I got a call about a spill," I replied, my gaze sweeping the room. They froze on the pad resting on the far side of the desk, its transparent face blank, the power apparently off. Could it be Hzzt's pad?

"Do you see a spill here?" the woman griped.

"Huh…Oh…N…no, ma'am," I stuttered, suddenly gripped by anxiety. Had the woman lifted the pad from Hzzt, or had someone brought it to her? "I'm sorry for the interruption."

"What's your name?" The woman asked. "When were you hired? I don't recognize you."

"I…uh…I need to go get that spill," I replied, backing out of the room. The moment the door closed, I sprinted back the way I had come. There had been no sign of Hzzt, but there was a good chance the pad on the desk belonged to him. I wanted to confirm it, but how could I? At least I could report back to the others and tell them that yes, the pad was likely here, and yes, someone in the casino knew something.

Stumbling through the door into the storage room, I hastily began removing the coveralls, hoping to escape back into the casino and blend in with the other patrons before making my getaway with Tyler and Lantz.

Nearly finished, Archie sensed something that made him squirm warningly against my back. I tossed the coveralls aside, reaching for my blaster as approaching footsteps stopped just outside the door.

"Did you see which way he went?" a rumbling voice asked.

"No," another deep voice replied. "There's only one way out. If he had used it, you would have seen it."

I swallowed hard, adrenaline flooding my system, certain I was about to be caught. So much for avoiding trouble. Archie's tendrils poked anxiously over one shoulder as one of the goons kicked the door open. The other one pointed a hand cannon right at my face. I didn't even bother to draw my weapon. What would be the point?

"Well, look what we have here!" one of the guards rasped harshly, his eyes cold. "Somebody's gotten himself lost back in places he's not supposed to wander. The boss doesn't like it when thieves start sniffing around restricted areas."

My denial emerged instinctively. "I'm no thief! I'm just looking for the bathroom."

The Hemid woman ducked between the two bruisers, eyebrow raised. "And you accidentally found yourself in a janitor's coveralls? What are you doing here? Answer me quick and make it believable, or you'll have an even worse night."

# CHAPTER 8

"I...I can explain," I stammered, panic threatening to steal rational thought as I raised both hands to placate the woman and her two goons. One goon's weapon never wavered. Beside him, the other goon cracked his apish knuckles. They looked ready to smear me across the walls.

"You'd better have a damn good story," the woman warned again. "Start talking."

I met her glare, reaching for calm. Matt's training took over, helping to calm my fear and steel my nerves. "You're right. I was snooping around. But…it's not what you think. I'm not a thief!"

"No? You're telling me there are other reasons to sneak into the back room of a casino beyond a desire to steal?"

"A…actually, yes." I lowered my voice conspiratorially. "I want to join Markan's syndicate."

The admission caught all three off-guard. The nearest goon's threatening scowl morphed into surprise before hardening. The other one glanced uncertainly at the woman, who studied me intently, her brow creasing.

"Don't tell me you don't know who Markan is," I said,

seizing the initiative before she could speak. "The looks on your faces already confirmed you do."

The woman huffed out an impressed breath. "You've got some nerve, kid. I'll give you that. But are you sure you know what you're requesting?"

"I want to join his crew," I repeated firmly. "I heard he takes on new blood, and my skills could prove useful to him."

"This isn't a recruitment center!" The nearest bruiser regained his bluster. "Markan isn't hiring, especially not some poor excuse for a thief!" His partner rumbled agreement beside him.

"I'll do the talking, Grell," the woman snapped, simultaneously silencing both goons with an upraised hand, her gaze never leaving me. "He's right, though. You couldn't pick a more impressive way to audition. Sneaking around back here dressed like custodial staff? My nephew has more subtlety and skill when he plays superheroes."

"I know, I didn't put my best foot forward," I admitted. "But desperation makes fools of us all." I met her stare evenly, willing her to believe. Archie squirmed warningly against my back. Whatever sixth sense the little guy had, it didn't seem the woman was going for my spiel. "I'm just a guy trying to get his foot in the door. Trying to find a place I belong."

"Failing spectacularly isn't how to accomplish that," the woman replied.

"Fine, I'm not good at stealing. But I do have other skills. For example, your servers communicate with the guards through hand signals. I knew they were watching another pair of patrons who entered the place when I did." I paused, waiting for her to accuse me of being with Lantz and Tyler, grateful when she didn't. If they had security cameras, she had yet to check the footage. "I used that to my advantage to sneak into the back. I also noticed that pad in your office. It isn't yours."

"Why do you say that?" the woman replied.

"For one thing, it was powered off. Probably not a good idea for the head of security. You are the head of security, right?"

"I am," she admitted.

"Do you have the pad on you now?"

She stared at me a moment before shaking her head. "No. I left it in the office."

"If it were yours, you would have grabbed it when you came tearing out here after me. Which supports my deduction that it belongs to someone else."

My reasoning earned another swift glance between the two goons. The woman's eyes narrowed, reassessing. After a taut moment, she pursed her lips. "You're not nearly as thick as you first appeared. But what makes you think that device has anything to do with Markan?"

I shrugged, affecting nonchalance. "What use would a place like this have for a stolen pad? It's not especially valuable as an electronic device. But what about the data it carries? What about the ILF you took it from? Maybe I'm wrong, but I think it belonged to someone Markan wanted dealt with. You handled the problem and kept the pad, hoping to crack the encryption and see what your target was up to. Am I close?" I had to hold back the wave of fear that shivered through my spine. If she confirmed the sequence of events, she would also confirm that Hzzt was likely dead.

"Almost too close," the woman answered after a pause. "You got all that just from seeing the powered-off pad on my desk?"

I nodded, pressing my momentary advantage. "What does it hurt to pass the word up the chain that I'm available and eager to sign on? The worst that happens is nothing, right? But if your boss is interested, I might make something of myself."

The woman stared intently, digesting my unexpected audacity. For several anxious seconds, the only sound was the muffled noise of the casino beyond the door. The two goons fidgeted, awaiting her command. With a sharp nod, she abruptly turned on one heel and strode out. My gut twisted, wondering if I'd made a terrible miscalculation. Then the door swung shut behind her with an ominous thud, leaving me alone with the pair of scowling toughs.

The nearest cracked his huge knuckles again, his grin cold and jagged with missing teeth. "Meel and I will reacquaint you with the rules about restricted areas."

As Meel stepped back to block the door, Grell lumbered toward me. I had no way to outfight him, so I hastily backpedaled. Unfortunately, I had nowhere to go and no choice but to drop into a defensive stance. I braced myself for the goon's first punch.

Archie stirred against my back, preparing to strike. I knew the Aleal could take out Grell without much of a problem. But could he do it before Meel put a round from his hand cannon squarely in my chest? I didn't think the underlay would stop a caliber as high as that thing probably fired.

The thought was enough to force Archie to stand down. We both remained still as Grell lifted a ham fist, cocking it back. I closed my eyes when it started forward, the breeze of its passing cold against my cheek.

The two guards laughed uproariously as I opened my eyes, surprisingly unharmed.

"We're just messin' with you," Grell rumbled. "Boss didn't signal us to rough you up, just to keep an eye on you."

"How come you didn't guess that one, smartass?" Meel teased.

A pounding on the door interrupted their fun. Meel pulled it open, revealing the rock-man bouncer. He held Ben by the scruff of his coat, the ripped garment hanging half off his narrow shoulders.

"Look who I found loitering in the shadows outside." Rock-man gave Ben a rough shake, a swelling bruise below one eye evidence of the brief struggle they must have engaged in. "Says he was just minding his own business, but I watched him eying this place like it's a piece of meat." My eyes met Ben's, my gut sinking at being responsible for his predicament.

"Friend of yours, wiseguy?" Grell asked me.

Ben started to shake his head, suggesting I deny our acquaintance. But he remained at the edge of the situation while I was stuck in the middle. "He's my brother," I replied. "It was his idea to come here and try to see if we could locate Markan."

For a brief moment, Ben looked like he wanted to strangle me.

"He's your brother?" Meel asked. "You got such different eyes. His are like this." He made a circle with his thumb and forefinger. "Yours like that." He compressed the orb.

"My brother from a different mother," Ben explained.

"Oh," the goon replied. "Okay. Grrk, toss him over here with his brother."

Grrk let go of Ben, pushing him at me with what had to be his gentlest shove. The force nearly knocked us both over.

"I'm going back to my station," Grrk announced, vanishing from sight. I didn't know how he moved without breaking or at least shaking the floor.

The two goons watched over us, and we spent the next few minutes standing side-by-side in silence. I hated dragging Ben into the mess I had made, but either intuition or stupidity had convinced me it might be the least painful option for him.

The door behind Meel opened again, admitting the woman. "Nice of you to join us," she said to Ben before looking my way. "It's your lucky day, kid." She motioned toward the door. "Bring them both. We're going upstairs."

The guards quickly moved to comply. Meel spun Ben toward the door while the other grabbed my shoulder in a crushing grip, propelling me after them. We headed back down the utilitarian hallway to the main corridor, my thoughts in worried turmoil. She had said it was my lucky day. Was she playing me straight or just being facetious? Would going upstairs be a good thing? Or the worst ever?

Beside me, Ben seethed in frustrated anger but didn't struggle against his captor's firm hold. The two bruisers marched us through the kitchen area to a small utility elevator. It carried us up a handful of levels to what I guessed were the executive suites.

Low lighting revealed plush furnishings with subtly patterned fabric replacing the glittering chaos of the gambling floor. The goons directed us down a paneled hallway lined with dark metal doors, finally halting us before the large door at the very end. A red beam scanned the woman's face before the door clicked open, and she ushered us inside what turned out to be some kind of meeting room. She gestured for us to sit at a round conference table that dominated the spacious office. I gratefully sank into the offered chair, exhaling my fear. This room was way too nice to be bloodied up.

Ben slowly lowered himself into the adjacent seat, gaze darting around the room. A bank of darkened vid screens took up one entire wall, adjacent to a fully stocked bar and entertainment space more at home in a corporate penthouse.

After seeing the woman safely inside, Meel and Grell

retreated to the other side of the secured entrance to stand guard. The woman moved behind the desk in the corner, settling gracefully onto the chair behind it before tapping the transparent surface. The dormant vid screens instantly flashed to life, showing columns and grids of alien data interspersed by numerous security feeds. I unconsciously braced, wondering if she was about to reveal Tee and Lantz in custody or the footage of me chatting with them, proving I hadn't entered the casino alone. Nothing on the monitors seemed to indicate that was a concern. Yet.

"Relax," she said, noting my anxious posture. "You aren't on the verge of being tortured or harmed in any way, for that matter. But I need you to explain why you're so bent on joining Markan."

"I told you," I replied. "I want to make something of myself."

"You could join the military if you want to be all you can be," the woman replied. "What you're asking to be brought into is something much different than that."

"I know. But..." I paused, lowering my voice. "I despise the Warden."

# CHAPTER 9

The woman's eyes narrowed in surprise, a smile tugging at the corners of her mouth. "I see. And how do you know Markan feels the same way?"

"Observation," I replied, remaining as obtuse as possible. "Tell me I'm wrong."

"You aren't wrong," she answered, returning to Ben. "What about you?"

"What about me?"

"Are you interested in joining the syndicate as well?"

"I go where he goes," Ben replied.

She smiled. "Of course. Do you two have names?"

"I'm Hondo," he said, "and that's Katzuo."

"Interesting names. I'm Janella, Chief of Security for the Blazing Star Casino, as well as Local Prime for Markan's network."

I struggled to hide my exuberance, which bubbled up despite our predicament. Confirmation that we were in the right place. The excitement failed before it could get going. Hzzt had likely paid for this meeting with his life. That was nothing to celebrate.

The vid screens all changed from security feeds to

different recordings, all containing me, playing different scenarios in the Asterock Arena. "This is you?" she asked as I grabbed an attacker by the wrist and flipped him to his back, kneeling on his chest and chopping him in the throat to take him out of the match.

Ben glanced over at me, obviously impressed. "Yeah, that's me," I replied.

"Why in Warexia did you ever attempt to ingratiate yourself to the syndicate by looking like a thief when you have skills like this?"

Another feed showed me ducking beneath a knife, moving into the attacker's guard, disarming, flipping, and stabbing him in one smooth motion.

"You already have plenty of muscle, I'm sure," I replied. "Besides, that was just an arena game."

"Not to us," she countered. "The arena is a proving ground. And your scores are some of the highest we've seen from a new player. Where did you learn to fight like this?"

"My brothers," I replied. "Hondo, here. And my other brother, Stang."

"Good job!" she gushed, looking at Ben.

As she opened her mouth to continue talking, a muted chime announced an incoming call. The woman activated a projector in the center of the conference table. After a burst of pixelated rainbow static, a smiling fat human-adjacent appeared in crisp holographic focus. With a ridged forehead and tiny mouth nearly swallowed up by thick cheeks, he reclined behind a large, ornate desk. A dark suit jacket draped his enormous shoulders, and he'd laced all eight of the bejeweled fingers of his ham-hands on an obese paunch.

He had to be Janella's boss. I immediately disliked his smug expression. It vanished when he took note of our presence, replaced by a look of disgusted irritation. "These are your so-called prospects?" he asked incredulously.

Janella hesitated, shooting Ben and me a slightly nervous glance. If she was worried, I figured we should probably be worried, too.

"Yes, sir," she replied. "They've expressed significant interest in joining the fold. And as I mentioned in my communiqué, the younger one's already playing at an advanced level in the arena, despite only having a week of experience."

The large alien reappraised us, eyes narrowing. "Are you certain you have the correct identifier?"

"Yes, sir. We scanned it as soon as he entered the casino, and Jathian confirmed the authenticity through secondary validation protocols. I agree, his stats seem unlikely given his appearance, but the results are legitimate."

He shifted his gaze back to me, staring for longer than felt comfortable before speaking. "Where did you learn to fight?"

"My brothers, Hondo and Stang," I replied. "This is Hondo."

"Janella, you only sent me arena scores for one of them."

"Sir, Hondo doesn't have an identifier."

"You've never played in the arena?" the alien asked Ben.

"No, sir," he replied, matching Janella's respectful tone. He knew how to play the game, and he played it well.

"Yet you taught your younger brother everything he knows?"

"Not everything, sir. But a lot of what he knows."

"So why haven't you participated in arena competition?"

"It wouldn't be fair to the other players, sir," Ben replied with surprising sincerity. He even convinced me that he believed it. Of course, the statement would have been true if he could access chaos energy the same way here as he had back on Earth.

The caller started chuckling before the seriousness of

Ben's tone sank in. His laughter trailed off. "Interesting. Tell me, how did you come to learn about our operation?"

I tensed in panic, unsure how to respond to the question. Thankfully, Ben didn't miss a beat. "We followed rumors that turned into whispers, that turned into actionable intel over a two-year period. It ultimately brought us here to the Blazing Star."

"Persistent. I like that. But why? What makes you interested in a position with us? Certainly, with your aptitude you can chart your own course."

"We are charting our own course, sir," I said. "That's why we're here. We understand that your organization is unfriendly with the—"

"DO NOT say his name!" The alien screamed, his voice rising so high it hurt my ears. Then, cool and controlled once more, "Do not say that name."

"I wouldn't think that M—"

"Don't say that name, either," he spat, silencing me. "One can never be too sure of who might overhear, or how."

"Understood," Ben replied. "Our apologies, sir."

"Consider that your first lesson in handling the delicate nature of our business. Those who speak so openly tend to disappear quickly and permanently." He leaned forward, placing his beefy fingers on his desk. "I assume our mutual acquaintance is the reason you went to such a desperate measure to attract our notice?

"That's correct, sir," Ben said. "We both relish an opportunity to...compete in that arena, so to speak."

The bloated alien chortled. "A delicate way of framing the situation. Do you know anything of value regarding our shared associate?"

Ben caught my eye briefly, weighing how much he wanted to say. "I know our parents are dead because of his actions," he replied. "That's all I need to know."

"And let me guess, you think coming here, talking to me, will get you the revenge you're after."

"No," Ben answered. "But it feels a lot more like freedom than the alternative."

The alien nodded. "Good, because you won't find revenge on the menu here. That's not what our association is about. We take care of our own, it's as simple as that. Wait there." His hologram abruptly vanished.

We sat in silence for the next few minutes, until my nerves began to fray in direct relation to the length of the delay. I couldn't imagine why Janella's superior had cut us off like that, unless new information had come to him revealing our association to Tee and Lantz, or maybe even Hzzt, Levain, or Zariv. Had someone in Markan's employ discovered we weren't being totally up front with them and passed the intel along?

"Is this normal?" Ben asked, apparently feeling the same tension but handling it with experienced calm. On the outside, at least.

Janella hesitated before responding. "Not completely," she admitted. "I'm sure it's nothing." She sounded worried, too. She had put us forward as candidates. If we came back dirty, she would be on the hook, too.

Archie squirmed against my back, reacting to my emotional state. I focused on my breathing, trying to calm myself. Finally, nearly ten minutes later, the portly alien flashed into holographic existence once more.

"Janella," he said.

"Yes, sir?"

"We've decided to move forward, mostly because of the younger one's arena scores. Make sure they're on the transport out tomorrow morning."

"Of course, sir. It will be done."

The holoimage and vid screens winked out simultaneously, leaving Ben and I facing an enormously relieved underboss. She sagged back into her chair as residual tension rapidly evaporated.

"It looks like you're in," she remarked. "I have to say, you both have more guts than brains."

"We knew that already," Ben replied lightly. "But thank you anyway."

Her lips twitched, a reluctant smile tugging free at his easy retort. Leaning forward, she accessed her computer terminal. "There's a cargo ship named Deepling leaving Asterock tomorrow morning, four sharp. It's at Asterock Central Docking, Level Three, Berth Seven. Be there no earlier than thirty minutes and no later than fifteen minutes before departure. When you arrive, you'll be challenged. Provide the phrase Melzat brep nye and let them scan your Arena identifier. That will get you on board."

"Where will the ship take us?" I asked.

"To the first day of your new life," she replied. "Don't waste this opportunity. Our leadership is fair, but we do expect results." The door to the office opened behind us. Meel and Grell entered. "Escort them back into the casino. They're free to go."

Grell scowled but provided no argument. The sudden reversal confounded him.

Casting one last look around the office, I sent Janella a relieved nod of thanks. To my surprise, she returned a warm smile. Her appreciation for my apparent abilities seemed genuine. My legs felt rubbery, weak from the abrupt release of tension, as we stood and exited the suite.

"I don't know how you did it," Grell said on the way back down in the elevator. "But you did. Welcome to the family."

"Yeah," Meel agreed. "You're gonna love initiation."

"If you survive it," Grell countered. Both of the burly guards laughed.

The elevator reached the bottom floor. The doors

opened. Meel pointed through the kitchen. "You know the way from here."

"See you around, Simbo," Grell added. He practically shoved us out of the cab.

"Simbo?" I asked Ben once the doors had closed and we started threading through the kitchen, avoiding the chefs, bots, and servers. Unlike before, nobody spared us a second look. Or even a first. Word of our acceptance into whatever we had been accepted into had traveled at faster-than-light speed.

Ben shrugged. "No idea."

We retraced our steps from the kitchen back to the casino floor. Tyler and Lantz were nowhere to be seen, and I figured they had made themselves scarce after failing to breach security.

"Hey softskins," Grrk said when we reached the foyer. "No hard feelings, eh? I'm just doing my job."

"Aren't all your feelings hard?" I asked, drawing a chuckle from the rock-man.

"No hard feelings," Ben agreed. "Everything worked out in the end."

"Have a good night," Grrk said.

"You too," I replied.

We exited onto the concourse, heading for the platforms that would bring us back to the top level. I started raising my hand toward my face to call Tyler and find out where he and Lantz had gone when Ben stopped in his tracks, turning and grabbing me by the shoulders.

"Are you insane?" he asked, furious worry sweeping his face.

"What did I do?" I replied.

"We were supposed to make contact with Markan's agents, not join his merry men. This isn't how these things are supposed to go."

"What else was I supposed to do?" I answered defensively. "They would have killed us both back there if I hadn't made something up. We should both just be glad they bought that awful excuse."

"We can't get on that cargo ship, Noah. If we do, we might never see Earth again."

"That ship is our path to Markan," I replied. "Remember, the sooner we wrap things up with him, the sooner we can get Mission Return to Earth back on track."

"You heard what Grell said. Initiation. Markan's a crime lord. What do you think that initiation will be? Not a pie eating contest or stupid fraternity hazing."

I swallowed hard, suddenly nervous about what we might be expected to do. "I understand, but..."

"Hey!" Tyler said, stepping out from the doorway of a bar with Lantz right behind him. Their unexpected appearance surprised me enough that I stiffened and felt the color blanch from my face. Tee cringed. "Sorry, man. Didn't mean to scare you. Are you both okay? What happened?"

"We're fine," I reassured him quickly. Ben opened his mouth to answer, and I swiftly cut him off. "We just had a little misunderstanding. Everything's fine."

Catching my pleading look, Ben let his unfinished reply die away with a grudging shrug. There was no point in telling them how narrowly we'd escaped disappearing like Hzzt or how artlessly I'd landed us in this situation.

"I don't buy it, but whatever you say." Lantz reluctantly fell into step beside me. "Luckily they only politely requested we leave with a warning not to come back. I was starting to worry they'd dragged you both downstairs for a more...permanent dismissal."

"Nothing quite that dramatic," I replied.

"Did you find any sign of Hzzt?"

My entire body tensed, a cold shiver running down my spine. I didn't need to say anything.

"I don't need details," he replied. "But I'll have to reach out to his wife."

"We don't know he's gone for sure," Ben said. "We didn't see a body or get a confession."

"It just doesn't look good," I added. "They had his pad."

"So what happened in there?" Tyler asked. "I thought we were all goners when Rocky snagged Ben."

I squinched up my face and admitted, "I might have accidentally volunteered Ben and I to join Markan's syndicate."

"You what?" Lantz said in the same are-you-out-of-your-mind tone Ben had taken moments earlier.

"Wow," Tee responded. "I guess that's one way of getting it done. Personally not my first choice, but whatever works, right?" He patted me sympathetically on the shoulder. "Nice knowing you guys."

I glanced at him, cold with fear once more. What the hell had I just done? The ominous words of the goons returned to haunt me.

*Initiation.*

*If you survive it.*

# CHAPTER 10

We hurried back to Head Case, my head still spinning over the implications of the trouble I had gotten us into. As soon as the ramp lifted behind us in the hangar, Ben rounded on me, picking our conversation up where he had left off. Only now, Tee and Lantz were around to serve as witnesses.

"Noah, no matter what happens from here forward, there's no way we're getting on that transport tomorrow. Is that understood?"

"Ben, I know you think it's dangerous, but—"

"I don't think it's dangerous," he interrupted. "I know it is. But worse than that, if we get on that ship, if we subject ourselves to Markan's initiation..." He paused, shaking his head. "There's no going back from that, Noah. Whatever we do, it can't be undone."

"I understand, and I'm willing to accept the fallout."

"That's because you don't understand the fallout. I do."

"I know I'm not eighteen yet, but I'm not a child. You don't need to treat me like one. Markan wouldn't have even accepted us if not for my Arena scores."

"And you say that like it's a good thing."

"It was better than having Meel and Grell crush our skulls!"

Ben sighed in frustration, forcing himself to calm down. "Look, Noah. I know you aren't a child. I don't mean to treat you like one. Matt and I, we've been through some stuff. Bad stuff. It changes you." He paused, collecting his thoughts again. "You're a smart, strong, caring young man with a solid moral foundation. I don't want this place to steal that from you."

The concern etched on his face stole any chance I had at a powerful rebuke, deflating my defensiveness. "I don't want to lose myself, either. But we decided that dealing with Markan is our best chance to get the Warden off our backs long enough to check out his ship. And joining his gang would be the easiest way to get closer to him. Hzzt may have paid with his life for us to have the opportunity."

"Uh, guys?" Tee said, stepping between us. "I hate to interrupt this tremendously dramatic argument, but aren't you both forgetting something? We can't split up without the Warden blasting us with a Level Five shock. Trust me, we don't want that."

We both stared at Tyler. In our frantic upset, both Ben and I had forgotten about the Warden's warning.

"One light year," I said. "You're right. Thanks, Tee."

"No problem."

"We still need to do something."

"I'll assemble the crew," Ben replied. "We can get their input on options." Without waiting for a response, he headed toward the elevator. I trailed after him, the other two on my heels.

No doubt Ben had planned to contact everyone and direct them to the Lounge or maybe the conference room adjacent to the flight deck. There was no need. We found the rest of the crew on the flight deck, gathered around the brand-new communications array. Multiple information feeds in a mix of translated and untranslated Warexian languages scrolled across the large display behind the station. Like excited children with a new toy, they were busy familiarizing themselves with the advanced interface, but seeing our grim expressions, their smiles of greeting faded to concern.

"What happened down there?" Ally asked. "You all look terrible. Did you find Hzzt?"

I quickly explained everything that had transpired over the last hour, from sneaking to the back searching for clues about Hzzt's fate to my panicked lie about wanting to join Markan's operation and its unforeseen consequences. When I reluctantly revealed the standing order to board Deepling in the morning, exclamations of dismay erupted around the circle.

"You can't get on that transport!" Leo looked almost as agitated as Ben had been earlier. "If you get more than one light year out of range—"

"The Warden shocks us all into crispy critters," Tyler finished.

"Exactly," Leo agreed.

"Not to mention, infiltrating a crime syndicate that's managed to slip the Warden's noose to attack it from the inside seems beyond reckless and stupid," Matt said. "Even for us."

Ben nodded, mouth compressed into a tight line. "At the same time, Noah's right that we can't afford to let this opportunity completely slip away." He glanced at me with a wink, his way of apologizing for his earlier outburst. "Even if we don't board Deepling as recruits, it would serve us well to track that ship wherever it's going. Meg, Leo, Lantz —can it be done?"

The three engineers remained silent while they considered the possibility. Meg spoke up first. "We'd need a tracking beacon that works from super-long distances. Or at least syncs through the Commweb. Lantz, does that kind of transmitter exist here?"

"If it does, it would be pricey as all get out," Lantz replied. "And even if we did manage to score one, we would need to get it onto Deepling."

"We could stick it to the hull," Leo suggested.

"Sure, but how are you going to get to the hull? All external activity around central docking is approved and monitored. Unless one of you got an invisibility boon, that's not going to happen."

"So we'd need to sneak it on board," Matt said.

"Yeah. But good luck doing that. I don't need to know much about Markan to guess that any ship of his will be well guarded. It's not like you can just walk on board."

"Well, we can," I countered. "We just can't get off again once we do."

"I have another idea," Leo said. "Forget the tracking beacon. What if we can remote hack into Deepling's PCS and pull out the ship's destination? We can get there before they do."

"It's not that easy to remote into a starship's primary control system," Lantz replied. "At least, it shouldn't be, if the engineer who built the security protocols is any good."

"But what if they weren't very good?" Ally asked.

"I mean, it's possible," Lantz said. "But it might not be helpful. Most ships don't enter their jump coordinates until they leave the dock, and I'd think that would go double for one of Markan's ships."

"What if we could get the jump coordinates as soon as they're entered?" I asked. "If we have access to the network, we should be able to intercept the entry, right?"

"A good thought, but also not that simple. Even on Head Case, the nav computer is on a subnet, firewalled from the rest of the ship's controls. Good thing too. I can only speculate what the Warden might have done to you if he could send you anywhere in the galaxy he wanted."

We fell silent as a group, the quick burst of wind stolen from our sails.

"I wonder..." Lantz said, breaking the silence before trailing off.

"What is it?" I asked.

I could almost feel his mind churning as the skin of my arms prickled with chills. "Well, I did work at one of the largest shipyards anywhere nearby, installing the very network software and equipment we're talking about hacking into. If, and it's a big if, Deepling happened to be made by Cacitrum Shipbuilding, Incorporated, then we may be back in business."

"A long shot is better than no shot," Ben said. "How do we find out if today is our lucky day?"

"Arrivals and departures of commercial vessels should be public domain," Lantz replied, pointing to our new comms array. "And we just so happen to have a fancy new Commweb interface. Levi, do you have Commweb access?"

"Commweb access confirmed," the ship's AI replied.

"Enter the Asterock node and run a query on the commercial vessel manifest for a ship called Deepling."

Less than two seconds later, Levi replied. "I've located Deepling."

'Wow, that was fast," Tyler commented.

"What's the make and model?"

"Deepling is an Ionicum Deep Hauler, manufactured more than forty years ago."

"Damn," Matt said. "There goes that."

"Hold on," Lantz said. "Let's not be too hasty. Levi, are you able to access the ship's service records?"

"Service records require authorization from a certified technician."

"Please use my identifier for authorization." He lifted his

pad from a wide pocket inside his coat. "I'm sending you the passkey now."

"Passkey received. I have gained access to the service records."

"Has Deepling undergone refurbishment or refit within the last twenty years?"

"Confirmed. Deepling underwent refurbishment six years ago. Work included upgrades to the thrusters, reactor, comms array, and control modules."

"Where did the control modules originate?"

"It appears they were salvaged from a vessel damaged during a pirate raid, later sold at auction as scrap."

"And who manufactured that ship?"

"The builder of record is Cacitrum Shipbuilding, Inc. The control module serial numbers are—"

"That's enough," Lantz said, cutting the AI off. His eyes swept across us, his grin widening. "It looks like we may have a winner."

"It's about time something went right for us," Tyler said.

"Let's not get too ahead of ourselves," Lantz cautioned before I could ramp up my excitement. "It may be possible to remotely hack into Deepling's network, but it won't be easy by any means. And there's no guarantee of success."

"Come on, man. You aced Zariv's systems. You even stole a robot carriage. You've got this one in the bag."

"I appreciate your faith in me, Tee, but nothing's ever a given." He looked at Ben. "Captain, I know we don't have a lot of time, but give me a few hours and I'll see what I can do."

Ben nodded. "Of course. As for Plan B, if this approach doesn't work out, we'll have no choice but to cut and run and hope we can find another way to approach this task."

"No pressure, Lantzy," Tyler said.

"Let's all let the man get to work," Ben said. "Dismissed."

# CHAPTER 11

I was in my quarters with Tyler and Archie, the Aleal beating me again at chess when Ben's voice crackled over the ship's comms.

"All hands, report to the conference room immediately for a briefing."

I sighed, moving my king into checkmate. "Good game, Archie." The Aleal's tendrils wiggled happily as I got to my feet. "Just wait here. I'll be back soon."

"I wonder what's so urgent," Tyler remarked, getting up from his mat on the floor. Archie started resetting the chessboard as we headed out into the passageway. We met Matt as he stepped out of his new quarters wearing sunglasses. "Gentlemen," he said in greeting.

"Too cool for school, Boss?" Tee asked.

"You try resting in a room with pink polka-dotted walls," Matt replied. "I can't repaint soon enough."

"Are you enjoying the downsize?" I asked.

"Not at all. But thanks for rubbing it in."

We made our way to the elevator, waiting a minute for any stragglers down in the lounge to join us so we could conserve the scaling supercapacitor.

"Hey guys," Ally said, joining us, along with Meg, just before we boarded the waiting car.

"How are you ladies enjoying the room upgrade?" I asked.

She glanced at Matt before shrugging. "Eh. It's okay." Meg chuckled beneath a hand, clearly excited about their new digs.

"How about you, Matt? You on pink overload yet?"

"It's fine," Matt said. "Besides, I never needed that much space."

Tyler clapped Matt's shoulder in support. "Poor guy's wearing sunglasses so you can't see him cry."

Our banter helped disguise rising tension as we rode the elevator up to Deck Four and headed for the conference room next to the flight deck. When we entered, the others were already gathered. Ixy crouched in the shadows, barely visible save for the reflections in her many eyes. Lantz slouched in a chair beside Ben, a deep frown creasing his forehead, Leo across from him. I slid into a seat between Matt and Ally as Ben cleared his throat, shifting forward to lean his elbows on the table.

"Thanks for coming on short notice. Lantz has an update on his progress that we need to discuss. Go ahead, Lantz."

Looking dog-tired, the engineer scrubbed both hands down his face before lifting his eyes to Ben's and then sweeping his gaze over mine. "I've been working nonstop for the last four hours, trying every trick I know to hack into Deepling's network. No luck."

My chest tightened at the news, a sense of disappointment filling the room.

"Must be some crazy tight security if super-Lantz can't crack it," Tyler said.

"Yes and no," Lantz replied. "Even using your new comms array, my rig couldn't handshake with the ship, let alone access anything. I kept at it, thinking maybe I was just looking in the wrong place. I finally got desperate enough to slice into central docking's monitoring systems to pull Deepling's network identifier, confirming the ship does have external access and has used it before. Honestly, that only frustrated me more since I couldn't even ping the bastard. Anyway, I spoofed a maintenance inquiry to the listed address, which should have triggered an automated response from any receptor node with external connectivity."

"But Deepling didn't reply," I guessed from his body language.

"Not a peep. My best guess is that the ship's comms and control systems were modified from their defaults to allow them to fully disable remote access. Whether it's simply disconnected at the moment or has gone permanently dark, trying to hack in remotely was never going to work."

A brief silence settled over the assembly while we all digested the news. My earlier elation evaporated, replaced by dark irritation. What other options do we have? Ally unknowingly echoed my thoughts.

"I assume that means we're leaving Asterock. But to go where?"

Ben frowned, the reality of our situation weighing heavily upon him. "We aren't leaving," he announced.

"So what are we doing?" Tyler asked. "Feeding you and Noah-san to the sharks?"

Ben glanced at me, the simple look telling me everything I needed to know. Another mood shift followed, from frustration to fear with a tinge of excitement. "That was the plan I'd put forward earlier," he admitted. "But I've since reconsidered. Noah's right that tracking Deepling is still our best shot for getting closer to Markan. And Lantz has an idea that I think mitigates enough of the risk to make it worth consideration."

"I don't need to consider," I said. "I'm in."

"Let's hear Lantz out before you dive in headfirst."

The others around me reacted with varying expressions of guarded hope as Ben gestured for the engineer to continue. Before Lantz could say anything, the conference room door opened, revealing Twama looking uncomfortable. I imagined it was because she was off Deck Three, though I supposed she already had Ben's permission to leave berthing.

"Perfect timing," Lantz said, looking over his shoulder. "Come on in. I was just about to explain my idea, and you being here will mean I won't have to explain it twice."

She crossed the threshold into the room, slapping her hands to her thighs and bowing her head, her people's way of paying respect to Ben. I noticed her right hand was closed around something. "Captain."

"At ease," Ben replied. "Have a seat. Lantz, go ahead."

"So yeah, like the Captain said," he continued as Twana took the only open seat directly across from Ben at the table's head, "since I can't pull data from Deepling remotely, the next best thing is to plug in directly. That would accomplish two things. First off, we can create a peer-to-peer network between Head Case and Deepling, allowing us to siphon data from the cargo ship's network. Secondly, placement between the primary command systems and the hyperdrive will let us bypass the subnet problems I would have encountered regardless of how we plugged into Deepling."

"I didn't know we had that kind of tech on board," Matt said.

"We don't," Ben replied.

"That's why I am here," Twama said. "Captain Murdock and Lantz requested procurement of certain technologies from me, and I from Princess Goloran, who remains invested in your ultimate success." She opened her hand, revealing a black disc the size of a quarter. "This transmitter bears much of the same comms technology we recently added to your flight deck. Obviously, the systems are miniaturized and as a result are less powerful, but they do have a range of a quarter light year. That's certainly enough to transmit Deepling's jump coordinates at interception."

"And then some, if needed," Lantz added. "The transmitter's also loaded with some tools I can use to take advantage of backdoors I wrote into the command modules."

"That sounds highly illegal," Meg said.

"Oh, it is," Lantz confirmed. "I would have been arrested on the spot if anyone had ever discovered them. But one, I was careful. And two, AI engineers struggle with anything that falls outside their learned parameters. Tarvik would have noticed the pointer hacks and buffer overflows. A stupid bot? Not a chance."

"That's so awesome," Tyler laughed.

"That still requires physically attaching it to Deepling's internal network," Matt pointed out.

"Which is where Noah and I come in," Ben explained.

"Hold up." Tyler sat straighter, his gaze darting between Ben and me. "I must have missed something. You're planning to join Markan's syndicate?"

"Like I said before, that transport represents our only solid lead on Markan. It could take months to get another chance like this, if at all. We don't have forever, especially with the Warden likely trying his damndest to get the coordinates to Levain's station."

"I'm all for anything that potentially gets us home faster," Ally said. "But what if we fail? You might end up like Hzzt." She turned her eyes to me. "I don't want anything to happen to you on my account."

"I appreciate that," I replied. "I don't want anything to happen to me, either. But this is the best option for everybody. Besides, with the transmitter, you'll literally be right behind us."

"Close enough to avoid the Warden's punishment," Lantz agreed. "Both en route and when we arrive."

"Which is great," Tee agreed. "But we're still sending our Captain and Noah into a den of vipers, with no guarantee we can get them out if things get dicey."

"We'll get them out," Matt said with his usual calm, confident bravado. "You can count on that."

"Can we just slow down for a second?" Meg asked, holding up both hands. She didn't look comfortable with the notion of deliberately putting Ben and me in harm's way. "Before we all just accept this is our only option, maybe we should pause to consider other possibilities one more time?"

Ben smiled faintly. "By all means. I'm open to alternatives."

"What about having Archie sneak aboard with the sniffer?" Tyler suggested. "We know that little guy can get just about anywhere undetected."

My gut tightened anxiously. The idea of sending Archie alone into a dangerous situation aboard a smuggler's ship struck me as an awful risk. "For one thing, Archie may not be human or adjacent like the rest of us, but he's still a crew member."

"And smarter than me by a mile, at least when it comes to chess," Ally added.

"And solving Rubik's Cubes," I agreed. "Besides, that only shifts the risk to a different crew member instead of eliminating it."

"Plus, how do we know he won't eat anyone's brains on the way?" Matt said. "We want to track down Markan, not have his entire organization hunting us."

"He won't try to eat anyone if I tell him not to," I replied.

"Are you one hundred percent sure of that?" I opened my mouth to confirm before thinking better of it.

"It still might make sense to bring the little booger along," Tyler said, accepting the rejection of his idea. "He's great protection, especially since I doubt they'll let you carry a blaster until they trust you more."

"Protection we hopefully won't need," Ben said. "But you're right. He's even better at remaining hidden than Shaq."

The Jagger buzzed something from somewhere near Ben. I hadn't even realized he was part of the meeting before that.

"He said he could hide that well too if he were made of gelatin," Ben explained. "Are there any other ideas?"

The compartment fell silent for nearly two minutes before I spoke up. "Ben's right. We need to move forward with the original plan. I'll carry the transmitter aboard with me and get it where it needs to go. Lantz can walk me through how to connect it after the meeting."

"Sure thing," Lantz agreed.

"I still don't like this." Ally glared at Ben and then at me. "If we're voting, my vote is against this plan."

"Are we voting?" Tyler asked. "Because I don't love it either." He paused for dramatic effect. "But I still don't know any other way we can accomplish our objectives. If there's one thing I've learned being here in Warexia, it's that nothing ventured really is nothing gained. And I don't want you, me, Noah, or Ben stuck here indefinitely."

"Sorry, Ally," I said. "I don't know if we were voting either, but you're outvoted if we are."

She sighed, disgruntled but out of arguments.

"Then it's decided," Ben said. "Matt will remain close by with Head Case if things go sideways. Hopefully, we won't require unscheduled extraction."

"You know me, always ready to pull your butt out of the

fire," Matt answered easily. Behind his casual tone I sensed tightly held concern for our wellbeing.

"Then let's get to it."

The others rose from the table, various expressions revealing worry for our pending infiltration. When Ben also stood to take his leave I lingered a final moment.

"Hey guys," I said, waiting until everyone was paying attention. "I know I got us into this mess, but I give you my word I'll do whatever it takes to get us back out."

"We know that, Noah," Ally said gently. "This isn't your fault."

"True enough." Tyler came around the table to grip my shoulder. "If it had been me, we'd probably already be taking a permanent dirt nap right now. Besides..." His grin flashed his familiar bravado. "...if you don't make it back I get our room all to myself. It's a win-win."

His jest yanked a strained chuckle from me. "Thanks, Tee," I replied before glancing between Lantz and Twama. "Let's run through this a few times, to make sure I have it."

"Of course," Lantz replied.

"We have about two hours," Ben said. "I'm going to get some rest before we need to leave. Noah, I'll meet you in the hangar when it's time."

I nodded to Ben. He filed out of the conference room with the others, leaving me with the two Warexian engineers.

"It's actually pretty simple," Lantz said, proceeding to train me on how and where to place the transmitter.

Hopefully, fortune favored the bold over the desperate and unprepared.

# CHAPTER 12

Janella was waiting for us when we arrived at Deepling's docking bay, her sharp gaze locking onto us from across the bustling outer concourse. My footsteps faltered in surprise before I caught myself, quickly resuming pace beside Ben. Her presence set my nerves on edge. Clearly, our new handler wanted visual confirmation we planned to honor the agreement to board the transport. Our chance for cold feet had expired. There was no going back.

"I was beginning to wonder if you'd lost your nerve," Janella remarked once we'd drawn close. Amusement colored her tone, though her eyes remained calculating. "You're right on time."

"I'm surprised you went through the trouble of coming down here to see us off," Ben replied. "I feel special."

"Unfortunately, since I vouched for you, I'm responsible for you until you're off Asterock."

"Responsible how?" I asked. "What if we hadn't come?"

"You may have thought you had a choice to be here or not. That choice was an illusion. If you no-showed, I would have seen to it that someone found you, and dealt with you accordingly."

My bones shivered at the thought of those consequences. Despite the anxious pitching of my stomach, I struggled to keep my tone casual. "We said we'd be here, and here we are."

"I'm glad. I didn't want to have you killed." Without waiting for a response, she spun on one heel and strode briskly toward the docking tube connecting Deepling to central docking. Ben and I exchanged tense glances before following. My fingers reflexively brushed the hidden transmitter sewn into the lining of my coat collar, drawing confidence from its presence and Archie's presence as well; the little booger literally had my back.

Janella led us into the utilitarian boarding tunnel, gesturing curtly for us to proceed ahead of her through the oval hatchway. I tried unsuccessfully to control another attack of nerves stepping over the threshold onto Deepling proper. While we'd already passed the actual point of no return, this represented the physical exclamation point at the end of the sentence. Ben crossed just behind me. He may have looked relaxed, but his eyes swept our new surroundings like targeting lasers. I had no way of knowing if he felt the same stomach-churning anxiety that I did. I guessed not. He was too experienced to panic.

Beyond the airlock we entered a compact operations bay, currently empty save for a handful of bots offloading cargo containers. Familiar with the vessel's layout, Janella waved us on without breaking stride. We followed her lead through the ship, the passages wider than on Head Case but still tight enough to create occasional close quarters when passing other crew members heading in the opposite direction. The assortment of Warexian species, all appearing to be human-adjacent, barely paid us any mind.

After twisting through a series of passageways, we eventually entered a larger junction at the ship's midsection. Nearby, an open lift stood ready for passengers.

Several passageways branched off toward unknown compartments.

My breath caught when a hulking rock man shouldered past us, craggy head nearly brushing the overhead. The massive ILF didn't even excuse himself, continuing without a backward glance. Beside me, Ben shifted subtly away, likely having flashbacks to our tussle at the casino's entrance. Or maybe he just didn't want to be flattened against the bulkhead.

Janella remained as focused as ever, not sparing the rock man or other crew so much as a glance as she led us to wherever we were going. A couple of minutes later, we paused outside an unmarked door. I glanced at Ben, who tapped his wrist impatiently. We had to get the transmitter placed before Deepling would go to hyperspace. That gave us an hour tops before the ship was underway and made enough distance from Asterock to jump.

Our guide banged her fist on the door. "What do you want?" a tiny nasally voice spat out. "I've got a ship to run!"

"Kobiack, it's Janella."

"Oh. Damn." The door opened a few seconds later. I had to look down to get a glimpse of the woman who answered. Barely three feet tall, with a petite build, big eyes, and smooth skin, she could have passed for a seven-year-old human if not for a cyborg eye surrounded by scarring covered by a dark tattoo. Her uniform suggested she was the ship's captain.

"Sorry, Janella. Nobody told me you were coming aboard." Her eyes snapped from her to Ben and then to me. "What's with the bilge rats?"

"New recruits," Janella replied. "They're the reason I'm here. This is Hondo and his brother, Katzuo."

"Welcome aboard, I suppose. I'm Captain Kobiak, though most of the crew just calls me CK. I'll be hauling your ass across the galaxy for initiation with the four other recruits we picked up along the way. This is the only time you'll see me, so if you have any questions, better ask them now."

Ben and I glanced at one another, both shrugging. "No questions," he replied.

"Good. I like you two already." She turned back to Janella. "I guess I'll take them from here. Always good to see you."

"Liar," Janella answered. "Just get them there in one piece, okay?"

"You know I don't make promises like that," CK answered, sending another nervous tingle down my spine.

Janella returned her attention our way. "Good luck out there. Try not to make fools of yourselves. Or me." She turned again, leaving without another word.

"Follow me," CK said, waving us down the opposite passageway. "There's only two rules for recruits on this ship. One, stay out of where you don't belong. You'll know those areas by the red triangles on the access hatches. There's no locks, but if anyone catches you in there, you'll wish you never stepped foot on my ship."

Ben and I snuck another glance at each other. Lantz had grabbed schematics of the ship from the shipyard that had upgraded it and walked me through placing the transmitter multiple times based on his best guesses about where we might wind up berthed. All of those placements would be behind the red triangle-marked hatches, no doubt.

"Two, don't do anything else stupid that makes me have to get involved. I don't want to see or hear from you again once I unload you in recruit berthing."

"We'll be on our best behavior, Captain," Ben promised.

We spent another few minutes winding through corridors, using the lift to drop to Deck Three, then more corridors, and finally stopping outside a portal spray-painted in alien lettering. The Warden's pill translated it to *Lower Berthing, enter at your own risk.*

The captain huffed when the door didn't open at our approach, cursing under her breath while she kicked it near the motor. It groaned as it rattled aside, exposing a small cabin containing stackable bunks crammed in so tightly there was barely room to walk by them. Four of the nine available berths already contained minimal personal items, the other five vacant and ready for occupants.

"Stow whatever gear you've brought and head forward through the next hatch. It leads to the rec area, galley, and head. It isn't much, but you haven't earned much yet." Without waiting for a response, she spun and marched away, closing the hatch behind her.

"She seemed nice," I said, channeling Tyler in a feeble attempt to calm my nerves.

"Yeah, home sweet home." Ben selected an empty lower berth and placed his coat and small pack on the thinly padded surface. Dropping my meager satchel on the adjacent empty rack, I sank beside him, pulse still racing. We now occupied a space barely larger than a walk-in closet. Trying not to feel trapped, my gaze darted over the compartment's spartan amenities—a metal light panel, two storage drawers and a shelf for clothing and personal items set into the end wall. It was a far cry from my shared quarters aboard Head Case. My gut twisted, wondering if I'd ever sleep in my comfortable bunk again.

Voices outside the oval portal on the opposite end of the compartment heralded the arrival of our bunkmates just before the hatch whisked open. Three males and a female entered, their laughter cutting off abruptly when they spotted us. For several seconds, we simply stared at one another in surprise. Taking in the unexpected familiarity of their appearances, my own shock doubled. All three males sported the large, Hemid foreheads along with blocky frames and blunt features reminiscent of Levain. I didn't know the females' species, but she had pale skin, orange eyes, and twisting ebony horns jutting out of her head while a thick tail protruded from oversized coveralls.

"Who the hell are you?" The largest Hemid demanded, breaking the uneasy silence. I tensed, unsure of how to respond. These recruits out-bulked us by a significant margin. Getting off on the wrong foot could prove bad for our health.

"That's Katzuo," Ben replied calmly. "I'm Hondo."

"What kind of name is Hondo?" the female asked. She moved in close to us, ignoring any concept of personal space as she sniffed my head. She smelled like cinnamon. "Where are you from?"

"Right here," Ben answered. "Asterock."

"What species are you?"

"Seriously, Lavona?" the smallest Hemid said. "You've never seen a human before?"

"I guess not." She pulled back, treating us like a couple of vermin. "You don't smell good."

"It's probably the beans I ate for breakfast," Ben said straight-faced. He had no intention of letting the other recruits intimidate him, and I was determined to follow his lead.

Lavona didn't understand his tongue-in-cheek humor, so she ignored it. "I'm Lavona." She pointed to the Hemids from largest to smallest. "Larev, Karpov, Yurt."

"Good to meet you," I said.

Our largest bunkmate grunted, his focus already moving beyond the conversation. He chose a top berth and levered himself up into it with ease despite his bulky frame. The other two followed suit, making no effort to be friendly. Lavona looked like she might try, but I got the impression she didn't want to upset the big guy, which I understood. Within moments, Ben and I were left to ourselves.

My fingers curled along the transmitter's reassuring outline, my thoughts circling to the vital task ahead just as Ben gently nudged me. "Time's wasting." I nodded, rising from my seat beside him. "Be careful," he added in a whisper.

I nodded again and moved to the exit, which opened ahead of me.

"Where are you going, new blood?" Lavona asked from her rack above mine.

"I want to see more of the ship," I replied.

"Why? It's a standard cargo hauler. Nothing special."

"I get claustrophobic." I hurried out before she could ask any more questions, the hatch shuddering closed at my back.

# CHAPTER 13

I moved further into the passageway and away from berthing before pausing to consider my best route to an engineering space housing the equipment Lantz needed to establish remote access to. Considering we were located in the lowest occupied decks aft of the superstructure's midpoint, it was a safe bet critical systems like the hyper-drive and power regulation were located somewhere nearby. Just some welcome good luck on our part that we'd been placed closer to the source, where network nodes able to siphon nav data would be in greater abundance. With that in mind, I hurried to the nearest red-triangle-marked hatch I found, not slowing before ducking through it.

Staying alert to avoid the crew, I set off into a warren of narrow access passages behind the main corridors and compartments, trying not to feel overwhelmed navigating the maze. Every shadow held a potential threat, and each faint echo rattled my strained nerves. Not to mention, the clock was ticking. I had plenty of time to finish the job, but I couldn't say that forever. Breathing deeply, I pressed on.

Approaching footsteps ahead pulled me up short. Two entities appeared from a narrow accessway, pausing to talk just long enough for me to melt unseen into another side passage.

Pressed against cold metal, I listened to their fading conversation—something about a damaged item, requesting authorization and rerouting mechanics to handle the repair—until it no longer reached my ears. I crept from hiding, angling down the corridor the pair had appeared from. Two turns revealed another unlabeled hatch. I stared at it, wondering where I had made the wrong turn. By now, I should have reached one of the control nodes.

"You appear lost." The lightly accented voice nearly startled a yelp from me. Whirling toward the unexpected greeting revealed an unfamiliar alien—the same species as Hzzt—studying me curiously from several paces down the passageway. Naturally, his features were arranged in a suspicious expression.

"Yeah, still getting my bearings," I replied, heart hammering. "This deck's kind of a maze." I nodded back the way I'd come. "I'm a new recruit. I was trying to locate the um...head." The last word came out so flat and awkward I was sure the alien's suspicion would lead to a quick call to CK. From there, I just knew it wouldn't be long until I got to examine the inside of an airlock.

The spindly figure chuckled. "Did Captain Kobiak not explain that you are to stay away from hatches with red triangles?"

"Captain Kobiak?" I faked. "Oh, you mean CK. She might have mentioned something about triangles. Honestly, the whole recruitment process has been such a whirlwind, I definitely don't have all my senses oriented."

"Well, you are deep within aft engineering, close enough to the reactor that discovery here by the wrong crew member would put you in mortal danger. Thankfully, I found you first. I'm Romdall, one of Deepling's engineering assistants. Follow me and I'll guide you back to an unrestricted area."

I did my best to hide my dismay. I didn't want to go back. Not yet. For a moment, I considered siccing Archie on the alien so I could get back to finding an engineering junction. The Aleal squirmed against my back, ready to act, until I changed my thoughts. Going back to an unrestricted area would help me get my sense of location back, which would make it easier to sneak back into the restricted areas and find what I was looking for.

"Lead the way, my new friend," I said.

Romdall chittered in amusement. "This way."

I fell in beside Romdall, retracing familiar steps toward an unrestricted junction. "Thanks for the assist," I offered. "I would've hated wandering around lost on my first day."

That drew easy laughter. "I imagine so! The last thing you want is to leave a bad first impression. Especially given your role."

"Role? I'm not sure what you mean. All I'm trying to do is find my way around."

Romdall answered after brief consideration. "I know only rumors passed along by friends who have participated in...collections. I also know better than to speak openly of such things, so let's leave it at that." He winked conspiratorially. "No need to explain your position. I'm no fool."

My skin prickled uneasily. Clearly, "collections" was a euphemism for less savory operations. Had he just tacitly confirmed trafficking activities? The notion sickened me. How did such an obviously decent being end up participating in something so evil?

Dour thoughts permeated my thinking. Beside me Romdall joked about near disasters befalling past newcomers. Preoccupied, I managed occasional murmurs and weak chuckles at appropriate moments before we finally reached the far side of a triangle-marked hatch.

"Here we are, safe and sound!" Romdall stopped beside me, his smile fading as he examined my expression more closely. "You seem troubled. Is something else wrong?"

The genuine concern caught me off guard. Forcing another smile, I met his earnest gaze. "I appreciate all your help. I think I'm just anxious now that we're getting underway."

"No need to worry, new recruit. When you arrive, your team leader will provide a thorough briefing covering all required protocols. I believe you will do well."

"I appreciate that. Thank you again."

"Of course." Romdall nodded toward me before disappearing back into the restricted area. I loitered in the passageway for a minute, about to follow behind him, when I felt Deepling's shudder as It separated from its docking clamps. We were getting underway.

Which meant I was rapidly running out of time.

Tracking through the restricted area once more, I mentally compared my turns to the schematics I had reviewed with Lantz, more careful to follow them precisely this time. The passages around me remained clear and silent. Reaching the junction where I had zigged instead of zagged, a course correction quickly found me outside of one the seemingly endless rows of oval hatches lining Deepling's corridors. Nothing differentiated this portal from any other save my crash-course in Deepling's layout.

I slipped inside the moment the hatch parted. Low lighting revealed a compact compartment stacked floor to ceiling with humming equipment—junction boxes, converters, and data cores—exactly what Lantz promised I would find. I dropped to one knee and tore the lining of my coat collar to retrieve the transmitter. After checking connections as Lantz had demonstrated, I located an open data port and carefully fitted the device in place. Holding my breath, I powered up the transmitter, immense relief flooding me when tiny indicator lights flashed steady confirmation of active linkup with the ship's network.

We had our connection!

After concealing my handiwork amidst the surrounding equipment, I turned back toward the hatch, ready to exit. Archie squirmed against my back, tendrils gripping my collar so the Aleal could pull itself into the open.

"Archie?" I questioned, surprised by his unexpected behavior. It slid down my coat and dropped toward the deck, its tendrils shrinking quickly, its body expanding. By the time it had reached solid plating, it had assumed the perfect form of a rat, hair and all.

The hatch opened, but I didn't trigger it. I caught a glimpse of Romdall approaching before Archie scampered out through the portal's expanding crack, racing right toward the alien. Romdall shrieked with unbridled fear, throwing himself against the bulkhead to allow Archie past. Using the distraction, I slipped out of the compartment and down a side junction.

I hadn't gone far before Archie came around a corner ahead, leaping toward my chest and melting back into his primary form before grasping my coat.

"You're full of surprises, aren't you?" I said as the Aleal climbed back beneath my collar and under my shirt. "Thanks for the save, bud."

He tapped my back with a tendril as if to say, no problem. Shifting my right hand to the call-me gesture, I thought about Tyler.

"Hello?" his voice emanated softly from my thumb. "Is this thing on?"

"Tee, it's me," I said into my pinkie. I felt ridiculous, but as long as it worked… "The transmitter's set and connected. We're in business."

# CHAPTER 14

I hurried back to recruit berthing, moving quickly now that I had returned to unrestricted corridors and didn't need to worry about being seen. Tyler had passed my success on to Lantz, who in turn promised to gain access to Deepling's control network before the ship could get far enough from Asterock to engage its hyperdrive. I shuddered when the berthing door rumbled open, the grinding of the mechanism worsening with each use. The vibrations pulsating through the bulkhead threatened to disturb the other recruits and draw attention to me at the worst possible time.

Fortunately, I had no reason for concern. Crossing the berthing threshold, I found Lavona and the three Hemid tucked into their racks with their backs to the narrow aisle, already asleep. Only Ben remained alert and swiveled his head out from his rack, eyebrows up in question. I flashed him a smile and a thumbs-up. In return, he silently motioned us to continue through the opposite hatch into the as-yet-unseen galley.

Cautiously skirting around Larev's bulk that spilled out from his bunk at chest height, I trailed Ben through the inner hatch. The galley here made Head Case's tiny area seem almost normal. While recruit berthing had enough bunks for nine, the table in the center of the compartment was only large enough to seat six under the best circumstances. With three oversized Hemid as part of our recruit collection, there was no way we could all use it at the same time.

It was just as well. The galley didn't have an assembler or even a microwave. The side bulkheads were lined with cabinets, and a curious check of their interiors revealed loads and loads of what looked like protein bars. A sink beside the hatch into the head provided water poured into ridiculously small paper cups, the waste container beside it already overflowing with them.

"They really pulled out all the stops," I commented quietly to Ben as he settled on the bench that circled the table.

"Hopefully, this will be a short trip," he replied. "Those Hemid don't have any qualms about letting it rip, and saying it isn't pleasant is a major understatement."

"And Lavona said we smell bad."

Ben smiled, closing his hand into the call-me gesture and bringing his pinky to his lips. "Matt, do you copy?"

It took longer than I expected for him to answer. "Damn, I hate this so-called enhancement," Matt replied. "My natural instinct is to fight the involuntary movement."

"That's not a bad thing," Ben answered. "What's our status?"

An uncontrollable urge brought my hand up to my face in the same position.

"Hey, can you guys hear me?" Tee asked.

"I could already hear Matt through Ben," I replied.

"I hear you," Ally said.

"Cool, conference call works," Tee remarked. "I thought about all of you at once."

"Tee, this isn't the time," Matt grumbled.

"If not now, then when?" he replied.

"I'm standing right next to you."

"And I don't hear an echo. That's better than Zoom."

"Tee," Matt warned.

My urge to hold my hand up faded when Tee disconnected.

"I'm going to hold my…phone…up to Lantz," Matt announced. The idea of him putting his hand to the engineer's ear earned a headshake and chuckle. No one could argue that the Warden had no sense of humor.

"Lantz, what's your status?" Ben asked.

"Hey, Boss," Lantz replied. "Wow, this is so weird talking to you through a finger. Anyway, everything's coming along as expected. I'm inside Deepling's network, almost done adding backdoors to all the control nodes. If I wanted, I could open all the outer airlocks and shut down life support."

"Please don't," Ben replied, drawing a laugh. "You ready to intercept the destination coordinates?"

"Ready and waiting," he replied. "Meg and Leo are standing by to patch them into our system. I had to add a delay to the packet forwarding to adjust for the differences in processor speed so Deepling wouldn't get too far ahead of us. Fingers crossed that I got the math right."

"My fingers are crossed," Tee offered.

"Nothing to do now but wait," Lantz added. "Three minutes to jump range. How's life aboard the Markan Express treating you so far?"

"We're here with four other recruits," Ben answered. "Three Hemid almost as big as Levain, and a female of a species with horns and a tail, like a devil."

"They're called Vicon. It's not very common to encounter one this far from their homeworld. I've only seen one in person before, in downtown Portus. That was a while ago."

"Berthing is tiny, especially with the big Hemids. But we'll—" Ben fell silent, his eyes snapping to the hatch behind me. I glanced over my shoulder as it opened, and Lavona entered the galley, her face already twisting in confusion over Ben's strange position.

"What are you two doing?"

"Two minutes, Boss," Lantz reported before Ben could cut the connection and lower his hand. The thumb mic wasn't loud, but in the galley's silence, it was loud enough to be heard by others.

"Who are you talking to?" she demanded. "What is this?" She copied Ben's gesture as he flattened his hand on the table.

"I don't know what you're talking about," Ben replied, playing innocent. "We just came in here to get away from the Hemids' flatulence."

"Don't play me as a fool, human. I heard the voice coming from your appendage. Who was that? Two minutes until what?"

"It's nothing," I said, turning around to face her. "Just a comms implant. Hondo was saying goodbye to our brother. He's tracking the ship out. Two minutes until we enter hyperspace, in case you were wondering."

She relaxed only slightly. "I do not trust you." Without another word, she turned on her heel and left the galley.

"That was close," I said, exhaling in relief.

"She went to get the Hemid," Ben replied, rising to his feet and returning his hand to his face. "Matt, we've got a situation on our end. Keep doing what you're doing; we'll be in touch."

"Do you need recovery?" Matt asked. "Lantz can cancel Deepling's trip."

Of course, he said it just as the hatch into the galley opened again, with Lavona leading Larev through. The

Hemid was impressively quick on his feet for such a big guy.

"No, I'll handle this," Ben said. "Hondo out." He lowered his hand back to the table.

"Nothing strange about that," Larev grunted, beady eyes sweeping from Ben to me and back. "What are you two plotting?"

"I don't know what you mean," Ben replied. "We're not plotting anything."

The big Hemid shouldered past me to plant his meaty hands on the table, leaning in toward Ben. "Don't get smart with me, puny. I heard that voice say they can cancel our trip to pick you up."

The other two Hemid, Yurt and Karpov, ambled into the galley, leaving little free space in the compartment. "What's the problem here?" Yurt asked.

"I think these two are up to no good," Lavona said. "They're in contact with someone outside the ship."

"Our brother," Ben replied. "I told you that already."

"That wasn't the same voice as the first one I heard," she replied.

"We have two brothers. So what?"

My jaw clenched, my body tensing as the threat of confrontation intensified. We didn't stand a chance against the Hemid bruisers, yet Ben seemed unconcerned. It had to be a bluff and maybe the only way to navigate out of this sudden mess without violence, but what if Larev reported us? My hand reached for a blaster I didn't have, Archie squirming beneath my collar, ready to defend me if it came to that. It was my secret weapon, but even the Aleal couldn't fight them all at once.

"So, you seem like you're trying to hide something, and I don't like it," Larev answered. "Especially when you look and smell like a plant for the Warden."

My heart jumped to my throat. We'd been on Deepling

less than an hour and Larev already had us figured out. I slowly began raising my hand toward my face, ready to tell Matt to get us and Lantz to shut down Deepling's engines.

"Don't be stupid," Ben replied, still graceful under fire. "Do you really think Janella would have brought us on board if we were plants? You don't think she or her boss would have seen right through whatever weak cover we devised?"

I nearly laughed out loud. Our cover couldn't have been weaker if we'd tried, but Janella and her overlord ignored it because of my arena scores—scores I'd only managed because I had Ally, Tee, and Lantz backing me up.

"I'll be sure to let them know how little you think of them," Ben added.

Larev eased back some, straightening up.

"Don't tell me you believe that line of garbage," Lavona said. "That's exactly what a Warden plant would say."

"What if he's telling the truth?" Larev countered.

"He isn't," she insisted.

"You don't know that," I said.

"There's an easy way to find out," she replied, tapping Larev on the shoulder and motioning to me. "Grab him, and start squeezing the life out of him until his brother fesses up."

Larev smiled and lunged at me, again faster than I expected. His hand easily wrapped around my throat like Levain's had weeks earlier. Archie shifted again, bunching to attack.

Wait! I tried to order the Aleal in my mind. Let Ben handle this. It seemed to work. Archie remained poised but didn't strike, even as Larev shoved me into the bulkhead while looking at Ben.

"Well?" He grumbled. "What's the truth?"

"I told you the truth," Ben calmly repeated.

"Then how can your brother cancel the trip?" Lavona asked.

"He used to date CK," Ben lied. "He still has her identifier. She'd let us off if he asked her."

"Why would you want to get off?"

"Maybe because some big dumb Hemid is choking my little brother to death?" Ben answered. "I didn't sign up for that. We're supposed to be on the same side."

"That's right, we are," Lavona said. "So why does everything about you scream plant?"

"You seem like you have sharper senses than the rest of us. Maybe you're picking up something else about me that's making you suspicious."

"Yeah, like what?"

I felt the sudden shift as Deepling entered hyperspace. Cut off from Head Case, unable to breathe, Archie growing impatient beneath my collar, there was suddenly no way off this ship before we reached our destination.

And Ben was about to do something drastic.

His hands glowed on the table, his lips barely moving. At once, the pressure on my throat vanished, and Larev flew from one side of the galley to the other, tossed like one of the paper cups in the waste container. He hit the bulkhead with a solid thud as Ben reached his feet.

"I'm not with the Warden, you idiots," he said calmly. "I'm his worst nightmare."

# CHAPTER 15

The other recruits joined me in staring at Ben as he stood on the far side of the galley table. They probably didn't notice how heavily he leaned on his hands, the glow slowly fading from them, or the beads of sweat forming at the edge of his curly hair. But I did.

The Hemids and Lavona remained frozen in shock as I moved to join Ben, ready to support him if he lost his balance. He had exerted a lot of energy to create his show of force, a risky maneuver that seemed like it might pay off.

"How...How did you do that?" Larev said, shaking off his impact with the bulkhead.

"That's impossible," Lavona agreed. "Who are you? What are you?"

"I told you already," Ben replied. "An enemy of the Warden's. Which by my estimation makes me a friend of this cargo ship's owner. That's why we're here. That's why we signed up."

"But...how did you do that?" Yurt asked, echoing Larev.

"I'm different," Ben answered vaguely. He slowly sat back down. I could sense his relief to get off his feet, exhausted by his use of chaos energy. "The more important question is, do you still want to question our loyalties?"

"Not me," Lavona said, hurrying to sit to Ben's left while I sat to his right. The other recruits joined us at the table, though Larev didn't have space to sit. He stood behind Lavona. "From what I understand, we don't challenge the Warden directly," she continued. "That's not what this is all about."

"It's about family," Karpov agreed. "Watching each other's backs."

"That's not what we heard," I said. "I mean, that's part of it, but there's also a rebellious nature to the business."

"Who told you that?" Larev questioned.

"We know about all of this the same way you do," Ben said. "Rumors and hearsay tinged with truth."

"So what do you have against the Warden?" Yurt asked. "He's a hero to some of Warexia, the closest thing to a god to the rest."

"What do you have against the Warden?" Ben countered.

"Nothing."

"Then why are you here?"

"I heard it was an easy way to make a lot of quark, so long as you're willing to do whatever you're told without question. Which is better than spending my life at some menial task, ultimately replaced by a robot."

"I've been to Cacitrum," Ben said. "Why not buy a bot of your own and let it work for you, like the other Hemid?"

"Yeah, it seems great, right?" Larev said. "Except those machines are third or fourth generation, traded out and replaced for new models, but their base pay rate is grandfathered in from the initial rollout of the program. To buy in now means you'll earn just about enough to make the monthly payment on the bot, and if you're lucky, have enough left to buy food, forget about shelter."

"We didn't see any poor on Cacitrum," I said.

"How much of the planet did you visit?"

"Portus and the capital," I admitted.

"Just like a tourist. You see what they want you to see and think it's all wonderful. A lot of Hemid have left Cacitrum because there's nothing for them there. No opportunity at all. All three of us are here for the opportunity. The shot at a better life."

"And you don't care what you have to do to get it?"

"No. Neither do you, or you wouldn't be here."

I tensed, realizing I'd broken character and slipped on my own morality.

"We're not in it for the quark," Ben said, covering for me. "Not that we're going to send whatever we earn to charity, but we're hoping to make enough of an impression to get an audience with the Chief Executive."

"You want a personal meeting with Ma—"

"Shh!" Lavona snapped before Yurt could say the name. "If I hadn't seen what I just saw, I would have said you're crazy to try to get all the way up to the top of the food chain. But you just might pull it off."

"We plan to move up quickly," Ben said. "And you know, you can never have too many friends."

"I don't know," Karpov said. "I'm not too keen on the idea of doing anything against the Warden."

"And you think the Warden is in favor of this operation?" I asked. "You can't get rich if he shuts us down. And you're obviously worried about it, or you wouldn't have accused us of being plants."

"You're pretty observant," Lavona noted. "The kid's right. We all know this kind of business isn't sanctioned." She looked at Ben. "If you're interested in friends, consider me one of them. I knew you were different from the moment I saw you, and now I know why."

"I appreciate the vote of confidence," Ben replied. "What about you, Larev?"

"I'm not ready to commit to anything," the big Hemid replied. "Glowy hands and telekinesis notwithstanding, I don't know anything about you two. But you're right about one thing. We're on the same side. So, if you're good with me and my crew, then we're good with you."

"Truce, then," Ben agreed. "I felt the shift to hyperspace, so it seems Katzuo and I are committed. I'm glad we won't have to hurt any of you. Do you have any idea where we're headed?"

"No," Lavona replied. "All the recruiter told me was that we'd be delivered to a training center. I don't know where it is, or what we'll be training to do."

"I heard the bulk of the business is in cargo," Yurt said. "With a side of salvage and scavenging abandoned colonies and former war zones. Based on that, I think most recruits are assigned to work on ships like this one. It isn't glamorous, but like I said, I hear the pay is ten times better than with more traditional shipping lines."

Nobody said the quiet part out loud, and nobody needed to. We all understood the general nature of the cargo in question.

"Yeah, well, now that the fun's over, I'm going back to my rack," Larev said. "There won't be much to do until we get where we're going, however long that takes. They didn't give us a gym, so I might as well sleep." He waved dismissively before leaving the galley. Karpov and Yurt followed his lead, returning to their racks.

"I want to know more about what you did to Larev," Lavona said, leaning closer to Ben. "Is it some kind of magic or something?"

"You could say that," Ben replied.

"Can you teach me?"

"I'm afraid not. There's a genetic component."

She made a face and slid away from him in response.

"Well, we can still be friends. But you get what you give. If you give nothing, then you get nothing."

"Fair enough," Ben replied. It wasn't like he had asked her for anything. "You never said. Are you here for the quark, too?"

"That's one motivation, but not the only one."

"What's the other?"

She smiled slyly. "Like I just said, you get what you give. I'm going back to bed, too." She stood up. "If you're hungry, avoid the darker bars. They taste like Hemid farts."

"Thanks for the advice," I said.

"Anytime." She winked at Ben and me before exiting the galley, too.

"That was risky," I whispered once she had gone.

"I know. I didn't have any other choice. I'm just glad it worked."

"How do you feel?"

"I don't think I can stand without falling over. Did I hide it well?"

"They probably wouldn't have been so amiable if they suspected it was a one-shot deal."

"Good point. Hungry?"

"A little."

"Let's try the snacks while I rebuild enough energy to make it back to my rack without collapsing. Let's just steer clear of the dark ones."

# CHAPTER 16

The next eleven days aboard Deepling crawled by at an agonizing pace. Ben and I remained confined to cramped recruit berthing with our hulking Hemid bunkmates and the fiery Lavona. Lavona's attitude toward us had started to thaw after Ben's use of chaos energy. The others remained wary, keeping us at arm's length whenever possible in the tight quarters.

Ben tried his best to use the interminable days of forced idleness to better acquaint himself with each recruit. Watching him employ his easy charm, wit, and confidence like well-aimed ion cannon blasts quickly became another learning experience. It impressed me how easily he connected—or at least tried to connect—with the other recruits, working to slowly breach their standoffish exteriors.

He started with Lavona, complimenting her horns and expressing interest in her homeworld of Viconia. Flattered by the attention, she dropped her guard enough to share tidbits about growing up in the war-torn city of Valma. Over repeated conversations, Ben unlocked more details about the long-lasting civil war that had left the entire planet in disarray, subtly steering each exchange to focus on her motivations for signing on and digging for her feelings toward the Warden. I suspected Ben believed the laughing wanna-be god had a hand in starting the fighting on Viconia. Then again, it was easy to suspect the Warden had a hand in everything.

"I want to earn enough quark to get the rest of my family off Viconia," she finally admitted over the mostly bland protein bars. Despite her earlier warning, I had decided to take a chance on the darker ones and found them to be the best of the bunch. They tasted almost like chocolate. Considering she had told Ben and me that we smelled bad, I probably shouldn't have been surprised. "The Vikers, the currently recognized government, control the flow of information in and out of the planet," she went on. "They've convinced so many people there's nothing else out here that's any better than what they already have. That the whole galaxy is in flames."

"So how did you discover the truth?" Ben asked, relaxing on the galley bench.

"That was my brother's fault," she replied. "Kersho and some friends of his joined the opposition Respers. My parents tried to warn us away from it, but he was always so headstrong, he refused to believe the Viker propaganda. He sent me coded messages, telling me how the Respers were importing weapons and electronics from other planets. That they had gained access to the commweb and learned the truth about Warexia. That the war was only on Viconia." She paused, her eyes misting. It was an odd sight to watch a devil cry. "I decided to join the opposition, but Kersho was killed before I could make contact."

"I'm so sorry," Ben said.

"Me, too," I agreed.

"I didn't want to end up like him, so I decided to leave. I convinced one of the incoming cargo ships to take me on as a crew member, and I served there for a year earning my passage. After that, I took on whatever work I could find. I haven't spoken to my parents or my sisters since, but I keep tabs on the situation there. I know things have gotten worse. My parents, they will probably never leave, but my two sisters might if I can reach them. The recruiter said the syndicate takes care of its own. Maybe that would extend to them, too, and they'll help me get them away from there."

"The syndicate would be stupid not to value someone of your resourcefulness and experience," Ben replied smoothly. "I hope you succeed."

His focused sincerity brought color to her cheeks. After that her residual suspicions vanished. While she had mainly buddied with Larev and his Hemid friends before meeting us, she began spending increasing time with us instead.

Emboldened by Ben's progress with Lavona, I attempted to engage the Hemid trio's leader in idle conversation. The hulking recruit indulged my initially tentative small talk with grunts and single-word replies. When I shifted topics toward his origins, his responding glower cut my effort short.

"You and your mouthy brother should just mind your own business," he rumbled. "Just because Hondo's got glowy hands doesn't mean I trust either of you."

Rebuked, I left the sullen Hemid to his thoughts. Ben flashed an encouraging grin across the tiny aisle separating our racks before picking up where I had failed. Within a couple of days, even Larev's perpetual scowl softened toward something almost resembling camaraderie when interacting with Ben. His easy leadership style never ceased to impress me. Meanwhile my attempts at fostering rapport slowly met with increasing success. My original awkwardness smoothed out over time, my nerves steadying and allowing me to present with greater sincerity, building my confidence. I even got Larev to say four whole sentences at one time.

By day four, the forced isolation had begun fraying everyone's sanity. A bit of relief arrived via Grint, one of Deepling's Lycene crew. The elven-style ILF ducked into cramped berthing to inform us our vacation was officially over, and it was time for us to make ourselves useful. From that moment forward, we would spend most of our waking hours cleaning corridors and maintaining air scrubbers. Despite the promise of long days spent swabbing the poop decks, it beat the heck out of lazing around cramped quarters. The announcement sparked excited chatter as we eagerly filed from claustrophobic berthing into the ship's passages beyond. Menial labor sounded infinitely preferable to staring at the same five faces for another minute.

My excitement evaporated by the end of the first cleaning day. The long, tedious hours spent endlessly mopping floors and cleaning membranes left me tired and sore. The work itself wasn't complicated, yet the sheer mind-numbing monotony of the tasks drained me almost as quickly as the physical exertion.

Not to mention, I worried about Ben. He managed to keep pace beside me for the first couple of days, but by the third day of cleaning it became increasingly obvious that the grueling routine was taking its toll. Dark circles formed under his eyes as each shift dragged endlessly by, sweat beading his too-pale face. Yet he refused to slow down or lessen his efforts, pressing on without complaint despite the visible toll the labor extracted. Determined to shoulder my responsibilities and as much of his as I could, I redoubled my efforts to spare him as much work as possible without drawing undue attention from the others.

Regardless, Lavona noticed, but that was where Ben's efforts to befriend the other recruits paid off. She surprised me by also picking up the slack for him, sharing silent glances with me as we worked harder than anyone else. Later, Ben informed her of his condition without mentioning chaos energy, drawing sympathy and a promise not to reveal anything to the others.

Four more excruciating days of toil crawled past before a new voice interrupted our work detail. "Recruits, gather your gear immediately! We've reached your final destination." The sharp order echoed down the waste reclamation passageway.

"It's about time," Lavona said as she walked down the corridor, dropping her mop to the deck.

Excited by the prospect of freedom, we hurried after Ben back to berthing. My gut churned with a mixture of anticipation and nerves. After nearly two weeks of uneventful travel, Deepling had finally emerged from hyperspace over a yet-unknown planet. But where exactly had we ended up? And of greater concern, what came next for Ben and I?

Questions swirled as I hastily threw on my jacket and gathered my small satchel. Ben finished donning his long coat, movements stiff with exhaustion. Our arrival couldn't have come at a better time. I couldn't be sure he would have made it another day without more time off his feet resting.

I reached up to give Archie a reassuring pat. I knew the little shapeshifter might prove our only ace up a sleeve should events go sideways. The Aleal squirmed gently beneath my shirt, tendrils gripping firmly around my shoulders in silent confirmation of readiness. I took some comfort knowing that no matter what awaited us, my tiny guardian would defend me without hesitation.

As the others gathered their personal items, Grint returned to rush us impatiently toward Deepling's main hangar. I fell into step beside Ben, sharing a knowing glance. Since neither of us had suffered internal shocks that would suggest Head Case had fallen more than a light year behind, we both knew the others were nearby, ready to swoop in at a moment's notice should we need them.

Stepping into the ship's hangar brought me up short. The outer bay door already sat open, an invisible force field protecting the interior from the danger of space while affording an arresting view of the planet looming large beyond it. Swirling clouds enshrouded the orb, which I immediately related to a more primordial, extreme version of Earth. Even at this distance, I could make out towering snow-capped mountains and deep yawning canyons carved across the massive land masses below. Random expanses of inky blackness across the landscape hinted at vast forests and seas. It was at once staggeringly beautiful and deeply imposing. I tore my attention from the view only when Grint roughly shouldered past, grumbling about the delay. Shooting Ben a nervous glance, I quickened my pace to catch up.

My friend moved beside me, expression set in rigid lines. Pain bracketed his dark eyes. Our arrival had permitted his body to relax a little, emphasizing his overall exhaustion. My chest constricted with sudden fear over what awaited us. Ben read my thoughts in my anxious expression.

"Almost there, Kat," he offered with forced lightness. "Let's hope they roll out the red carpet for us."

"No offense, but you look like you need them to roll out a gurney for you," I replied, trying to match his lightness.

"It's nothing fourteen hours of sleep won't fix," he replied.

I swallowed hard and managed a weak grin in return. It wasn't as if we could change course now.

Deepling's crew directed us toward a compact shuttle docked along the hangar's aft bulkhead. We filed in silently, cramming against the oval cabin's inner hull beside the other recruits. My heart hammered as the shuttle disengaged from the ship with a slight lurch, fully exposing the planet still looming large beyond the forward viewports. Soon, we passed beyond the reach of Deepling's artificial gravity, beginning entry into the pull of the unnamed world below.

Like the primordial Earth I imagined this place to be, a violent atmosphere greeted our descent. I gripped my harnesses nervously, the progressively sharper buffeting threatening to shake the shuttle apart and even my teeth lose. Another few minutes and the violent quaking eased as our pilot navigated a pass through the wispy cloud cover. Craning my neck to see out the flight deck viewport, I glimpsed a breathtaking landscape of sheer peaks and narrow valleys spread out below us. Ice and snow brushed even the lower elevations. Our pilot deftly maneuvered the now steady shuttle inside a deep gorge between two imposing cliff faces before finally descending into a shadowed surface opening.

Our shuttle entered a cavernous hangar already loaded with additional shuttles, larger transports, and hundreds of stacked crates. Robotic loaders lurked around the crates, ready to move them in and out of the apparent base. Squeezing between two similar shuttles, we touched down with a slight bounce.

Grint emerged from the flight deck as the side hatch opened. "All right, move it recruits!" His gruff shout sent all of us scrambling from the opened shuttle.

We stepped onto smooth, dull metal decking, unease churning in my gut. Overhead, an enormous dilating gate began grinding closed, further concealing the hangar. Panic threatened to have me contact Matt immediately, telling him we needed recovery before we vanished deeper into the mountain base. I firmed my resolve, glancing at Ben, who nodded slightly. I noticed Lavona also looking my way, seeking comfort in these alien surroundings. I nodded to her, and she returned the gesture, her confidence rebounding.

"Welcome to Marin!" Grint said as a very tall, severe-looking woman with midnight black skin sidled beside him. She was completely bald and dressed all in black. Grint gestured toward her. "This is Miss Asher. She'll be your boss during your time here. It's her job to ensure that you have what it takes to become a valuable member of the family."

Her dark lips split, revealing a fanged grin. "It's my pleasure to welcome you, as well. These next few weeks will not always be easy for you, but by the end of your time with me, you'll either be fully prepared to succeed in your initiation, or you'll be dead. Come along."

# CHAPTER 17

A cold spike of fear lanced through me at Asher's blunt declaration. I exchanged an uneasy glance with Ben, noticing his jaw tighten. We knew about the initiation and expected some aptitude testing, but nothing quite like the ordeal she suggested.

We fell into an anxious formation behind the woman, trailing her out of the hangar into a maze of smoothly bored stone passages. I took in little of the sparkling, mineral-rich corridors as Miss Asher guided us deeper into the mountain base.

Finally, we reached our mysterious destination, a pair of doors emblazoned with stylized daggers that whisked aside at her approach. Halting just over the threshold, I stared in surprise at a huge auditorium with terraced seating angled toward a wide sunken combat circle. Various melee weapons bristled from racks scattered across the arena floor, revealing glimpses of brutal sessions to come.

Asher intended to waste no time.

"What if I just want to mop floors on a cargo ship?" Yurt

mumbled softly behind me. As the smallest of the Hemid, it made sense he didn't want to be a combatant.

"Question," Ben said, speaking out for us.

Asher's sharp gaze settled on him. "What is it, recruit?"

"I thought the business was more focused on acquisitions and logistics," he said, choosing his words carefully.

Asher smirked. "And we do. What you'll be exposed to during your time here will primarily assist the appropriate stakeholders when filling assignments..." Her eyes turned my way. "...though some of you were accepted based on pre-existing skill sets, which we intend to both rank and hone." She looked back at Ben. "Does that answer your question?"

"Yes, Miss Asher," he replied.

"Good. Recruit Hondo, and your younger brother, Katzuo, isn't it?" she drawled without blinking, eyes shifting uncomfortably back to me. "Janella spoke quite highly of your arena performance at Asterock. Let's see if her glowing praise lives up to reality."

She motioned for me to follow her into the combat circle. I looked to Ben, hoping he could save me, but he nodded in support, leaving me no choice. I squared my shoulders and trailed the dark vampire woman, refusing to let nerves get the better of me.

Reaching the circle, Asher's next razor smile sent my pulse galloping. Selecting an ebony shock rod from the rack closest to her, she dropped into a fighting stance directly across from me.

"Katzuo, show me what you've got."

My breath caught as adrenaline flooded my system, my eyes darting to the nearest weapon rack. While I had achieved impressive arena combat scores, it was as part of a team with Ally, Tee, and Lantz. Without them, I probably didn't stand a chance. This wasn't the Asterock Arena. The swords, glaives, nunchucks, and other melee weapons would do real damage. Still, I knew my only option was to obey or risk her wrath.

"Well?" Asher chided. "I won't wait forever."

I steadied my breath like Matt had taught us, closing my hands into fists, eschewing a weapon. I sank into a balanced stance, knees bent, hands loose and ready, eyes tracking her every move. Asher darted forward without warning, her shock rod almost a blur as she unleashed a series of blistering thrusts. I desperately dodged and wove, narrowly evading her initial lightning strike. My reaction was just a hair too slow. The rod's tip grazed my shoulder in a flash of white fire, muscles instantly locking up. I stumbled back with a choked cry, barely regaining my feet in time to avoid a follow-up jab to my ribs.

Asher pursued me relentlessly around the combat circle, her superior speed and reach keeping me scrambling on the defensive. I couldn't evade every attack. A particularly skillful feint knocked me aside before she landed a painful kick to my right thigh. My leg buckled, and I sprawled onto the stone floor, barely catching myself against the hard earth. Asher closed in, rod poised to deliver a finishing strike. Desperately, I flung a handful of debris toward her face. She recoiled reflexively, and I used the precious second to roll clear as electricity sizzled the ground where I'd collapsed.

Clambering upright and dancing back, I raised my fists just in time to deflect a vicious follow-through. We exchanged a flurry of strikes. Her unnaturally quick blows forced me onto my heels until another got through my faltering guard. It caught me squarely across the ribs, dropping me to my hands and knees and leaving me gasping through the aftermath.

"Not bad, but I expected more." My ears were ringing, but I still heard her soft voice.

Ribs throbbing, sweat streaming down my face, it was

all I could do to catch my breath, but I dragged myself upright through sheer force of will. Across from me, Asher paused, idly spinning her shock rod while she observed my struggling recovery.

"Well, don't stop now," she purred. "I'm just getting warmed up."

Before I could rejoin the contest, Larev's rumbling voice echoed unexpectedly through the arena.

"Leave the runt alone! I'll take you on instead."

I turned in surprise to find the hulking Hemid recruit approaching. His heavy features were set with challenge. Asher's violet eyes narrowed, gaze raking his muscular form. After a moment, she smiled again.

"How gallant of you to volunteer. By all means, show me your skill...if you can." Her tone dripped with mockery. Still, she spun lightly on one heel and dropped back into a fighting stance without hesitation. The rod's tip sparked. "Give me your best shot."

Larev bared his teeth in a feral grin. Head lowered, he charged straight at our instructor like an enraged bull. Even I could tell it was a disastrous opening gambit. Asher stood her ground before slipping aside in a blur of supernatural grace. Larev thundered past her flickering shadow. At the last instant, she pivoted, bringing her weapon up and around to jab him hard in the back. The shock rod discharged in a visible arc of energy. Larev's roar sputtered out. Every thick muscle spasmed as he crashed face-first to the arena floor.

My gut lurched in dismay. So much for gallantry. If Larev represented our best fighter, we had no chance against this woman. Her soft, cruel laughter raised every hair on my neck.

"Pathetic," Miss Asher scoffed, circling Larev's massive twitching form. She prodded him contemptuously with the tip of her boot, rolling him onto his back. "Is this really the best you can muster?" The hulking recruit groaned, eyes glassy and unfocused. Asher glanced my way, disappointment etched across her angular features. "Thus far, you've all failed to impress."

Sudden movement at the corner of my eye drew my attention. I turned to see Lavona striding fearlessly into the arena. "You want impressive?" she called out. "It's my turn."

Asher regarded her new challenger with renewed interest. A smile teased the corner of her full lips. "My dear, you may actually give me a worthy fight."

Lavona matched her instructor's expression, baring sharp incisors in anticipation. Without another word, she launched herself across the intervening distance. I watched spellbound as she unleashed a blurring combination of strikes and kicks, forcing Asher onto the defensive for the first time since we arrived. For all the conversations Ben and I had with Lavona during our trip here, she'd never mentioned that she knew how to fight.

She and Asher battled back and forth across the arena, neither giving quarter. My nerves jangled with every tense exchange, certain our supervisor would prevail. Somehow, Lavona managed to counter her blinding speed, even landing several solid blows despite the shock rod's paralytic effect.

I glanced at Ben and read the same burgeoning hope in his tightened expression. When I turned my attention back to Lavona, she was flat on her back, Asher standing over her.

That's when it hit me. None of us could best Asher alone in single combat, and she knew it. But together...

"Do you submit?" our supervisor asked Lavona, who flipped backward to her feet, baring her devilish fangs.

"I'm just getting warmed up," she replied in the same tone Asher had used earlier.

I understood what Asher wanted, what we needed to

demonstrate here and now. Gritting my teeth against the aftershocks still coursing through my frame, I staggered back toward the ongoing melee. Lavona reengaged our instructor, keeping her occupied as I circled toward her unprotected back. Asher remained oblivious to my presence, attention consumed trying to penetrate the recruit's whirling defense. I tensed as Lavona disengaged by several steps, chest heaving from exertion. In that instant, I struck, launching a running jump kick squarely between Asher's shoulder blades. Our instructor sprawled forward with a surprised grunt as Lavona charged back in, seizing immediate advantage. Within moments she had Asher pinned, and the shock rod knocked well out of her reach.

"Do you submit?" Lavona growled at Asher, shooting me a fierce smile over her shoulder. As I moved, intending to help Lavona back to her feet, the pinned woman began emitting a strange wheezing. My steps faltered. Was she...laughing?

Sure enough, a moment later, her rich laughter echoed around the arena. Still chuckling as Lavona released her, she flowed easily back to her feet. Retrieving her fallen weapon, she flashed an approving smile our way.

"Well done, both of you. It seems you *do* understand the most basic lesson after all—the syndicate is more than a business. It's more than a network. It's more than contracts and quark. The syndicate is a family, and we have each other's backs. Always." She glanced meaningfully around at all of us. "Remember that, recruits. Rely on and protect each other, and there's no limit to what you might achieve here."

Though we all remained wary of what else our ruthless supervisor might demand, a collective breath of relief swept the arena in the wake of Asher's unexpected praise.

Once the last of the paralytic tremors finally faded from my limbs, a new concern entered my scattered thoughts. Ben had yet to undertake his own assessment. What if Miss

Asher still meant for him to fight? They certainly made a more equitable match in size and reach. However, I doubted even Ben's special abilities could counter the woman's terrifying speed and skill. And as tired as he was, he had a zero shot at defending himself without chaos energy.

Thankfully, Asher showed no interest in further evaluations for the time being.

"That concludes your welcome drill," she announced. "Even with such a woeful beginning, you have clear potential." She bestowed another smile upon Lavona and me. "It seems Janella's faith may not have been entirely misplaced."

A muted groan echoed from the arena floor as Larev slowly collected himself under Asher's indifferent stare. "Your form and approach are on the wrong side of pathetic. But how you tried to protect your smaller fellow recruit is commendable."

A trio of subordinates filed into the arena, dressed similarly to Asher. Two were of her same species, while the third appeared to be human.

"Take that one to the infirmary for treatment," Asher ordered, pointing at Larev. "Show the others to their barracks."

"Yes, Mistress," they replied in unison.

With that, Asher turned and exited the auditorium without a backward glance.

"Nice moves earlier," Lavona commented, dropping into stride beside me as we trailed after the others toward the exit.

"Are you kidding?" I replied. "She kicked my ass."

"She's a Nyrian. The entire universe is moving slower for her than for anyone else here, except maybe me. That you didn't lose as quickly as Larev is a real accomplishment."

"You mean she has supernatural reflexes?"

"Supernatural for a human," she answered. "You did well. Believe me."

I flashed a sheepish grin at the unexpected praise. "Yeah, well I can't take too much credit. Arena matches got me accustomed to reacting rather than thinking." I lowered my voice, brow creasing. "Do you think we can really hold our own here?"

Lavona blew out a breath as we stepped through the training hall doors into a stark corridor. "Honestly? No clue. But the first lesson was a good one. We'll pull each other through, no matter what she throws at us next. I've got your back, little human. Yours and your brother's."

She briefly squeezed my shoulder in reassurance before she slipped past to catch up with the others, leaving me staring after her in surprise. That had sounded almost like the beginnings of friendship.

If days under Asher's tutelage lay in our near future, at least Ben and I wouldn't face them alone.

# CHAPTER 18

Our guides led us from the combat area down several winding passages before stopping at a nondescript door. One of the subordinates placed his hand on a sensor beside the portal. The slab whisked aside at his touch, exposing a barracks space similar to recruit berthing aboard Deepling, only far more spacious.

I followed Ben and Lavona across the threshold, excitement and nerves seesawing through my gut. I had apparently passed my first test with flying colors. But what else would we need to endure to satisfy the Warden's whims?

I abandoned my inspection of our new quarters when I noticed we weren't alone. Three unfamiliar beings already occupied a few of the available bunks. At our entry, they ceased their casual chatter and swiveled their heads around to study us with obvious interest.

Two of the three were Lycene, androgynous figures with elongated limbs and ears, alabaster skin and ruby eyes. Add in their high cheekbones and delicate features, and they brought to mind the elves of Tolkien's Middle Earth. They were dressed in brightly colored, form-fitting clothing. The third recruit's physical appearance was outwardly human, her shirt and trousers a contrasting muted gray. All three radiated a mix of curiosity and stand-offish intensity. I tensed, wondering if our welcome would prove as uneasy here as our initial introductions aboard Deepling.

An awkward pause ensued until Ben stepped forward, his hand extended toward the nearest elven recruit. "You must be another batch of new recruits. I'm Hondo." His easy grin widened a fraction. "Did you just get here, too?"

After a split-second hesitation, one of the elves stepped forward and accepted Ben's proffered hand. "We arrived two days ago. I am called Cade." His mellow voice barely rose above a whisper. Releasing Ben's grip, he motioned toward his twin. "My brother Rhis. And this is Mak." Ben made the introductions for our own motley group and mentioned that Larev had gone to the infirmary but would probably join us soon.

"How did you fare against Miss Asher?" I asked the trio.

"What do you mean?" Mak replied.

"Didn't you have to fight her when you arrived?" Lavona clarified.

"No," Rhis replied. "We were escorted directly here, and told we were waiting on additional arrivals before beginning our assessments."

"What the heck?" I said, glancing at Ben.

"Asher did say that your reputation preceded you," Ben pointed out. "Maybe not in so many words, but still."

"Well, we're sorry to keep you waiting. But we're here now."

Cade smiled. "You are here, and I for one am glad. We're eager to move on to bigger and hopefully better things."

"What are you aiming for, assignment wise?" I asked.

"We're willing to serve wherever we're needed," Rhis answered. "As long as we can serve together."

"I've heard recruits who train together usually stay

together," Mak said. "I think we're supposed to bond while we're here or something."

I shifted my glance to Lavona, silent understanding passing between us. We'd already started down that road.

"I don't know about the rest of you, but I need to lie down," Ben said before claiming an empty lower bunk. He shrugged out of his long coat with a barely audible groan. The simple act seemed to accentuate his overall fatigue. The sooner he could rest and recover from cleaning Deepling's decks, the better.

An awkward beat passed before Lavona broke the lingering silence, heaving her own exaggerated sigh of relief. "I call top berth." She scooped up her discarded duffle and scrambled to the bunk above Ben's. "After being jammed in aboard that stuffy transport, I can use a little breathing space."

Yurt and Karpov began shedding their gear and moving to select one of the remaining empty bunks. I dropped my satchel on the lower berth across the aisle from Ben before turning my attention back to our fellow recruits.

"Anyway, nice to meet you all. Please excuse my brother if he doesn't seem overly excited right now." I offered Ben a teasing smile. "Someone partied a little too hard last night."

My quip finally pulled a quiet chuckle from him as he scrubbed both hands wearily down his face. "You know me too well, Kat."

I flashed the same grin over one shoulder toward Cade and the others, hoping to smooth any residual awkwardness and start the bonding process. The sooner we gelled as a unit, the easier things would be for everyone. "So, how was your trip here?" I asked Cade, curious if it was as long and cramped as ours. "I was sore from swabbing the deck before Asher planted me in the dirt."

Predictably, Cade's tentative half-smile widened toward

something more relaxed. "It was long, tedious and uncomfortable. We were assigned cleaning tasks, too."

Rhis released an indelicate snort. "We couldn't stretch out the kinks without knocking someone unconscious."

"Well, hopefully training here will prove more exciting than dusting light fixtures and cleaning toilets," Mak remarked.

"No doubt it will," Lavona agreed. "If that first welcome test was any indication, this next phase will be anything but boring."

"Let's hope Miss Asher plans to let us rest a bit before the next round." I sank down on my thin mattress with a tired huff. "That shock rod packs a heck of a punch. How's the food here? Is it any good?"

"Nothing special, but it's adequate. Galley's that way," Mak said, pointing to one of a pair of hatches that split the berthing in half. "Head's that way," she pointed to the other. "Uniforms and equipment are through that one." She motioned to the hatch at the rear of the room.

"We were told we didn't need to wear the uniforms until everyone arrived," Cade said. "They're dark and dull. About like the food bars."

"I can imagine you aren't a fan," I said. But by his comment, I hoped I would find a full stock of the chocolate-tasting food bars. It wasn't my fault if none of the Warexians could stand them. They ate weird purple paste and liked it.

Considering a trip to the galley, my eyes drifted to Ben, once more grateful Miss Asher hadn't picked him out for combat. He looked awful enough that I decided stuffing my face could wait. "It's been a long day. I think I'm going to get some shuteye, too. It was good to meet the three of you. I look forward to working with you and getting to know you better."

"And also you," Cade said. "I hope you find your rest refreshing."

"Thank you. You, too."

I lowered my head to the pillow, trying hard to ignore the throbs of pain from my ribs where the shock stick had nailed me and let the exhaustion carry me off to sleep.

It felt like I'd just closed my eyes when sudden blinding light and deafening klaxons jolted me awake. I had just enough time to reach a panicked upright position and bang my head on the overhead berth before Miss Asher's magnified voice blasted through unseen speakers:

"On your feet, recruits! Your assessment starts now!"

# CHAPTER 19

"So much for getting enough rest," Rhis practically snarled before joining the rest of us as we slid out of our berths.

While Ben and I had gone down for the count without removing our coats or boots, the rest of our group frantically began reaching for discarded clothes and footwear. The barracks hatch whisked open, and Asher's three subordinates rushed in wearing dark combat armor and toting rifles.

"Move it, recruits!" one of them growled. The three mixed with our group and shouldered us toward the exit.

"I'm still in my underwear," Lavona complained, gripping her baggy coveralls in one hand. I'd never seen any part of her skin beyond her head and hands before, and I did my best not to stare now. She was in incredible shape, her body layered with lean muscle. But her body also told a painful tale. Numerous scars mottled her flesh, drawing my immediate sympathy for whatever plight had caused them. The war on Viconia, I assumed.

"Grab your boots and move," Asher's underling snapped, pushing a shirtless Karpov toward the door.

I went forward on my own accord before any of the

subordinates could shove me, filing in beside Ben, who suddenly seemed a lot more energetic despite limited sleep.

"Restore?" I asked. He nodded silently.

Asher's three trainers guided us from the barracks into the corridor, urging us into a sprint with shouts and threats. One took the lead, guiding us through a maze of passageways that went by too quickly to keep track of them. The overhead lighting grew dimmer as we forged on, maintaining the pace as the air grew colder. I estimated we'd run almost two miles by the time we reached an open metal hatch leading into an impossibly dark room.

The lead trainer stopped at the door. "In you go," she ordered, waving us through.

"What is this?" Yurt questioned, trying to slow down. Another trainer on the other side of the door shoved him, stumbling into the center of the dark cubicle. The rest of us piled in behind him, with Cade and Rhis bringing up the rear. The trainer inside the room slipped out as the lead trainer grabbed the edge of the door, ready to slam it closed.

"Hold up!" a fourth trainer shouted, coming around the corner. Larev followed right behind him, still slightly bent over from the blow he had taken to his back. The trainer veered off, but the Hemid continued, without hesitation, into the room with us. The door slammed shut behind him, leaving us in pitch black.

I could sense the tension in the room, and while the space seemed large enough for us to spread out, we stuck tight, using one another's body heat for warmth and comfort. No matter what happened next, at least we were all in this together.

"Bastards didn't even let me put my clothes on," Lavona hissed.

"What do you think they're going to do with us?" Mak wondered out loud.

"Everyone, just stay calm," Ben said. "It'll be fine. Right now, they're probably just trying to unnerve us."

"It's working," Karpov said.

"Larev, how do you feel, man?" I asked to normalize the situation. "I appreciate you sticking up for me with Miss Asher."

"Kinda wish I hadn't now," Larev replied gruffly. "My back is killing me. You owe me, Kat."

"He didn't ask you to volunteer," Lavona answered. "I took you for a fighter, but...I guess not."

"I'll show you who's a fighter," he threatened.

"How do you plan to do that?" Yurt asked. "None of us can see a damned thing."

"Everyone, calm down," Ben repeated sternly enough for the room to fall silent. "Our singular lesson so far is that we can only succeed by working together. So let's try that before we try anything else."

"You're the one that can make your hands glow," Larev replied. "We could use some illumination."

"What do you mean, make your hands glow?" Mak asked. "I want to see that."

"It's not a parlor trick, Larev. Besides, they're not going to keep us in the dark forever."

As if in response to Ben's statement, the room shuddered, the vibrations traveling through the floor and up into our feet.

"I think we're moving," Rhis said.

"We're definitely moving," his brother replied.

"My eyes are adjusting," Lavona said. "I can see a little. Yurt, either move your hand or lose it."

"Sorry, I didn't know that was you," he replied.

"Right."

"The walls are lined with racks of clothing," Lavona continued. "Looks like cold-weather gear. I see packs.

Weapons, but not standard ones. Looks like training models."

"Training models?" I asked.

"Low energy, with sensors in the gear," Mak explained. "If you're hit, it'll register a small shock and harden the clothing. Too many hits and you won't be able to move anymore."

"This is another test, then."

"Looks like it."

"We must be heading to the surface," Ben said. "Lavona, since you can see, start passing out gear. They won't expect us to get a head start."

"Who died and made you the boss?" Larev asked.

"Someone has to take charge," Ben answered. "How many battles have you fought? Or obstacle courses have you run?"

"None yet. You?"

Ben's voice lowered, his tone revealing a heavier past than I'd even guessed. "Too many." He perked up right away. "Lavona?"

"I'm fine with you taking charge," she replied, brushing past me to get to the gear. Her skin inadvertently slid along my hand, revealing its damaged roughness. Then her hand found mine, and she pulled me through the group. "I need help passing stuff out."

"I can't see a thing," I replied.

"I'll give you directions."

Her hand vanished, replaced by material with a nylon-like feel, much lighter than I expected. Not that I needed it as much as the others, with the underlay still beneath my regular clothes.

"It's a single piece," Lavona explained. "The front is open. Find the legs with your hands, step into it, and then close the front. The material on the chest will cling to itself.

There's also a cowl you can raise to cover your neck and head. It will stretch."

"That sounds like a Yamari Coldsuit," Mak said. "Their military uses them. It's high-end kit to modify and pass out to recruits."

"I'm sure they can afford it," Karpov said.

I pulled the suit on, noticing how it shifted and stretched around my existing clothes, creating a comfortable fit, though I worried about Archie being suffocated beneath it. The Aleal sensed my concern, and in the darkness climbed from beneath my shirt, circling to my chest and waiting there while I finished joining the front of the coldsuit together. From there, Archie crawled around my neck and under the suit.

"Kat," Lavona said softly. "Are you—"

"I'm fine," I replied, cutting her off. I had to assume she had caught a glimpse of the Aleal. "It's fine. Trust me."

"I do," she answered.

"What's fine?" Larev asked. "What's going on?"

"Nothing you need to know about," Lavona answered. "Take this, Kat, and hand it to your brother. He's right in front of you, about three steps."

I accepted the offered coldsuit sight-unseen and took three steps forward, pushing the suit into the first hand I found.

"Got it," Ben said.

Half of our group were outfitted in the suits when the room finally shuddered to a stop. The door clanged and swung outward without warning, immediately allowing a freezing wind inside. The sudden light blinded us all, Lavona worst of all. She cried out softly, covering her eyes.

"Recruits," Asher's voice said over hidden speakers. "The Marin assessment course lies ahead. Your first true mission has begun. You have three minutes to gather whatever gear you can and evacuate the lift. You will be terminated from candidacy if you are still inside when it descends. The clock starts...now."

"Do you think she meant terminated, as in dead?" Rhis asked.

"I don't think it was an accidental choice of words," Ben replied. "If you can see, grab gear for the others."

"Are you kidding?" Larev asked, already pushing the others aside to grab a pack and a rifle racked near the door. "I'm not being terminated."

My eyes adjusted quickly, and I moved for the coldsuits to hand them out to Mak, Cade, and Karpov. Lavona held her head in her hands, still trying to adjust to the light.

"We have three minutes," Ben answered. "Plenty of time, thanks to our head start."

"Maybe I don't want to stick with the rest of you, then," Larev insisted. "Yurt, Karpov, you coming with me?"

"I'm not ready yet," Karpov replied.

"Then I'm leaving you behind. Who else is with me?"

"Are you stupid?" Lavona said. "Or did Asher crack you in the head, too? Our one and only lesson was that we need to work together."

Larev glared her way for a moment before shrugging. "Fine. I'll be waiting outside."

He practically knocked Ben over in his eagerness to get out. Yurt caught Ben before he could fall.

"Wait!" Ben cried. "It's—"

Larev stepped through the door, only making it two steps before a heavy barrage of what resembled small energy blasts poured into him, leaving him shuddering as if he'd been electrocuted. His coldsuit stiffened in response to the charges, and he toppled face-first into deep snow.

Ben sighed. "We have two and a half minutes to get him out of that coldsuit and into another one. Kat, help me grab his legs and pull him inside."

"You should just leave him," Mak said, pulling on her coldsuit.

"No," Ben answered. "We'll do this together, or we won't do it at all."

"Larev is dead weight," Lavona complained.

"I'm sure he'll prove himself later," Ben replied convincingly.

I joined Ben at the doorway, blinking against the blaze of sunlight spilling across the snow-encrusted landscape. My breath plumed as I stared in surprise at the vista of craggy white peaks and a towering evergreen forest. If I didn't know any better, I would have thought we were back on Earth in maybe Colorado.

We leaned out of the room, each of us grabbing one of the Hemid's legs and pulling him back inside. I expected the effort to drain Ben completely, but he held up well as we dragged the four-hundred pounder to safety.

"Cade, Rhis get him out of the suit. Mak, grab another one for him." Ben barked orders with a sense of urgency, no doubt tracking the time in his head.

"Kat, Hondo, here," Having recovered from her light blindness, Lavona held out a rifle to each of us.

"Thank you," Ben said, accepting the weapon. "Yurt, Karpov, do you have any combat experience?" They both shook their heads. "Not even the Asterock Arena?" Another shake.

"I have plenty of experience," Lavona said. "Too much. Like you."

"Okay, Kat, you're with us. The rest of you get Larev changed and back on his feet. We'll see if we can suppress the incoming fire."

"I don't need your help," Larev complained, still awake. He tried to move his arms, but the suit had hardened like iron.

"Looks to me like you do, friend," Cade said, separating the material and adjusting it so Larev could get his arm out.

"Are you two ready?" Ben asked. The last time he had looked so alive was in the cornfield of Jackson Farm when he had snuck up behind Tee, Ally, and I to introduce himself and Head Case.

"Ready," Lavona and I replied.

"I'll take the right flank. Kat, use the door as cover and take the left. Lavona, there's a boulder about twenty meters ahead. Try to get there."

"Try?" she said. "Let Larev try. I'll get there."

Ben grinned. "Let's go."

# CHAPTER 20

Ben counted down from three, and we sprang into action, bursting through the doorway with weapons up and ready. I followed Ben's directions, using the metal frame of the lift door for cover while spraying suppressive fire toward the hilly treeline on the left flank. Ben did the same toward the right flank on the other side of the threshold. Lavona moved like a blur, sprinting forward across a couple of feet of snow and diving behind the convenient cover of a large boulder that just happened to be sitting there for our use should we be smart enough to take advantage of it.

The opposing fire slackened as we popped up and down, taking turns laying down bursts from our training rifles. The energy blasts felt real enough when one hit my thigh, sending a solid shock through it and hardening the area. I grimaced but pushed through the pain, thankful for the minimal blast damage.

Behind us, Cade and Rhis finally freed Larev from his locked-up coldsuit and helped him shrug into a fresh one. Mak finished distributing the rest of the gear to Yurt and Karpov.

"Thirty seconds!" Ben shouted over the whine of our

rifles. "Lavona, cover our egress! Everyone else, grab your packs and move!"

With Lavona pouring suppressive fire from her advanced position, the rest of the group grabbed their assigned kits and sprinted from the lift. As one, we fanned out, pushing toward the treeline. A reduced hail of energy bolts sizzled around us, but Lavona's steady barrage helped prevent any accurate shots. Catching up to her at the boulder, we all took cover to regroup.

"Nice shooting," I said to Lavona, crouching beside her.

"You too," she replied with a fanged smile before noticing my thigh. "You're hit."

"Nothing serious."

"This is fun, isn't it?"

I might have offered a resounding yes if we had been in the arena. But this was way too real. Before I could answer, a shout rose from nearby.

"Rhis!" Cade cried. "What are you doing?"

My head whipped around, searching for the other Lycene. My breath caught when I found him still standing inside the lift. His trembling hands held his rifle at the ready, but he'd frozen on the spot, shaking his head. "I can't do it," he replied. "I'm sorry. This isn't what I came for."

"Rhis, I'll protect you," Cade shouted. "Come on, you're running out of time!"

"Ten seconds," Ben said before raising his voice. "Rhis! We can do this! *You* can do this! Come on!"

"Rhis!" Lavona shouted. I shouted my support. So did the rest of us. He looked back into the room before setting himself and stepping toward the door. It swung closed in front of him, cutting him off.

Five seconds early.

"Noooo!" Cade cried, rising to return to the lift. Larev grabbed his arm before he could move, holding him fast.

Out in the open between the boulder and the lift, he would have been gunned down in seconds.

"Bastards!" I snapped. "He still had time."

"There's nothing we can do," Lavona said.

"If they kill him," Cade growled, hands clenched around his rifle, "I'll—"

"You'll what?" Larev asked, letting go of the other man's arm. "Fight back against the entire organization? Good luck with that. Might as well go out there and get yourself frozen stiff." Cade glowered at him but didn't leave his position. Larev's attention turned to Ben. "Thanks for saving my ass. I'm going to listen to you from now on. No hard feelings?"

"None at all," Ben replied. "Let's just stick together, okay?" He said to everyone, and the nodding heads from the group confirmed what Lavona and I already knew. "Lavona, do you think you can get to the treeline?"

"I know I can," she replied.

Ben nodded. "Kat and I will cover you. Engage any targets you encounter."

"Gladly."

Ben and I peeled out from opposite ends of the boulder, opening fire into the trees. Lavona rose from behind the boulder, scaling over the top of it in a single, graceful leap. She bounded ahead with astonishing speed, zig-zagging to throw off the limited incoming fire. Several shots nearly hit her, but she never slowed, reaching the treeline at full tilt and vanishing into the shadows beneath the thick canopy. A few light flashes lit the shadows before the incoming fire stopped completely. Lavona reappeared at the edge of the trees, signaling all-clear.

"Maybe the rest of us should just wait here while she finishes the entire course," Mak said dryly.

"If combat is her thing, good for her," Karpov replied. "Better than us having to go out there."

"This test has only just begun. We need to put some distance between us and the lift, then get our bearings." Ben adjusted his grip on his rifle, meeting each of our gazes in turn. "Everyone stay close and keep your eyes peeled. Miss Asher seems fond of surprises. Move out!"

With Ben on point, we made for Lavona's position at a dead run, my senses straining for any hint of a threat. Though I had no idea what other challenges lay in store, one fact remained crystal clear—united, we stood a real fighting chance. Divided, we'd be lucky to survive.

"Nice job," I said when we reached her.

"Not that impressive," she replied, motioning to her right, where I found an automated gun turret toppled on its side.

The icy wind threatened to cut through even our high-tech coldsuits as we pushed onward, forcing us to raise our cowls. I discovered it covered the back and top of my head, neck and entire face, providing much-needed warmth and protection from the frigid air. Furtive rustles from deep within the woods kept us on high alert, rifles tracking each new sound. Knowing nothing about the planet Marin, I figured that anything could lurk in the trees, waiting to pick us off. I tried not to let the tension get to me, focusing instead on watching my footing over the uneven terrain. The last thing I needed was a twisted ankle slowing me down.

We hiked silently for almost an hour, guided as much by the terrain as anything else. I welcomed the strenuous effort of ascending a series of progressively steeper ridges. It helped keep me focused on the moment. At this point, the environment was the greatest threat to our survival.

As if to punctuate that reality, a particularly strong gust of wind caught me off-guard. I stumbled and would have tumbled back down the incline if Larev's meaty hand hadn't shot out to snag my arm at the last instant.

"Watch yourself, runt," he grumbled, effortlessly setting me back on my feet. "I won't be around to yank your tail out of the fire every time."

"Thanks," I replied breathlessly, offering a glance toward Lavona. By her cognizant expression, I knew she understood the meaning right away. If Ben had left the big Hemid behind, I would be at the bottom of the incline, seriously injured, if not dead.

We crested the ridge a short while later, trees thinning out to provide an elevated vantage point. Ben raised a fist, signaling a halt. Gratefully, I sank to a knee to catch my breath, shoulders and legs burning from the physical exertion. The others did the same, establishing a loose perimeter while sucking wind.

A resurgent Ben unslung his pack and knelt to dig through its contents. After a moment, he produced a compact case and cracked it open, revealing what appeared to be a survival kit—food bars, a medkit, a multi-tool, some rope, and a palm-sized electronic device I took for a compass. He powered on the small gadget and stared intently at the display, brow furrowed in concentration.

"Looks like they provided a basic map," he said, angling the screen to see the pulsing dot indicating our position imposed over a topographic map. "The terrain gets even rougher to the north, nothing but cliffs and deep ravines. To the east and west, more of the same. Forested ridges as far as the eye can see. My guess is that we're supposed to continue south." He traced a line on the display. "It looks like there's a bridge here, over an especially deep ravine, and if I'm reading this right, there's a small installation here."

"Can I see that?" Cade asked. Ben handed him the device. The elven alien moved the map, zooming in on the installation. "It's a military base. Look, there's a shuttle parked on a small launch pad. And those are robot guards."

"This is an assessment trial, right?" Mak said. "How much you want to bet we need to infiltrate the base and steal that shuttle?"

"Sounds reasonable," Ben agreed. "Any pilots in the group besides Kat and me?"

"Soldiers and pilots, too?" Lavona said, looking at Ben and then at me. "Impressive."

"Not that impressive, at least for me. I only know how to fly one kind of ship. I can figure that shuttle out if needed, I suppose."

"I'm a pilot," Cade said. "I haven't flown military, but I've flown a civilian version of a similar model."

"Let's make sure we get you there alive, then," Larev said.

"South it is," Lavona said, pushing to her feet. "We can follow this ridgeline for a few more klicks before we'll need to find a way down."

No one argued with the plan. We set off again, Ben taking the lead with Lavona close behind. I fell into step beside Mak and Cade. Larev, Yurt and Karpov formed a sort of rearguard, alert for any signs of pursuit.

We spent the next hour following the ridge south, thankfully unimpeded as we descended from the hilly terrain into a more even expanse of forest. The shape of the topography seemed to push the bitter cold wind toward our backs, buffeting nearby tree limbs and giving me an occasional shove forward. The air howled as it passed around wide trunks, rattling branches in a cacophony of natural sound. The din forced us to remain more visually alert, constantly scanning in all directions so we couldn't be taken by surprise.

Ben kept the map device in hand the entire time, monitoring our progress and ensuring we remained headed in the right direction. We remained another hour from the gorge, splitting our route and the bridge that crossed it, but in my estimation, we were making pretty good time.

I could only hope Miss Asher would agree.

The gales from the downslopes eased up somewhat as we forged deeper through the forest interior, the howling wind reduced to a stiff breeze. The overhead branches shook without crashing violently against one another or dropping smaller twigs on us. Passing between two sentinel evergreens, we entered a small, unblemished clearing. Halfway through, Lavona suddenly stiffened.

"Lava?" I said, using a nickname that just popped into my head. "What's wrong?"

She glanced at me, shaking her head. "The shape of this clearing is too perfect."

"What does that mean?" Larev asked.

Before she could answer, a loud metallic clank reverberated directly beneath our feet. I barely had time to register it before the ground abruptly fell away in a screech of buried hinges and pistons.

"Trap!" Ben shouted. But it was too late.

We plummeted into a hidden pit, tumbling in a confusion of limbs and curses to land in a graceless heap twenty feet below. I hit hard on my side, the impact blasting the air from my lungs.

Gasping, I rolled slowly off Larev to my hands and knees and stayed there, trying to pull air into lungs that didn't want to work. The others were doing the same, groaning and checking themselves for injuries. Miraculously, I didn't think I'd broken anything. The coldsuits and my landing on Larev had cushioned the worst impact.

"What...the hell..." Mak coughed. Lavona spat a curse that didn't get translated.

Ignoring our collective distress, Ben was already on his feet, though he was holding his ribs, his attention focused upward to the trap door in the process of sealing off the sky.

"Looks like another test," he said, glancing at the unscalable metal walls. The whole thing was too elaborate to have been placed accidentally.

"Another test that could have killed us," Larev complained, getting off the dirt floor.

"That *will* kill us, if we can't pass it," Karpov replied.

"Now what?" Yurt asked.

"Now we find the way out." Ben moved to the nearest wall, running a hand over the smooth surface. "There's got to be a release mechanism somewhere."

We spread out, searching the walls for any sign of a control panel. We would either pass this test or die here, trapped like an animal in a cage.

"Over here!" Karpov suddenly called. "I found something!"

We converged on his position to find the Hemid crouched before a small access panel, barely visible against the wall. A series of colored diodes winked on its surface in an intricate, ever-changing sequence.

"It looks like some kind of code lock," he said, squinting at the flashing lights. Each light appeared over a series of ten simple toggles in seemingly random up-and-down positions.

I doubted there was anything random about it.

"The lights create a pattern," I said. "We need to flip the toggles in the right order, to the right position, based on that pattern."

"How do you know?" Cade asked.

"I don't, for certain. It's just a guess."

"A good guess," Ben said.

"Some of them are flipped already," Yurt pointed out. "Maybe we just need to reverse them all." He reached over Karpov's shoulder to flip one of the toggles.

"Wait!" Ben snapped. "What if changing the position is irreversible? We'll be stuck here."

Yurt snatched his hand back. "I didn't think of that."

"Maybe we should get on each other's shoulders and try to force the trap door," Larev suggested, eyeing the unyielding metal. "If I push it from underneath, maybe I can dislodge it."

"We'd likely just end up with broken bones for our efforts," Mak replied. "And none of us want you standing on our shoulders."

All eyes turned back to the panel. Karpov's face was already set in deep concentration, watching the flashing lights. Ben and I joined him, watching them flicker on and off in different colors. Red, Green, Blue. It felt like another Warden game.

"No pressure," Yurt joked weakly. No one laughed.

"There are three colors," Ben noted. "I'll take red. Kat, green. Karpov, watch blue. Hopefully, we can build a pattern from a single color."

I stared at the panel, watching green. Nearly ten minutes had passed before I realized the sixth light never displayed that color. Did that mean the toggle was already in the correct position? But that would mean none of the others were. I didn't think that would be likely.

"It isn't green," I decided, explaining why.

"Then it isn't blue, either," Karpov replied.

"Or the pattern is multi-colored," Ben said.

We resumed watching the lights, minutes stretching to an hour before I couldn't look at the flashing any longer. Lavona paced like a caged animal while Cade kept glancing up at the sealed door, face tight with barely suppressed panic. Mak chewed her lip; rifle clutched white-knuckled to her chest.

"Nothing yet?" Yurt asked.

"If we had anything, we wouldn't still be staring at the lock," Karpov replied.

"This is taking forever," Larev said.

"How about instead of whining, you come help?" Ben said.

The big Hemid lumbered over from the other side of the pit. "Okay, I will." He replaced me over Ben's shoulder. Lavona joined me near the center.

"Lava?" she asked.

"In my language, Lava is superheated rock that becomes liquified. It's smooth-flowing, can be fast-moving, and very dangerous. Like you."

She smiled. "I like it."

"Which positions only have two lights?" Larev asked.

"Six," I said.

"Seven," Ben replied.

"Five," Karpov answered.

"Flip those three," Larev barked, his voice smug.

"Why those three?" Ben asked.

"It's another trick to make it seem harder than it is. The colors don't mean anything. Because what would three colors stand for when there are only two positions?"

Ben, Karpov, and I all stared at Larev. "You have to be kidding me," Ben said, the answer obvious now that the big Hemid had pointed it out. "Karpov, flip them."

He did. The access panel emitted a cheerful beep and flashed solid green. A mechanical thunk echoed above, and a hidden door in the side of the pit unsealed with a hiss and cracked open.

"Got it!" Larev crowed triumphantly, wearing a huge grin. He eyed Lavona. "Not such dead weight after all."

"No," she agreed. "I'm sorry I suggested we leave you behind."

"Apology accepted."

"Nice work!" Ben said, cracking a broad grin.

"I really thought we were done for," I said, clapping Larev on the shoulder. The Hemid ducked his head, pleased embarrassment coloring his round face.

"We're not out of the woods yet," Mak reminded us. "This trap is just the beginning. We need to stay sharp."

Larev grunted in agreement. "All the more reason to reach that installation and find our way off this rock."

No one could argue with that. With renewed urgency, we gathered our gear and set off once more. The distant bridge and sprawling base waited ahead, promising escape.

All we had to do was survive whatever gauntlet of additional hazards lay between us and salvation.

# CHAPTER 21

The sun hung low on the horizon by the time we finally cleared the dense forest and emerged at the edge of the gorge. Ben consulted the map once more before pointing to our left.

"The bridge should be two klicks that way. We're close."

"It's about time," Larev grumbled. "It's frigid enough that I can feel it through the coldsuit."

No one else had the energy left for verbal replies. Bone-weary, we fell in behind Ben and Larev, picking our way along the ravine's rim.

The bridge, constructed of massive metal girders and heavy deck plates, quickly came into view. I pulled up short, blinking in surprise. Whatever I had expected to find, it certainly wasn't the imposing structure spanning the yawning chasm between the sheer cliff walls. Standing at the very end of it was a lofty embattlement and tower that looked like something straight out of an Arthurian legend. While the portcullis stood open, the entire central span of the bridge was raised to form an impenetrable wall.

"Great," Mak complained, slumping against a nearby boulder. "Now what?"

"Did you expect this to be easy after our exit from the lift and escape from the pitfall?" Lavona asked.

"Look there." Ben pointed at a small stone building sitting off to the side of the bridge's initial span. "I think that's some kind of control station. If we can get inside, maybe we can find a way to bring that middle span back down." He paused, glancing at Lavona. "I don't expect it to be easy getting into that castle, but we can't just give up and not try."

"You're right." she said. "Let's do this."

We cautiously followed Ben as he approached the squat two-story structure, all of us alert for automated defenses or additional traps. Reaching the reinforced door without incident, Karpov stepped forward and rapped his knuckles against the metal.

"What are you doing?" Cade asked, alarmed. "What if there's someone inside?"

"That's the whole point of knocking," the burly Hemid grunted. "To see if anyone is inside."

"Like they'll just open up to greet a group of rifle-toting strangers? If there's someone in there, you're giving them time to hide or worse, jump out and ambush us."

"There's no one inside," Karpov insisted. He tried the handle. Locked. Bracing himself, he slammed one beefy shoulder into the portal. It shuddered beneath the impact but held. "Stand back," Karpov warned, backing up several paces before charging it like a rampaging bull. This time, the abused metal screeched and flew open, swinging inward to reveal a dark interior. "After you," he said, motioning grandly for us to enter.

Lavona, Ben and I led the way, sweeping the control room beyond for threats. Dim emergency lighting revealed banks of silent machinery. I moved to the nearest console and tapped several keys experimentally. No response.

"Looks like the whole system is down," I announced. "Maybe there's a backup generator somewhere?"

"Down there, if I had to guess." Lavona pointed toward a recessed hatch in the corner. I swallowed, trying not to imagine what fresh hazards might await us below.

Ben knelt beside the portal, examining the wheel lock. "Okay, we're going to need to split up. Some of us remain here and watch the bridge. The rest head down and try to find the backup power."

"I'll go," I immediately volunteered. No way was I letting Ben out of my sight.

"Me, too," Lavona said.

Larev grunted, jerking his head at Cade. "Flyboy, Mak and I will cover things up here. Yurt, Karpov, go with them. Your tech skills might come in handy."

"Good idea," Ben said. "Larev, a little help?"

The big Hemid moved to the hatch. He gripped the wheel lock and heaved it counterclockwise. Metal ground together in protest before the mechanism released with an echoing clank. Foul air wafted up from the dark shaft as he hauled the hatch aside. I wrinkled my nose.

"Smells lovely," Lavona said wryly, turning on a flashlight she had found in her equipment pack, angling it into the gloom.

"Probably just stale air," I replied, doing the same. The beams revealed a ladder down to a utilitarian catwalk.

Ben went first, slinging his rifle over his shoulder. I followed close behind, Lavona on my heels, and Yurt and Karpov took up the rear. The catwalk ended at another sealed hatch, emblazoned with warning symbols I couldn't read. I tensed, expecting some final failsafe or boobytrap to bring the whole thing crashing down on us.

The wheel lock spun smoothly under Karpov's hands and the door opened without protest, exposing a larger chamber. We cautiously advanced onto a wide grated landing overlooking banks of silent machinery. Overhead, a confusing web of cables and piping crisscrossed the ceiling, snaking into shadowed recesses. The huge room felt cavernous, our lights swallowed up by the oppressive darkness. I swept my light in a slow arc, unable to shake the sensation of unseen threats lurking just beyond the feeble illumination.

"Looks like the whole place is offline," Yurt commented.

"I bet the reactor's busted," Karpov replied. "That'll be fun to try to fix with a multi-tool."

"But can you do it?" I asked.

"If the problem isn't too severe."

"Any ideas where the reactor might be down here?" Lavona asked.

"Your guess is as good as mine," Karpov answered.

"Fan out," Ben said softly.

We moved to comply, spreading across the platform. Reaching a junction box, I played my light over the alien labels, searching for anything I recognized. Behind me, Lavona sucked in a sharp breath.

"What did you find?" I abandoned the fruitless effort and moved to join her. She angled her light to a schematic bolted to the bulkhead nearby.

"Here." Her slender clawed finger tapped a section of the blueprint. "Looks like there should be a backup generator on this level."

"Good eyes," Ben said, coming up on her other side. He turned and raised his voice slightly. "Yurt, Karpov, we've got a lead on a generator. Lavona's going to need your expertise."

"On our way," Yurt called.

I glanced back to see the pair moving to join us, my earlier unease returning. Before I could dwell on it, a hint of motion in my peripheral vision made me whip back around, my nerves jangling as I searched the darkness.

"There's something moving down here." I jabbed my light toward the far end of the platform, certain I'd glimpsed a large shape slinking through the shadows.

"I don't see anything," Lavona replied. Beside her, Ben frowned as he swept his own light back and forth.

My skin prickled. I knew I had seen movement. "Something's in here with us."

"That hatch was shut tight. How could anything get down here?"

"There could be another entrance from the outside," Ben said. "Or maybe something dug its way in."

"Or Asher's people put something in here before we arrived," I replied, shivering at the unsettling thought. "Maybe it's what smells so bad."

Yurt and Karpov reached our position, expressions puzzled.

"What's the hold up?" Karpov asked. "I thought we were looking for the generator."

"Katzuo thinks he saw something moving," Lavona explained.

"Probably just your imagination," Yurt said dismissively. "It's creepy down here."

Before I could respond, an echoing clatter rose from below, the sound of something substantial knocking into the machinery. We all froze, all arguments forgotten as we strained our vision to pierce the darkness. The sound came again, closer this time, followed by an unmistakable dog-like huff. Definitely not my imagination. And definitely bigger than any dog I'd ever seen. My finger tightened on my rifle's trigger.

"There!" Karpov shouted.

I jerked my light up as an enormous shaggy shape exploded from the shadows in a blur of snapping fangs and sharp claws. Yurt screamed. The monster slammed into him with the force of a locomotive, sending them both tumbling across the deck in a tangle of thrashing limbs. His screams turned gurgling and wet before falling silent.

More hulking shapes poured from the darkness below as the first beast reared back from Yurt's body, its crimson muzzle drawn back, blood dripping from its saber-toothed snarl.

I backpedaled in horror, my brain struggling to process the enormity of the threat. Vaguely wolf-like in appearance, each beast stood waist high at the shoulder, at least two hundred fifty pounds of solid muscle and bristling fur. They had broad, blocky heads, twisted horns, and eyes that glowed an unnatural green. As they stalked closer on silent paws, I counted at least six of them before panic sent me scrambling away, all thoughts of finding the generator forgotten.

Lavona and Karpov opened fire at the same instant. Maybe if we had real guns, we might have stood a chance. Our low-power blasts were barely enough to stun the nearest saber-wolf. It stumbled beneath the barrage before its pack mates surged forward as one.

"Back to the hatch!" Ben shouted. "Move!"

We sprinted for the ladder leading back up to the access shaft, the beasts hot on our heels. There was no question they would run us down before we could return to the surface. They were simply too fast, their fangs certain to drag us screaming back down into the depths of the darkness to share in Yurt's fate.

"Archie!" I shouted as I reached the ladder. Desperate, I ripped the cowl back from over my head. "Help!"

The Aleal responded, surging instantly from beneath my collar. It launched itself over my shoulder, stretching its body impossibly long to intercept the lead beast. I watched the alien slam into the saber-wolf, tendrils coiling tight around the monster's skull, its midsection hardening into a spike that stabbed into the beast's skull. The thing managed one startled yip as Archie leaped free of its massive body and it crashed to the deck. Rolling end over end, it finally collapsed dead at our feet.

We stumbled to a halt, the creature's pack mates coming to a halt on the other side in momentary confusion. The respite lasted only a heartbeat before the largest male shook itself and leaped over its leader's dead body, charging toward us. Coming around from the side, Archie again shifted into a lethal spike. Meeting the attack almost head-on, it sheared straight through the beast's forehead, splitting the creature's skull wide open before penetrating its brain and killing it instantly.

Covered in blood and gray matter, Archie shifted back to its original transparent form. Leaping onto the creature's snout, the Aleal brandished its dripping, spiked tendrils at the remaining wolves in clear warning. The pack skidded to a halt, snarling in fury and fear. For a moment I was certain they would attack despite the threat. Then as one they turned and fled, vanishing back into the darkness. Heaving for breath, I collapsed against the railing. Adrenaline left me lightheaded and shaking.

"What...the hell…is that…that thing?" Karpov gasped, pointing at Archie. "Where did it come from?"

"That's Archie," I replied weakly. "My friend.." The Aleal remained watchful a moment longer before returning to the gaping crater in the creature's forehead. It wrapped its tendrils around the wolf's skull and slithered inside.

Rather than disgusted, Lavona approached the downed saber-wolf and Archie with curious interest. She toed the beast with her boot. "I've never seen anything move as fast your little friend there. What is it?"

"It's called an Aleal," Ben answered.

"Where did it come from?"

"That's a long story," I replied.

"It eats brains?"

"Among other things," I replied as Archie uncoiled itself from the wolf's head, its body dark from the matter it had absorbed. No longer a secret, it climbed up my body to rest across my shoulder. "We need to keep moving before those things decide to take another pass at us."

Ben's troubled gaze met mine before he gave himself a visible shake. "Agreed. Let's find that generator and get out of here."

It took us several minutes to navigate to the ladder leading down to the floor and the access hatch in the back corner of the room. The schematic proved accurate. I nearly cried in relief when Karpov pulled the handle and the heavy metal door easily swung open, revealing a large backup generator. Acutely aware of the darkness pressing around us, the Hemid wasted no time setting to work bringing the machine back online.

"It's not really damaged," he reported, following a quick examination. "The starter wires are disconnected, and a couple of other parts weren't coupled.

"Another puzzle for us to put together," Ben said.

"Looks that way. It won't take long to fix, even with the multitool."

He dug the tool from his pack and set to work. Curiosity tugged me toward watching him work and maybe learning something. Given the deadly creatures still potentially lurking nearby, I was all too happy to take advantage of an engineering lesson.

"That should do it," Karpov announced within a few minutes. Flipping the starter switch triggered a low hum that built steadily to a deeper rumbling whir. All around us, dormant control panels flickered to life, bathing us in cool blue illumination. I had never been so happy to see indicator lights.

"You did it," Lavona said with a tired smile.

"Nice job, Karpov," Ben added.

"Now let's get out of here before those wolf-things come back," I suggested.

We sealed the generator room and hurried back to the access shaft, giving Yurt's body a quick nod of respect along the way. I assumed someone from the training facility would be along to recover the remains once we had left. Halfway up the ladder, my arms started shaking so badly I struggled to maintain my grip on the rungs. Residual shock and fatigue made me clumsy and weak. From below, Ben offered wordless encouragement, all but pushing me upward.

We spilled back into the control room to find Larev and Cade crouched tensely on either side of the door, rifles aimed into the deepening twilight. At our less than stealthy entrance they spun around, relief and confusion warring across their faces.

Relief quickly shifted to comprehension as they scanned our group and noted the missing member. "What happened down there?" Cade asked.

"Yurt didn't make it," Ben replied shortly. "We were attacked by native wildlife."

"At least, we assume they're native," I added.

Mak swore colorfully in words the implant didn't translate.

"But Karpov fixed the generator," Lavona quickly added. "I think I saw the main control panel when we entered."

She moved across the room to the far wall. A few keystrokes brought the terminal humming to life. A few more and a loud mechanical grinding sounded from outside. Rising from my seat against the wall, I looked out to see the central bridge span lowering into place, locking down with a quaking shudder.

"Alright!" Mak cried. "It worked! We can get out of here!"

Despite my exhaustion, a smile tugged at my mouth. She was right. We had made it past this latest challenge. Only one remained. The sprawling military base waited on the other side of the gorge, promising escape.

If we were strong and resourceful enough to make it off the planet.

Sensing my weariness, one of Archie's tendrils brushed my face, offering comfort and encouragement. Larev, Mak, and Cade noticed the Aleal but didn't comment, too tense and tired to care where the alien had come from. I would have felt the same way if I were in their shoes.

We needed all the help we could get, and my little squishy friend had proven to be just the backup we needed.

"Should we rest here a while?" I asked, looking at Ben. Inexplicably, he seemed to be growing stronger over time rather than weaker. Not that it was a bad thing.

"No," he replied. "Let's finish this."

# CHAPTER 22

The frigid wind picked up again as we emerged from the control room into the snowy night. Fresh flakes swirled on icy gusts, limiting visibility to only a few feet. Archie ducked back beneath the coldsuit as I pulled my cowl back over my head and face to keep out the stinging cold. Beside me, as we started across the bridge, the others did the same.

Metal groaned beneath our boots, the only sound beyond our labored breathing. No one spoke, too weary and focused on reaching the far side for idle chatter. I fell into step beside Ben, noting his tight expression. As the leader of this expedition, Yurt's loss weighed heavily on him. The Hemid recruit's absence was a stark reminder of what awaited the unwary or unlucky. How many more of us would fall before this trial ended?

We reached the other side of the gorge without incident, trekking another half-mile before pausing at the beginning of a steep trail leading, with several switchbacks, down the far side of the terrain. Below, the sprawling military base sat nestled between our ridge and a second—more sheer cliff face to navigate. Perimeter walls rose in concentric rings to protect the inner facilities.

Lights from the base twinkled like stars amidst the whirling snow, their nature making them more night-marish than idyllic.

"Looks like a tough nut to crack," Mak observed quietly. "Mountains on two sides. Double walls. Plenty of guard positions. And if they have sensor arrays on the peaks, we won't be able to get close without setting off a proximity alarm. That place is locked up tighter than a bank vault."

"Every fortress has a weakness," Ben countered. "We just need to find it."

"I can't imagine what kind of weakness a place like that would have," Cade said, looking down on the base. "We're done for."

"That's the spirit," Larev grumbled. "We didn't spend all day traipsing through the cold for your lousy attitude, especially after we passed the last two tests."

"Yeah, well, it isn't your brother who got left behind and is probably dead."

"No, but Yurt was a friend of mine," Larev growled back. "And your brother chose to stay behind. We didn't leave him."

Cade threw his rifle into the snow. "You son of a—"

"Enough!" Ben snapped, stepping between the two. "Be quiet, both of you. You're going to bring that whole base running making so much noise."

"Sorry, boss," Larev said. Cade stared at Ben, remaining silent.

"There has to be another way into the base," I said, looking down at the facility. "Ben, can we see the map again?"

He nodded, retrieving the device and showing me the map. I navigated around the installation, looking for signs of another entry outside of the immediate area. A place like that was bound to have a bolt hole or something.

"There!" Lavona pointed to what appeared on the map

as a handful of white speckles a short distance from the bridge.

"What are we looking at?" I asked.

"Runoff," Mak said, growing excited. "Wastewater, or maybe water from a cooling unit."

"That could be coming from the bridge," Cade said.

"No, it's on the wrong side," Karpov said. "If that is water flowing out to the ravine, it's most likely from the base. Which means—"

"There's a tunnel leading from the ravine to the facility," Lavona finished. "If we can get inside, it should take us straight there, past the outer defenses."

"Sharp eyes," Ben praised. "But what about security? A tunnel like that has to be monitored."

"Probably," Lavona agreed. "But it's still our best shot at getting inside without a major fight. One we're sure to lose with these undercharged zappers. We'll just have to stay alert and move quickly."

"You found the outflow. Lead the way."

We followed Lavona back to the bridge. She and I crossed a second time, stopping halfway and turning back toward the side where Ben and the others waited. Even in the starlight, it was too dark for me to make out anything along the ravine's rocky cliffs, but she pointed excitedly.

"I see it." She paused thoughtfully. "I'm just not sure if we can reach it. I don't see an easy passage down."

"We all have rope in our packs," I reminded her, though I was frightened by the idea of repelling down to the tunnel.

"That's right, we do. Let's tell Ben."

We returned to the group, and Lavona guided us to where she had seen the outflow. As we neared, I could hear the water splashing against the rocks and running down into more water at the base of the ravine that somehow hadn't frozen. A hot spring, perhaps?

"It's about halfway down," Lavona said.

Ben retrieved the rope from his pack. It wouldn't be long enough on its own. "Kat, pass me your rope."

Once I did as he asked, Ben quickly joined the two lengths of rope and searched the immediate area for a tree or rock to secure it to. "I don't see anywhere to anchor this end," he said, looking at the two Hemid. "One of you will have to stay behind to hold the rope while we climb down. We'll pick you up once we have the shuttle."

"I'm the strongest," Larev said. "I'll stay."

"Thank you," Ben replied.

"I'll wait for you in the control tower. You just better come back for me."

"We will. I promise."

Larev tied the end of the rope around his waist and gathered the excess before planting his feet.

"How are we going to get the gate open?" Karpov asked. "I might not be strong enough."

"I'll go down first," Ben said. "I can open it."

"Hondo, are you sure?" I asked, fresh concern blossoming.

He nodded. "I'm sure." He tied the other end of the rope around his waist and moved to the edge, slowly lowering himself over it. "Okay, Larev. I'm ready."

The big Hemid slowly lowered Ben toward the outflow. I watched from the edge with Lavona, more nervous observing him than I figured I would be doing it myself. It was risky for him to use more chaos energy now when he had only just recovered some strength.

"Larev, stop!" Lavona ordered once Ben reached the gate. He grabbed onto the bars, putting his feet down on the bottom of the tunnel, the water sluicing over them. Tugging on the gate bars a couple of times, he tested to see if it would open easily. It didn't. Examining the gate, he shifted his hands, which glowed only slightly.

"You weren't kidding about glowy hands," Mak said, watching the proceedings.

"How does he do that?" Cade asked.

"It's magic," I replied.

"You two are full of surprises, aren't you?"

He had no idea. I shrugged in response. Down below, Ben's use of chaos energy pulled the bolts from the tunnel stone and then from the gate. Shifting to the side, he tugged on the bars again. This time, the six-foot-diameter metal circle tumbled away with little effort, crashing against the cliff face before splashing into the water below.

"I don't see any evidence the gate was wired," Ben called up to us as he removed the rope from his waist. "Come on down."

Larev spent the next half hour lowering each of us in turn until finally he was alone at the top of the cliff.

"We'll be back for you!" I shouted.

"Nah," he replied. "I don't want to wait here. You can go ahead if you want. I'll be along shortly." With that, the big Hemid dropped the rope and began picking out foot and handholds as he made his way down the mountain.

"He's going to fall," Cade said breathlessly, watching Larev descend.

"Nah, I think he can make it," Karpov replied.

We all remained at the edge of the opening, heads craned upward to watch Larev, his muscles bulging as he slowly moved from crevice to crevice in the nearly flat cliff face. It was as impressive a feat of strength and dexterity as I had ever seen, especially for someone so large.

Within twenty minutes, he loomed some twenty-five feet above our heads. Pausing, he glanced down at us, a big grin spreading across his face. "Almost there," he said, shifting his weight to another foothold. The portion of the cliff beneath his left foot suddenly crumbled away, and he lost his grip. He reached for another handhold, scrabbling with his feet to find purchase as he slid down the cliff face. When his foot landed on a rocky protrusion, it wasn't the help he needed. He cried out as he tumbled backward, his arms flailing as he fell.

I heard Ben's unintelligible mumble beside me, and an invisible hand seemed to slow his descent and then push him toward Karpov. The smaller Hemid braced himself, getting his hands up to catch Larev. The pair tumbled to the stone floor in a heap. By the time I looked at Ben, the glow of his hands had almost fully subsided.

"That was close!" Cade exclaimed. "How did you manage to change direction in mid-air like that?"

Looking perplexed, Larev shrugged. "I have no idea." Stretching out a hand, he helped Karpov up. "I'm an experienced climber. I know how to fall right, but that was…" Finding himself without words, his eyes flashed to Ben, suspecting had been saved from certain death. For his part, Ben wiped away a line of sweat on his brow. Though his face was paler than before, he seemed to be holding up pretty well despite using chaos energy. I couldn't explain it unless…I gaped at him. He merely grinned back at me, clasping Larev's shoulder as he passed him, heading for the service tunnel that loomed before us.

Exchanging stunned looks, Larev and I hung back as Lavona crept cautiously forward, her rifle up and ready. Ben, Cade, Karpov and Mak followed in her footsteps. Larev and I, finally shaking off our sopor, brought up the rear.

We crept forward quickly, the narrow entrance depositing us into the cramped tunnel beyond. Our only light came from dim red lights stretching off into the darkness. Our senses strained to hear any hint of security patrols or automated defenses over the sound of the overflow water that was a constant pressure against our ankles. We heard nothing but our own cautious movements.

Over time, pipes and conduits began crisscrossing the low ceiling, turning the tunnel even more claustrophobic. Splashing ahead stretched my nerves to their breaking point, my hands tense around my rifle, only to discover we'd reached the ingress point of the water but not the end of the line. We pressed tight against the sides to get past the water without getting soaked. As we continued into what appeared to be maintenance access, the wiring became more dense and split off in multiple directions, disappearing into the overhead. Beside me, Lavona's tension matched my own, her hand flexing around her rifle.

"We must be under the main complex," Ben whispered in response to the changes.

We didn't have to go much further before a ladder appeared ahead, leading to an overhead access hatch. Lavona reached it first. Examining the locking mechanism, she called Karpov up to look at it. Like an alien MacGyver, the Hemid pulled out his multitool, and in moments, the hatch popped open with a hiss of pneumatics.

Bringing his rifle up from where it hung on its shoulder, Karpov climbed up through the hatch, his feet disappearing from view. After a tense pause, his hand reappeared, beckoning us to follow before again vanishing from view.

I trailed Lavona up the ladder, emerging into what appeared to be a storage space. Crammed with crates and unused machinery, it looked like a repository for broken equipment. Combat bots hung lifelessly in inactive charging stations. Motion lighting flickered on in the overhead at our approach.

"Some kind of maintenance bay," Cade said, sweeping the room with his rifle.

"Look." Mak pointed toward an open doorway on the far wall. "That should lead further in. If we can find a terminal, I can try to access a map of the facility layout."

Ben nodded. "Good idea. Everyone stay alert. We don't know what's waiting for us deeper inside."

With weapons ready, we followed Mak through the doorway into the dimly lit corridors of the base proper. The stark metal walls seemed to press in from all sides as we wound past unmarked doors and silent intersections. I shifted my grip on my rifle, uneasiness building with every step. The entire place felt like a tomb.

Where were all the guards?

Expecting us to try to sneak in from outside when we were already inside?

We emerged into a larger room dominated by humming data banks and chirping consoles, an apparent server hub. Mak made a beeline for the nearest workstation, fingers flying across the input keys while we silently took up guard positions, rifles aimed at the doors.

"Got it," Mak announced after a few tense minutes. "Main armory is two levels down, northwest quadrant. The lift to the landing pad is on the same level, at the other end of the compound."

"Can you pull up any info on security?" Ben asked.

Mak frowned at the display, shaking her head. "No. I only have basic access permissions. The map is about the only thing I'm able to read. Let's just assume the worst and plan accordingly."

"Which is what, exactly?" Karpov crowded in to squint at the console. "Shoot our way in and blast out again?"

"Only as a last resort," Ben replied. "Our main priority is reaching that shuttle in one piece. Anything else is a bonus."

"We should go for the armory," Mak argued. "We'll be better equipped to push through any resistance between here and our exit."

"Unless your little friend is as good at short-circuiting bots as it is at eating brains," Lavona said, looking my way.

"Archie has trouble with bots," I admitted, glancing at Mak. "What exactly is your background, again? I never got to ask you back at the barracks."

Mak offered a sly smile. "A girl's got to have her secrets. So what do you say, boss? Armory?"

"Okay, change of plans," he decided. "We're going to secure the armory first. Mak, Lavona and I will clear the room. Cade, Kat, you'll watch the door and cover our backs. Once we've hit the depot, we'll all move on the landing bay together." He paused, mouth quirking into a humorless smile. "If everything goes well, we'll be sipping hot drinks back at the training base inside of an hour."

"And if it doesn't go well?" Karpov rumbled.

Ben's grin hardened. "Then I guess we'll be too dead to care. Let's move."

We followed Mak's directions through increasingly utilitarian corridors toward the armory. I couldn't shake the sense that we were being watched, though we encountered no signs of activity—mechanical or otherwise—as we traversed the base. More than once, I found myself glancing behind me, certain we were being shadowed. If the others felt the same unease, they hid it well.

After descending several levels via maintenance ladders, we finally arrived at a reinforced hatch stamped with alien lettering I assumed spelled armory. Mak examined the locking mechanism, lips pursed.

"Think you can get us in?" Ben asked.

"I've got this," Karpov said, replacing Mak at the door. Again, he employed the multitool to pop open the control panel and hotwire the door.

Ben shot him an approving look before taking point into the next room, Mak close on his heels. I hung back with Cade, scanning the silent hallway for threat.

Barely a minute passed before the others returned,

triumphant grins in place and laden with new toys. With a wink, Lavona tossed me a high-powered plasma rifle.

"Merry Christmas," Ben said.

"Let's see them stop us now!" Mak crowed.

"Just remember," Ben cautioned as we distributed the upgraded arsenal, "we want to reach the shuttle with as little fuss as possible. These are a last resort, nothing more."

"You worry too much," Mak scoffed.

"You should worry more," Lavona retorted, smoothly checking the charge on a sleek energy rifle. "Overconfidence is what gets you killed before anything else."

We formed up and resumed our trek toward the hangar. We encountered no resistance along the way, a fact that kept me firmly on edge rather than bringing any relief. This had all been too easy. Something was bound to go wrong. I just hoped that when it did, we'd be ready for it.

After countless twists and turns through the maze of corridors, we arrived at the final intersection separating us from our means of escape. Mak motioned us to a halt.

"The hangar should be just ahead, through those blast doors at the end of the passageway."

"Finally," Larev grunted. "The sooner we're off this rock, the better."

"I hear that," Mak agreed fervently. "This place is seriously giving me the creeps. It's like a—"

A sharp hiss of pneumatics cut her off, all our eyes fastening on the heavy doors at the end of the hall as they ground open. Lavona swore under her breath, bringing her weapon to bear. We were so close. If we got pinned down now...

My spiraling fears froze as the doors finished retracting and a single figure stepped into the junction.

Miss Asher.

# CHAPTER 23

Our handler regarded us with a small, dangerous smile; arms folded almost casually across her chest. My grip tightened convulsively on my rifle. My fury rose in tandem with my fear. If she seriously expected us to gun her down in cold blood to prove our devotion to the syndicate, she was out of her damned mind.

"I wondered how long it would take you to get this far," she said, unconcerned by the firepower bristling in her direction. "I'm impressed. You're the first group to raid the armory in a very long time. In fact, I think my group was the last to do it. Everyone else goes straight for the shuttle and runs into some pretty thick defenses along the way. But we can't have you destroying our combat bots. They're expensive and difficult to replace." Her smile widened. "Congratulations recruits, you passed your assessment."

Shocked silence met her pronouncement. I struggled to process her words, half-expecting a cruel punchline to follow.

"Wh...what?" Lavona managed.

Cade looked equally flummoxed. "You mean... that's it? We're done?"

"Done?" Miss Asher's tone dripped condescension. "Hardly. You're just getting started. What did you think we hauled you out to the armpit of nowhere for? To pick daisies? Vacation at a luxury resort? No, this is your proving ground." She cocked her head, eyes glittering. "Most of you performed...adequately."

"Adequately?" Karpov snarled. "We played your game. Fought your monsters. Watched two of ours die!"

"A pity about Yurt," Miss Asher acknowledged. "He showed promise. But the maulvas need to eat, too. As for Rhis..." She paused, a mockery of thoughtfulness. "Well, he had his chance like the rest of you. He simply lacked fortitude. May he rest in peace."

I felt Ben tense beside me, no doubt remembering Rhis's final moments. A single word from this woman could have spared him.

Motion to my left drew my attention. "You didn't have to kill him!" Cade cried, raising his full-powered plasma rifle toward Miss Asher. She didn't move a muscle or say a word, observing unconcerned while he squeezed the trigger.

Nothing came out. No noise. No blast of plasma. Nothing.

He pulled again and again, roaring in frustration and agony before throwing the weapon to the floor.

"You didn't think we would actually let you fire the guns from the armory, did you?" Miss Asher said. "That would be incredibly reckless of us. Unfortunately, we have many enemies across Warexia, and some will go to great lengths to infiltrate our family."

Coincidentally or not, her eyes landed on me at the same time she mentioned infiltration. It took all of my focus to maintain my poker face instead of looking away. Of course, Miss Asher's cold treatment of Rhis had only made it easier to keep following the Warden's directive.

"You might as well put down your weapons," Miss Asher continued. "Your shuttle awaits. I know you must be eager to return to the comforts of the training base."

"Yeah, I bet you know exactly how eager we are," Lavona muttered. She shifted closer to Larev. "Is it just me, or does this feel like another trap?"

"Definitely another trap," the big Hemid rumbled.

If Miss Asher overheard the exchange, she gave no indication. She turned on her heel, heading toward the shuttle bay. After a tense moment that seemed to stretch out for the longest time, Ben leaned his rifle against the wall and followed her. I did the same, falling into step on Ben's right, Lavona on his left. The others trailed uncertainly behind us.

A long corridor led to the shuttle bay. Passing through blast doors, I noticed four transports in the underground hangar, with one positioned on a lift that would bring it to the surface for launch. Miss Asher crossed the open area to it, taking a position beside its open hatch.

"In you go," she said, smiling sweetly like a stewardess, but her candy grin no doubt hid poison behind it. None of us believed this would be a smooth ride back to the base, and the plasma turrets mounted on the top of the shuttle's delta wings reinforced the feeling.

"Are you riding back with us, Miss Asher?" Lavona asked, looking for further confirmation.

"No, dear," she replied. "I have to oversee the cleanup and repairs to the training course."

Larev huffed at her response but continued behind us as we climbed aboard.

"Cade, you said you can fly this thing?" Ben said.

"Yes," the elf answered. "I'm not quite sure how to work the weapons system, however."

"Katzuo can help you with that. Kat, join Cade on the flight deck."

I nodded, following Cade to the front of the shuttle. The

controls reminded me of Nyree's vessel on Cacitrum. I could fly it in a pinch but was glad I didn't need to. Instead, as Cade began tapping the touch screen and flipping switches, I concentrated on figuring out the weapons system, starting with what I knew about Head Case's fire control.

Meanwhile, the shuttle's hatch closed, and Asher moved off the platform to stand near the door. An overhead portal clanked and groaned open while the floor rose to carry the ship into the cold.

"Recruit-1," a voice said over the ship's comms. "You are cleared for liftoff."

Cade tapped the control screen. "Copy that." Igniting the thrusters and manipulating the stick, the shuttle lifted from its launch pad into the air. Inertia pushed me into my seat as Cade opened the throttle, sending us rocketing away from the military installation.

Immediately, warning beeps filled the flight deck, cut off a moment later by an aggravated tap.

"The reactor barely has enough juice to get us to the landing site," Cade explained, pointing to the marker on the sensor grid.

"They're not taking any chances we might try to leave," I replied.

Cade banked the shuttle to put it on course for the marker. Again, warning tones sounded on the flight deck. Instead of angrily clearing the alert, Cade's head swiveled my way. "A surprise to no one, but we've got contacts incoming."

Thankfully, I had found the fire control. A quick glance at the interface revealed all of the settings were locked out except manual turret control. Again, I wasn't surprised. As four bogeys appeared on the sensor grid, coming in fast, I activated the switchover so the stick would guide the turrets and not the shuttle.

All I had to do was not miss.

I took a deep breath to calm my nerves and focus on the task at hand. The bogeys closed rapidly, blinking red on the sensor display. The shuttle lurched as Cade banked hard to starboard, throwing off their initial approach vector.

"I'll try to keep them off our tail," he called. "You take them out!"

Swallowing hard, I swiveled the stick, aligning the targeting reticle with the nearest bogey, a dark wedge too small to have an organic pilot. My first burst went wide, missing the drone by several feet. It whipped past, its thrusters flaring. I tracked it doggedly, continually adjusting my aim. It jinked and wove with inhuman precision, easily evading my fire.

"Come on, Kat!" Cade urged as he sent the shuttle into a stomach-churning dive. The other drones swarmed after us, plasma cannons blazing.

I gritted my teeth, narrowing my focus to the targeting reticle. My world shrank to that small blue circle with the ex inside. I squeezed the trigger again, longer this time. A hail of superheated energy connected in a satisfying explosion. Trailing smoke and fire, the drone spiraled away.

"One down!" I announced.

"Great shot! Don't celebrate yet, three more to—"

Cade's warning morphed into a startled curse as the shuttle bucked violently. Alarms shrieked, red lights bathing the flight deck. "We're hit! Port stabilizer's offline." My stomach clenched as Cade fought with the shuddering stick, barely keeping us level. "We can't take another hit like that."

The remaining drones pressed their advantage, moving to line up shots we'd struggle to evade. Heart hammering, I swung the turret after the next attacker. The drone swooped and rolled, plasma stitching dangerously close. Cade juked hard to port, helping me to line up my shot. I went after the bogey with sustained fire but most blasts went wide. Frustrated tears pricked my unblinking eyes. We were so close! I refused to fail now.

Sucking in a steadying breath, I adjusted my lead, tracking the drone's erratic path. My next burst punched through one wing, sending it cartwheeling out of control. Luck was on our side an instant later when its wild spiral intersected with the third bogey. Both vanished in a satisfying collision, sending debris raining down on the snow-covered landscape.

"Two more down!" Fierce pride surged through my veins, tempered by grim focus. "One to go."

"Let's finish this," Cade growled.

The final drone whipped past on a strafing run, its lasers searing our hull. The shuttle lurched drunkenly, Cade wrestling the damaged stick. I could hear the groan of over-stressed metal, feel the deck shuddering beneath my boots.

Time was running out.

The drone looped around in a tight arc, lining up for the killing blow. White-knuckled, his face set in stubborn determination, Cade gripped the stick. Somehow he managed to flip the crippled shuttle in a nauseating one-eighty, again putting the bogey right in my crosshairs.

I didn't hesitate. The instant the drone flashed past, I squeezed the trigger, walking blasts down its center. The drone detonated spectacularly, disintegrating into a million flaming pieces.

I collapsed back in my seat, gasping. My hands shook uncontrollably, my body still pumping unspent adrenaline. Distantly, I heard Cade's labored breathing, a perfect match to my own.

"We did it." His voice emerged rough and unsteady. "I can't believe it but we actually did it."

I managed a shaky laugh. "That makes two of us. Can you land this thing?"

"We're about to find out."

Angling for the landing marker on the sensor grid, he painstakingly coaxed a few more percentage points from thrusters low on fuel. Each second dragged like an eternity. Despite the drone's destruction, I kept scanning for additional threats, but the grid remained mercifully empty.

Finally, after an interminable descent, the dark hole we had entered a little over a day earlier appeared ahead of us. Mumbling what sounded like a prayer, Cade hit the reverse thrusters as we dropped into the opening.

The shuttle screamed a final mechanical protest before dropping the last few feet and slamming into the hangar deck with punishing force. Out of fuel. The impact nearly rattled my teeth from my skull. Horrible grinding sounds followed until we rocked to a stop.

Ears ringing, every inch of me ached and throbbed. Then Cade's unsteady laughter cut through my daze. A second later I was giggling right along with him, the release of tension too powerful to resist.

After everything we had just been through, what else could we do but laugh?

# CHAPTER 24

Euphoria from surviving the assessment trial mixed with sheer exhaustion as I stiffly extricated myself from my harness. My movements felt stiff, muscles already beginning to knot from the abuse. I couldn't imagine how badly the others would be hurting. The flight had been punishing on so many levels.

Already out of his harness, Cade noticed my wince as I rotated a shoulder. "You okay?"

I waved off his concern. "Nothing a few days of sleep won't cure. We should check on the others."

"Good idea."

Together, we limped from the ruined flight deck toward the main cabin. My heart rate picked up, my worry tempering elation. The shuttle had been built for combat drops, not comfort. I could only hope Ben and the others had endured the brutal evasives and crash landing without major injury.

"Is everyone okay?" I asked, finding them shaken and undoubtedly bruised, but each one of them appeared to be in one piece.

"That's the most fun I've had since being woken up from a sound sleep, thrown out into the cold and shot at," Mak replied.

"It looks like we all made it," Ben said, grinning. "Nice job getting us here."

"We couldn't have done it without everyone pulling their weight," I replied.

"I don't know about the rest of you, but I can't wait to get out of this deathtrap," Larev said, unbuckling his harness and stumbling to the hatch. When it refused to open, he cursed and kicked it with so much force it burst off its track and clattered on the hangar floor. I could only hope nobody was in its direct line of fire. "Serves you right, stupid door," he muttered, climbing out.

The rest of us followed in short order, some more unsteady on our feet than others. I kept an eye on Ben, expecting him to collapse from exhaustion at any moment, but if he felt tired, he didn't show it.

Miss Asher's subordinates spilled into the hangar, armed and wary despite our battered state. Clearly, they didn't fully trust that we wouldn't turn our hard-won skills upon them, given the slightest provocation. They ushered us from the cavernous chamber to the barracks in silence, remaining outside until we were all back through the main door. The possibility they locked us inside existed, but none of us cared at that point.

"I don't know about the rest of you, but I desperately need a shower," Mak said, tiredly running her hand through her lank, sweaty hair.

Karpov grunted his agreement. "You and me both. I think I panic-sweated through my clothes at least three times out there."

"Only three?" Mak answered.

That earned a few weak chuckles. Even filthy and exhausted, it felt good to laugh.

"First a meal, then a shower," Ben said. "I don't know about any of you, but I'm running on fumes. A few minutes more won't make much difference."

We moved as a loose group to the small galley, snagging ration bars from the cabinets before sinking gratefully onto the benches to devour them. Despite a lack of the chocolatey bars I enjoyed, I had never tasted anything so delicious. Across from me, Lavona tore into her own bar, ivory fangs flashing.

"I can't believe we actually pulled it off!" Mak exclaimed around a mouthful of protein. "We should do a toast or something."

"With what?" Karpov gestured at his half-eaten bar. "These?"

"It's the thought that counts," she retorted.

Ben raised his ration in salute. "To survival in the face of impossible odds," he declared. "And to fallen comrades who should be here celebrating with us." He paused, humor fading into solemnity. "To Yurt and Rhis. They were part of us, comrades, even if only for a little while."

"To Yurt and Rhis," we echoed.

Conversation lapsed after that, the reminder of those we had lost a sobering damper. We finished our meager meals in silence.

"Okay, enough brooding," Mak announced, getting to her feet. "I'm hitting the showers." When no one else moved to join her, she smiled. "There are partitions, if you're shy," she explained, separating her coldsuit and letting it drop in a heap on the galley floor. She wore simple gray underclothes beneath. "I'm not shy, but Kat doesn't look old enough for a peek." She smiled and vanished into the head.

"How old are you, anyway?" Lavona asked, all eyes turning my way.

"Seventeen," I answered. "But I'll be eighteen in four months."

"Just a baby," Larev commented.

"Don't listen to him, Noah," Lavona said. "I'm barely a year older than you."

"Have you ever seen a naked female before, Kat?" Larev pressed. "Your species or otherwise?"

I could feel my cheeks heating, my reply a little too slow to come.

"I think we should let the ladies shower first," Ben interjected to rescue me from Larev's attention. "Partitions or not."

"Good idea," Lavona agreed, relieved by Ben's decision. She stood and made her way toward the door to the head.

"Well, just don't use all the hot water," Larev grumbled, shaking his finger at them before joining the rest of us as we adjourned to berthing to wait our turn. I shrugged from my coldsuit and collapsed gratefully onto my rack, muscles crying out in relief. My underlay had thankfully absorbed most of my sweat and had dried, though I was too tired to care anyway.

Cade glanced around the room as he stood beside his bunk, a pained shadow darkening his eyes. I felt a pang of sympathy, knowing he was missing his brother among us, whole and healthy instead of left behind to an unknown fate.

"I know it probably doesn't help much," I offered quietly, "but for what it's worth, I'm truly sorry about Rhis."

His shoulders tensed. "Thank you," he murmured. I...I don't know what to do." He shook his head, hiding his face with his hand. "What to think. What to feel. He panicked. That's all. They didn't need to kill him."

"I know. It's not right. I figured Markan ran his outfit without mercy, but seeing it so coldly demonstrated..."

"I wanted to believe they let him live," Cade said. "I still need to believe it."

Mak and Lavona's return interrupted any further discussion. The women entered in an explosion of floral scents, towels wrapped around their bodies, and hair still dripping.

"All yours, boys," Lavona declared.

"I hope you saved some of that shampoo for us," Larev said. "I want to smell like a girl, too." He rose from his bunk and moved between the two females on his way out the door. The rest of us, gathering fresh clothes, followed at a more sedate pace. As I passed, my gaze caught on the scars along Lavona's bare shoulder.

Of course, she noticed. "See something you like?"

My face warmed immediately. "What? No! I mean, not no, but I wasn't...I just....sorry." I clamped my mouth shut before I could shove my other foot into it.

To my relief, she seemed more amused than offended by my babbling. "Relax, Kat. I'm just teasing."

"Right. I knew that."

Her smirk softened. "We've all got our scars, right? Ones you can see and ones you can't."

I nodded, throat suddenly tight as my mind flashed back to the night of the accident that killed my parents. "How did you get yours? If you don't mind me asking."

"I don't mind you asking. But ask me again some other time." Her eyes danced to Mak, suggesting she didn't want to tell the story to a larger audience.

"I will," I replied, our eyes meeting briefly before I left her and Mak to get dressed.

The shower was little more than a basic square with nozzles lining the walls, separated by half-walls that didn't offer nearly as much privacy as Mak's claim of partitions suggested. Stripping out of my underlay, I carefully transferred a sleepy Archie to a fluffy towel nest on a nearby bench before joining the others beneath lukewarm sprays. For several minutes, we simply stood there, letting the water sluice away the sweat and grime of our trial. Never had a shower felt so good. I tipped my head back, savoring the clean scent of regulation soap while wondering where Mak and Lavona had procured their floral cleanser.

"So," Karpov said, lathering shampoo through his barely-there hair. "Any bets on what torture Miss Asher has in store for us next?"

Larev grunted, muscles flexing as he scoured his gorilla chest. "With our luck? Probably hand-to-hand combat against her. Again."

I winced at the thought, ribs still aching from our initial disastrous encounter. "Maybe it won't be so bad?" I offered without much hope. "I mean, we passed the assessment, right? How much harder can she push us?"

"I'd rather not find out," Larev answered.

"Where's your sense of adventure?" Karpov questioned. "Don't tell me our little near-death experience was enough to make you want to quit."

"Little near-death?" He gave Karpov a disbelieving look. "We nearly got eaten. And shot down. And blown up."

"Yeah, but it was exciting as hell."

"Maybe for you," Cade commented, voice still distant.

"Aww, I'm sorry," Karpov said. "I don't mean to make light of your brother's death."

"Or Yurt's," I said. "Wasn't he a friend of yours?"

Karpov shrugged. "We met on Deepling, so not much more than you and I are friends."

"What's the story with your little brain-eating gelatin monster?" Larev asked, pointing to Archie. "Is it your pet or something?"

"My friend," I replied. "It's an ILF, just like you and me. It's actually an amalgamation of many. It's smarter than me in a lot of ways; it just can't speak."

"What planet is it from?"

"I honestly don't know," I replied. "It was a stowaway on our ship."

"You two have your own starship?" Karpov asked.

Ben threw me a cautioning glare before answering. "We did. We lost it in a bet."

"That happened to a buddy of mine," Larev said, laughing.

"Maybe Rhis is still alive," Karpov suggested after a brief silence, still trying to make up for his earlier callousness.

"Maybe," Cade agreed. "The question is, what should I do if he isn't?"

"What do you mean?" Larev asked.

"I couldn't kill Miss Asher back at the military installation. But what if I get another chance?"

The question turned the mood from quiet to somber. "I wouldn't if I were you," Larev replied.

"Why not? They can only kill me once."

"Maybe, but there are worse things than death. And if you don't think Miss Asher knows all of them, you're delusional."

Cade stared at Larev. "I promised him this would be our ticket to a better life," he said before turning to the wall and sobbing quietly.

"It still can be for you," Ben said. "I know it hurts, Cade. But you aren't responsible for Rhis' death."

He raised his head. "No. You're right. Markan is." His expression hardened, and he remained silent for the rest of his shower despite ongoing banter between Larev and Karpov.

We finished our showers and quickly toweled off, exhaustion dragging at our limbs. Gathering Archie and my underlay, I followed the others back to our bunks, where Mak and Lavona were already fast asleep.

"They've got the right idea," Larev said, throwing himself onto his rack and rolling over to face the wall. "Goodnight, recruits."

"Goodnight, Rev," Ben replied.

Karpov and Cade retired to their respective racks, leaving Ben and I alone. "How are you holding up?" I asked him again.

"Surprisingly well," he replied. "I feel better than I have since we got here."

I knew he didn't mean the training facility. He meant Warexia. "Do you think...?" I asked, stopping short of saying anything curious ears might pick up on. The others all seemed to be asleep, but looks could be deceiving.

"I can't rule it out," Ben replied. "Though it does make me wonder why me, and why that."

"Incentive, if I had to guess." I looked around the room. While bonding with the other recruits had helped us survive the assessment, it would also make it harder to betray them when the time came.

But if the Warden really had cured Ben's cancer with a boon, that sure would take the edge off.

"Let's just see how things progress from here," Ben said, in reference to both his illness and our predicament. "Goodnight, Kat."

"Goodnight, Hondo."

Still wrapped in the towel, I lowered the dozing Alleal onto my bunk, climbing in after it. Around me, the soft sounds of my companions settling in lulled me towards unconsciousness.

The next thing I knew, an urgent grip was shaking me awake. Heart hammering, I blinked futilely against the darkness, momentarily disoriented. Memory trickled back as the vestiges of sleep fell away. The assessment. Our unlikely victory. Collapsing into bed with the others. I had been certain nothing short of an orbital strike could rouse me. I had been sure our trainers would leave us alone for a while and give us a chance to recuperate.

Apparently, I was wrong.

"Katzuo, wake up," an unfamiliar voice hissed urgently. "Miss Asher wants a word with you."

# CHAPTER 25

The insistent grip on my shoulder gave me another firm shake. "Katzuo, I won't ask you again. On your feet."

Groggy and disoriented, I struggled into an upright position, nearly slamming my head against the base of the upper rack. Blinking rapidly to clear my vision, I found one of Miss Asher's subordinates looming over my bunk, her severe features set in obvious impatience.

Unease chased the last cobwebs from my brain like a cold breeze. Why would she want to speak to me alone, especially after we had just completed our assessment?

I swept my gaze around the barracks, realizing with a sinking feeling that I was the only recruit present. The other bunks lay conspicuously empty. Had I slept longer than I thought? "Where's everyone else?"

The woman didn't reply, crossing her arms over her uniformed chest. She had no intention of revealing anything beyond Asher's summons.

Knowing I had little choice but to comply, I hurried to extricate myself from the warm confines of my blanket and don my boots. My muscles protested the sudden movement, sore from the prior day's punishing exertions. When

Archie stirred sluggishly beneath his towel, I pressed a hand down on it in warning, nervous the Aleal would give its presence away. Oblivious to my actions, the subordinate waited with visible impatience.

Once ready, I followed her out into the dimly lit corridor. We traversed the empty passages in tense silence. My apprehension grew with every step. Had I done something wrong during the trials? But that made little sense. Asher had praised our collective performance. Was there something I had said or done that might have made her suspicious of Ben and my true reasons for being here?

I wracked my brain for another explanation as we wound our way deeper into the heart of the facility, but by the time we arrived outside an unmarked door, I still had no idea what awaited me on the other side.

My guide pressed her palm to the secured access panel and the portal swished open. Asher's subordinate motioned me inside without preamble. I stepped across the threshold into what could only be Asher's private office. The space held an air of muted opulence, from the rich fabrics adorning the walls to the elegantly carved furniture dominating the room's center. Display cases housed strange artifacts I assumed were from all across Warexia. My curious gaze flitted over the eclectic collection as I ventured further inside. It immediately reminded me of Levain's apartment in Cacitrum. Did every wealthy ne'er-do-well in Warexia have an art collection?

Behind me, the door slid shut, leaving me alone in the chamber. Without my guide's disapproving presence, my fear receded enough for me to consider inspecting the artwork and artifacts more closely. Bioluminescent vines twisted up the wall in one shadowed corner, delicate leaves pulsing with violet light. An ornate clay vase occupied a niche across from it, the fired surface depicting a grisly battle between grotesque insectoid aliens and sleek silver starships. The macabre imagery sent a shudder down my spine.

My attention settled on a nearby display featuring a floating holo image of the Warexian galaxy. Thin ribbons of text in a flowing alien script I couldn't comprehend wound lazily around the hologram's edges, reminiscent of our own solar system displays back on Earth. Except this one held ominous red markers that, when touched, described present-day conflicts. There were far too many markers for my liking, most clustered around the system's outer boundary. It made sense that the galaxy's edge would be more lawless than the center, though it did call the Warden's grip on Warexia further into question.

I began turning away when one final case caught my eye. Resting on a bed of crimson silk, an ornate ring glinted beneath the recessed lighting. Its dark metal band was incised with intricate geometric patterns that tugged at my memory. I leaned closer, realization striking like an electric shock when I placed where I had seen its like before.

A Sigiltech ring that could have easily passed as a companion to the bracelet Jaffie had stolen for Zariv.

Before I could do more than suck in a startled breath, the office door swished open behind me. I whirled around guiltily as Miss Asher strode inside, an unreadable expression on her dark face. Her gaze fell upon me before flicking to the ring. One slim brow arched.

"Exquisite isn't it?" she asked, standing at my shoulder.

I swallowed, trying to gather my wits. I had to tell Ben about the ring the first chance I got. He would know what the sigils inscribed on it could do. "It's beautiful," I managed. "Wh…where did you get it?"

She waved her hands across the entire bounty of her collection. "All of these items were gifts to me from upper management for a job well done. Honestly, I don't know where most of them originated. But that one has always been my favorite. It speaks to me on a deeper level than any of the other artifacts. You clearly hear it speaking to you, too."

"I do," I replied.

"Perhaps we can discuss artwork in the future, once you've graduated from training and are a full member of the family." She stepped away, gesturing to the pair of chairs fronting her wide desk. "Please, have a seat."

I did as she instructed, trying to ignore the way my heart hammered against my ribs. Asher settled into the seat across from me, her unblinking gaze assessing me like an exotic insect pinned to a specimen board. A heavy beat stretched between us, my apprehension ratcheting up with every second.

Finally, Asher put her hands flat on her desk, an approving smile gracing her lips. "I'm sure you're wondering why I called you here."

"Yes," I replied. "I'm also wondering where everyone else went. The barracks were empty when your subordinate woke me."

"I called each of your fellow recruits to meet with me in turn, though I spoke to most in the meeting room, not in my private office."

"You also called me in last," I said, relieved I hadn't been completely singled out. "To what do I owe the honor?"

"You've impressed me greatly, Katzuo. I've had recruits come through here before with strong scores in the Aste-rock Arena. But there's a big difference between reality and a simulation, even one that seems real. Because in the back of your mind, you always know it isn't real. You've matched your Arena scores with your real-world perfor-mance during our combat session and the assessment trial. Recruit Lavona said you managed to kill two maulvas and scare off the rest. I believe you may have a real future with us. One that few attain."

I blinked in surprise, caught off guard by the unexpected praise. Of course, Archie had killed the wolf creatures, not me. But Lava had kept her promise not to reveal the Aleal's existence. "Thank you," I said carefully. "But I didn't do it alone. We all worked together."

"As you should have." Asher inclined her head. "Family is the foundation upon which this organization is built. Without it, we would crumble. Your ability to set ego aside and cooperate speaks well of your character."

She paused, studying me with renewed intensity. I resisted the urge to squirm beneath her penetrating stare. "In fact, your skills have earned you a place in our advanced operative training program. You'll be working with recruit Lavona to hone skills so valuable to us that only one in a thousand recruits is selected. To have two in one unit is unheard of."

My stomach simultaneously flip-flopped with nerves and soared with relief. At least now I knew I wasn't in some kind of trouble. "I'm honored by the opportunity."

"As you should be." Asher's gaze sharpened. "I trust you'll give it your all."

"Of course."

"I will warn you. The training won't be easy. If you found the assessment grueling, you're in for much more of the same, if not worse. But the skills you learn will be invaluable as you make a name for yourself with the family."

"I can't wait to get started," I said as sincerely as possible, while dread tried to take root in the back of my mind. "Can I ask you an unrelated question?"

"You've earned as much."

"What about my brother?"

"Family first, as usual. Recruit Hondo has been assigned

to our management program," Miss Asher replied, a note of amusement coloring her tone. "It seems he has a natural talent for leadership."

"He always has. When will I see him again?"

"You'll cross paths with him in the barracks, if not sooner. Since we believe we're strongest together, our goal is to maintain the bonds formed during the training process beyond the walls of the Marin facility. Upon successful completion of training, as many of you as possible will be assigned together. Reflecting on the makeup of your unit's natural composition, I can already guess where you'll provide the most value."

"Where is that?" I asked.

"Oh, I'm not going to spoil the surprise. Besides, you all need to complete your training before those plans might come to fruition. For now, your singular focus is on your next phase of training." Asher rose smoothly to her feet. "I suggest you get some rest. We'll begin after lunch."

"You'll be training Lavona and me personally?" I asked.

"Yes. I began my career as a special operative like you are now. There's no one here better suited to the job. Is there a problem with that?"

"Not at all," I replied. "I'm looking forward to working with you, Miss Asher."

"And I, you, Katzuo." At the implied dismissal, I stood up. Rather than head for the door, I stared at her until she met my gaze. "Something else, Recruit Katzuo?"

"I have one more question."

"What is it?"

"Did you have to kill Rhis?"

She stared at me intently before answering. "Would you trust Rhis with your life?"

"That's not really a fair question. I hardly got a chance to get to know him."

"Let's pretend you knew him well. Based on the last time you saw him, would you trust him with your life?"

I knew the answer immediately, but I didn't want to say it. Not when Cade was so distraught over his brother's death.

"I appreciate your concern for your fellow recruit. Cade will overcome his grief in short order, once he realizes how much Rhis would have held him back."

"For an outfit that stresses family, that doesn't sound very supportive of Cade."

"He has a new family now. As do you. I'll see you after lunch, Katzuo."

This time, there was no countering her send off. I turned on my heel, head spinning with the revelations of the last several minutes—a Sigiltech ring, advanced training, and Ben being groomed for bigger things. I can't say I had expectations on how our efforts to reach Markan's orbit would go, but at the moment, everything seemed to be coming along better than I might have hoped.

Her office door swished open at my approach, and I stepped out into an empty corridor. Apparently, Miss Asher no longer felt like I needed a chaperone to get around the base. The portal shut behind me with a soft snick, leaving me alone with my racing thoughts.

As I navigated back through darkened hallways, I turned Asher's words over in my mind. From the moment we arrived on Marin, our handler had taken a keen interest in me. Now I knew why. I didn't know whether to feel flattered or unnerved by her assessment.

Regardless, one fact remained inescapable. My place in Markan's syndicate, for however long Ben and I had to maintain this ruse, came with strings attached. Asher would push me relentlessly, seeking to shape me into a loyal weapon for her precious organization.

My fingers curled into fists, fresh determination surging

through my veins. I refused to become anyone's mindless tool. I would play the part I had to for now, learn what I could from Asher and her specialized instruction. But in the end, those skills would serve my goals, not hers. Those skills would help finish the Warden's task and get Tyler and Ally back to Earth where they belonged. It didn't matter who or how many friends I might make here. My loyalty would always be to them, first.

Speaking of which…

I peered down both ends of the corridor, hunting for signs anyone else might be nearby. Satisfied I was alone, I raised my hand to my ear, curling my middle three fingers into my palm and thinking of Tyler. "Tee, you there?" I whispered.

"Noah-san!" he replied excitedly, his voice practically booming out of my pinkie compared to my hushed tone.

"Shh!" I admonished. "Not so loud."

"Sorry," he whispered. "I'm just happy to hear from you. How's everything going?"

I spent the next few minutes giving him a summary of Ben and my adventures, from the moment we'd entered hyperspace on Deepling to my meeting with Asher.

"Wow. Sounds like you're having a blast," he said. "Wish I was there."

"Are you serious? I could've been killed multiple times by now."

"Maybe, but it has to be better than hanging around Head Case, just waiting for some action. I must've watched the entire John Wick series four times already. Even watching Keanu kill people is getting stale. It's great to hear that the Warden may have cured Ben's cancer. I'll be sure to pass that on to Matt."

"I'm not sure how great it is. Everything the Warden does has a price, I'm sure. We just don't know what it will be."

"Yeah, I guess you're right. So, what's the exit strategy?"

I didn't answer right away, a faint echo of footsteps sounding from an adjacent passageway. Tyler didn't press, waiting for me to continue. "I'm not sure yet. We're still playing it by ear until something reveals itself."

"Which means more waiting for us. We'll never make it back to Earth at this rate."

"We're doing the best we can. How's Ally?"

"Same. She loves her new digs. Apparently, Captain's Quarters has space for three queen-sized mattresses and a huge closet. Every night is a slumber party."

"I'm sure you aren't exaggerating at all."

"Nope," Tee laughed.

"I should go," I said. "I just wanted to check in. I'll be in touch soon."

"Stay safe, man."

"I'll do my best." I disconnected the comms and padded through the corridors, returning to the recruit barracks. In the darkness, I crept to my bunk, noticing Lavona was asleep in her bunk. Asher must have met with her right before seeing me. I settled my weary body onto my own mattress, hoping a few more hours of rest would grant me much needed clarity regarding the road ahead.

Just before slumber claimed me, my mind drifted back to the Sigiltech ring in Asher's office. Once more I couldn't shake the feeling that everything was connected. And now, I had this sense that Asher had brought me into her private office expressly so I could see the inscribed jewelry.

I just needed to figure out her endgame. Or Markan's. Or the Warden's. Or most importantly, my own.

But those mysteries would have to wait. Tomorrow would bring fresh challenges. Taking a steadying breath, I let my eyes drift closed and embraced the oblivion of sleep.

# CHAPTER 26

The next two weeks passed in a blur of intensive training. True to Miss Asher's word, I spent nearly every waking moment drilling alongside Lavona in advanced combat techniques under our handler's watchful eye.

From the moment we stepped into the training hall each morning until we dragged our exhausted bodies to the showers each night, Asher ran us through a punishing gauntlet of martial forms, weapons drills, and brutal sparring matches. She drove us relentlessly, imparting skills to transform us into living weapons at the syndicate's disposal.

I lost count of how many times I hit the mats, muscles screaming in protest as I labored to master each new lesson. Lavona became my constant shadow, her devilish smirk an odd comfort during our most trying sessions. She took to the advanced instruction with a natural ease that kindled a flare of envy before I viciously beat it down. Her assistance proved invaluable, shortening my own learning curve as I struggled to retain the onslaught of new techniques and applications.

Despite our progress, neither of us managed to best

Asher. The deadly Nyrian possessed reflexes bordering on precognition, her lithe body poetry in motion as she effortlessly countered our most determined efforts to break through her defenses. More than once, I limped away from our training space, wondering if I could ever possess anything near her level of skill. In the quiet moments before sleep claimed me, I wasn't certain I wanted to be that lethal.

No, I was certain I didn't want that. More than ever, I wanted to go home.

When we weren't trading blows, Asher introduced us to an array of sophisticated tech that put anything I'd seen in spy thrillers to shame. We spent hours perfecting the art of crafting disguises to mold full-spectrum holomasks into flawless copies of alien features and program nano-fiber bodysuits that made my protective underlay seem archaic. We learned to mimic everything from bulky musculature to intricate scale patterns or the delicate avian plumage of aliens resembling chicken people. Voice-modulating mouthpieces and customizable pheromone signatures rounded out the deception, rendering us unrecognizable as our original selves.

I took particular satisfaction in honing this new skill set, the thrill of successful subterfuge preferable to continually getting my butt kicked. My confidence grew with each mission Asher assigned us to test our budding proficiency. Lavona's approving grins bolstered my daring, our easy camaraderie blossoming into a solid friendship that made the pressure of constant evaluation more bearable. I appreciated her sharp wit and indomitable spirit, finding solace in our shared triumphs as Asher heaped on fresh challenges.

Late one evening, nursing a veritable constellation of new bruises, curiosity finally won out over my better judgment. Sprawled across a low bench beside the sparring mats, I watched Asher and Lavona exchange a dizzying series of strikes across the room, their movements a lethal dance.

"So what kinds of missions will we be running once we graduate from the program?" I asked during a lull.

Asher disengaged from Lavona. Her glare immediately forced me to second-guess interrupting to pose similar questions in the future. "Your role will be to carry out sensitive tasks vital to the organization's interests. Infiltration, reconnaissance, acquisitions, and the like."

I frowned, parsing her words. "That sounds an awful lot like fancy terms for spying and theft."

Her answering smirk held a dangerous edge. "Call it what you will. But if you do, you're discounting the nuance that turns simple thuggery into enterprise."

"Different rules that just so happen to benefit the cause." I made no effort to hide my skepticism despite the hard gleam in her gaze.

To my surprise, she released a throaty chuckle. "You're a sharp one." Humor vanished as quickly as it had come, replaced by warning. "We do what we must to ensure the security and prosperity of our own. If certain external parties find themselves caught in the crossfire, so be it."

I bit back a retort, recognizing the dismissal in her tone. Asher wouldn't be revealing anything more, no matter how I pressed. Unease stirred in my gut, the implications of her statement impossible to ignore. Just how far was the syndicate willing to go in the name of protecting their interests? And what would that mean for innocents unlucky enough to cross their path? I recalled her star map's stark red conflict markers, my disquiet intensifying. How many of those conflicts had the Warden and maybe even Markan gotten involved in?

As if sensing the direction of my thoughts, Miss Asher leveled a pointed look my way. "I trust you'll exercise discretion with your newfound skillset. What happens in this program is not to be shared with the other recruits."

I ducked my head, successfully chastised. "Understood."

"Good. From here out, your only concern is to master the tools we place at your disposal. Leave the rest to upper management. Like your brother."

With that she signaled Lavona to resume their bout. I leaned against the wall, trying to shake the chill slithering down my spine. Our trainer's choice of deflection felt rehearsed. How many cynical recruits had she fed similar lines to over the years? On the other hand, the syndicate operated under a shroud of secrecy by necessity. Revealing too many sensitive details presented an unacceptable risk. Of course, those were exactly the details we needed to pin down Markan and find a way to finish this task.

My eyes landed on Lavona, desperately fighting to prevent Asher from once again knocking her flat on the mat. Two weeks ago, I was willing to sacrifice her and everyone else to satisfy the Warden and improve our shot at going home. Now, I wasn't so sure. When the time came, given a choice, would she pick me or the syndicate?

I feared the time might come when I would have no choice but to find out.

Exhausted in mind and body, I cornered Ben during a rare break, dragging him away from the other recruits to a quiet section of the corridor. He looked equally wrung out, fatigue carving deep lines around his eyes and mouth. Still, his smile held genuine warmth when I plopped down across from him, my tray piled high with rations.

"Hey, little brother. I feel like I've barely seen you lately."

"That makes two of us. Asher's had me and Lavona running drills nonstop. I'm pretty sure even my bruises have bruises at this point." I glanced around to ensure no one was within earshot before continuing. "Please tell me you've got something good to share."

"I'm not any closer to discovering Markan's location, if that's what you mean," Ben replied.

"I didn't expect an easy win. How high up the food chain have you managed to reach?"

"It's hard to say. The syndicate is huge. Way bigger than I imagined. And they keep their org chart pretty close to the chest. Honestly, the more I learn about how this place is run, the more I feel like the Warden set us up to fail. Even if we somehow managed to find Markan and take him out, there are hundreds of others waiting to take his place. And, they not only have the ability to replace him, at least a few of them likely have his blessing."

"Like Hydra," I said.

"Exactly. Cut off one head, two more take its place."

"So how do we bring him down?"

"Like I said, I'm not sure we can. But what we might be able to do is find a way to expose Markan and his assets to the Warden, so the Warden can bring the syndicate down himself."

"The Warden can't stop them because he hasn't been able to track them," I said. "That makes sense."

"It's also much easier said than done. I'm working on getting higher level clearance to the syndicate's networks so I can trace more of the personnel and logistics. If I master what I'm learning, I think I can compile a pretty comprehensive database of assets and resources."

"And I thought getting beat up every day was the short straw."

Ben laughed. "It's definitely not exciting, except for the fact that if I overstep and get caught, I'll be executed. Once I have the list, do you think you can summon the Warden again?"

I made the call-me gesture. "I think I could give him a call. But no guarantees he'll answer."

"Well, we can worry about that when we get there."

A shout from the end of the passageway put any further discussion on hold. We both glanced up to find Karpov waving to us, an excited grin splitting his craggy face.

"Come on, you two! Cade's going to fill us in on his new piloting gig."

We followed Karpov into the barracks to the galley. The others were already there, listening attentively as the normally reserved Lycene bounced on his heels, green eyes bright with barely contained enthusiasm. I knew how much the loss of his brother weighed on Cade. To see genuine excitement from him now was a welcome change.

He was in the middle of an animated description of the starship he'd been learning to fly. The same starship, it turned out, that Larev and Mak had also been assigned to learn their skills on. They followed Cade in the conversation, energetically discussing their roles, which had them building off one another's expertise. It struck me then how much their assignments complemented each other, reminding me of what Asher had said about keeping recruits together. At the time, I'd asked her what kind of plans the syndicate might have for us. Knowing now what I didn't know then, I had a feeling I knew exactly what she was thinking.

The sour taste of foreboding flooded my mouth anew. Our training was quickly progressing. Sooner or later, Asher and her cohorts would order us to put our abilities to practical use in service of the organization's ambiguous goals. Ben and I needed to be ready for anything when that time came.

Lost in thought, I nearly jumped out of my boots when Asher's voice exploded through the barracks loudspeakers.

"Attention recruits. Your presence is required in the main hangar bay immediately. Further instructions will be provided upon your arrival."

I traded an uneasy glance with Lavona, finding my

dread reflected in her eyes. Around us, the others shifted restlessly, a current of trepidation bleeding through earlier camaraderie. Without a word, we filed into the corridor.

Whispers flew between the recruits as we made our way toward the hangar, tension winding tighter with every step. This was the first time Asher had summoned us as a group since our assessment. A sinking certainty settled like a lead weight in my gut. Whatever awaited us, it had to be serious.

Normally innocuous, the hangar doors loomed as a foreboding sealed portal. I sucked a steadying breath, feeling more than seeing Ben on my left, Lavona a solid presence at my right shoulder. A quick backward glance confirmed the rest of our ragtag band at our backs, faces set in identical lines of resolve beneath the apprehension.

We'd come this far together. At that moment, I knew that no matter what Asher threw at us, we would endure. Adapt and overcome.

As a unit.

Miss Asher awaited us in the center of the hangar, hands clasped at the small of her back. Her lips curled into a cryptic smile as we assembled before her, the expression sending a shiver down my spine. She swept her gaze over our ranks.

"Recruits, the time has come to prove your worth to this organization. You are being activated for your initiation mission." Her smile sharpened. "Your first true taste of service to the syndicate begins now."

# CHAPTER 27

Ben's brow furrowed in confusion as Miss Asher's words sank in. He stepped forward, a frown tugging at his mouth. "With all due respect, ma'am, we've only been in training for two weeks. Are you certain we're ready for a real mission so soon?"

Asher's gaze cut to him, sharp as a blade. "Your concerns are noted, Captain Hondo. And under normal circumstances, I would agree with you. However, a time-sensitive opportunity has arisen that cannot be ignored. You are simply the closest assets we have available to act upon it."

My gut clenched at the implications. Whatever this mission entailed, it had to be important enough to warrant throwing a bunch of half-trained recruits into the field. I tamped down on the urge to protest, knowing it would only earn me a reproachful glare and a biting reprimand about the chain of command.

"Did you say Captain Hondo?" Ben replied, surprised by the sudden title. I wanted to be excited for him, but the suddenness made it hard.

"I did," Asher replied. "The Nakata is your ship for the

duration of the mission. From what I've heard about your progress during training, she's in excellent hands."

"Thank you, Miss Asher," Ben replied. "What are our orders?"

Approval flashed across her angular features. "Your orders are to board the shuttle behind me and enter the coordinates on this data chip. She picked it out of her pocket and passed it to Ben. "Further instructions will be provided when necessary." Once more, her gaze swept over our assembled group. "You've all shown great promise these past weeks. Now it's time to put that potential to use in service of the cause."

She spun neatly on one heel and strode out of the hangar, expectation clear in the set of her shoulders. We fell into step behind Ben, trading uneasy glances as we crossed the hangar. I caught his eye, reading the same trepidation in his dark gaze that churned in my gut. This felt wrong. Too fast, too soon. But what choice did we have? Our path had been laid before us the moment we agreed to infiltrate Markan's organization. All we could do now was play our roles and hope our training held up under pressure.

We filed into the shuttle, the cramped interior doing little to ease the tension crackling through our group. Cade made immediately for the cockpit, his tightly coiled energy betraying his nerves. The rest of us strapped in, restless as the hatch sealed shut with a hiss.

Cade's voice crackled over the internal comms a moment later. "Strap in and hang on. We'll be docking with Nakata in T-minus three minutes."

The shuttle lifted off with a lurch, the press of acceleration driving me back into my seat. We rose off the deck and exited the hangar, entering Marin's turbulent atmosphere, the gray clouds giving way to a star-strewn expanse of hard vacuum as we rocketed upward. Curiosity momentarily overriding my unease, I craned my neck for a better view out the forward viewports.

The Nakata loomed ahead, a boxy silhouette against the infinite darkness. At first glance, the vessel appeared to be little more than a standard short-haul cargo transport, squared-off and ugly. But as we drew closer, I caught signs of concealed weapon emplacements and the unmistakable shimmer of high-powered shields. This was no ordinary freighter. It was a wolf in sheep's clothing, a predator built for speed and stealth.

We slid into Nakata's docking bay with barely a shudder, the shuttle's skids meeting the deck with a muted clang. No sooner had we touched down than the bay doors were cycling shut behind us, sealing us in.

"Cade, Katzuo, Lavona, you're with me," Ben said as we departed the shuttle. "Larev, Karpov, Mak, report to engineering. Run us through all standard checks and diagnostics and report to me on the bridge when they're complete."

"Yes, Captain," Larev replied, showing no hint of resistance to Ben's position. The assignment came from the syndicate, and by now, we all knew better than to question or even be jealous about the roles each of us had been given. With such a small crew, every job was important, every member essential.

Lavona and I followed Ben to the bridge, Cade trailing close on our heels. We emerged onto a surprisingly spacious command deck, all gleaming consoles and hi-tech interfaces. Ben moved confidently to the command station, his bearing every inch that of a seasoned captain, though as far as Lavona and Cade knew, this was his first time running a starship.

Ben beckoned Cade forward. "You'll be serving as our pilot on this run. I trust you're up to speed on the specs of a vessel of this class?"

Cade nodded sharply. "Yes, sir. I've trained extensively

on the systems installed on Nakata. I should have no trouble at the helm."

"Good." Ben sat at the command station, withdrawing the data chip. "Take your position at the helm. I'll read you the coordinates Miss Asher provided for upload to the nav computer."

Cade hesitated only a fraction of a second before moving to comply. I watched him slide into the seat and rapidly input commands, preparing the ship to get underway.

"Captain, I'm sure the chip was programmed for a direct transfer to navigation," Lavona said.

Ben's eyes paused on me before shifting to Lavona. "Are you telling me how to captain my ship?"

"Uh. What? No, sir," she replied. "I just wasn't sure if you knew—"

"I've been training on these ships over the last two weeks, too," Ben said.

"Yes, sir," Lavona answered, lowering her head in silent affront. I felt bad for her, especially because Ben wanted to read out the coordinates so I could have them to pass back to Head Case.

"Captain, it's Larev," a rough voice said over the comms. "Initial diagnostics and systems checks are complete. Everything is nominal."

"Thank you, Larev," Ben replied. "Your only job now is to keep it that way."

"Yes, sir."

"Captain, I'm ready to receive the coordinates," Cade said.

Ben read the coordinates to the pilot, slowly and clearly enough for me to commit them to memory. "Get us a solution, but wait for my signal to initiate the jump."

"Yes, sir," Cade answered.

"Captain, permission to be dismissed?" I said. "Sorry,

sir. I need to visit the head before we get underway."

Ben played the request well, frowning as he jerked his chin toward the exit. "Be quick about it."

"Yes, sir." I hurried out into the passageway. As soon as the bridge door swished shut at my back, I raised my hand in the call-me gesture, my heart pounding, while I fast-walked to the head we had passed on the way up. Focusing my thoughts on Matt, I whispered urgently into my pinkie.

"Matt, it's Noah. I don't have a lot of time. They've sent us out on a priority mission, and we're about to leave the system. I have coordinates."

"Noah, I'm here," Matt replied. "What are the coordinates?"

I recited them, and while I was sure I had gotten them right, nagging doubt sent chills down my spine. If I was even a little wrong, we would all be in for a lot of pain. How would we hide that from the rest of the crew?

I reached the head and tapped the door control, slipping inside and pausing near a sink.

"Let me confirm," Matt said, reading the numbers back to me.

"That's it," I replied once he had finished. "Sixty seconds. I need to—"

"Katzuo?" The hatch whisked open.

I whipped around, heart in my throat, to find Lavona watching me from the hatchway. Her orange eyes narrowed, suspicion and confusion warring across her fine features.

"What are you doing?" Her gaze darted from my face to my oddly contorted hand. "Talking to your brother again? Why? Did you tell him where we're going?"

I forced a weak smile as I lowered my hand, brain scrambling for a plausible excuse. Or any excuse, for that matter. "No. Of...of course, not. We just check in from time to time."

"And you decided that time was now?" Her brow furrowed and for a moment I was certain she would push harder against the lie. But then she shook her head, apparently deciding to let it slide. "Yeah, it's a lot to take in," she allowed. "But we'll get through it together." She jerked her chin toward the corridor behind her. "If you're done in here, clear out. I need to pee."

I exhaled shakily and exited the head, waiting for her before returning to the bridge. I fell into step beside her, leaving me painfully aware of her sidelong glances as we double-timed it back to the bridge.

I nodded as subtly as possible to Ben as we entered. He nodded back before returning his attention forward. "Cade, initiate jump."

"Yes, sir," Cade replied. Not much later, the ship shuddered faintly and then we were away.

Ben activated ship wide comms while turning to face me and Lavona. "Attention all hands. This is your Captain speaking. We've just entered hyperspace with an ETA of a little under twenty hours. If your training has been anything like mine, you're probably eager for a chance to rest. We'll be receiving further mission parameters upon arrival. Until then, you're all off-duty. Get some rack time while you can." He exited the ship wide comms and fixed us with a stern look. "You, too. Cade and I will be joining you shortly. Dismissed."

We chorused a "Yes, sir!" and filed off the bridge, eager to investigate our new accommodations. I kept my eyes forward, uncomfortably aware of Lavona's gaze boring into my back. Silently, I vowed to be more careful going forward. We were walking a razor-thin edge and I couldn't afford any further slip-ups.

To my surprise and delight, our assigned quarters were a significant step up from what I expected. Instead of rows of impersonal bunks, we each had our own small but well-appointed cabin, complete with a real bed, shelving and drawer unit, computer terminal, and private head.

Larev approached from the other side of the corridor with Mak and Karpov, coming up from engineering. He let out a low whistle as he palmed open his door and stepped inside. "Now this is more like it!" he exclaimed. "The sweet life, baby!"

I had to agree. After the spartan barracks back on Marin, this felt downright luxurious. The syndicate had clearly pulled out all the stops to ensure our comfort, a gesture that eased a bit of the coiled tension between my shoulders. At least we wouldn't be spending the next twenty hours crammed together.

Retiring to my cabin, I urged Archie out from under my clothing. The Aleal scrambled out and jumped to the bed, tendrils pressing into the soft gel mattress in fascination.

"Pretty nice, huh, bud?" I said.

It waved a tendril at me in agreement, noticing the head. Two more tendrils waved that way.

"Yeah, I know," I replied, opening the door and poking my head inside. The space was as cramped as an airliner lavatory plus a tiny shower. I grabbed a towel and balled it up, putting it at the end of the bed for Archie. The Aleal wasted no time rearranging it the way it wanted and vanishing underneath. I kept my clothes on, just in case, and collapsed on the bed.

Despite the unexpected creature comforts, I couldn't fully relax. The looming specter of our mysterious mission haunted me, a thousand unanswered questions churning in my gut.

Rolling onto my back, I flung an arm over my eyes and exhaled heavily. Worrying endlessly wouldn't change our circumstances. The best thing I could do now was grab some shuteye.

And hope this mission didn't turn into a total disaster.

# CHAPTER 28

I sat in Nakata's small galley, nursing a mug of gish and trying to ignore the palpable tension radiating from Lavona across the table. A tension I shared as a gnawing in my gut that only bit harder with the more time that passed. We had both been on edge since dropping out of hyperspace, the unspoken knowledge that our mission would soon be upon us lending a strained quality to the silence. As so-called special operatives, I knew we would play an important role whatever this mission was.

The comm panel beside the door chimed, shattering the uneasy quiet. Ben's voice emerged from the speaker, clipped and all business, though I knew him well enough to sense the unease behind his words.

"Katzuo, Lavona, report to the briefing room immediately."

"Yes, sir," we both replied, trading a loaded glance as we pushed to our feet, the coffee stand-in abandoned. My stomach knotted with accelerating trepidation as we went through the corridors, the moment of truth nearly upon us at last.

To my surprise, only Ben awaited us in the briefing

room, standing at the head of the central holotable. His expression remained tight as he manipulated the controls, bringing up a glowing star chart.

"What's going on? Where's everyone else?" Lavona asked.

"This briefing is need-to-know only," Ben said without preamble. "Take a seat."

We did as ordered, pulling out side-by-side chairs at the table.

Ben zoomed in on a planet in the same cluster as Marin, a topographical map of a sprawling cityscape materializing above the table. "This is Quintain, the capital city of the planet Hixia," he continued, maintaining his stiff, formal tone and posture. "Population, sixty-four million, mostly Hixian, who for all intents and purposes look externally like Kat and me, but whose internal physiology distinguishes them as a unique species. A high-value target has been traced to this location. Our orders are to make contact and eliminate the threat, quietly and efficiently."

My heart stuttered in my chest. "Eliminate? You mean—"

"We're to assassinate the target," Lavona finished, something dark and unreadable in her orange eyes. "This is what we've been training for."

I stared at her, a chill snaking down my spine. I knew we would be expected to get our hands dirty in service to the syndicate. But this? It was too much, too soon.

"Who is it?" I managed. "Who are we supposed to...eliminate?"

In answer, Ben tapped on the table. The star map dissolved, replaced by the rotating image of a young woman. She couldn't have been much older than eighteen, her delicate features arranged in a shy smile and her auburn hair tumbling to well past her shoulders. Pretty, in a girl-next-door sort of way, she looked about as threatening as a kitten.

"This is our target. Rena Maringan."

"Is that her real name?" I asked.

"I don't know. That's the name the syndicate provided."

"What else do we know about her?" Lavona questioned.

"We know she betrayed the syndicate, and now the syndicate wants her dead."

"Betrayed us how?" I stared at the holo, struggling to reconcile the fresh-faced girl with the severity of our assignment. What could she possibly have done to warrant a death sentence?

Ben shook his head. "That information is above our pay grade. All we need to know is that she turned traitor. Now it falls to us to mete out the consequences."

He fixed us both with a hard look. "Miss Asher has arranged everything we need. Identities, requisition codes, mission-specific tech. It's all waiting in a prep module adjacent to the hangar." His voice gentled a degree. "I know this may not be what you were expecting for your first assignment. But we have our orders. The organization is counting on us to resolve this matter cleanly and completely. I expect you both to do whatever is necessary to neutralize Maringan. Understood?"

Lavona nodded fiercely. "Yes, sir. We won't let you down."

I opened my mouth to echo her affirmation, but the words stuck in my throat. Ben's gaze bored into me, a silent warning not to be too obvious about my distaste for the situation. I swallowed hard. "Actually, sir, I was hoping I could speak with you privately."

Lavona shot me a sharp look, but I steadfastly avoided her gaze. Ben's eyes narrowed a fraction as he nodded. "Of course. Lavona, head down to the prep module. Katzuo will join you shortly."

Her jaw tightened, but she rose from her seat and strode out of the room. The door whisked shut behind her, leaving Ben and me alone. He crossed his arms, regarding me compassionately.

"I know. This is exactly the kind of situation you were afraid we would run into."

"Weren't you?" I replied. "We can't do this, Ben. We can't just murder some girl in cold blood."

His eyes narrowed. "Lower your voice," he warned. "You never know who might be listening."

"Sorry," I said, tone just above a whisper. I continued shaking my head. "This is why the Warden sent us here. Because Markan and his syndicate are out there trading in illegal cargo and killing people with impunity."

"Yes, you're right. But I'm sure you know the saying. You can't make an omelet without breaking some eggs. I don't like it either. But we don't have the luxury of backing off right now. We're so close to becoming full members of the syndicate, which will open up all kinds of data streams and possibilities for us. It's too late to cut and run and start over. We have to play along until we find a way to bring Markan down from the inside, or we have to face the consequences of failing the Warden's task."

"He said he would go easy on us if we failed."

"And do you really believe that? You saw what happened to the Achai."

I pushed to my feet, pacing away a few agitated steps. "And how many innocent lives are we supposed to take before we can get close to the top? How much blood has to be on our hands? I should have been home burying my parents, and now look at me."

Ben's eyes fell as he exhaled a mournful breath. "I know. Believe me. I think about that every day. This whole situation is hell, and it's spun so far out of control it makes my gut ache. But we can't do anything about it now. I laid out the only two options we have, like them or not. I don't know what Rena did to run afoul of the syndicate. I agree it seems extreme to order her death. But this would have happened to her whether we were here or not. Her outcome isn't going to change. But ours might by following through with this. I hate to sound like such an asshole, but I've learned the hard way that sometimes it's necessary to turn off compassion and just do what needs to be done."

"At what cost?" I scrubbed a hand over my face, suddenly soul-weary. "I didn't sign up to become an assassin."

"Then let Lavona take the shot," he offered.

I rounded on him. "Letting her do our dirty work is no better than pulling the trigger myself and you know it."

He raised his hands in supplication. "Then what do you want to do? Abandon the mission?" He formed his left hand into the call-me gesture. "Because I can have Head Case here in minutes. We can steal the shuttle and escape. But then what?"

I stared at him, torn. As much as it galled me to admit, he wasn't wrong. We had come too far to turn back now. There would be consequences for failing the Warden, and truth be told, the laughing demi-god looked more and more like the good guy with every action the syndicate took.

And yet, the thought of participating in a summary execution made my stomach churn. It was the antithesis of everything I believed in, every moral line I had drawn for myself. Even if Rena had betrayed the organization, she deserved better than a blaster shot to the head from a pair of faceless killers.

I squeezed my eyes shut, dragging in a shuddering breath. When I opened them again, Ben watched me, resignation and sympathy warring in his dark gaze.

"I don't know if I can do this," I said quietly.

He reached out to grip my shoulder. "I know this feels wrong. It is wrong. But we have to see this through."

I met his gaze squarely, resolve hardening in my chest. "I won't kill her. I can't. But I'll do my part to locate Rena and give Lavona her shot." I held up a hand to forestall his protest. "On one condition. If I can come up with an alternative plan that satisfies the syndicate, the Warden, and my morality, we go with that."

"I have no idea how you'd manage that heavy of a lift, but okay," he agreed. "I'll agree to those terms. But if you come up empty, we take her down. No hesitation. Clear?"

"Clear," I echoed. It wasn't a promise I could make with any sincerity, and we both knew it. But it bought me time. A chance to come up with an alternate solution that didn't end with a young woman dead in a dirty alley.

Ben clapped my shoulder once more before tipping his head toward the door. "Go on. Lavona's probably wondering what's taking you so long."

I exited into the corridor, the weight of the mission lending urgency to my stride. But my mind was in chaos with conflicting emotions and half-formed plans. I had somehow found my line in the sand. A moral boundary I could not, would not cross, no matter the consequences.

Now I could only hope to find a way to save Rena before we had to breach that line.

# CHAPTER 29

I stepped into the prep module, still reeling from the implications of our assignment. The compartment turned out to be a treasure trove of advanced technology, every surface packed with sleek cases of unfamiliar devices. Racks of clothing in a dizzying array of styles and colors lined one bulkhead, while another held an arsenal of familiar and strange weapons. Shelves along the third bulkhead provided access to many tools we'd learned about and practiced with during Miss Asher's training sessions.

Everything we could want or need, from small biometric security cracking devices to the nano-fiber underlay that could allow us to completely change our appearance, was available for our use.

Lavona stood in front of a mirror, fingers probing her face. It took me a moment to realize she had already fitted herself with a holomask. The thin material molded seamlessly to her skin and activated millions of microscopic pixels, rendering her features strikingly human. Or Hexian, in this case. Gone were her orange eyes, elegantly twisting horns and sharp fangs, replaced by basic brown eyes, a smooth forehead and a straight line of pearly whites. I couldn't see through the disguise even though I knew it for what it was.

"How do I look?" she asked, facing me fully. "Think I'll blend in?"

I blinked, still taken aback by the transformation. "Yeah, definitely."

She flashed me a smile that was at once foreign and familiar on her altered face. "The texture of the material takes a bit of getting used to, but it beats the hell out of makeup."

I nodded along before another question occurred to me. "What about…" I gestured vaguely at her lower half. "Won't your tail be kind of a dead giveaway?"

"Got it covered." Without warning, Lavona shrugged out of her plain gray coveralls, leaving me unable to avert my eyes before I got a glimpse of her in just her underwear. Heat flushed my cheeks as I turned away. "I appreciate your respectful attitude, Kat, but it isn't necessary. The syndicate partnered us up from now until one or both of us die. It'll make things easier if we're physically comfortable around one another."

I hesitated before turning back toward her. She had already snagged a band of material from one of the racks and was tucking her tail into it. Our eyes met, and she offered an approving smile to help calm my nerves. My parents had taught me to be respectful, and looking at a half-naked female, alien or otherwise, consensual or otherwise, still felt awkward.

"The tail sheath is a bit uncomfortable, but it works," she said, pulling up the compressed band and reaching for one of the nano-fiber underlays. She tossed it to me. "Don't just stand there and stare."

"I'm impressed," I said honestly, catching the light-weight material while she picked out one for herself. "Miss Asher didn't teach us that one."

Lavona shrugged off the praise, but I caught the pleased glint in her eyes. "Spend enough time with the wrong people and you pick up all kinds of tricks." She looked at me expectantly. My face heated up more as I removed my issued utilities. Sensing my unease, she continued talking as if we were having a normal conversation under normal circumstances while we dressed. "I wasn't always the upstanding citizen you see before you," she said, tone forcibly light. "Believe it or not, I used to be a bit of a troublemaker."

Despite myself, I felt my lips quirk. "Why do I get the feeling that's an understatement?"

She huffed a laugh. "Because you're smarter than you look." She paused, running a hand over the top of her scarred chest. "You asked me once how I got these."

The abrupt change in topic caught me off-guard. "I did. But you don't have to tell me if you don't want to."

"I want to." I could see the memories weren't easy for her to relive, her gaze distant as she drew a steadying breath. "It happened not long after my brother Kersho joined the Respers. He was so fired up, so certain they were the key to a brighter future for Viconia. I bought into the dream too. I thought that if I joined the cause, we would change things for the better." A bitter twist of her lips. "I was an idiot." She paused. I remained silent, sensing she needed time to get the story out. After a moment, she continued. "I made it to the Resper safehouse where Kersho was staying. But the location had been compromised. I got there about thirty seconds before the Vikers stormed the building."

An involuntary shudder rippled through her. "They launched explosives through the front door, which set the place on fire. They charged in afterward, protected in their armored envirosuits. I did everything I could to escape them and reach Kersho. I still remember the look on one Viker's face when I punched right through his visor with my claws and raked his eyes to get away from him. The smoke...the heat...it was unbearable. The whole place started coming down around me. I don't think the Vikers expected it to fall, and I've always wondered if the Respers rigged it, just in case they needed to destroy all of the evidence of their activities in a hurry. Either way, I barely made it out before the whole building collapsed. My brother...he—"

"Lavona..." I extended a hand, gently gripping her shoulder.

She met my gaze, eyes haunted. "I never found Kersho's body. Never got to say goodbye. These scars? They're a daily reminder of my failure. Of all the things I couldn't change no matter how hard I tried."

"I'm so sorry," I murmured.

Lavona held my gaze a moment longer before shrugging off my hand and turning away. "I spent three torturous months healing. Honestly, I should have died. After that, I needed to get off-world. The Vikers would have executed me for sure if they'd caught me. And like I told you before, I'm trying to earn enough quark to at least get my sisters off Viconia. So, I fell in with a rough crowd and started taking jobs to get by. The good news is, those jobs put me on the syndicate's radar and them on mine. I tracked down a contact who got me a berth on Deepling, and you know the rest."

I watched her square her shoulders, burying her old hurts beneath a mask of determination. "This life...it's not pretty. But it's all I've got in the here and now. The syndicate is my family. You're my family, Katzuo. And I'll do whatever it takes to protect that. To protect you."

Including murder. The thought sat like a stone in my gut.

I opened my mouth, desperate to find some words of

comfort, but Lavona was already moving on, all business once more."We should finish gearing up," she said briskly. "Wouldn't want to keep the captain waiting."

Seeing her shut down as if a curtain had fallen over her face, I nodded and crossed to the racks of equipment. Within minutes, we had both donned the form-fitting nano-fiber bodysuits and dressed in clothing similar to Rena's in the image Ben showed us. We each added a pair of blasters, an assortment of concealed blades, and other goodies. Lavona also slung a nondescript duffel over one shoulder, the bag clinking softly with surveillance tech.

No sooner had we finished our preparations than the comm panel beside the door chimed. "Katzuo, Lavona," Ben's voice crackled into the room. "We'll reach Hixia's orbit in approximately thirty minutes. Wrap up your prep work and report to the shuttle bay for deployment."

The connection cut off with an audible click. I met Lavona's gaze, an uncomfortable mixture of dread and resignation sitting heavy in my chest. This was it. In less than an hour, we would be on the ground and hunting our target in earnest.

"Any final words of wisdom for your new partner?" Lavona's eyes glinted with dark humor.

I tried for a smile. "You're the one with the experience in this sort of thing. The only other time I tried to be stealthy, I got captured and almost killed."

She laughed. "I'd like to hear that story."

"It ends with me and Hondo on Deepling."

We crossed to the adjacent hangar in silence. The shuttle was already sitting there, facing the bay doors, its engines online—ready for insertion. We boarded through the open hatch and took seats in the cabin, strapping in.

A few minutes later, Cade stepped into the shuttle."Hey Katzuo, Lavona," he said. "The Captain told me to tell you he's got more intel for you, which he'll share once you're planetside. You brought comms, I assume."

I nearly cursed at my stupidity when Lavona retrieved a pair of tiny earpieces from a pocket and handed one to me. "We're good, Cade," I said, accepting the gift and tucking it into my ear canal.

"We already have clearance for landing. Shouldn't be more than fifteen minutes to the surface."

"Taking the express lane?" Lavona asked, smiling at him.

"You know it," Cade said before moving to the flight deck.

We launched less than a minute later, blasting out of the hangar bay and angling toward Hixia. The planet resembled Earth in many ways, with smaller continents but similar landscapes and atmosphere. Beside me, Lavona sat in stoic silence, features remote. The time for soul-searching had passed. Now, only the mission mattered.

As the shuttle sliced through clouds and glided in toward a bustling spaceport, a final certainty crystallized in my mind. No matter what happened from here on out, I would leave the planet diametrically both better and worse off.

Fun times.

# CHAPTER 30

As the shuttle touched down at Quintain Central Spaceport, my stomach churned with a potent mix of anxiety and dread. The weight of our impending mission sat like lead in my gut. The hum of the engines faded slowly as we settled into our landing zone.

Before Lavona and I could disembark, the comms device in my ear crackled to life. "Katzuo, Lavona, I have an update for you," Ben said, maintaining his uneasy, businesslike tone. "New instructions just came through from the manager in charge of this situation. You're to proceed directly to the Warton Hotel in the city center. A room has been reserved in the names and identifiers listed in the pads you were provided. You're to meet a syndicate agent in the hotel restaurant. He goes by the title Master Gun."

I could almost hear Tyler's voice in my head, enthusiastically expressing how awesome it would be to have the name Master Gun. "Understood," I replied, doing my best to keep unease from my tone. Lavona seconded the confirmation.

"Good. Hondo out." The comms fell silent.

We exited the shuttle, joined the bustle of activity, and

entered the terminal. I couldn't shake the feeling of being watched. Just in front of me, Lavona seemed to share my unease, her shoulders tight beneath her orange overcoat.

I leaned over her shoulder as we stepped into the arrival line. "I assume you have my pad?" I asked, leaning over her shoulder.

She smiled at me, unzipping her duffel and passing me the personal access device. "I'm sure you'll be more detail-oriented next time."

"Definitely," I replied, accepting the pad. "Thanks for the save."

We quickly advanced toward the automated scanners at the front of the line, where security scanned our identification and passed us through without incident. The guards nearby didn't pay us any mind either, eyes slipping over us like we were as insignificant as the tourists and business people surrounding us. Within minutes, we'd exited the terminal and boarded a sleek maglev shuttle headed for the city.

It wasn't until we emerged from the spaceport proper that I got a breathtaking look at the crystalline spires jutting high into the lavender sky. The light of Quintain's twin suns glinted off their faceted surfaces, forming dazzling prisms of shifting colors. Maglev trains wove between the buildings just above ground level, ferrying passengers in silent efficiency. Everywhere, from the spotless streets to the iridescent foliage lining the pedestrian walkways, the city was a shining example of Hixian advancement and clean, modern technology.

Picking up a map of Quintain on my pad at the downtown station, we headed on foot for the Warton Hotel. Within moments of reaching the street and getting out among the population, it became obvious to me that, for all its beauty, there was an ugliness to Hixia. While my appearance and Lava's disguise hid our origins, I watched as a mother clutched her child closer to her when a Hemid passed them. On the other side of the street, a shopkeeper backed away from a catlike alien browsing his wares as if he weren't interested in selling anything to the off-worlder. Consequently, for all of the sixty-plus million packed into the sprawling metropolis, I saw very few non-Hixians, and the ones I did see wore expressions that suggested they knew they weren't welcome here.

"This place gives me the creeps," I said to Lavona as we walked along a wide pedestrian thoroughfare. Vehicular traffic buzzed along on roads beneath us, but the skies kept clear—maybe to maintain the view.

"Agreed. I'd never choose to come here on my own."

"Had you heard about Hixian discrimination before we arrived?"

"No. It's disgusting. I'm thankful for the holomask."

The Warton Hotel rose in glittering splendor at the end of an especially large promenade, also ringed with high-end boutiques and eateries that probably wouldn't have let Lavona inside without her disguise.

A soaring monument of glass and chrome, the hotel's towering lobby dwarfed us as we entered, the vaulted atrium disappearing into the hazy distance. Layered with the tinkle of ornamental fountains, soft music played from what seemed like every vertical surface. Everything gleamed, not a speck of dirt or wear to be seen anywhere.

"We should check in after we meet Master Gun," Lavona suggested.

"Agreed," I replied. "I'm eager to hear what he has to say."

We followed signs and stopped to ask a bellhop where to find the hotel restaurant, uncreatively named Warton's at the Warton. Located on the fortieth floor in the tower's midsection, we boarded an express elevator that took us up to the eatery. When the cab doors opened, we stepped out into a dimly lit space filled with the scent of exotic spices. Diaphanous curtains cordoned off intimate dining alcoves while ambient music thrummed at the edge of hearing. A burbling water feature cast shimmering reflections across polished stone tables at the center of the room.

"Can I help you?" A man with thick mutton chops and a trimmed mustache immediately approached. Wearing a heavy tailcoat, fancy breeches that bled into socks, and buckled shoes, he looked as though he had just escaped a Jane Austen novel.

"We're meeting someone here," I replied.

"Dressed like that?"

"Is there a dress code here?" I asked.

"No, but some semblance of propriety is always appreciated." Apparently, the Hixians were as snobbish and condescending toward one another as they were with outsiders.

"Maybe next time," Lavona said. "We're with Master Gun."

The host turned his palm over, a hologram projecting above it. Quickly flicking his opposite pointer, he scrolled the list of guests and their tables. "Here we are. This way." He gave my outfit another disparaging glance before guiding us to a booth in the back corner.

A shadowed figure with square shoulders beneath an impeccably tailored suit waited there. He had silver, collar-length hair and hawkish features. His piercing amber eyes watched our approach without blinking.

"Sit," he instructed by way of greeting. Two place settings already awaited us, plates carrying tiny morsels of alien fare that hardly passed as a full meal.

Our host turned on his heel and returned to the entrance while we slid into the booth. Lavona's hand never strayed too far from the concealed weapons at her hip. If our contact noticed, he didn't comment.

"I must admit," he began without preamble, "I was expecting operatives with a bit more...seasoning." His eyes flicked speculatively between us. "Markan must really be desperate to assign two so...fresh...to the task." He smiled playfully, picking up a flute of something bubbly and swishing it in his hand. "Or, maybe he doesn't think the odds of survival are very high, and doesn't want to waste experienced SpecOps people on the run."

Beside me, Lavona bristled, but her voice remained coolly professional when she spoke. "I assure you, we are more than capable of handling the job—not that a *gizzap* would know anything about it."

"Gizzap?" I asked.

"A gizzap is a small reptilian creature that, once fed, will follow the feeder mercilessly for the rest of its life. But it will never gather any food for itself."

"A Viconian, then," Master Gun said, lips quirking humorlessly. "Let us hope you have the necessary talents. For all our sake." He plucked a data chip from his breast pocket and slid it across the table. "Everything I've managed to compile on the target's current whereabouts. I tracked her to a safe house on the outskirts of the shopping district. Likely one of Erach's bolt holes." At our blank looks, he sighed impatiently. "A local thorn in the syndicate's side. Fancies himself a rival of sorts to Markan's authority in the area. It seems our little runaway has sought refuge with him."

I accepted the data chip, turning it over in my fingers as my mind raced. A safehouse likely meant defenses. Guards. Lines of defenses between us and Rena.

"Is there anything we need to know that isn't on the chip?" Lavona asked.

"No. As a gizzap, I know not to bite the hand with shoddy work. I trust you're smart enough to understand the same." His smile was cold. "Markan doesn't look kindly upon failure." He slid from the booth with fluid grace. "I'll leave you to...enjoy your meal."

And with that he was gone, vanishing into the restaurant's dim interior. I stared after him, my appetite vanishing along with him.

"Charming fellow," Lavona muttered, poking at her food with a distinct lack of enthusiasm.

"No kidding. What do you say we take this upstairs?" I motioned to our meal.

"I'd rather eat a gizzap," she replied, standing up. I joined her, and we almost made it to the exit before the host intercepted us.

"Leaving so soon?" he asked.

"You can put the meal on our tab," Lavona replied, holding out her pad.

The host quickly scanned her identifier. "You haven't checked in yet."

"Can you check us in?" I asked.

He sighed and made a face like we were mistreating him by asking him to do something he considered menial. But he did it anyway.

"Room seventy-eight twenty-four," he said, perking up. I could tell by the sudden shift that the room that the syndicate had reserved for us didn't come cheap. "A corner suite. An excellent choice."

"It'll do," I replied. "Thank you for taking care of it. Please add a reasonable gratuity for yourself."

"Thank you, sir," the host replied.

The ride up to our room passed in tense silence. My thoughts whirled, the gravity of the tasks pressing down on us—overcome a defended safe house, eliminate the target, and get out clean. Nothing about this would be easy, and getting Rena out alive felt damned near impossible.

Our room, all muted tones and plush fabrics, proved to be a welcome haven after the restaurant's tension. The panoramic windows showcased a breathtaking view of Quintain's glittering skyline, though I couldn't fully appreciate the spectacle. Lavona wasted no time sweeping the room for listening devices and other bugs. Only then did some of the tension bleed from her slender frame.

"Well," she sighed, sinking onto the room's jelly-like sofa, "this just got much more complicated."

"No arguments there." I joined her on the opposite end, passing the data chip to her. "Let's see what our friend was able to dig up on this safe house."

Sliding over to my side of the couch so I could share the screen of her pad with her, she inserted the chip into a hidden port. A few tense minutes passed as we scanned schematics and personnel dossiers, my unease growing with every new detail. The compound was a veritable fortress—blast-shielded doors, state-of-the-art bioscanner checkpoints, and enough professional mercenaries to hold a company picnic with two full softball teams. Breaking in would be no easy feat. If Rena was smart, she'd be holed up in the most secure room, far from any windows or access points.

Finally, Lavona sat back with a sharp exhale. "I count no less than twenty armed guards on rotating shifts. And the perimeter is locked up tight."

"Not to mention, all indications point toward this Ear Ache guy knowing Markan will send someone to take Rena out. We can forget about the element of surprise."

"Perhaps we can get a position across the street on higher ground. A well-aimed bullet through a window would keep things simple."

"Except the windows are probably bulletproof; if Erach is smart, he won't let Rena anywhere near them."

"Good point. So if a remote kill is off the table, do you have a different approach in mind?"

"Not yet, but no one has given us a deadline yet."

"I think it goes without saying. The deadline is asap, before the target can change location."

"Right," I sighed. "Can I see the pad again?"

The next few hours passed in a blur of meticulous study, as we attempted to put together an approach that would leave us alive and the target incapacitated. We poured over every scrap of information— no matter how seemingly inconsequential—from guard rotations and staff credentials to service bot specs. Anything that might give us an edge. The more the facts sank in, the more I started to feel like Gun's second reasoning for our selection was the right one.

We were more expendable than seasoned assassins.

As the seed of an approach took root in my mind, a desperate half-formed notion sprouted along with it. One born of equal parts altruism and pure defiant recklessness. One that, if I was very clever and even more lucky, just might see Rena live another day.

Of course, I couldn't share this secret hope with Lavona. She was too dedicated to the mission, too loyal to the syndicate. If she suspected I was trying to find a way to spare our target, she wouldn't hesitate to take matters into her own hands. No, for this gambit to have even a chance of success, I needed to play my cards very close to the vest.

"I think I have a plan," I said at last, returning from the bathroom, where I had made a quick, quiet call to Matt. I would need his help if I had any chance of making this work.

Lavona glanced up from the datapad, one brow arched. "Do you always do your best work on the toilet?" she joked.

"Pretty much," I replied, leaning over her to bring up the schematic of the safe house on the pad, enlarging the northwest perimeter. "The guard rotation is weakest here, at the service entrance. Only one man on duty at any given time, with sightlines from the other guard position obscured by the irregular corner. If we time it right, I can neutralize him quietly and take his place. Disguised as a member of the security team, I'll have a far better chance of getting inside and close to Rena."

Lavona frowned, considering. "And where will I be during all this?"

"Overwatch," I replied promptly. "We'll set you up in this building across the way. It has a clear line of sight to the compound. You can monitor my progress and provide support if things go sideways."

"Support?" she echoed skeptically. "Kat, if you're made, there won't be much I can do from that distance."

"I know. But a sniper on my side can only help my odds of getting out in one piece." I met her gaze squarely. "I need you watching my back,"

For a long moment, she simply stared at me, searching my face for any hint of hesitation or doubt. Finally, she sighed, shaking her head. "I really hope you know what you're doing."

"Trust me."

She huffed a mirthless chuckle. "That was one of the last things Kersho said to me." But there was no real heat in her tone. Just a weary acceptance of the inevitable.

"I won't end up like your brother," I replied. "Not with you on overwatch."

"No," she agreed, confidence returning. "You will not."

"According to the rotation timing, we have forty-five minutes to get across town to the safehouse and get set up."

"Not a lot of time."

"No. That's probably a good thing. I won't have a chance to chicken out."

"Chicken?" she replied, the word going untranslated.

"I won't have a chance to change my mind," I rephrased. "Don't tell me you aren't nervous."

"I'm terrified," Lavona admitted. "But this is my chance

to make my mark with the syndicate, and earn my family's respect and freedom. I intend to make the most of it." She paused, her next words freezing on her lips before spilling out. "I'm glad to have you with me, Katzuo."

My return smile was genuine. I'd come to care as much about Lavona as I did Tee or Ally, if not more. "I'm glad you'll have my back," I replied.

We finalized our preparations before exiting our room and going down to the street. I fell into step beside my partner, and together we set out to meet our fate.

# CHAPTER 31

Lavona at my side, I crept through darkened streets toward the safehouse where Rena was being kept. Night had fallen, casting long shadows across the deserted back alley, where we crept toward a nondescript apartment building directly across from our target. I had resolved my plan in my head, but that didn't stop my heart from hammering against my chest. Rena's blood would be on my hands if my desperate gambit failed.

I couldn't let that happen.

We entered the apartment building from the rear, bypassing a pair of strangers smoking something that smelled enough like weed that it might as well have been marijuana. Finding an emergency stairwell, we ascended to the seventh floor, high enough for Lavona to get a good angle on the safehouse across the way. She removed a small device from a pocket and placed it against each door. Interior sounds echoed through our earpieces, the devices filtering out anything that didn't come from activity inside. The tech made it easy to locate an empty apartment, and a second device allowed us silent entry.

"We're running out of time," Lavona said, dropping the

duffel on the floor and unzipping it to remove the broken-down pieces of her sniper rifle.

"We'll make it," I replied. We had to.

She efficiently assembled the weapon while I shed my outer layers down to the form-fitting nano-fiber underlay. I took a steadying breath, trying to calm my nerves.

"You're sure about this?" Lavona asked without glancing up from the gun.

"No," I admitted. "But it's the best plan I've got."

She huffed a mirthless laugh. "That's not exactly a ringing endorsement."

"I know. I need to get into position before the next guard rotation." I met her gaze squarely, allowing my resolve to show. "I'm trusting you to watch my back in there."

Something unreadable flickered through Lavona's eyes before she nodded. "I won't let you down. Now go, before you miss your window."

I flashed her a final tight smile and slipped back into the hallway, taking the stairs three at a time to get back outside as quickly as possible. The smokers outside barely saw me as I hurried through the alley and shot across the street into an adjacent back passage. I froze in a shadowed alcove with a clear view of the safehouse's side entrance.

Precisely on schedule, the guard emerged for a cursory perimeter sweep. I held my breath, muscles coiled. The instant the man turned away, I lunged from concealment, jabbing a stun rod against the guard's neck. The Hixian crumpled with a muffled grunt. Working fast, I dragged the unconscious sentry deeper into my hiding place in the alley before stripping off his suit and pulling it on over my slimmer frame. I must have looked comical in his way-too-big jacket and pants.

The look wouldn't last for long.

Lifting my pad, I initiated a biometric scan, a dim matrix of light washing over his still form. With a few taps,

I transmitted the scan data to my holomask and nano-fiber underlay. The advanced tech shimmered and reshaped itself, sculpting my features into a perfect replica of the guard. The underlay expanded and hardened, bulking up my physique to match the older man's larger proportions. Within moments, the transformation was complete. I straightened, now a dead ringer for the neutralized guard.

Using a security override device, I hacked the biometric protection on the service door, unlocked it and slipped inside the safe house. My senses strained for any hint of discovery as I crept through utilitarian back halls. The building's blueprints flashed through my mind. Based on Gun's intel, Rena was most likely being kept in a secure suite near the structure's core, far from windows and external access points.

I tracked deeper into the compound, hugging the walls and pausing at every corner to listen for approaching foot-steps before proceeding. Yellow lighting cast an eerie glow across the featureless corridors, disorienting in their same-ness. I relied on memory to guide my steps, mentally ticking off turns as I followed the path to my destination. .

My nerves taut, I was certain any moment I would round a corner and find myself face-to-face with another guard. But through some miracle, the halls remained empty. The almost preternatural quiet set my teeth on edge. Where was everyone?

After an eternity, I had nearly reached my destination. Only one more corridor lay between me and what I had taken for a series of bedrooms near the building's center. I had just crossed the halfway point when another guard turned the corner in front of me, freezing in surprise to see me coming his way. It took all of my focus not to turn and run. That would ruin everything, and I was too far down the passageway to escape, anyway.

"Orven? Why aren't you at your post?" The guard asked.

My mind raced, and my mouth turned to cotton. I had prepared an excuse just in case something like this happened, but now my insta-panic made it hard to think.

The guard's eyes narrowed. "Well? What's your problem?"

"No problem," I finally replied, hoping my voice modulator sounded natural. "Just needed to hit the head. Laric's covering for me." I knew the guard's name from the dossiers Gun had provided. It was probably the only thing that made me believable.

To my immense relief, the guard huffed in understanding. "That's Laric. Always trying to score brownie points with his betters." The suspicion bled from his stance. "Well, hurry it up. The package is restless tonight and the boss wants everyone sharp."

"Roger that." I nodded and continued down the hall at a faster pace. Once safely out of sight, I released a shaky breath. Too close for comfort.

I swiftly moved through the empty halls, using the listening device against each door to check the rooms for occupants. There was a chance more than one room would have someone inside, but I had also prepared an excuse for that.

Putting the device against the fourth door down, I quickly snatched it away from the blasting music, which remained inaudible on my side. The door was clearly reinforced, and there was definitely someone inside. The odds seemed pretty good that it was Rena.

My fingers trembled as I switched the device over to its lock-cracking option and employed it. I could hardly believe what I was doing. What would my parents think of all this? With an almost inaudible snick, the lock disengaged, dragging my focus back to the moment. I sucked in a sharp breath as I gave the door a light shove inward.

Cool recycled air washed over my face as the door to

Rena's quarters swung open...revealing the business end of an energy pistol leveled right between my eyes.

"Don't. Move," a soft voice hissed.

The music stopped, thick silence hovering between us.

Despite the spike of fresh fear, I raised my hands slowly, keeping my posture as non-threatening as possible. "Rena Maringan?" I asked, turning my eyes from the gun to the most striking violet eyes I'd ever seen.

"Who wants to know?"

"My name is Noah. I'm here to rescue you."

"Rescue me?" The pistol never wavered. "I'm in a safe-house. Why would I need to be rescued?" Her eyes were fiery orbs above the thin line of her mouth

"Because the syndicate knows you're here, and they've sent assassins to kill you. If you know the syndicate, you know they have the means and won't stop until they succeed."

"How do you know about the syndicate?"

"Because I'm one of their assassins," I replied, stretching my fingers to emphasize I wasn't a threat. "But... but like I said, I didn't come to kill you, or you'd already be dead. I came to help you."

"Why?" Rena's brow furrowed. "What's in it for you?"

"My soul," I answered. "I'm not a killer."

She glared at me a moment longer before lowering her weapon. "That much is obvious. She barked a harsh laugh, grief and bitterness written across her face. "Dear old dad never could stand having his authority questioned, could he."

I blinked, thrown by the twist. "Dear old dad? You mean, Markan?"

"The one and only." Her smile faded. "His wicked little secret. The daughter who saw through his lies to the cruelty beneath and dared to defy him. Instead of showing me love, he sends his goons to take me out. So damn predictable."

The reveal hit like a jackhammer. I swallowed hard, my resolve crystallizing into diamond clarity. I had to get her out of there and keep her safe.

"I didn't know," I said quietly. "But that only makes it more critical that I get you somewhere safe."

"I'm supposed to be safe here," she replied. "How can you promise that when you got in so easily?"

"Because they trained me for this. Which means I know their tricks."

For an eternal moment Rena stared at me, suspicion warring with desperate hope in her eyes. Then, all at once, the fight drained out of her. "Why are you doing this? Why risk yourself for me?"

"Because it's the right thing to do. Because if I don't, I won't be able to live with myself. And because I need your help as much as you need mine. Please. We need to go… now…before anyone realizes what's happening. Especially my partner."

Rena hesitated only a fraction of a second before nodding. I held out a hand and after a moment, she took it, allowing me to guide her into the corridor.

We nearly made it out of the residential wing before a cold voice stopped us in our tracks. "Orven. Care to explain what you're doing?"

Krex, the safehouse commander, stepped from an adjoining passage, flanked by a pair of hard-eyed guards. His gaze flicked from me to Rena and back again, an ugly sneer twisting his mouth. My blood turned to ice in my veins. Of all the rotten luck.

"He's helping me escape my father," Rena said, squeezing my hand. I glanced at her in surprise but her gaze never left Krex.

"Is that so?" the Hixian growled. "And what makes you think I'll allow that?"

"Because Markan knows I'm here, and you want me to live."

"How do you know that?"

"Markan sent me to kill her," I said. "But I'm not going to do that. I'm taking her somewhere safe."

"You expect me to believe that? Maybe you're taking her somewhere safer for you to blast her between the eyes."

"How reckless would that be, when I could have dropped her in her room and snuck out before you knew she was dead?"

The color drained from Krex's face, and then he stepped aside, his expression twisting with fury that I had overcome his defenses so easily. Embarrassment quickly reddened his cheeks. "Go then. But if you leave, don't expect my help a second time."

"I won't need it," Rena replied. Krex and his goons watched in silence as we slipped past and hurried out of the building.

The night air tasted impossibly sweeter as we burst from the safehouse into the alley beyond. My knees nearly buckled. We had done it. Against all odds, Rena was out of there alive. Now all I needed to do was...

My train of thought derailed violently as I caught sight of a familiar figure standing in the mouth of the alley.

Lavona.

She was supposed to be covering our escape from the sniper's perch. Why was she on the ground?

A jolt of adrenaline crackled down my spine as I locked eyes with my partner. Lavona's gaze raked over us, confused surprise melting into something infinitely harder. I had only a fraction of a second to register the blaster rising to point at my chest before she spoke, each word thick with accusation.

"What are you doing, Katzuo?"

I swallowed hard, mind spinning. This definitely wasn't part of the plan. It had gone so smoothly, I should have guessed something would go wrong. "Lava. I can explain," I said, sweeping Rena behind me, out of her direct line of fire.

"I knew it," she said, voice taut with anger and grief. "I knew you were going to betray us. To betray me. Just because she has a pretty face and no horns doesn't mean she isn't a threat."

"What? No!" I held up a placating hand. "That's not what this is."

"Really." It wasn't a question. "Then what exactly do you call helping our target escape?"

My mind raced, thoughts turning in futile circles. How could I possibly convince her when I had orchestrated this entire charade? "I call it the right thing to do. And I think you know it's the right thing to do, too."

Lavona's eyes narrowed dangerously as she laughed. "You can't be serious. I trusted you, Katzuo! But you're nothing but a traitor to the cause."

"The cause is wrong! Markan is wrong. He sent us to kill his own daughter!"

Lavona's aim never wavered, but I saw the briefest flash of uncertainty cross her face. I desperately seized on it.

"Rena hasn't done anything to deserve a death sentence. Her only crime was disagreeing with her father and trying to get away from him. Is that really something you don't understand, after everything you went through back home?"

For a moment, anguish flickered through Lavona's eyes. Then her expression hardened once more. "It's not our place to question the syndicate."

"Yes, it is!" Finding the courage to face down the barrel of Lavona's weapon, Rena stepped back around me. "You have no idea how terrible my father really is. The things he's done…the number of individuals he's hurt. He's not a good man. He's a monster." She took a ragged breath, tears standing in her eyes. "The syndicate is built on a foundation of innocent blood. What you're fighting for...it's a lie."

Lavona's composure cracked, doubt and turmoil plain on her face. In that moment of vulnerability, a new voice rang out.

"I'd listen to them if I were you."

As one we spun to see Matt step from the shadows, blaster trained on Lavona. My knees nearly buckled in relief. My backup had arrived in the nick of time.

Matt's gaze never left her. "The way I see it, you've got two choices here. You can either lower that weapon and help us get Rena to safety...or you can die where you stand, loyal to a monster."

"Lava," I said softly. "Trust me. Please."

The moment stretched, tension near unbearable. I barely breathed, afraid the slightest provocation would shatter our precarious balance. I could only watch as Lavona visibly wrestled with herself, her blaster trembling noticeably.

A lifetime passed in a handful of galloping heartbeats. Then, slowly, incredibly, Lavona lowered her weapon. She met my gaze, and in her eyes I saw a maelstrom of emotions—anger, grief, uncertainty. But beneath it all, a grim resolve.

"Damn it, Kat. Despite myself, I do trust you. But what am I going to do?" she pleaded, emotion filling her voice. "My sisters…"

The breath left me in a rush, my knees watery with relief. A fragile, disbelieving smile tugged at my mouth. "We'll find a way to help your sisters. I know you didn't leave Viconia to fall into something even worse."

"Did you say Viconia?" Rena said.

Lavona deactivated her holomask, revealing her true face. "Yes."

"Are you with the Respers?"

"I'm not with anyone now. But I was."

"My father armed the Vikers, and helped arrange for the assassination of your President. He's still making deals with them to this day. Not only for military hardware. Viconians, too. When the Vikers take prisoners, they don't hold them. They trade them to the syndicate. He's as responsible for the desolation of Viconia as anyone."

Lavona's face twisted into a new kind of fury. "What?" she hissed, free hand curling into a tight fist.

"That's what he does...whatever it takes to make a profit. To take care of his so-called family, while he sends assassins to kill his flesh and blood."

I glanced at Matt. The Warden's part in this as a benevolent entity was impossible to ignore.

"Whoever you are, get her out of here," Lavona growled, looking at Matt.

"You'll be safe with him," I told Rena, guiding her to him.

"Hi, I'm Matt," he said, offering her a warm smile as he took her hand.

"Rena," she replied.

"We should get out of here," Matt said. He shifted his attention to me. "So should you."

"We will," I replied. "We'll be in touch soon."

Matt nodded, leading Rena back down the alley, the two of them disappearing into the shadows.

I turned to Lavona, clasping her shoulder. "Thank you for trusting me."

She gifted me a tight smile in return. "You're just lucky you have such a sweet, trustworthy face," she replied, but there was no heat to her words. Exhausted humor was more like it. "What do we do now?"

"We go back to the spaceport to wait for pickup and report back to Hondo that the target is eliminated."

"Hondo. Is he…"

"Yeah. It's a long story. I'll give you all the gory details along the way. But you need to keep it between us."

"I'm certainly not going to betray you to the syndicate after what Rena said. If it's true…" She shook her head. "I might not have been able to rescue Kersho, but I sure as hell can avenge him."

"Yes, you can. And you will."

They were tough words, and I could only hope our conviction would remain strong enough to carry us through the days ahead. Because one thing was certain. Once Markan discovered our betrayal, all hell would break loose.

And when it did, there would be nowhere left to run.

# CHAPTER 32

I sat in the rear of the shuttle, my mind reeling from the revelations of the past few hours. Lavona and I had returned to the ship without incident, though the weight of Rena's true identity sat like a stone in my gut. Markan's own daughter. I could still hardly believe it. What kind of father sent assassins after their child, no matter their perceived duplicity? The thought made me sick. For all the Warden's sins, at least he didn't target family.

Not that I knew about, anyway.

That uncertainty led my thoughts down darker pathways. What if Markan and the Warden were equally awful? What if, by completing the Warden's task, we defeated his primary rival and freed him up to do even worse things to the rest of Warexia? I already knew we were pawns in his games, but this was about more than just sick entertainment. Still, if we ever wanted to get back to Earth, what choice did we have?

None right now.

"Are you okay?" Lavona asked, noticing my silent tension.

"Not really," I replied.

"The Warden?" she questioned in a hushed tone so Cade wouldn't overhear.

I had explained as much as I could on our way back to the spaceport. There hadn't been time to go into too much detail, and she still didn't completely understand how the Warden managed to trap outsiders in Warexia and use them to do his bidding, but that was okay. I still didn't completely understand that part, either.

"Yes," I replied. "And Markan. And everything else that's happened to me in the last three months. My restless brain is trying to figure out how it all fits together."

"Maybe it doesn't," she suggested.

"What do you mean?"

"I mean you're trying to make everything make sense. And I understand why. But maybe it never will. Maybe it never can."

"I'm just afraid helping the Warden take down Markan will make everything worse."

"Worse than the destruction of my homeworld? If you had grown up there, you wouldn't think so."

"I think the Warden has destroyed planets, too."

"Maybe, but at least he's part of the fabric of Warexia. Perhaps he had a good reason. Markan is a criminal. His only motivation is profit. Those are his daughter's words, not mine."

"Good point," I said. The short conversation helped ease my mind, at least a little. For now.

Cade guided the shuttle into Nakata's hangar bay. Karpov was there when we arrived to run post-flight diagnostics and handle any maintenance needs.

"The Captain's waiting for you in the briefing room," he told us as we stepped out of the craft. "How did it go?"

"Mission accomplished," Lavona replied.

As promised, we found Ben in the briefing room. We'd already reported our success earlier, though I left out any of the details with the assumption our comms were being recorded and possibly transmitted back to Miss Asher. Because of that, I had yet to tell him how Lavona's allegiance had shifted.

"Welcome back," he said as we entered. "Take a seat. We need to report back to Asher."

"You haven't done that already, Captain?" I asked, sitting beside Lavona.

"I figured it could wait until you returned." He activated a comm unit built into the table.

"Captain Hondo," Miss Asher greeted crisply. "I trust you have good news for me."

"Affirmative," Ben replied. "I have Katzuo and Lavona here with me. The operation was a success. The target is neutralized, as ordered."

"Excellent. I had a good feeling about your unit, Captain, and you haven't let me down. Well done, Lavona and Katzuo. Let this mission be the first of many contributions to the family."

"Thank you, Miss Asher," Lavona and I replied in tandem, looking at each other and grinning at our natural rapport.

"They performed admirably," Ben said smoothly. "I'm proud to have them under my command. Should I set a course for Marin?"

"Don't be too hasty," Asher drawled. "You've already proven your mettle during a difficult assignment, completing it in record time. I'm questioning if further training may be necessary for your group, at least in the short term. For now, maintain position in orbit around Hixia while I discuss your availability with additional members of upper management. I'll provide further instructions once the matter is settled."

"Yes, Miss Asher," Ben replied. "We'll hold position until we receive new orders."

"Thank you, Captain. Please consider the delay a reward for a job well done. I firmly believe you're fated to do great things for the syndicate." Asher cut the connection without further comment, and the comms disconnected.

Ben immediately turned toward us, his eyes landing on Lavona. "So what really happened down there?"

I briefly recapped the sequence of events, starting with our meeting with Master Gun and concluding with Matt's arrival. When I finished, Ben leaned back in his seat, his expression unreadable.

Finally, he blew out a long breath. "This just got a whole lot more complicated."

"More like a whole lot more personal," Lavona muttered.

"What do we do next?" I asked.

Ben straightened up. "Our first order of business is to touch base with Matt and Rena. If she really is Markan's daughter, then I assume she knows where to find him. That's what we joined the syndicate to learn, so this could be a major shortcut for us. She might also have access to other intel that would come in handy. Like Princess Goloran said, knowledge is the strongest currency."

He closed his hand into the call-me gesture and raised it to his ear. Matt's voice only took a few seconds to emerge from Ben's thumb. "Hey Cap," he said, the strange method of communication drawing a thoroughly confused look from Lavona. "I assume Noah and Lavona made it back okay."

"They're sitting here with me now. How's Rena?"

"She's just fine. I snuck her out of Dodge and got her back up to Head Case on the hop racer without drawing any attention. The real question is, where is she going to sleep?"

"It sounds like you two are destined to become room-mates," Ben replied.

Matt sighed. "How did I know you were going to say that?"

Ben chuckled. "Our little crew is going to grow by at least one more."

"You mean Lavona?"

"Yes."

"She can bunk in the Captain's quarters, or with Rena. There's space in both. Anyway, let's not get too far ahead of ourselves here."

"Agreed. I need to speak to Rena directly. Can you put her on?"

"I can't move my hand too far from my head without disconnecting," Matt said. "Hold on." A brief pause followed.

"This is Rena."

Ben leaned forward intently. "Rena, my name is Ben. Thank you for trusting us. I know this can't be easy for you."

"Easy?" she laughed, her tone devoid of humor. "None of this is easy. But it's necessary. What do you need from me, Ben?"

"We need to find your father," Ben said. "Noah says you might know how to do that."

"I do," Rena confirmed. "It's probably the number one reason my father wanted me dead. That and the confidential syndicate data I uploaded into my DNA before I ran." Ben and I locked eyes. Confidential data sounded promising. "But it's not as simple as just giving you coordinates. The station is hidden in deep space, beyond the explored boundaries of Warexia. It's…not easy to get there."

"I see," Ben replied. "But you came out. I assume you know how to go back."

Rena's voice hardened. "Of course." She paused. "But it took me two years of planning to get away from him. What makes you think I'd be willing to go back?"

"Revenge?" Lavona blurted. "He did send us to kill you."

"That's not a good enough reason. It's much more likely we'll be killed, and if that happens, then I escaped for nothing."

"I understand your hesitation," Ben said. "And I don't blame you for not wanting to go back. In truth, I don't want you to go back, especially if you're carrying valuable, irreplaceable intelligence. Are you sure you can't just give us directions?"

"I could try, but you're bound to make a mistake, and there's no margin for error."

"Then I'm sure you also understand why we need your help."

"He tried to kill you," Lavona said. "We want to kill him."

"I don't blame you for that. But I also don't see the point. The syndicate is bigger than my father. Removing him wouldn't change much of anything."

"Not right away," Ben agreed. "But given enough time, we aim to erode the syndicate from the inside out."

"I appreciate you saving me," Rena said after a brief pause. "I really do. But I can't go back there. I didn't escape just to be captured or killed back where I started."

"Then what did you escape for, if not to bring your father down?" I asked, my voice coming out more forcefully than I intended. The idea of getting so much closer to Markan and being denied didn't sit well.

"What does that matter?" she replied.

"You stole information about the syndicate. You ran away because you learned your father is a criminal warlord and a monster—your words, not mine. So you could what? Buy a bikini and bake on a beach somewhere? Or so you could stop him from committing crimes?"

Ben looked my way, surprised by the strength of my

reply. I had even surprised myself. Lavona eyed me with fresh admiration.

A long silence followed while we waited for Rena to reply. "If I lead you there, what can you do to stop him? How will you get close enough to kill him?"

"We have a few tricks up our sleeves, "Ben answered.

"And we got to you easily enough, didn't we?" Lavona added.

Another pause followed. "I can guide you," Rena finally decided, exhaling sharply. My entire body flooded with relief as I sank into my seat. "But we'll need to move fast. If he discovers I'm still alive before we make our move, all of his defenses will be on high alert when we arrive. We won't stand a chance."

"I understand the need to move quickly," Ben said, "but we can't rush into this blind. We need time to formulate a plan."

I could almost hear Rena's frown through the comms. "Captain, with all due respect, we may not have that kind of time. Every minute of delay adds to the risk."

"I hear you. But charging in unprepared is a good way to get dead fast. Your father isn't some two-bit thug. He's smart, ruthless, and commands a pretty large army. I know it's not ideal, but for now, just sit tight. We've got to do this right or there's no point in doing it at all."

"I understand," Rena replied, disappointment spiraling with her resignation.

"Thank you, Rena. You have no idea how much your willingness to lead us to your father means to us, and to all of Warexia. We'll be in touch soon with a plan."

"I'm counting on you, Captain. I'm putting all of my trust in you. Please don't let me down."

"We won't," Ben replied. He lowered his hand, looking deeply thoughtful.

I shifted in my seat, warring slivers of anticipation and

doubt worming beneath my skin. "Are we sure this is a good idea? I want to take Markan down as much as anyone, but this..."

"Feels like a suicide mission," Lavona finished. "That's because it probably is."

I flinched. Ben ran a hand through his hair. "The odds aren't great. But this is our best shot." He pinned us with a hard look. "We've got a chance here. One I didn't expect. We can't afford to pass it up. A chance to not only cut the head off a snake and do some good for Warexia, but also get us closer to going home. It won't be easy, but I believe we can do it."

"How?" I asked.

"We need to figure that out," he admitted. "The crew of Head Case is my family. But the individuals here onboard Nakata are like family too. We can't hide this from them. We need to give them a choice."

"I don't know if that's a good idea," I said. "If even one of them turns on us, Markan will find out about Rena before we can make our move."

"Not to mention, they might try to kill us," Lavona said.

"If we have to fight, then we'll fight," Ben said. "Our first lesson was that we're strongest together. The assessment proved it, and I'm a firm believer." He turned to me. "Do you have Archie with you?"

I nodded as the Aleal shifted on my back, poking a tendril up from beneath my clothes. "I don't go anywhere without it."

"It was with you the whole time?" Lavona said, surprised. "I never saw it."

"Yeah, it's been practicing stealth. I think you passed, bud."

Archie waved its tendril in celebration.

"I'm going to tell the others to meet us here," Ben said. "Let's hope we don't end up regretting it."

# CHAPTER 33

Ben activated the ship-wide comms, his voice echoing through the halls. "Attention all hands. This is your captain speaking. Report to the briefing room immediately."

Within minutes, the rest of our team filed in, expressions ranging from puzzled to wary. They knew something significant must have occurred for Ben to call a meeting so soon after our return. The tension in the room was palpable as they took their seats around the table, looking expectantly at Ben.

He wasted no time getting to the heart of the matter. "We have a situation," he began without preamble. "The mission...didn't go according to plan."

Cade sat up straighter, eyes narrowing. "What do you mean? Did something happen to the target?"

Ben met his gaze steadily. "You could say that. The target was Markan's daughter. We told Miss Asher that we neutralized her, and as far as the syndicate is concerned, she's dead. But she's very much alive. We didn't kill her. We saved her."

Shocked silence followed his words. I could practically see the gears turning in everyone's heads as they processed his bombshell. Cade recovered first, leaning forward intently.

"His daughter," he repeated. "And you saved her? Why?"

"Because she doesn't deserve to die," I said.

"Who made it your job to decide who does and doesn't deserve to die?" Mak asked.

Larev shook his head, confusion and disbelief warring across his craggy features. "Yeah. I don't understand. Why would you directly disobey orders like that? We had a job to do!"

"A job that was wrong," Lavona interjected, voice hard. "Rena is innocent in all this. Markan only wants her dead because she learned the truth about what he really is—a monster who profits off the suffering of others."

"This is insane," Mak said, eyes wide. "Do you have any idea the kind of trouble you've brought down on us? When the Big Boss finds out—"

"When Markan finds out, it'll be because we're storming through his door," Ben interrupted. He swept his gaze around the table, taking in each crew member. "Rena knows how to find him. She can get us through his defenses. We have a chance to kickstart the decline of the syndicate."

"But...why?" Karpov asked. "You joined up like the rest of us. You aced the assessment. You're the Captain! Why would you want to give up everything you worked for?"

"Noah and I joined the syndicate to destroy the syndicate," Ben replied. "We needed to work from the inside to get closer to Markan. That Asher sent us to kill his daughter was dumb luck, and saved us a ton of time and effort."

"Noah?" Cade said. "I thought your name was Katzuo?"

"It's Noah," I replied. "And that's Ben. I'm sorry, Cade. I'm sorry we had to lie to all of you. To use you. But we have an opportunity here to do something that matters. To make a real difference."

"You're talking about betraying the syndicate," Larev growled. "You might want to throw away everything you've worked for, but I don't."

"Everything you've worked for?" Lavona shot back. "You mean being a nameless cog in a machine powered by the suffering of innocents?" Her eyes flashed with barely contained fury. "Let me tell you what your beloved syndicate is responsible for, Larev. They orchestrated a devastating war on my homeworld, Viconia. They armed the Vikers and sat back to watch the slaughter, all so Markan could get rich on weapons sales and the sale of slaves. Countless dead, including my brother. Even more displaced. Families like mine torn apart. That's the legacy of the syndicate. That's what you're working for."

Larev shifted in his seat, looking uncomfortable. But he set his jaw stubbornly. "I didn't sign up to be a hero. I signed up to earn my keep and live comfortably doing it. You're asking us to throw all that away."

"You all joined the syndicate for different reasons, but none of us knew the full extent of what they were really about. Now we do. We have a responsibility to do the right thing."

Karpov shook his head and groaned, clearly torn. "I hear what you're saying. And I'm with you. The kind of messed up stuff the syndicate does isn't right. But this...this is big. Taking on an entire criminal empire? We're a handful of people. We don't stand a chance."

"We only need to take out Markan," Ben replied. "It won't be enough to topple the syndicate. Not right away. But Rena also has reams of intel on their interests and schemes. Once she passes that intel to the Warden—"

"The Warden!" Mak shrieked, interrupting. "You're going to bring him into this?"

"Is there a problem with that?" I asked.

"You can't trust the Warden."

"But we can trust Markan?" Lavona countered, her expression reflecting her disdain for the man.

Mak opened her mouth to speak but couldn't come up with a rebuttal. Instead, she folded her arms and scowled. Even so, I could see indecision and fear playing out across her face and the faces of the two Hemid. They were wavering, caught between the draw of an easier path and the harder road their consciences demanded.

Ben saw it, too. He rose to his feet, shoulders squared. "I won't force anyone into this. But I'm asking you, as your captain and your friend, to stand with me. With us. We have a real shot here to make a difference. Rena is the key to getting to Markan and if we act decisively, we can end his reign of terror once and for all."

Everyone remained frozen. Then Cade pushed back from the table. "I'm in," he said simply. When the others glanced at him in surprise, he shrugged. "You saw the way they treated Rhis. I only stayed on because I didn't want his death to be for nothing. But I'd rather have vengeance than comfort any day."

Karpov blew out a long breath, his broad shoulders slumping. "Alright. You can count me in too, I suppose. Working for such a shady outfit never felt right to me anyway. They treated Yurt's death like he was nothing, too."

Mak and Larev remained silent, glaring at the rest of us with thinly veiled hostility. My heart sank as I realized they wouldn't be swayed. Not with words, at least.

Larev abruptly stood, chair screeching across the deck. "You've all lost your minds if you think I'm going along with this insanity. I'm done here. Mak, let's go."

Lavona tensed, half-rising, but I beat her to it. I stepped

quickly into Larev's path, blocking his exit. He glowered down at me, muscles bunching.

"Get out of my way, runt. Before I make you."

"I can't do that," I replied evenly, refusing to be intimidated. "We already have the captain and the pilot on our side, which means this ship is already ours. We tried to appeal to your better natures and give you the freedom to make the right choice. But if you're not with us, then you're against us."

"So that's it?" Larev spat. "Join your little mutiny or get shoved out an airlock; is that it?"

"Of course not." I never took my eyes off the big Hemid. "We'll let you go, when we've accomplished what we're setting out to do.. But until that time, you're just going to have to be confined to quarters. *After* we remove your access to comms. We can't risk you blabbing to Asher about our plans."

Larev snarled, shoving forward to thrust past me. "Move aside!"

He outweighed me by a significant margin, muscled arms thicker than my head. Sheer size and brute strength should have sent me sprawling. Should have, but didn't. The last two weeks of training hadn't been a waste of time.

I shifted my weight, dropping low and twisting to redirect his momentum. Grabbing his wrist, I torqued viciously and heaved. The big Hemid had just enough time to blink in shock before he was airborne. He hit the deck with a thunderous crash and a pained bellow.

Mak gaped openly. "What the—"

She never got the chance to finish her thought. At that exact instant, a concussive boom shuddered through Nakata, throwing us against each other. The lights flickered and dimmed, emergency klaxons blaring to life.

I regained my balance. That had felt like weapons fire.

Were we under attack?

# CHAPTER 34

Another impact rocked Nakata, sending me crashing to the deck. My breath left my lungs in a pained wheeze as my head hit the deck. My vision swam, and for a moment, I simply lay there, stunned and disoriented.

Motion in my peripheral vision sent enough adrenaline racing through my system for me to ignore my pain and roll onto my knees just as Mak darted within my reach. My fingers barely brushed her sleeve as she slipped past me, making for the open hatchway. Clearly, she intended to head for the bridge.

"Stop her!" The words emerged from me as a strangled gasp, but it was enough to spur Lavona into launching herself at Mak. She caught the fleeing woman around the waist, the two of them snarling and clawing at each other as they slammed hard into the bulkhead

I had no time to intervene. Larev's meaty hands closed around my throat from behind, and I again lost my air. Spots danced across my vision as he squeezed mercilessly. Panic sent my pulse skyrocketing, but I forced it down, remembering my training. Gripping his wrists, I dropped my weight and twisted hard to the side. Larev grunted in surprise as I slipped free of his chokehold. Pivoting, I snapped my elbow back into his face. Cartilage crunched satisfyingly beneath the impact. Larev howled, staggering back, blood pouring from his nose.

I didn't give him a chance to recover. Grabbing the front of his shirt, I hammered my knee into his groin once, twice, three times in rapid succession. The Hemid's eyes bulged, all the air leaving him in an agonized wheeze. He crumpled to his knees, clutching himself.

I dragged in ragged gulps of air, adrenaline surging. Lavona and Mak still grappled nearby, trading blows. But my attention shifted to Ben and Cade as they scrambled past the brawling women and out into the corridor, clearly racing for the bridge.

With a final punt to Larev's head that knocked him unconscious, I leaped over his prone bulk and sprinted after Ben and Cade. The ship bucked and shuddered around me, and more hits from our mysterious attackers impacted the shields. I staggered, bouncing off the bulkhead without breaking stride. This couldn't be the syndicate, could it? There hadn't been time yet for anyone to warn them about our betrayal.

Or had there?

By the time I burst onto the bridge, Cade already occupied the pilot's seat, hands tight on the controls.

"Shields down to sixty percent!" he reported, voice tight. "Rerouting auxiliary power now."

Ben swung toward me, expression bleak. "Noah, I need you on weapons!"

"On it!" I slid into the co-pilot seat, hands flying over the controls, activating the weapons systems.

"Four contacts!" Cade shouted, my stomach lurching as another barrage struck the shields, shaking the deck plates hard enough underfoot to rattle my teeth. I zeroed in on the tactical display, watching the red outlines around the enemy ships arc across the screen. "They're positioning for another barrage!"

Without hesitation, I raised my hand to my ear and thought of Matt. "Matt, it's Noah! We're under attack! We need backup now!"

"Noah," Matt replied. "Damn. We're on our way. Just hang in there!"

"Easier said than done. We're being pounded. Hurry!" Needing both hands to shoot, I shut the comm down and reached for the targeting controls, returning my full focus to the tactical display. Hidden ion cannons lining the otherwise unassuming hull rotated into position, coming online one after the other. The enemy ships completed their turn, streaking toward us with clear intent. "Here they come!" I warned.

"Evasive maneuvers!" Ben cried. "Brace for impact!"

The first warship opened up at maximum range, cannonball-sized ball-lightning slamming into our shields, shaking us hard. I bit my tongue hard enough to draw blood. Slamming my teeth together to keep that from happening again, I concentrated on the other three ships joining the assault, their intensified barrage hitting us hard. We needed to fight back. Otherwise, there was no way we could outlast their combined firepower.

Eyes narrowed in concentration, I centered my targeting reticle on the lead warship, ground my teeth together, and squeezed the trigger. Nakata's forward guns erupted in a dazzling hail of return fire. Most shots defused harmlessly off the enemy's shields, but a lucky few found their marks. Minor geysers of molten metal sprayed into the void as my blasts chewed into the enemy's hull.

"Keep on that one!" Cade shouted. "Coming about."

Nakata made a hard maneuver, its aft swinging to the port side as Cade launched her bow upwards like a breaching whale. The move put my target full broadside to us, but facing the wrong direction to fire back with any authority.

I squeezed the trigger again, starboard cannons flinging heavy ions against the warship's hull. The attack overwhelmed their shields, punching into the superstructure. Atmosphere and ablated metal exploded from the ship's side, glowing like sparklers in the black. The ship's maneuvering stalled out, leaving them adrift as their ship continued venting.

"Nice shooting!" Cade cheered. He jinked hard and over, narrowly evading an answering salvo from another one of the enemy ships. "One down, three to go!"

I swung the guns after our next target, Nakata's superior agility and Cade's impressive flying allowing me to score multiple hits before the other ship could bring its weapons to bear. Explosions blossomed along the enemy warship's beam, stitching toward its engine array. One violent gout of flame later, the vessel tumbled away, leaking bodies among the smoke and debris.

A vicious smile curved my lips. We were giving better than we got, but Cade's urgent cry snapped me out of my dark elation.

"Shields critical! Thirty percent and falling!" Even as he shouted the warning, the bridge lights flickered ominously. The stench of burning insulation flooded the compartment an instant before a conduit above Cade's head exploded in a shower of sparks. He reeled back with a startled yelp, batting at the embers smoldering on his shirt.

I wrenched my attention back to the battle as the two remaining warships pressed their assault, energy blasts stabbing through our weakened shields to gouge molten scars across Nakata's hull. We couldn't take much more of this.

Where the hell was Head Case?

Snarling, I sent shot after shot hammering into the nearest enemy ship. Again, most of the blasts scattered harmlessly, allowing the warship to shrug off my barrage like Nakata was nothing more than an annoying insect, its guns never wavering.

Behind me, Cade cursed bitterly, fighting to keep us oriented against the onslaught. "We can't win this! We need to break off, put some distance between us!"

"Negative!" Ben shouted. "We run now, we're dead! We can do this!"

I bit back a curse, thumb tightening on the trigger. He was right. Damaged as we were, the warships would run us down long before we could escape. Our only chance was to keep fighting and hope the cavalry arrived in time.

That faint hope surged as my next flurry of shots found a weak point in the enemy vessel's shields, leaving glowing craters in the reinforced armor. Fire belched from a jagged rent in its flank, molten debris spraying into the void. The ship lurched suddenly, guns falling silent.

"Got him!" I felt a surge of savage satisfaction. Three down.

The feeling was short-lived. As if enraged by the loss of its brethren, the final warship redoubled its assault. The entire bridge bucked, a tortured groan reverberating through the deck and the bulkheads. I had one panicked instant to realize the shields had collapsed completely before a console behind me exploded, igniting a gout of fire from a ruptured plasma conduit.

"Archie!" I screamed, terrified by the heat searing my back and my little buddy. This was it. We weren't going to make it.

My phone hand suddenly slapped the side of my head

like an electrical jolt, adrenaline surging through my veins. "Noah!" Matt shouted. "Keep shooting!"

"I need more power!" I cried, hand dropping back to the console as I aimed the forward guns, placing the reticle over the last warship's thrusters.

"All power's diverted to the cannons," Ben announced. "Fire!"

A brilliant lance of pure destruction erupted from the guns at Nakata's bow. The ions smashed into the remaining warship, a shotgun blast through its primary drive core, joined by cannon fire from Head Case as it swooped in from overhead.

For a beat, nothing happened. Then, a miniature sun blossomed where the enemy vessel had been. I raised a hand to shield my eyes from the dazzling detonation, superheated gasses washing across Nakata's battered hull.

And then it was over. Blessed silence enveloped the bridge, broken only by the hiss of automated extinguisher foam smothering the fires as I slumped in my seat, not quite believing we had survived.

"Archie?" I suddenly remembered him. Anxious about his fate, I jerked forward to take my weight off his position at my back. "Are you okay back there?" The harsh rasp of my breathing eased into a weary smile as a tickle moved up my back, and a gelatinous tendril snaked up past my collar to pat my cheek. "Glad you're still with me, bud." I lifted my shoulder and pressed my cheek lightly against the tendril.

"Damage report," Ben croaked, looking as battered as I felt. He had a handkerchief out, mopping up a trickle of blood running from a gash above his eye. I figured he must've caught some shrapnel from the console behind us when it exploded.

Cade's hands flew across his instruments, assessing. "Shields are offline. The reactor is damaged but operational.

Multiple hull breaches all over, but the emergency bulkheads contained them." A relieved grin split his face. "I think Nakata's done for, but at least we're still alive."

Ben blew out a long breath. "Good to hear it. Noah, are you okay?"

"I'll live," I managed, grinning broadly despite feeling like my whole body had been worked over with a baseball bat. "Did we get all of them?"

"Scopes are clear," Cade replied. He pointed to a small silver sphere headed our way, a relieved smile tugging his mouth. "And it looks like the cavalry has arrived to pick us up."

"A sight for sore eyes," I replied.

"Captain, we're being hailed," Cade said.

"I've got it," Ben replied, opening the comms channel.

"Anyone alive over there?" Matt asked, relief obvious in his tone. "Or can I change quarters again?"

Despite everything, a laugh bubbled up my raw throat. "Afraid you're stuck with pink, Matt. In fact, you're going to have a roommate or two."

"You had me worried for a minute there," Matt drawled. "I thought you were toast. Tee even bet against you."

"I did not!" Tyler complained from somewhere on the flight deck.

"I thought we were toast, too," I admitted. "Thanks for the backup."

"Do you remember that time I put you on guns, and you froze?" Matt asked.

"No," I replied with an understanding grin.

"Me, neither. Nice job, kid."

I glanced around at the shattered remnants of the bridge, scorch marks and exposed wiring sparking from a partially collapsed bulkhead. We had come within a hair's breadth of destruction. Though the immediate threat had passed, we weren't out of the woods yet. This mission was far from over.

"Was this Markan, do you think?" Matt asked.

"I don't know how it could be," Ben replied. "Mak and Larev didn't make it to the comms to warn Asher about our little mutiny."

"Master Gun, maybe?" I guessed. "If he was watching Lavona and me move in on the safehouse…"

"If those were Markan's ships, we wouldn't be alive to wonder," Lavona said, leaning against the open hatchway onto the bridge. Her hair was a mess, and she had bleeding cuts along her cheek. "Erach figured out we tricked him, is my guess."

"Orven wasn't going to stay unconscious forever," I said. "But doesn't Erach care that he might have killed Rena?"

"It's a good sign," Lavona answered. "In all likelihood, even *he* thinks she's already dead."

"That would be good ," I agreed.

"At any rate, this boat is done for," Ben announced. "Matt, bring Head Case in for docking. We'll transfer over and get underway."

"What about Mak and Larev?" Lavona asked.

"Did you leave them alive?" I questioned.

"I figured the Captain would be cross with me if I didn't. Karpov's keeping an eye on them."

"We still need to take them with us," Ben said. "We don't know how long it will take to reach Markan, and we don't want them blabbing about what happened to Asher or anyone else."

"Won't Asher realize something's up as soon as she contacts Nakata and there's no reply?" I asked.

"Good point. We'll need to scuttle Nakata on our way out. They'll know something happened, but they won't know what. With any luck, Asher will think we're all dead."

"I can't believe I'm doing this," Cade said, rising to his feet.

"How does it feel?" I asked.

"Great, Katzuo. It feels great."

# CHAPTER 35

Lavona and I entered the briefing room, where Karpov stood over Larev and Mak, both seated at the table, staring back at the wrong end of a blaster. Mak had a bruise on her face, a split lip, and a broken nose. Larev's forehead sported a tremendous welt, forcing his right eye into a squint.

"Karpov," Lavona said. "Captain needs you to make Nakata go boom."

"What?" Mak cried. "You're going to destroy the ship?"

"With us on it?" Larev grumbled, tipping his head and looking curiously back at her.

"It's pretty much destroyed already," I replied, drawing his attention. "We're all lucky none of the occupied parts were breached. And no, we're the good guys, remember? You're coming with us."

"What happened to dropping us off somewhere?" Larev asked.

"Maybe if you hadn't tried to fight for the syndicate, we could have trusted you enough to leave you unsupervised. That's not happening now."

"I still can't believe you're willing to betray the syndicate like this," Mak snarled, eyes like daggers. "Doesn't loyalty mean anything to you?"

"It means everything to me," Lavona hissed back. "I'm loyal to my flesh and blood first, this crew second. That should have included you. What does Markan know about loyalty to his family? He would kill his own daughter to keep her quiet. That's the leader you're willing to die for?"

"She's got a point." Larev groaned softly. "Is it too late for me to change my mind about helping you? I'd like to join you."

"There's no way for us to know you mean it," I replied.

"Yeah, figured I'd ask. For what it's worth, I'm sorry, runt."

"Please," Mak complained. "They're not buying it, Larev."

"I'm not playing," Larev insisted. "I am sorry, Katzuo… Noah."

At that moment, a heavy shudder vibrated through Nakata's hull, the dull clang of docking clamps engaging.

"I'm sorry, too," I replied. I met Lavona's gaze, my gut churning with equal parts anticipation and trepidation. "Looks like our ride is here. Karpov, can you destroy the evidence?"

"Sure can," the Hemid replied. "I'll override the safeties and let the reactor overload. The blast should reduce everything to dust. But we'll need to be out of here inside of an hour."

"That shouldn't be a problem."

Lavona reached out toward Karpov's blaster. "May I?"

"With pleasure." Eying Larev with a look of disgust, he handed her the weapon and left the briefing room, ostensibly heading for engineering.

"Let's go," Lavona said, motioning with the weapon toward the hatch.

"I'm not going anywhere," Mak replied while Larev stood, locking his hands behind his head.

"I see you've done this before," I told him.

"I left Cacitrum for a reason," Larev replied.

"Do you want to stand up, or should I break some more of your bones?" Lavona asked Mak.

The other woman grumbled and rose to her feet. I could tell she wanted to make another run for it, but she knew she wouldn't make it.

We guided the pair through the ship to where Ben and Cade waited by the main airlock. Through the small viewport in the door, I glimpsed the corrugated plates of Head Case's hull, the smaller ship locked onto Nakata's crippled hulk, and felt the welcome relief of homecoming.

"Thank you for joining us," Ben told Larev and Mak.

"No trouble at all," Larev replied while Mak scowled.

Ben cycled the airlock. The heavy hatch hissed open, as did that of Head Case. We crossed into Head Case's hangar bay. Instantly, we were swarmed by the rest of the crew, including Rena, Lantz and Twama. Matt and Ally were armed, prepared to handle our two prisoners should they try anything stupid.

Tyler practically bowled me over, catching me in an exuberant hug. "My man!" he laughed, lifting me off my feet.

"Good to see you too, Tee," I wheezed, trying to breathe through his stranglehold. Over his shoulder, my smile widened as a familiar arachnid scuttled into view, multiple eyes bright with unmistakable relief.

"Noahsss," Ixy said. "Ssso goodsss to seesss yousss. Bensss too."

"Hey, Ixy." I replied as Tee finally put me down. "It's good to see you too."

"Shaq!" Ben cried, happy to see the jagger as he

launched from Matt's shoulder onto his. He immediately began nuzzling Ben's neck.

"Not worried," Shaq buzzed, with a definite undertone of *I totally was*.

Ben rubbed the jagger behind his ear and clapped Matt on the shoulder as they shook hands. "Thanks for the backup. You saved our asses back there."

"We do seem to be making a habit of that," Matt replied. His gaze slid to Mak and Larev. "What are we going to do with these two?"

"That's Mak and Larev," Ben introduced. "I figured they could *hang* out with Ixy while she keeps an eye or two on them."

"Yesss," Ixy agreed.

Larev shuddered, looking at her. "What do you mean by hanging out?" Ixy cackled, making him wince.

"The first chance I get, I'm going to kill you all," Mak growled, remaining defiant.

"You won't getsss chancesss," Ixy countered, rising on her legs to appear even more menacing.

"Captain," Karpov said, stepping through the airlock. "We're all set. We have forty-eight minutes to clear the area before Nakata blows."

"We'll make that with plenty of time to spare," Ben replied.

Matt's gaze shifted across Lavona, Cade, and Karpov, questions clear in his eyes. "I believe full introductions are in order."

I took that as my cue and made quick work of the introductions. "A pleasure," Lavona said when I reached her. She shook hands with Matt and Tee and nodded with a smile at Ixy and Shaq.

After introductions, I noticed Karpov had gravitated toward the towering Hunter mech, wonder overtaking his usual stoic demeanor. "Do you really use this machine?" he asked, running an appreciative hand along its leg joint. "It's incredible."

"It sure is," Leo said, looking pleased by the Hemid's interest in the mech. "We don't get a lot of chances to use it, but it's always good to have a little extra something waiting in the wings should we need it."

"Indeed," Karpov agreed. "I am very interested in learning more about it."

Leo approached him, and the two quickly fell into an animated discussion about the mech's specs and abilities. I had to hide a smile. Looked like the Chief Engineer had found a kindred spirit.

Ben finally cleared his throat to get everyone's attention. "We have thirty-eight minutes to disembark. Lavona, Karpov, Tyler, I want you to head down to the prep module on Nakata and grab as much gear as you can in one trip. Some of that Inspector Gadget stuff might come in handy."

"Yes, sir," Karpov said, leaning down to Tee as they headed for the hatch. "Who's Inspector Gadget?" he quietly asked.

"Funny you should ask," Tee said, clapping him on the back as they disappeared through the hatch.

"Ixy, Shaq, Ally, please show Mak and Larev to their sticky accommodations on Deck Five."

"Mmmhmmm," Shaq hummed, hopping from Ben's shoulder to Ally's.

"Cool," Tyler said. "We weren't allowed on Deck Five when we first came on board."

"I wouldn't call being stuck to Ixy's web cool," Matt replied.

"Stuck to her web?" Larev cringed. "Please, Captain. I told Noah, I changed my mind. I want to help you."

"I would confine you to quarters, but we don't have enough space," Ben admitted. "and I can't trust you enough to let you roam freely around the ship. I'm sorry, but it has to be the web."

"Can't you handcuff us to the railing or something?" He pointed to the steps leading to the elevator. "Please, Captain."

Ben sighed. "Lavona, are there restraints with the gear Asher provided?"

"Yes, Captain," she replied. "They're still in the prep module."

"Okay. Ixy and Ally, wait here with Mak and Larev until Tyler and the others get back. If we can restrain you two, then we won't drag you up to Deck Five."

"Thank you, Captain!" Larev said.

"Matt, Rena, Noah, let's get to the flight deck. Lantz, you and Cade might want to tag along, too."

"Sure, Cap," Lantz replied. Cade merely nodded.

"Meg, Leo, Twama, as you were. We'll all sync up once we're underway."

"Goodsss to havesss you baacksss," Ixy said, easing up beside me and stroking my hair with a pedipalp.

"It's good to be back." I started up the steps at a sedate pace, Lantz, Cade and Rena right behind me.

After the destruction on Nakata's bridge, Head Case's flight deck offered welcome familiarity as I strode onto it.

Ben, seated in the command chair, motioned me toward the helm. "Take the pilot's station, Noah."

"Aye aye, Captain," I replied, crossing to the pilot's seat and lowering myself into it. He slid me a broad smile.

Behind us, Ben swiveled his command chair around and seated Rena in the stadium seat closest to him. Lantz and Cade slid into the seats beside her. "Thank you for agreeing to help us, Rena," Ben said. "I know this can't be easy."

She bravely lifted her chin. "I'll do whatever I can to stop my father." Blowing out a nervous breath, her gaze turned distant. "Like I said before, getting to him won't be easy. His station is hidden deep within a massive asteroid sphere, maybe the largest in the galaxy."

"Wait," I said. "Did you say sphere? Not a belt or field?"

"Yes. The asteroids are arranged in a spherical form around the base. Of course, they didn't naturally organize that way. They were moved into position to hide and protect the station."

"You said earlier that the station is located beyond Warexia's fringe," Ben said.

"Yes. Not only is the station not on any star map, my father's seen to it that very few individuals can plot a direct course."

"But you can?" I said.

"Obviously, jumping in anywhere close to the base is impossible. The field is too thick, the risk of collision too high. The only way to reach the station is to come out of hyperspace at the field's edge and navigate through it to the center."

"We've flown in asteroid fields before," Matt said, turning to face them. I followed suit. "How hard could it be?"

"The base is nearly impossible to reach by design," Rena warned. "Not only do you have to contend with the asteroids themselves, but Markan has the whole thing seeded with automated defenses. Proximity mines, autoturrets, and more."

"But you do know a route through," I prodded. "A safe path."

"I know the route that existed when I fled the base a few days ago. But my father has been known to close off certain approach vectors and seed new ones without warning. It's another way to keep potential enemies and deserters from returning."

"It's a wonder you were able to escape at all," Ben murmured.

She glanced away, voice soft. "I almost didn't."

"Wait, back up a second," Matt said "You said you left Markan's base only a few days ago?" At Rena's nod, his frown deepened. "That doesn't add up. It should have taken you weeks to reach Hixia."

Rena hesitated before answering. "My father has some tricks up his sleeves, too."

"What kind of tricks?" I asked.

"Wormhole generators." Rena exhaled, uncomfortable with revealing one of Markan's secrets, despite their soured relationship. "They're scattered throughout Warexia, hidden from the Warden. They create portals that enable near-instant travel from one place in the galaxy to another."

"That's amazing," Ben said. I could almost sense him thinking what I was thinking. Did the Warden have wormhole generators too? Had Levain had them? Might one of them have planted one near Earth?

"That also explains how the syndicate is able to work around the Warden and move without a trace," Matt added.

"There's a gate station not far from here. On a planet called Marin."

"Are you serious?" I said, taken aback. "Marin is the syndicate's training facility. We just came from there yesterday."

She looked surprised by the news. "You're trainees? Recruits?"

"Technically, we graduated when we killed you," I replied.

"I suppose my father worried I would disappear before he could reach me. He sent recruits. And you got through Erach's defenses like they were nothing."

"Your father does have a lot of tricks," I reminded her.

"Still. Either a terrible showing from Erach's guards, or you're very skilled."

My face heated up at the compliment. "Must be the former," I replied.

"In any case, I didn't use that wormhole, for obvious reasons. But it is the closest. I had hoped by entering further away and backing up closer to my father's forces, I might be able to avoid attention, as he would expect me to be running away. Clearly, that didn't work."

"How do we access the generator on Marin?" Ben asked.

"The generator itself is always active. The wormhole is located in the crater of the Musu Volcano. What looks like the dark depths of the mountain is actually empty space in another part of the universe."

"But all the wormholes go back to your father?" Matt questioned.

"No, of course not. The Marin wormhole will lead to a hub, a space station built to generate dozens of wormholes to different locations. That's where we'll enter the portal closer to home."

"Assuming it's still online," I said.

"Yes. Assuming it's still online. Since star maps don't have a record, we'll have to construct the hyperspace route ourselves once we arrive. Or more accurately, I'll have to reconstruct the route."

"And even if we get to the asteroid sphere, we have to hope Markan hasn't closed off your escape route," Ben said, circling back to the earlier part of the conversation. "Is there any way to know for certain before diving in?"

Rena shook her head. "No. But it's possible he expected me to try to come crawling back, and so he might have left the route intact. I don't know if he'll change the pathway now that he'll soon believe I'm dead."

"And what happens if the route is closed?"

"You would need to be a better pilot than anyone else

who has tried to defeat the sphere, or we'll all end up dead."

"Matt's a pretty damn good pilot," I replied. "If the path is gone, I'm sure he can get us through."

"Thanks for the vote of confidence," Matt said. "I wish I could share it. This sounds like no matter what happens, it'll be hairy."

"It sounds like we need to set a course for Marin and fly into the middle of a volcano first," Ben said. "We can worry about being crushed in an asteroid sphere when we get there."

"Yeah," I agreed. "Going back to Marin means having Asher to contend with again. You'd have to be crazy to think she's going to just let us waltz right into the wormhole."

"Noah, set a course for Marin," Ben said. "We've got twenty hours to prepare for what comes next. Which means we don't have another second to waste."

# CHAPTER 36

Eight hours later, after the most pressing preparation had been completed and Ben ordered us to rest up, I settled on the sofa in the lounge, sinking gratefully into the plush cushions. The familiar surroundings provided a much-needed sense of normalcy after spending the last few weeks as a recruit for Markan's syndicate. Tyler and then Ally flanked me on my right, their presence a reassuring comfort. Rena and Karpov claimed the chairs across from me. Lavona and Cade sat to my left, Lavona so close her thigh touched mine.

"So," Tyler said, the first to break the silence. "Sounds like you two had quite the adventure down there." His attention shifted back and forth between Lavona and me. "Care to fill in some blanks?"

I exchanged a glance with Lavona. Where to even begin?

"Well," I said. "The fun started the moment Ben and I boarded Deepling. I thought we would be the only recruits on board, so I was surprised when we were brought to berthing and Lavona and Karpov were already there, with Yurt and Larev."

"Larev's that big guy we locked to the railing in the hangar bay, right?" Tyler asked.

"Yeah, that's him."

"And I thought Levain was a brute. That Larev dude is swole."

"Levain?" Karpov said. "You know him?"

"We met once," Ally said before Tee could say too much. "Did *you* know him?"

"Only by reputation. I mean, I wouldn't have minded working for him, but last I heard he was using his robots for everything, so no real opportunity there."

"You heard right," I said.

"Did you know Levain is dead?" Tyler asked.

"Tee!" Ally snapped.

"No way!" Karpov replied. "When did that happen?"

"A few weeks ago. Not that I know anything else about it."

"Crazy to think he's gone. He had so much influence on Cacitrum. Him and Zariv. I guess the industry is all his now."

Tee opened his mouth to tell Karpov that Zariv was gone, too, but I kicked him in the shin before he could.

"Ow! What the heck, man?"

"I was telling you about our time with the syndicate," I reminded him.

"Oh, yeah. Carry on."

"The trip to Marin felt like it took forever," I said. "Between having to scrub the decks every day and the cramped quarters, I thought I would go insane."

Lavona snorted. "That's putting it mildly. I thought Larev was going to drive me insane with his snoring."

"Hold up," Tyler said. "Who's Yurt?"

"Another Hemid," I said.

"He didn't come along?"

"He died," Cade said. "Killed by maulvas."

"Maulvas?" Ally asked.

"They're like wolves, only bigger," I explained. "We all would have died if not for Archie."

"Where is the little booger, anyway?" Tyler asked. "I haven't seen it since you got back."

"Archie missed its nest," I replied. "And it's Rubik's Cube."

"That's so cute," Ally decided.

"My brother, Rhis, died too," Cade added.

A somber silence swiftly descended, the tension thick. Lavona laid a comforting hand on Cade's shoulder.

"I'm sorry for your loss," Rena said. "I can't imagine how difficult that must be."

He managed a tight smile. "Thank you. It's not something I'll ever forget."

We remained silent for a few more heartbeats. I expected Tee might be the one to break it with a joke, but Lavona picked up the slack instead, continuing the story from our arrival on Marin. Tyler especially liked her description of Miss Asher, though he seemed more intrigued than disgusted by her domineering ways. Soon enough, even Cade was laughing along with the rest of us. Despite the circumstances that had brought us together, bonding as a crew felt good.

Lavona and I were discussing our training sessions with Miss Asher when Lantz appeared at the lounge's entrance.

"Who's hungry?" he called, grinning around the stack of flat cardboard boxes he carried. "I come bearing gifts!" The tantalizing scent of hot cheese and savory toppings wafted through the room, making my mouth water.

"Is that what I think it is?" Tyler asked, practically vibrating with excitement.

"Pizza!" Ally cheered. "Lantz, you beautiful man. Where have you been this whole time?"

"In my quarters, patching my security protocols. The

Warden hasn't given up trying to crack the encryption. Every time we're out of hyperspace, we get activity across the spectrum. I think I figured out how to rate-limit the access, though. He's going to be pissed."

"What does the Warden want with you?" Karpov asked.

"Our first-born sons and our souls," Tyler joked. "He sent us on this mission to deal with Markan. It's his under-handed way of keeping us from learning more about him."

"He's the most powerful entity in Warexia. What else is there to know?"

"How to get back to Earth," Ally said. "He caused us to be trapped here in Warexia. And he knows how we can get home, but he won't help us. He says we belong here, working for him."

"Against your will? That doesn't sound like the Warden."

"Yeah, well, maybe you don't know him as well as you think you do. Not every story you hear about him is true."

Another tense silence descended, quickly dissolved by Lantz. With a flourish, he flipped open the top pizza box, releasing a fresh wave of deliciousness. "Dig in, everyone!"

Lavona leaned closer, sniffing tentatively. Her nose wrinkled. "It smells...pungent."

I couldn't help but laugh at her dubious expression. "It's an acquired taste for some. But trust me, it's delicious."

Rena politely waved off Lantz's offer. "Thank you, but I'm not very hungry right now."

Karpov, on the other hand, wasted no time claiming an entire pie for himself. "What is this yellow stuff?" he asked, taking a huge bite before anyone could answer.

"It's called pineapple," Lantz replied. "A classic pizza topping."

Ally made a face. "Pineapple on pizza is an abomina-tion," she declared.

"Are you kidding?" Lantz said. "Pineapple and Canadian bacon, with barbecue sauce, mozzarella, cheddar, and goat cheese is absolutely perfect."

"Or perfectly disgusting."

"More for me then," Karpov mumbled through his mouthful, his first slice already obliterated.

Lavona shifted uncomfortably, still eyeing the pizza like it might bite her. "Do you have anything else on board? Even those food bars like we had on Deepling would be preferable."

I shook my head apologetically. "Sorry, Lava. We've only got Earth food programmed into the assembler at the moment."

"I can help you find something you might like," Tyler offered. "The galley's got all sorts of stuff programmed in. And the best part is, if you don't like it, you toss it into recycling and none of it goes to waste."

Lavona hesitated before nodding. "I suppose it wouldn't hurt to look."

The two rose and headed out, Tyler already chattering about culinary possibilities. Karpov turned his attention to Rena in their absence, curiosity gleaming in his eyes.

"So, what's it like being Markan's daughter?" he asked.

Rena stiffened, her gaze dropping to her lap. For a moment, I thought she wouldn't answer. Then, haltingly, she began to speak.

"Growing up, I had everything I could ever want," she said softly. "My father doted on me, showered me with love and affection. Anything I asked for, I received without question." She looked up, meeting Karpov's gaze. "But then I discovered who he really is. What he's truly capable of."

"What happened?" I asked gently.

Rena swallowed hard. "I was just a child. Eight years old. I was having lunch. One of my caretakers accidentally spilled soup on my hand, burning me. It was a minor injury, but my father..."

She trailed off, a shudder rippling through her. "I woke up that night to the faint sound of screaming. Worried it was my mother, I left my room and followed the sound. What I saw...I'll never forget or forgive. My father, standing over my caretaker, a knife in his hand. She was already bloody by then. Tortured for hurting me. And..." She broke off, tears streaming down her cheeks. "She looked at me, and all I saw in that moment was her love for me. He killed her because she had caused me the slightest harm. He never even considered the harm losing her did to me."

A horrified silence followed her words. I felt sick to my stomach, fury and revulsion warring in my gut.

"All the love in the universe couldn't make up for that kind of cold cruelty," Rena whispered through suddenly hushed sobs. "From that moment, I realized my father was a monster. And I knew I could never be a part of his world."

She took a shaky breath, visibly collecting herself. "I still love him. Despite everything, he's my father. But that love isn't enough to let him keep hurting others."

Karpov lowered his gaze, clearly regretting his intrusive question. "I'm sorry," he said gruffly. "I shouldn't have asked."

"No, it's alright," Rena replied. "You deserve to know the truth. All of you do."

This heavy silence hung longer and thicker than the prior two. It was abruptly shattered by Lavona and Tyler's return. Tyler looked thoroughly amused. Lavona just seemed disgruntled.

"Well, that was a bust," she announced. "Apparently all Earth food is comparable to fecal matter."

Tyler failed to stifle a snort of laughter, earning a fiery glare from Lavona. He held up his hands in mock surrender.

"It's not my fault you have a weird sense of smell and

no taste," he said. A sly grin tugged at his mouth. "Though I think we can all agree she's right with regards to pineapple on pizza."

"Hey!" Karpov protested.

The good-natured ribbing successfully cut through the earlier tension, startling a laugh from Rena. I felt a rush of gratitude toward Tyler and his uncanny ability to lighten even the darkest of moods.

"You know what we need right now?" Tyler said, flopping back onto the couch. "A movie. Nothing like a so-bad-its-good flick to relax and bond over."

"A movie?" Lavona echoed skeptically.

"I think a movie sounds perfect," Ally said. "Something fun and lighthearted."

"Fun and lighthearted, coming right up!" Tyler declared. He started scrolling through the ship's datastore. "Hey, what about Cats?"

"Are you trying to give us all nightmares?" I replied.

"Madame Web?"

"That one's so bad it's bad," Ally said.

"I got it! The Adventures of Pluto Nash!"

"Fine," I said. "At least it shouldn't totally go over the heads of our new Warexian friends."

As the opening credits began to roll, I settled back into the cushions. The hardest part of our journey was still ahead, but for the moment at least, everything felt just a little bit easier.

I would make sure I enjoyed it while it lasted.

# CHAPTER 37

I gripped the co-pilot's controls tightly as Head Case shuddered around us. Matt and I watched intently through the forward viewport, the tension palpable on the flight deck as the smudged orb of Marin swelled to consume our field of view. Beside me, Matt's face was a mask of concentration as he guided us toward the planet's surface, his hands steady on the stick. As always, I had no idea how he could be so outwardly calm. My heart threatened to pound out of my chest with every inch we closed on our destination.

Only days ago we had been on Marin as syndicate recruits in training, a part we needed to play to get closer to Markan. Now we had returned as traitors to burn the whole operation down, starting with using the planet's wormhole gate as a springboard to jump right to Markan's front door. I had expected this place to be locked up tighter than a bank vault, so the fact that we had cut through Marin's orbit unchallenged left an uneasy feeling in the pit of my stomach.

Marin looked completely abandoned from this distance, but I knew it wasn't. I had just spent weeks down there struggling through harsh survival trials and brutal instruction. The base within those jagged peaks was likely a hive of activity, lookouts monitoring sensors and observing our arrival, Miss Asher standing in the control center, trying to figure out who we were and what we wanted with *her* planet.

Twenty hours had passed since we'd left the vicinity of Hixia. Had she tried to contact Nakata since then? Did the syndicate know they had been tricked into believing Rena was dead? Or were they playing possum down there, hoping we didn't know this planet belonged to the syndicate? Hoping we would fly over and return to orbit? I couldn't bring myself to believe that as much as I wanted to. They knew we were coming. They didn't want us here. It was that simple.

They were down there. Watching. Waiting.

Ben's voice broke into my racing thoughts, unnaturally loud in the tense silence.

"ETA to the volcano?"

"On approach," Matt replied, his focus never wavering from his station. "ETA, ten minutes."

On the surface, the plan was straightforward. Get to the massive crater that hid the entrance to the wormhole and fly straight down its maw. Once on the other side, Rena would direct us to the correct wormhole at the waystation. Once we crossed through the second portal, she would guide us through the asteroid sphere protecting Markan's hidden base.

Of course, plans had a way of going sideways fast, especially ones that involved charging headlong into hostile territory with no backup beyond believing we could pull it off. I had no doubt Matt's piloting skills were top-notch, but I couldn't shake the dread pooling in my gut. So far, this all felt too easy.

Famous last words.

In a single heartbeat, the threat grid went from dead to very much alive, with multiple contacts appearing from points all across Marin's surface.

"We have incoming!" I announced, unable to hide my nervous quiver. "Multiple targets are rising fast."

"Looks like the welcome wagon finally decided to make an appearance," Matt replied, watching the same contacts on his projected display. "Missiles coming in hot." His grip tightened on the controls. "Increasing power to forward shields." The ship hummed around us as he adjusted our defenses. "Noah, you're on guns. Let's give them a proper greeting."

I activated the automated firing system and quickly set up the targets. I felt the vibrations ripple through Head Case as the ion cannon turrets rotated into position, ready to open fire. A cold sweat prickled my forehead as I waited for the missiles to arrive. "Almost within range," I announced.

I engaged Head Case's forward cannons, hurling spheres of heavy ions into the void. One missile vanished in a plume of fire. Then another. And another. But there were simply too many targets. Relentless, they kept coming.

"Hold on!" Matt warned.

He juked and jinked, throwing off the missiles' targeting locks and buying me precious seconds to draw a bead on them. Gritting my teeth, I struggled to mark them on the firing computer and then pick them off, one by one.

Proximity alarms blared an instant before a missile slipped past my curtain of fire and impacted our forward shields directly in front of the transparency. The sudden flare of bright blue energy nearly blinded me. The ship lurched violently; the impact would have thrown me from my seat if not for my restraints.

"Shields at eighty percent!" Meg shouted from her station.

"Captain, we're being hailed," Ally announced from hers.

"Miss Asher," I said.

"Ignore it," Ben replied. "We don't want to give ourselves away."

"Aye, Captain," Ally agreed.

"Noah, stay sharp!" Matt exclaimed. "Looks like we've got a new problem to deal with."

I momentarily turned my attention away from the incoming missiles to the threat display, my throbbing heart catching in midbeat. A fresh wave of contacts swarmed across the sensors—smaller, faster, and more numerous than the missiles. They were drones. They had to be. In the wake of the missile barrage, they arced through Marin's atmosphere, clearly intending to mop up anything that had survived.

"They're moving to intercept," I confirmed bleakly. "ETA sixty seconds."

Matt's expression tightened, but he simply nodded. "Stay on target," he ordered. "We're punching right through them."

I swallowed hard, trying to stay focused and at least fake Matt's unerring calm as I continued marking missiles for the guns. We all expected resistance, but this was insane. There was no way we could fight our way past—

"Noah." Matt's voice cut through my whirling panic. I glanced over and met his steady gaze, a wealth of understanding in his blue eyes. "We can do this," he said simply. "*You* can do this."

I stared at him for a heartbeat before resolve hardened in my chest. He was right. We had to do this. For Rena. For Lavona. For the rest of Warexia. For a chance to strike a blow against Markan and his twisted organization.

For a chance to finally go home.

I blew out a sharp breath and gave a single nod. "Damn right we can."

The swarm of drones closed the distance rapidly, a glittering cloud in the distance. As one they opened fire, energy blasts stitching lines of molten destruction across our shields.

"Shields at sixty percent," Meg reported.

I barely heard her, all my attention consumed in the struggle to mark the last of the missiles and the multitude of drones behind them. Our cannons sang as flurries of ion blasts dispensed with the missiles and then tore into the drone swarm. The hits created dazzling explosions that filled the space ahead with shrapnel, our shields reducing them to sizzling sparkles as we flew straight through them. For each drone I destroyed, three more swept in to take its place. It was like trying to turn back a tidal wave with my bare hands.

We weren't going to make it.

"Thirty seconds to the crater!" Matt shouted over the cacophony.

I risked a glance at the forward viewscreen, and my breath caught. We were closer than I thought. The Musu Volcano filled our view, a massive caldera of jagged obsidian rising from Marin's frozen white landscape. At its center, a yawning abyss of perfect darkness swallowed all light.

The wormhole.

I stared at the void ahead, imagination running wild as I tried to picture the impossible tunnel of warped spacetime waiting to swallow us whole.

"Noah!" Matt snapped, dragging me back to reality. I'd lost track of the drones while I marveled at the wormhole in what could have been a stupid, fatal mistake. Fingers a blur on the controls, I quickly targeted as many drones as possible, ion cannons blasting them from the sky, focusing on keeping our path ahead clear.

"Shields at forty percent," Meg called out.

"Almost there," Ben said urgently behind me. "Stay on target!"

Collision warnings blared as we rocketed toward the void, the oncoming drones ruthlessly attacking. I kept firing, even as the blasts that missed their mark sank into the darkness, vanishing impossibly when they hit the black. The last of the drones slammed into our forward shields and detonated, sending a wash of flame up and over the transparency. By the time it cleared, the crater's darkness had completely enveloped us. That perfect nothingness consumed my entire world for an endless, terrifying moment.

Then, between one blink and the next, we were through.

# CHAPTER 38

I couldn't immediately make sense of our new location until I looked at our rearview. A massive space station floated static behind us, a singular celestial object lost in a sea of nothing.

Spidery docking arms radiated from the central structure, branching off like a tree and culminating in what looked like silver-ringed flowers. Their centers exposed pitch black pits, a star-encrusted expanse, or in a couple of cases, either the fiery glow of a close-up star or the distant view of a planet. Taking it all in, I struggled to wrap my mind around the entire idea of the station. The advanced technology involved made Levain's robots look as archaic as Twama claimed our original comms were.

Suddenly, the sensor grid stole my attention from the station. The drones from Marin hadn't peeled away from the wormhole.

They'd followed us through.

"Noah, keep them off us," Matt said as he threw Head Case into a stomach-churning flip that inverted my original view of the station while getting us headed back in the right direction. The inertial dampeners struggled against the move.

I barely had time to clench my stomach muscles before the G-forces hit. "On it," I replied through gritted teeth, the G-forces compressing me into my seat as I marked the drones for the fire control system. The turrets swiveled independently, each choosing a different target and unleashing new fury.

"Rena," Ben said. "Which gate leads home?"

"I'm looking for it," she replied, her voice weak and her face pale. "I…I think it may be around the other side."

"You think?" Matt asked. "We can't linger here."

"I know! I'm trying. It all looks the same from this angle, and the gate we want doesn't have any landmarks. It's pure black, just like the one that brought us here."

"Three-quarters of these gates are pitch black," Ben said. "How will you recognize the right one?"

"They don't change positions. I just need to remember the pattern. I'm sorry. I'm scared."

"It's okay," Ben replied calmly. "Forget about everything else. Just look at the station. Is it on this side?"

"No," she replied. "I'm sure of that much."

The words had just left her mouth when Matt opened the throttle, and the ship leaped forward as if kicked into high gear, colliding with two drones before we overshot them. The impacts sent fresh shockwaves across the hull but didn't penetrate the shields. Meanwhile, the monstrous station grew rapidly in my surround before rushing by in a dizzying blur as we scooted past.

"Do you see anything that looks familiar?" Ben asked, keeping his tone as soothing as possible given the circumstances.

"Not yet. I…wait. There! Around the side, toward the bottom. That one!"

"Are you sure?" Matt asked.

"I...yes. I'm sure."

She didn't sound completely sure. I glanced at Matt, who shrugged. We had no choice but to go for that one.

"Don't be shy if you change your mind," Matt said.

"New contacts!" I snapped, eyes drawn to the sensor grid. Warships of some kind, closing in from the space around the station. Eight appeared on the grid's edge, approaching from multiple angles. "Looks like station defense. They're still a ways out."

Not that I could draw any comfort from that. The fixed batteries on the station suddenly began to fire, sending huge energy blasts rolling toward us at top speed.

"Incoming!" I cried, powerless to do anything to stop the cannon fire. I continued targeting drones, watching the warships closing on the station. The first two energy blasts sizzled past us, far too close for comfort.

Matt jinked hard to port before sweeping back and sinking low, narrowly evading the hail of cannon fire from the station's fixed batteries. "They're too slow," he commented, guiding Head Case through the energy storm with practiced ease.

Despite the deadly stakes, a fierce grin split my face. I adjusted my aim, sending return fire toward two fixed batteries, disabling one before Matt sent us into a stomach-knotting dive. He threaded deftly between a tangle of docking arms in a bid to shake the remaining drones and limit the station's attack angle. A few of the drones collided with the arms, but most swept through without incident. They poured on speed, doing their damndest to detonate against our tail.

I marked the targets, the computer spraying return fire into their ranks. The barrage slammed home, reducing one drone to shrapnel. Another lost a wing and careened wildly into a third. Both vanished in an expanding sphere of flame and debris. Three still remained, clinging to our six.

Head Case shuddered as the drones' fire raked across our topside, shields working to absorb the energy.

"Shields at twenty percent," Meg informed us.

The flailing defenses forced Matt to send us into a wild corkscrew. We overshot the station and rocketed toward empty space and one of the incoming warships.

"Matt—!" I cried.

"I see it," he replied, a bit more edge to his voice than I was used to. Even he couldn't keep his total calm in this maelstrom.

"They're launching missiles," I told him, a dozen small blips appearing on the sensor grid. I could see the faint glow of their thrusters on my surround, creating halos around the otherwise invisible projectiles. Meanwhile, the three remaining drones continued peppering us from behind.

"Hold on, I'm going to hit the brakes," Matt said.

"Wha—? " My chest hit the restraints, stealing the rest of my breath as Matt fired full retrorockets, decelerating in a fraction of a second. Rather than colliding with our stern, the heat of our thrusters quickly devoured the three drones. Immediately, Matt swung Head Case back toward the station, putting the missiles behind us and closing fast.

"There!" Rena cried. "The gate is up ahead!"

"Can you repeat that trick on those tangoes?" I asked, in reference to the missiles.

"You need to take them out," Matt replied. "You can do it."

I cursed silently. I couldn't mark them all for the firing system in time. Instead, I switched the controls to manual and grabbed the stick, quickly rotating all the guns to the rear.

"Noah, do you have them?" Ben demanded urgently.

"Just...a second..." I gritted out. I couldn't afford to miss. Not now. Not this close to escape.

An eternity seemed to pass as I tracked the missiles, waiting for them to close ranks before impact. Closer. Just a little closer...there! My thumb stabbed down while I adjusted the stick in tiny increments, spreading fire across our contrail. The cannons thundered in response, hurling destruction at the projectiles.

My eyes remained glued to the rearview, watching the ion blasts swarm the missiles. One after another, the halos expanded into fireballs, the detonations exciting me like fireworks on the Fourth of July. Within a matter of seconds, all of the incoming warheads were gone.

Head Case plunged into the gate's yawning void, another wormhole swallowing us whole.

# CHAPTER 39

I clung to my station, my heart pounding as Head Case plunged into the wormhole's yawning void. Darkness consumed my vision, the inky blackness so absolute it felt like a physical weight pressing against my eyes. For an endless, terrifying moment, that perfect nothingness was my entire world.

Then, between one blink and the next, we were through. Stars once more dusted the viewport, and a distant sun glinted against the endless expanse. I sagged back against my seat, my knuckles aching from my white-knuckled grip on the controls.

For the moment, the sensor grid remained gratefully clear.

"Damn, that was so close I can't even think of something funny to say about it," Tyler said from the spectator seating. "I think I may have peed a little, though."

"Is everyone okay?" Ben called from the command station. A chorus of affirmatives rose from around the bridge. "Meg, damage report."

Meg grimaced, tapping rapidly at her workstation. "Could be a lot worse. There's a hull breach on Six that's sealed off, but we'll want to get it fixed ASAP. Thankfully, nothing important is affected. Shields are down to twenty percent. We came pretty close to losing them entirely. To be honest, if Noah hadn't blasted all those missiles, we might not have made it through the wormhole."

A swell of disquiet at how close we'd come to destruction swept through me, followed by a sense of pride that I'd come through for my crew when I was most needed. I'd remained calm enough to do something the Noah of a month ago definitely wouldn't have been able to accomplish, and for the first time, I felt like I was becoming a man my parents would truly be proud of.

"We'll need to replace some of the burnt out emitter nodes if we want a snowball's chance of getting through the asteroid sphere alive," Meg added.

"Understood," Ben replied.

"Captain," Rena said from the stadium seating before he could say another word. "We should get underway before we worry about repairs. Odds are those warships won't come through the portal, but that's not a guarantee. And we clearly won't survive another attack right now."

"Agreed," Ben answered, removing his safety restraints and rising from the command station. "Go ahead."

Rena hurried down to Ben's seat to replace him, immediately tapping on the controls to build the route.

"Why are the warships unlikely to come through the portal?" I asked.

"Like I said, there's no guarantee they won't. But getting this far is still only half the challenge of reaching Markan. They know what comprises the other half. There's little reason for them to worry we might make it through."

"What about destroying the gate we used?" I pressed. "Just in case. We can cut off any chance of them following at all."

"We could, but then if we want to get back out we'll

need to deploy a new portal. That's easy for my father to do. Not so easy for us. I don't mean to be rude, but can you let me work?"

"Sorry," I replied, shrinking in my seat as I returned my attention to the sensor grid. Still clear. Looking to my surround view, I saw that the wormhole portal and the stationary chunk of rock it and its power supply were anchored to had nearly faded from sight behind us. Rena was right. None of the forces from the wormhole station had given chase. They must not have realized, either, how close to destruction we had come.

"Jump coordinates are loaded, Captain," Rena announced after a brief silence. She rose from the command station, returning the seat to Ben. "ETA, four hours."

"Thank you, Rena," he replied. "Noah, take us out."

Anticipation coiled in my gut as I reached for the controls. "Aye, Captain. Engaging the hyperdrive." I flipped the toggle. Instead of initiating the jump, a warning flashed on the screen, complaining about the unknown flight path and risk of death.

"Levi, it's fine," I said. "We know where we're going."

"I require a verbal override to allow an uncharted jump," Levi replied.

"Override confirmed," Ben said.

"Override authenticated."

The warning disappeared. Within a minute, we were zipping through the universe faster than light.

"Okay, crew," Ben said, a sharper-than-usual edge of authority in his voice. "We have four hours. We'll need every second of it to get Head Case back in fighting shape. Meg, how many shield nodes do we have in inventory, and how many need repair?"

"Twenty-six in inventory," Meg answered from memory. "We also have enough resources for Asshole to assemble another fourteen. Let me simulate replacement." She tapped on her controls, eyeing a schematic of Head Case's shield system, a series of interlocking lines of various colors displaying their status. A lot more red than blue, which was bad. She tapped a series of nodes, simulating their replacement. Within seconds, the entire system turned blue again. "If we replace thirty-four nodes, we can bring shields back up to full. But it takes thirty minutes to replace a node, counting travel time. Four hours won't be enough time."

"That's all we have," Ben answered. "Karpov," he called, eyes cutting to the burly Hemid. "Do you know how to fix external shield nodes?"

"If you have a spacesuit big enough for me," he replied.

Ben looked to Meg for a response.

"We can make you one," she answered.

"Then I can pitch in, sure."

"What about you, Lantz?" Ben asked.

"I'm a software guy, Captain," he replied.

Ben nodded and tapped his comm badge. "Twama, do you copy?"

"Yes, Captain. How may I be of service?"

"We need some help fixing Head Case's shields. Do you have any experience with that?"

"Negative, Captain. But I am a fast learner."

"We don't have time to teach her right now," Meg said.

"Okay, I'll be in touch if we can use you." He disconnected. "That leaves us with three. Meg, what can you do with twenty-four nodes?"

She worked on the simulation. Even from my position, I could see the results were nowhere near as promising. The new structure left a lot of orange and yellow. Weak spots in our protection.

I cleared my throat, drawing Ben's attention. "What about Mak? I know she's not exactly trustworthy, but she's a skilled engineer. And we could really use another pair of hands."

Ben considered her for a long moment before finally nodding. "She has as much to lose as we do if Head Case is destroyed. But I want eyes on her at all times. The last thing we need is sabotage. Lavona, Noah, go collect her from the hangar and escort her to the airlock."

"Yes, sir," Lavona replied over my, "Aye, Captain."

We made our way down to the hangar, where Mak and Larev were still locked to the railing. Mak glared at us with open hostility as we approached.

"What do you want?" she spat.

"We need your help," I said bluntly. "The shields took a beating and we need another engineer if we're going to get them repaired before we need them again."

"And why should I lift a finger to help you traitors?" Mak sneered.

I leaned in close, holding her gaze steadily. "Simple. Because if this ship goes down, you die too. So you can either pitch in, or sit here twiddling your thumbs while the clock runs out on all of us. Your choice."

For a long moment she simply stared at me, a muscle jumping in her jaw. Then, with a muttered curse, she thrust her bound wrists toward me. "Fine. But don't expect me to be happy about it."

"I'll settle for cooperative," I replied, releasing her restraints.

"Hey, Noah," Larev said as we turned to go. "Take me with you. I can help."

"In what way?" I asked.

"Any way you need. An extra set of hands couldn't hurt, right?"

"It could if they're your hands," Lavona countered.

"Aww, come on. I'm not an idiot. I'd be stupid to try anything on a spacewalk in hyperspace."

I exchanged a glance with Lavona, conflicted. She

shrugged minutely, leaving the decision to me. Blowing out a breath, I turned back to Larev.

"Alright. But one wrong move and you'll wish we left you locked up down here. Clear?"

"Totally," he replied fervently.

I tapped my comm badge. "Meg, can you make one regular Hemid sized spacesuit and one huge Hemid sized spacesuit?"

"Noah? You aren't suggesting—"

"We need as many helpers as we can get, right?"

"Right," she replied before disconnecting.

I nodded to Lavona and she moved to release Larev's restraints. As soon as his hands were free, he jumped to his feet and rubbed at his wrists, grin splitting his face.

"You won't regret this," he laughed.

"I already do," Lavona replied, a none-too-happy look on her face.

We escorted them to the airlock. After a few minutes, Meg, Leo, and Karpov arrived with a hovercart carrying the two oversized spacesuits, tool belts, and multiple containers of replacement nodes.

"Reinforcements," I explained to Karpov before he could protest.

Meg still didn't look thrilled about letting our prisoners help out, but she jerked her head toward the stack of space-suits along the wall. "I've got Hemid suits here. The rest of you, grab a suit, and there's magboots for all of you."

We were suited up in minutes, the airlock cycling open to release us into the void.

We filed out onto the hull with Meg in the lead, our magboots clinging to the metal. Mak followed close on her heels while Lavona and I brought up the rear behind Leo, Karpov and Larev.

"First node is just ahead," Meg reported, pointing to a

blackened mess of rent metal. The hull around it was scuffed, having taken some of the energy from the hit that destroyed the node. "Mak, I need you to take the three nodes in this area. There are nine in total." She quickly motioned in the general direction of each. "Larev will assist you. Noah and Lavona will be watching you. Closely. Don't do anything stupid." She lifted one of the node containers and passed it to Mak. "Leo, Karpov, and I will work further from the airlock. Good luck."

Everyone split up, moving in different directions across the outer hull. We continued to the first node, where Mak knelt beside the wrecked node and set to work.

She definitely knew her way around the damaged equipment. With Larev acting as an assistant, she swapped out the burnt emitter for a new one, the new component humming to life a good five minutes earlier than expected.

"Not bad," Lavona allowed grudgingly. "Next one is fifteen meters portside."

I led the way, stepping carefully on the treacherous hull while trying to ignore the upside-down horizon, focusing instead on the task at hand. Replace the nodes. Get the shields back up. And give us a fighting chance.

"Noah!" Lavona's shout sent ice through my veins. I spun in time to see her bend backward to evade the swing of Mak's wrench. She wasn't fast enough. The improvised weapon silently collided with Lavona's helmet. She reeled backward, her magboots separating from the hull.

"Lavona!" Instinct sent me lunging after her as she began tumbling slowly away, her arms wheeling uselessly. One of my boots broke free of the hull beforeI managed to snag her ankle. Arresting her spin, I jammed my boot back down on the hull and dragged her back into full contact with it.

A glint of metal in my peripheral vision was my only warning of Mak's wrench coming my way. I jerked aside, the wrench flying past my faceplate, missing me by a hair's breadth. She snarled in wordless rage, already rearing back to take another swing. What the hell was she thinking? I could hardly believe her loyalty to Markan was already so strong she cared more about helping him than saving her own life.

Startled, I stared at Larev as his meaty paw closed around her wrist, checking her arm's forward momentum. The jarring force of his grab knocked the wrench from her hand, letting it float away.

Mak barely had time to gasp before the big Hemid swallowed her throat with his other hand. "I figured you would try something dumb," he growled, lifting her with enough force to break her magboots' hold on the hull.

"Larev, don't," I warned, taking a step toward them. He didn't bother to look my way, much less respond. All his attention was on Mak.

"Whose side are you on?" she snarled at him, reaching to grab hold of his arm.

"I think that's pretty obvious now, isn't it? I wanted to join a team. A family. Not a murderous cult."

"Larev, wait!" I cried, hoping I still had a chance to make him listen.

Ignoring me, he jerked his arm free of her grasp and shoved her clear of the ship before I could even make a grab for her. There was nothing I could do to save her. I watched her tumble slowly away from the ship, begging and then screaming for help. I reached for my comm control as quickly as I could, switching it off so I didn't have to listen to her terrified cries, and then I turned away.

She had made her choice and would suffer the consequences, but I couldn't stand there and watch her vaporize at the edge of the compression field. Instead, I faced the big Hemid and took a deep breath of relief, hoping it would allay the sick roiling in my stomach. "You saved us. Thank you."

"I told you," he replied gruffly. "I'm on your side now."

Lavona stepped up beside me. "Good riddance," she growled. "I just wish I had been the one to do it. I can't believe I let her catch me off-guard like that."

"Happens to the best of us," Larev answered.

"Yes, well, we still have eight nodes to replace and we've lost our engineer," I lamented. "We can't complete the repairs now."

Larev grunted and patted the toolkit around his waist. "I watched her do the first one. Looks easy enough." I blinked in surprise as he moved toward the next damaged emitter with confident purpose. "You and me, runt...we'll get it done."

I met his gaze, an unspoken question in my eyes. He nodded once, an almost imperceptible gesture but an affirmation of trust and common cause.

I found myself nodding back, a new understanding settling between us. "Alright then. Let's get to it. We don't have all day."

# CHAPTER 40

I found myself leaning forward in excited anticipation as I watched the compression field dissipate through the forward viewport and the universe regain its correct proportions. Thanks to Larev, we managed to repair the shield emitters with thirty minutes to spare. It had been just enough time to grab a drink and something to eat, check in on Archie to reset its Rubik's Cube, and rest my weary body for a few minutes before replacing Cade at the co-pilot's station.

Beside me, Matt's hands tightened on the controls, his jaw clenched with determination. Behind us, the rest of the crew had gathered on the flight deck, all eyes glued to the looming expanse of tumbling rock filling our field of view.

"Goodness gracious, great balls of...what are those asteroids made from?" Tyler asked, awestruck. "That thing is massive!"

"Mostly silicate and nickel-iron," Larev replied, occupying two seats beside him. "Lots of other minerals in smaller amounts, too. The important thing to remember is that they're hard as rocks."

The statement drew a nervous laugh from Tee. "Yeah, let's try not to test that equation first-hand."

The sheer scale of the asteroid sphere defied comprehension. It stretched as far as I could see in every direction, an endless sea of jagged stone and swirling dust. Individual asteroids ranged from the size of a small moon to chunks no larger than Head Case herself, all whirling in a dizzying, chaotic dance. The effect was mesmerizing and utterly terrifying.

"I've never seen anything like it," Ally murmured, echoing my thoughts.

"Well, I'll be damned," Lantz said. "Captain, you won't believe this."

"What is it?" Ben asked.

"Do you remember how I told you the Warden starts pinging us as soon as we come out of hyperspace?"

"Yes."

Lantz shook his head. "Not this time. He's gone silent."

"Or out of range," Tyler suggested.

"Where exactly are we?" Ally asked.

"Anywhere without the Warden is a good place to be," Matt said.

"Rena, you're up," Ben said. "How do we find the entrance in all of that?"

Rena stood beside the command station, eyes locked on the field. "I assume your running lights are customizable?"

"Full spectrum," Meg confirmed.

"Good. Adjust the wavelength to 612.4 nanometers."

Meg glanced at her dubiously but complied, fingers dancing across her station controls. A moment later, our forward beams shifted to a sickly red hue. The change swept across the churning asteroids, initially revealing nothing unusual.

Two larger asteroids suddenly emerged from the endless rock, their surfaces glowing strangely against the red light. A narrow gateway formed between them, and the path immediately beyond them was currently clear.

"That's it," Rena breathed. "The entrance."

I narrowed my eyes at the distant portal. It looked impossibly small compared to the titanic asteroids flanking it. "Are you sure? That's not much of an opening."

"I'm sure," Rena replied. "The spectrum doesn't lie."

"Get us in there," Ben said.

Matt squared his shoulders. "Aye, Captain. Noah, are you ready?"

I gripped the station's joystick, breathing in to quell my nerves. There was too much noise on the sensor grid from all the asteroids to leave the fire control system on automatic. "Ready as I'll ever be," I replied.

"I'm heading up to the sigibellum," Ben announced, rising from his seat. "Just in case we need a little extra defense. Rena, take the command station. Help guide us in."

"Yes, Captain," she replied, a nervous quiver in her voice.

"I have total confidence in all of you," he said before leaving the flight deck, Shaq affixed to his shoulder. His sincerity inspired me and helped me remain focused.

"Hold onto your butts," Matt called. "Here we go!"

Head Case leaped forward as he fired the thrusters, racing toward the entrance. I swallowed hard as we crossed the threshold, diving into the seemingly endless obstacle course. With the sensors practically overloaded from all of the targets whirling around us, I locked my gaze on my surround, eyes straining for any hint of automated defenses, targeting reticles centered.

At first, our passage remained unopposed. Matt guided the ship through an obvious course within the treacherous field, almost lazily maneuvering past asteroids whose orbits had cleared our route.

"Looking good so far," Matt commented.

"I think the route is still intact," Rena replied.

"Could we actually have it easy for once?" Tyler asked. "That would be nice."

"Don't jinx it," Ally warned.

I refused to let my focus drift, my attention relax. I had learned not to take *easy* for granted. It had a habit of disappearing well before its—

Sharp warnings cried out from hidden speakers, the sensor grid marking sudden flares of energy, which I spotted right away from an asteroid up ahead on the port side. Before I could react, flashes of energy streaked our way.

"Incoming!" I barked.

Matt juked hard to port, narrowly evading the first barrage of energy blasts. They seared past the viewports, close enough to bathe the flight deck in their dangerous light. I zeroed in on the closest turret and squeezed my trigger. Head Case's port side cannons spewed a flurry of high-energy blasts, quickly reducing the emplacement to glowing shrapnel.

"Nice shooting," Matt grunted as he sent us into a stomach-churning corkscrew. Without warning, the universe detonated around us, proximity mines releasing their payloads. Matt had somehow seen them coming, and his maneuvers allowed only glancing blows off our restored shields, shaking Head Case as she dove off-course and into the churning scrum.

"Why do I ever open my big fat mouth?" Tyler complained in a fearful cry.

"Yep. You jinxed it!" Ally shot back.

"Noah, the mines show as negative space against the asteroids," Matt explained. "Easier to spot when you know what you're looking for."

He guided us deeper into the field with deft skill,

weaving between the tumbling rocks as if performing an intricate dance. His hands were steady on the stick and throttle, constantly adjusting our velocity and trajectory as he slipped Head Case through gaps that seemed far too narrow.

I watched, heart in my throat, as a massive asteroid tumbled past mere meters from our starboard side, so close I swore I could have reached out and touched its pitted surface. Matt never flinched, his eyes narrowed in concentration. His uncanny ability to account for the constantly shifting gravitational fields and wells allowed him to smoothly angle us toward the next clear path.

Another boulder spun into view directly ahead, its jagged surface promising a messy end if we collided with it. I tensed, certain we were about to be pulverized. At the last possible instant, Matt fired vectoring thrusters and we leaped upward, the asteroid's bulk passing underneath.

"That was too close," Rena remarked.

"You ain't seen nothing yet," Matt replied through gritted teeth. He sent Head Case into a tight barrel roll, narrowly avoiding two asteroids converging on our position like the jaws of a celestial alligator snapping shut.

Around us, the deadly chunks of rock seemed to press in ever tighter, an inexorable vise slowly crushing the life from us. Still, every second forward brought us one second closer to the end of the field. And for a few seconds, at least, the asteroids remained the only obstacle.

Until once again, they weren't.

Following Matt's advice, I picked up the outlines of more mines approaching our forward path. I adjusted my aim and opened fire, picking them off as we shot toward them. Keeping the reticle trained on the mines while we rolled and twisted around the rocks was a challenge of its own, sweat beading my brow, my focus as steady as it had ever been.

So steady, it was as if I fell into a trance.

My jaw clenched as I identified and targeted incoming threats, at first frustrated when blue lightning from detonating mines washed across our shields. They failed to penetrate the hull but set off proximity alarms. Matt's brilliant flying was the only thing keeping us from being torn apart by the turret fire sizzling past us in an endless barrage of near misses.

No matter how hard I tried, it was impossible for me to negate every threat. Once I accepted that one cold truth, my success rate jumped, the pressure on me reduced even while the tension remained.

I fired another barrage at an automated turret up ahead, knocking it out of commission just before Matt rolled Head Case hard to port. He cursed loudly as an asteroid the size of a small frigate spun into our path. Quickly, he wrenched the ship into a climb so sharp I was certain our spine would break. The massive rock whipped past, near enough to fill the viewports with its cratered surface.

With a whoop of pure adrenaline, Matt coaxed a fresh burst of speed from the thruster and we shot forward, threading the needle between the asteroid and another of its brethren with barely a meter to spare on either side.

Of course, more mines came into view as we cleared the latest churn. Firing a steady stream across the black gaps between asteroids, I picked off nearly a dozen within the few seconds it took to reach the area. Despite my efforts, a handful more detonated against the shields, trying to force us into a collision as we bounced and rolled like we were on the high seas.

Matt somehow kept us on course. He rolled and tumbled the ship through an impossible slalom, constantly one step ahead of the asteroids filling our flight path. At one point, he neatly evaded a fresh barrage of turret fire by skimming Head Case along the surface of a planetoid, using its meager gravity to slingshot us onto an entirely new vector.

"That's the best you've got?" Tyler whooped as another turret exploded under our guns. "My grandma could program better defenses in her sleep!"

"Less goading, more shooting," Lavona growled from her seat. I barely heard them, too focused on not letting us all die.

A fresh salvo hammered our shields, and Matt juked us into a wild spiral, thrusters straining to change our vector. For a heart-stopping instant, I thought we wouldn't make it. That this time, the universe would call our bluff. Time seemed to slow, the massive asteroid ahead looming to fill my field of view.

At the last possible second Matt fired the port thrusters and put us into a hard slingshot around the obstacle. I sucked in a sharp breath, my knuckles white around my controls. My hands hurt from holding the stick so tightly. My eyes burned from not blinking nearly enough. My heart pounded so hard it felt like it might burst through my chest.

Just when I was sure I couldn't keep up anymore, the swirling rocks parted, a sudden, exalted peace descending as we broke out into open space, finally exiting the deadly gauntlet.

My elation quickly turned to dread as what could only be our destination came into view.

"You've got to be kidding me," I breathed, unable to tear my eyes from the sight of it.

Rising from the heart of the asteroid sphere like a malevolent god was the largest construct I had ever seen. It was a robot. Or rather, it had been a robot once upon a time. Now it appeared to be little more than a gutted shell. Half of one titanic arm was missing, sheared away and leaving a long trail of thick wiring and exposed broken mechanical parts. A missing foot created a similar effect. Massive rents marred its chest and torso, exposing dark chasms within.

"That thing is the size of a mountain," Lantz said slowly, as if even his genius brain struggled to process the scale.

The derelict metal monstrosity filled our forward viewports, so enormous it defied belief. Zooming in on my surround, I noticed swarms of shuttles and transports flowing in and out of the breaches in its massive frame, traveling from one part of the apparent station to another.

Ben's voice crackled over the comms, impossibly calm given the situation. "Rena, I assume there's a way inside that behemoth?"

"Yes," she managed. Her familiarity with her father's base couldn't negate its intimidating presence. She collected herself with visible effort, pointing to one of the larger rents. "There. The port landing bay is accessible through that opening in the chest. But we can't just let ourselves in unannounced."

"Are you sure?" Ben replied with a lightness in his voice that had been absent while his cancer spread. I still couldn't quite believe the Warden had cured it with what amounted to a snap of his fingers. "Because that's exactly what we're going to do."

# CHAPTER 41

"What do you mean?" Rena asked, confused by Ben's response. "The second we get close enough to stand out from the asteroids, we'll be fired upon."

"Not once Markan knows we have you onboard," Ben countered.

Rena flinched as if she'd been hit. "What? I didn't agree to that. You said I just had to get you here. You didn't say anything about me having to see my father."

"You don't need to see him again," Ben assured her. "You'll be on board Head Case the entire time."

"I...I'm very confused," she said.

"It'll all make sense soon enough. Ally, let's see what our new comms array can do. Try hailing the station."

"Aye, Captain," she replied.

Within seconds, an unfamiliar and unhappy voice pierced the flight deck through hidden speakers.

"Who is this, and how did you get on this channel?"

I looked back at Rena, half-expecting to accidentally be on the line with Markan. She shrugged and looked equally confused.

"My name is Murdock," Ben replied. "I'm the leader of the…the…"

"Stinking Badgers," Tyler called out.

"The Stinking Badgers," Ben repeated, unenthused with the moniker. "We have the Boss' daughter on our ship. We're returning her home to her father. Assuming the reward is still good?"

"I'm sorry," the man replied. "That's way above my pay grade. I don't know how you patched into my comms badge, but let me transfer you to Station Control."

Ben looked to Ally, who shrugged. "I guess I hit the wrong button or something," she replied, eyeing the console. "I think we're being hailed."

"Answer it," Ben said.

She tapped on the console.

"Unidentified intruder, this is Gargan Control. State your business immediately, or you will be fired upon." The voice echoed across the flight deck, caught in a feedback loop because it was live on two channels. I winced at the noise as the loop began squealing, imaging Gargan Control doing the same from their end.

"Ally!" Ben said, putting his hands over his ears. Panicked, she tapped random buttons on the panel until the echo subsided.

"Sorry. You should have put Twama on the comms."

"Gargan Control, do you copy?" Ben asked.

"I repeat, state your business immediately, or you will be fired upon."

"If anyone else along this route had given us a chance, I would have told them that we're the Stinking Badgers, and we have Rena captive," Ben answered. "We're here to claim the reward for her return."

"I see. Hold position and standby."

The line went silent. Matt immediately turned Head

Case in a one-eighty, using the thrusters to slow our approach.

"This is crazy," Rena said. "He tried to kill me on Hixia. Why would he offer a reward for my return?"

"For the same reason you don't hate him," Ben replied. "Because he's your father."

"If I had known this was your plan, I would never have agreed to it."

"Which is why I never told you my plan."

Rena frowned but didn't say anything else. We waited in tense silence for a long two minutes before control returned to the comms.

"Stinking Badgers, you are cleared to land in Heart Bay. Follow the markers illuminating for you. Someone will meet you there."

"Confirmed. We have the markers in view," Ben replied. "Matt, bring us in," he added as soon as control disconnected from the comms.

"Here we go," Matt replied, opening the throttle and sending us toward the gargantuan robot once more.

As we neared the station, the true scale became even more mesmerizing. Before long, what had started as a scar across the massive bot's chest had grown into a gaping chasm that could have easily swallowed the Warden's ship dozens of times over. The machine had to be ten miles tall, maybe more, and at least three miles wide. How could anything so large have ever walked around anywhere? Even in low gravity, the size and mass seemed impossible to keep upright.

Deftly maneuvering Head Case, Matt guided us into the hangar as part of the regular traffic flow in and out of Heart Bay, where an energy field prevented the intrusion of space but let us in without mishap. Monstrous girders large enough to hold up The Golden Gate Bridge crossed the cavernous space, with what looked like bridge abutments anchoring them at each end. The bay buzzed with activity in an impression of tightly controlled chaos, countless bots and transports going about their everyday business.

We were less than a gnat in comparison, wholly insignificant.

Monitoring the deck, I gawked at dozens of large ships, everything from transports and cargo haulers like Deepling to a half-dozen warships bristling with armaments. Workers scurried around the vessels like ants, loading and unloading or effecting repairs.

"There," Rena said, pointing from the command station. "Bring us in on the upper level, portside aft. It's a lesser used landing area."

"Copy that," Matt replied. He shifted our vector, slowing steadily as he approached the area. We sat down in the shadows with barely a bump. "We're in. What's the plan, Cap?"

"Noah, Lavona, I want you both outfitted in the specOps gear we brought over from Nakata. Lavona, once you're ready, I want you to scan Rena. You'll be going in as her."

Lavona grinned. "Sounds like fun."

"Cade, you'll replace Matt at the pilot station. Twama, you'll take over for Ally. Leo, take over for Noah. Lantz, make sure they don't try to pry into our systems. Larev, Tyler, Ally, Matt, meet me in the armory. We don't have much time to make ourselves look like generic mercenaries before our escort arrives. Oh, and Noah, don't forget Archie."

"Never," I replied.

"What are you going to do once you get to my father?" Rena asked.

"That's up to him," Ben replied. "But from what you've said, I don't see how both him and us leave the meetup alive."

"If you do kill him, please do it as quickly and painlessly as possible."

"I will," Ben promised.

I spared a glance at Ally. She hadn't blanched listening to Ben talk about killing someone. Neither did I. We'd both come a long way from naive tourists excited about a three-hour tour around Venus.

"Let's get moving, crew," Ben said.

"You heard the man," Tee said, jumping up from his seat in the back. "We've got a village to pillage!"

We all left the flight deck together, taking the elevator down. I got off on Deck Three and hurried to my quarters while the others continued to the armory.

Racing past the lounge and up to my cabin, I opened the door and froze. Where I expected to find Archie, I instead laid eyes on a miniature version of a transparent maulvas, complete with long teeth and fur.

"Archie?" I said as it lifted its head toward me. It whined in greeting, crossing the room and sitting in front of me. "This is…weird."

It shifted form, changing into a rat before returning to the more primal shape I was accustomed to. It waved its tendrils in greeting.

"I need to change into my stealth suit, and then we're going to confront Markan."

It wriggled tendrils again before moving to the bed to wait. I quickly stripped naked and pulled on the nano-fiber underlay while wondering who or what Ben intended for me to impersonate. He hadn't said, and I only had a few scans stored. Orven from Hixia, Lavona, and Miss Asher, the last two done while practicing with the gear. I threw fresh clothes on over the underlay, choosing something more mercenary in appearance: a long duster, ragged pants, and a simple shirt. I stuffed the holomask in my pocket for later.

"Come on," I said to Archie, who scrambled up my arm and slipped between the underlay and the coat, sliding out of sight.

When I reached the armory, Larev, Tyler, and Alyssa were already there. Tee and Ally were dressed in combat armor while Larev leaned against the threshold, arms folded across his chest.

"Hey, runt," he said in greeting.

"Where are Matt and Lavona?" I asked.

"You didn't notice Matt on the way down?" Ally asked. "He went to Three to have Asshole make Larev some armor that would fit."

"Lava is already in the hangar," Tyler added. "Or should I say, Rena is in the hangar."

"Do you really think this plan is going to work?" Ally questioned.

"It has to," I replied. "It's all we've got."

"How can it fail with Killshot over here?" Tee asked, patting her shoulder.

"I don't want to be the one to do it."

"You might need to be, though. You've got the best boon for it."

"Lucky me."

"At least we know Markan is a monster," I said. "That should make it easier."

I turned when I heard Matt approaching. He had a large suit of combat armor slung over his shoulder, a stern look on his face.

"We need to hurry. Our escort to Markan is already waiting outside."

"It'll only take a minute," Larev said, accepting the armor and quickly pulling it on. "This feels awful light."

"It's not to spec," Matt replied. "We didn't have enough materials to make a full suit your size. It won't protect you if you get shot."

"Maybe I should stay behind," Larev suggested.

"You're the only one who doesn't have that option."

"Still don't trust me?"

"One hundred percent? No."

Larev laughed and shrugged. "Fair enough. I wouldn't either."

Matt changed quickly, leaving me surrounded by military-grade mercenaries. Clad head to toe in dark combat armor, cradling plasma rifles and bristling with other weaponry, my friends looked downright terrifying.

"Let's go," Matt said, leading the group to the elevator and down to the hangar. We descended the steps to the deck, where Lavona waited with Ben, Shaq, and, more surprisingly, Ixy.

"The gang's all here," Tyler said, eyes bugging out when he moved beside Lavona. "Whoa. That is eerie." He reached out to poke her face, only to have her grab his wrist and twist. "Ouch! Okay. I just wanted to see how real it felt."

She let go, grinning at him with Rena's face. "Next time, if you don't ask for permission first, I will break your fingers," she replied.

"Noted," Tee answered, pulling his hand back when she let go.

"Remember, we need to make this convincing," Ben said. "Lavona is the key to this whole infiltration. She, Noah and I will take the lead. The rest of you stick close, but let us do the talking."

"Oh, believe me, I'm more than happy to leave the acting to you," Tyler said, hands raised. "I'll just hang back and look menacing."

"Remember," Ben continued. "No matter what happens, we can't break character. From this moment forward, Lavona is Rena. I'm Murdock, the leader of the Stinking Badgers. And you're my mercenary crew."

"Uh, Ben?" I said. "Who am I?"

"You're my little brother, Zuo."

"I don't get it. Why did you want me in the SpecOps underlay? I would have more protection in my regular setup."

"Because it's better to be safe than sorry," he replied cryptically. "Trust me."

"I do," I replied.

"Our escort is already waiting outside. Very impatiently, I might add. Rena, put out your hands."

Lavona responded without hesitation, extending her arms toward Ben. He approached with a pair of restraints, locking them around her wrists. Her entire disposition transformed instantly, head lowering, posture slumping as she took on the role of the captured daughter.

"Wow, she's good," Ally noted.

Ben grabbed Lavona's arm and tugged her toward the smaller hangar bay door. "Let's go, Rena. It's time to turn you over to your father and collect our reward."

# CHAPTER 42

The hangar door slid open, immediately sending a renewed jolt of fear and trepidation through my chest. I thought we looked menacing in dark armor and bristling weaponry, but we were cosplayers compared to what awaited us.

Arranged in a fearsome half-circle just outside the ship stood a dozen of the most dangerous-looking aliens I had ever seen. They wore sleek, dark body armor with purple and gold accents. Clutching advanced energy rifles of some kind, plasma blades and other weaponry hung at their hips. They were the real deal, not a group of individuals pretending to be mercenaries.

His muscles bunched beneath mottled green scales and an elaborately embroidered jacket, the hulking reptilian figure standing at the head of the group exuded an aura of authority and barely-leashed aggression. We stood quietly as he took a single step forward. "I am Izzak," he rumbled, his voice even deeper than Larev's. "I stand at the Boss' right hand. Which one of you is Murdock?"

Ben released Lavona's arm and stepped forward, chin raised. "I am. I believe your boss is expecting me."

Izzak's gaze raked contemptuously over our group,

lingering on Lavona's slumped form. "The Boss is expecting his daughter," he corrected. "There's no need for...all of this." He made a sharp gesture that encompassed the rest of the crew. "You and Rena come with me. The rest can wait here until we return."

I tensed, a cold sweat prickling along my spine. Splitting up in the heart of enemy territory was the absolute last thing we wanted. Ben shared my apprehension. His posture shifted, taking on a stubborn set.

"I don't think so," he said flatly. "If you don't want all this..." He swept his hand over us. "Then you shouldn't have brought all that." He swept his hand across Izzak's guards. "Your boss has a reputation. Call me paranoid, but I'm not walking into a meeting without backup."

A few of Izzak's guards bristled, hands twitching toward weapons. Their leader silenced them with a sharp hiss before turning a coldly assessing stare on Ben. "You don't trust us to honor a simple arrangement?"

Ben barked a harsh laugh. "I wouldn't trust you to tell me the time of day. No, either we all go, or the girl stays right here on my ship."

The threat hung in the air between them. I held my breath, certain we were seconds away from a firefight. Lavona kept her head down, her posture perfectly submissive, but I noticed her shoulders tensed, ready to spring into action.

Izzak's expression darkened, fury sparking in his obsidian eyes. For a long moment, I was certain he would call Ben's bluff and this would end in a bloodbath before it had truly begun.

Then, to my shock, he took a step back. "Fine," he laughed, tension draining. "Bring your so-called backup. But they had best remember their manners."

"They'll be on their best behavior. You have my word."

"For whatever that's worth," Izzak muttered. "Come

then." He spun on his heel, motioning for us to follow before looking back over his shoulder. "And don't wander off."

I fell into step beside Ben, fighting to keep my nerves under control as we followed Izzak and his goons back into the bustling chaos of the hangar. All around us, workers and cargo transports moved with controlled urgency, a discordant buzz of activity that had my head spinning. Despite the circumstances, I couldn't help staring in unabashed amazement at the gargantuan docking bay. The sheer scale of everything defied belief.

We garnered more than a few lingering glances as Izzak led us across the hangar and into the labyrinth of corridors in the station proper. I couldn't blame the onlookers. Our little group—a motley assortment of armored humans and aliens surrounding a captive girl—definitely stood out. The presence of Izzak and his hulking guards didn't help us blend in.

Not that blending in was our goal. We needed to sell the illusion that we were exactly what we appeared to be. A band of successful bounty hunters, cocky and eager to get paid. Anything less would arouse suspicion we couldn't afford.

Playing the part, we strode through the heart of Markan's operation, our chins held high and weapons openly displayed at our hips. I kept my hand near my holstered blaster, the solid weight a comfort. I tried not to imagine what it might be like to be trapped inside this hulking carcass, a rat in a seemingly endless maze.

As we ventured deeper into the bowels of the robotic colossus, the sleek lines of the hangar gave way to a more chaotic, almost organic architecture. Exposed synthetic musculature rippled along the walls, massive cables and hydraulic lines snaking overhead like the entrails of a great beast. Uneven corridors twisted and turned, often redirected by the bulk of a giant servo or other nonfunctional machinery. It was like traversing the fossilized remains of an ancient, mechanical god that had long since fallen into ruin and been repurposed for Markan's needs. I could only wonder how he had come into possession of the mega-sized machine.

After an interminable march through the twisting guts of the fallen machine, we finally reached an oversized elevator. Izzak ushered us in, his goons surrounding us once we boarded. For a moment, a shockwave of fear zipped through me, wondering if this was the part where we were overwhelmed, disarmed, and brought to an airlock for disposal. With a lurch, the platform began to rise, carrying us up through the robot's chest and into the neck. No one spoke during the journey, an oppressive weight squeezing the air from the confined space.

A few minutes later, the lift shuddered to a stop. The doors opened to reveal a large, utilitarian chamber. The dull gray metal of the bulkheads and deck looked almost black in the dim lighting, unadorned and starkly functional. Uncomfortable-looking metal chairs lined the bulkheads on either side, currently occupied by a handful of ragged, shifty-eyed aliens. They shot us suspicious glances as we filed out, their postures hunched and wary. I had to assume they were here hoping for an audience with Markan, too.

A single set of plain metal doors dominated the far wall, the only apparent exit. Izzak strode over to them before facing us, his expression unreadable.

"The Boss' sanctum is just through there," he rumbled, jerking his chin toward the sealed portal. "Only you, the kid, and Rena go any further." His obsidian gaze cut to Ben, brooking no argument. "Everyone else waits here, including your pet."

"Pet?" Shaq bristled on Ben's shoulder before Ben

touched him reassuringly. The Jagger buzzed unhappily and jumped from his shoulder to Matt's.

"What about your guards?" Ben asked.

"They will stay out here, as well," Izzak replied. "Happy?"

Ben gave a curt nod before turning to the others. "Sit tight," he ordered. "We won't be long." He caught Matt's gaze, and something unspoken passed between them. A promise and a warning all in one.

Then he grasped Lavona's arm again and inclined his head to me. "Zuo. With me."

I jumped to follow. The rest of our group moved to the seats on one side of the compartment. Izzak's crew claimed the seats on the other. I cast one last look over my shoulder as we approached those final doors. Matt met my gaze steadily, belief and reassurance in his eyes. I drew strength from that absolute conviction, squaring my shoulders as I turned to face forward once more.

Izzak knocked, the sound echoing like a death knell. A beat passed. Two. Then a cultured voice called out.

"Enter."

Falling into step beside Ben and Lavona, I followed Izzak through the portal.

Into the serpent's den.

# CHAPTER 43

As the blast doors slid shut behind us with a resounding clang, I found myself standing in a space unlike anything I had ever seen. Instead of the opulent office I had been expecting, we were greeted by a chaotic whirlwind of machinery and technology.

Workbenches stretched in every direction, their surfaces cluttered with a dizzying array of half-finished projects and gleaming components. Bits of circuitry and chunks of metal lay strewn haphazardly across the room, forming a treacherous obstacle course. Shelves overflowing with datapads, schematics, and strange devices whose purpose I could only guess at lined the walls.

It was like stepping into the mind of a mad scientist. Everywhere I looked, something new caught my eye—a spindly robot in the corner with its innards exposed, a rack of futuristic-looking weapons in varying stages of assembly, and a towering machine pulsing with an eerie blue light. The air practically crackled with barely restrained energy, and the hair on my arms stood on end.

And there, in the center of it all, stood Markan.

He was not at all what I had expected. Rather than the

hulking, physically imposing crime lord I had envisioned, the man before us looked more like a gentleman scientist from Earth's Victorian era. Beneath a tan apron heavily stained and scorched from his work, he wore a finely tailored suit of deep purple brocade. A pair of thick goggles sat perched atop his head, holding back pale hair threaded with silver at the temples.

He glanced up as we entered, his eyes twin chips of ice in a craggy, aristocratic face. Those eyes widened as they settled on Lavona.

"Rena," he breathed, setting aside the circuit board he had been soldering. "Is it really you?"

I held my breath, fearing Lavona would break character to kill the man who had started Viconia's civil war. Or that Markan would take one look at her and know she was an imposter.

"It's me, father," Lavona replied, disgust tinging her presentation of Rena's voice as she held up her shackled hands. "I'm not here by choice."

He stared at her as if trying to discern truth from fiction before his eyes shifted to Ben. "I don't believe I've ever heard of the Stinking Badgers before. Or of you, Murdock."

His statement did nothing to ease the sense that we were in over our heads. We had walked willingly into the lion's den without fully understanding the beast's nature. How much did we truly know about Markan and his operation? What secrets lurked behind his cold, calculating eyes?

"Do you know every bounty hunter and mercenary outfit in the galaxy?" Ben replied almost combatively.

I cringed at his tone, but Markan seemed to appreciate it. "Obviously, that would be difficult. I have much greater concerns than keeping track of scum, lowlives, and miscreants."

I noticed how Ben's jaw clenched in response to the

insult. He wanted to snap back, but he managed to keep his composure. "Well, this lowlife captured your daughter and got through your defenses to bring her back to you. She's yours. All I want is compensation for my trouble."

"Yes, of course. And I did offer a reward for her return." His gaze shifted back to Lavona. "But you seem to have misread the terms of the bounty. She was supposed to come back to Gargan in a casket."

"What?" Lavona hissed, leading the chain reaction of surprise that swept across the three of us. "How could you?"

"What did you expect?" Markan asked. "Not only did you rebuke me, you stole from me. And you thought I would just let you walk away? You claim to know so much about me, dear. Why would you ever believe I would let you get away with that?" He didn't wait for her to answer, shifting his attention back to Ben. "If you want your reward, you'll need to kill her." He crossed his arms over his chest. "I'll wait."

Ben and I shared a glance. Neither of us knew what card to play next, which quickly became painfully obvious to Markan, and to Lavona. Rather than waste more time, she took matters into her own hands.

The restraints were rigged to release with the lightest effort, allowing her to break them easily. She lunged over the debris on the floor between herself and Markan, clearing it with ease while he remained fixed in place, taken by surprise.

Or so we thought.

At the last moment, his hand raised, a soft glow emanating from one of the rings adorning each of his fingers. Lavona suddenly reversed course, thrown back across the workshop where she landed roughly on her back just before us.

"He's got—" I started.

"Sigiltech," Ben finished, fear audible in his voice, even as I could sense him pulling in chaos energy of his own.

Markan lowered his hand, surprisingly unperturbed by the attempted assault. Ben stayed his hand, not ready to reveal his secret yet.

"I could have killed you," Markan said, eyes on Lavona. "Whoever you really are. With little more than a word and a thought to do the deed. But, in case you haven't guessed, I'm a curious sort. I can't abide situations I don't understand and didn't see coming. Answers are more valuable than retribution." His gaze shifted to Ben again. "So tell me. Who are you really?"

"I think you already know," Ben answered.

"I have my suspicions." He removed the goggles from his head and placed them on the nearest workbench, running his fingers through his hair so that it cascaded down around his face. "But don't worry. Your assassin did an excellent job of playing my daughter. Even her disdainful tone was right on the mark. Where you went wrong was in making the assumption that I wouldn't know that she's the very same assassin Asher sent to kill my daughter." He pointed at me. "As is he."

"How?" I replied softly.

"My influence is everywhere," he replied. "Even among a tightly knit crew on a starship like Head Case."

"Twama," Ben immediately surmised.

"Military make the best spies," Markan replied. "They're presumed to be loyal. To her credit, she is. Mostly. The trick is to request the right information, with the proper reward."

"So you know why we're here?" I asked.

"The Warden sent you to kill me." He sighed, shaking his head. "He'll never learn."

"What do you mean?"

"Do you think you're the first of his players to be

assigned this task? What makes you special and the only reason you're still alive is that you're the first to reach me. The first to participate in this parlay. I know some of it was dumb luck. You were in the right place at the right time to pick up Rena and have her direct you here. But there's a measure of luck in everything, isn't there? Some of the greatest inventions of all time, from any part of the universe, happened by accident." His gaze flitted back to Lavona. "You can drop the disguise if you'd like, Lavona."

She deactivated the holomask, pulling it off her head. "You destroyed my home," she growled.

"Nonsense. Unlike the Warden, I don't fancy myself a god. I can only do business where there is business to be done. If Viconia's house had already been in order, I couldn't have gotten a foot in the door."

"Even if the idea existed, you enabled it," Lavona countered.

"Yes, I suppose I'm guilty of that," Markan replied with a shrug. "What can I say? I couldn't pass up such a profitable opportunity."

Lavona didn't react well to the comment. She shot back to her feet, lunging at him a second time. Again, he used his Sigiltech ring to send her crashing into the door behind us. She grunted when the air left her lungs and collapsed to her hands and knees.

"Lava!" I rushed over to help her, but fuming under her breath, she brushed my hand away.

"That's two," Markan said calmly. "The next attempt you make to kill me will be your last. I promise you."

"He wouldn't be so cocky if Ally were here," I whispered as she regained her feet. All I needed was a chance to call her. It would look suspicious, but she could get the job done like she did with Zariv.

"How are you doing that?" Ben asked Markan.

"I've been told you're familiar with chaos energy,"

Markan replied. "You needn't play the dumb mercenary with me."

"I mean, how are you using it so easily? It's barely present here."

"Not true. There's as much chaos energy in Warexia as there is anywhere else. If you understand the nature of the energy, then you should know that."

"What I know is that I can barely access it," Ben admitted, guessing his secret wasn't so secret after all.

"And why do you think that is?"

"I assume it has something to do with the Warden."

"It has *everything* to do with the Warden."

"How?"

"If you think of chaos energy as a basic natural resource rather than some weird cosmic power, then it all makes much more sense."

"Fuel, then?"

Markan nodded. "The Warden is absorbing nearly all the chaos energy available to be siphoned into Warexia. Which leaves you with nothing but scraps."

"But not you," Ben replied. "You've devised a workaround?"

Markan shook his head. "Regrettably, no. Ironically enough, I can only access chaos energy because of the Warden."

"You're not from Warexia," I said, the realization slapping me in the face. "You were one of the Warden's pawns once, too."

"Yes," Markan admitted. "My original home was—"

"The Manticore Spiral," Ben finished for him.

"You know it?"

"I live there. Part-time, anyway. How did you end up here?"

"The same way you did, I imagine. I was a Gilded on a Sigilship during the war. I opened a rift to bring my fleet through. But something went wrong after entering. My ship came out of the rift in Warexia. The rest of my fleet never made it out at all."

"The war was over a thousand years ago," Ben said. " You've been here that long?"

"I have. I'm sure you know some of the benefits of Sigiltech, especially concerning longevity. Not that there haven't been plenty of times I considered letting myself die. But I can't bring myself to do it. Not as long as the Warden remains."

"What happened?" I asked. "Between you and the Warden, I mean."

"You're familiar with the beginning. I had only started to get my bearings when a Wardenship approached and scanned us. Being a Gilded on a warship, I was subject to orders from the captain, who bade me to fight back. You can imagine how that went since I had little access to chaos energy. The Warden's pralls subdued the crew, and he boarded. Only he didn't want to talk to the captain. He wanted me. He seemed to know I was different. When the captain complained, the Warden killed him and placed me in charge. He told us we had to entertain him and sent us on our way. Of course, my immediate goal was to return to the Spiral."

"And the Warden started giving you tasks that made it harder for you to achieve that goal," I said.

"Impossible to achieve that goal. We spent the next ten years running errands for the Warden, the crew slowly accruing boons and benefits for our troubles. Finally, it was my turn. I don't believe the Warden controls the boons. My theory is that the nanites, once activated to grant the boon, seize on the most powerful subconscious thought within the psyche. In other words, the thing we want the most. There's no telling how that desire will translate to the machines."

I thought of Tyler and his rocket fist. Was that really what he wanted the most? In a way, it was. A weapon he could use to defend the people he cared about, the way he couldn't defend his brother. Something that wasn't a gun because he didn't like them. And Ally? A way to kill someone with a thought. It seemed such a singular, powerful desire. The kind of thing generally directed at someone in particular. I wondered who and why. There was something darker in her history that she had chosen not to share with us. Ben's boon was obvious. He didn't want cancer to kill him.

I didn't know what a Gilded was, but I could guess. And of course, what Markan wanted most of all was his power back.

"If you had your abilities back, why didn't you leave?" Ben asked.

Markan glanced at the machine with the pulsing blue light before answering. "Don't you think I tried? Every rift I opened led to another place in Warexia. No matter what I did, I couldn't escape, until one day I no longer wanted to. By then, I'd started building my empire. My network. My new family. I also began studying every field of science in this galaxy, all with one goal in mind."

"To kill the Warden," Ben said.

"Not exactly. I don't care if the Warden lives or dies. No, my goal is to render him impotent. Unimportant. Forgotten. To render him irrelevant." He crossed his workshop to a row of shelves and lifted a small device. "Do you know what this is?"

"A P.K.E. meter?" I guessed. Tee would have been proud.

"Freedom," Markan replied. "From the Warden, at least. It will disable the comms array in the nanite pill he made you swallow. Without the ability to communicate with the nanites, he can't make you do anything you don't want to do. He can't hurt you."

A wave of excitement crashed over me, quickly flattened by Ben's next comment.

"And you'll use it on us with no strings attached, out of the goodness of your heart, I'm sure," Ben said. In the face of being rid of the Warden, I had quickly forgotten that Markan was as much a monster as the Warden, if not worse. Thankfully, Ben hadn't forgotten.

"Of course, there's a price to be paid for everything. Freedom isn't free, after all."

"And what's this freedom going to cost us?"

"First, I know you have Rena on board your ship. I want her back."

"So you can kill her?" Lavona snarled.

"Yes," Markan answered flatly. "That equation hasn't changed because of this conversation. Secondly, I want you to work for me instead of the Warden. I know that you know where to find a Wardenship. You can imagine my interest in bringing it back here to reverse engineer."

"I don't think your wormhole gates are big enough for that," I said.

"I can open rifts, remember?" Markan replied.

"Let's say you succeed in your goals," Ben said. "You incapacitate the Warden. You become the preeminent being in Warexia. Then what?"

"Then nothing. Business as usual, without interference."

"All that trouble and ingenuity just to continue being a crime lord?" Lavona asked. "How sad."

Markan's hands clenched into fists, eyes burning into Lavona. For a moment, I thought he might throw her across the room again, this time with enough force to ensure she wouldn't get up. "Warexia is too large to rule directly. It requires a more subtle touch to steer. Besides, I'm content with where I am."

"What happened to you?" I asked, "to make you such a cold-hearted monster?"

"The war happened to me," he answered. "And then the Warden. This is what my life has made me. Power is always what I've most desired." He shrugged. "I am what I am. The question is, what do you want to be? Servant to a mad god or part of something greater?"

"Greater?" Lavona hissed. "You call this greater? Captain, you can't seriously consider this offer."

"And if we refuse?" Ben asked. "What happens to us? It isn't a choice if we can't say no."

"I'll allow you to leave. But you will return my daughter to me first. After all, that was the pretense by which you were permitted to land."

Ben nodded, looking at me and then Lavona. "There is something appealing about getting the Warden out of our lives."

"There is," I agreed, picking up on his tone.

"You...you can't," Lavona said. "I trusted you."

Ben's gaze flicked from us to Markan and back. "I'm sorry, Lava. I can probably only give you a few seconds."

He whirled back toward Markan, hands glowing.

Decision made.

# CHAPTER 44

Whatever Markan tried to do next didn't work. Instead of the rings on his fingers glowing, his body emanated light from beneath his shirt. His mouth moved to utter a cantrip, and his expression twisted with frustrated surprise when he didn't get the effect he was going for.

Just like that, he was out of time.

Lavona barreled into Markan at full force, sending them both crashing into a pile of electronics.

"Cover his mouth!" Ben shouted just before his glow faded, and he collapsed to his knees, exhausted by the effort of countering Markan's power. "Noah, get help."

Blinking, I broke out of the surprised stupor Ben and Lavona's sudden actions engulfed me. Realizing what I needed to do right away, I put my phone hand to my ear and thought of every member of Head Case's crew who had the Warden's pill. "Help!" I cried out, not waiting for a response before lowering my hand to draw my blaster.

"Katzuo!" Lavona shouted. I looked her way in time to see the nanite disabler flying toward me, ripped out of Markan's hand. "Run!"

Never good at sports, especially baseball, the disabler bounced off my hand as I tried to catch it, clattering to the metal decking. Before I could move, the twin doors behind me ground open, and Izzak squeezed through the increasing gap. Behind him in the outer room, I could see that all hell had broken loose. Our two groups were attacking one another while the unaffiliated petitioners dove to the deck, hands over their heads, to avoid getting hit by the crisscrossing plasma bolts.

Lavona cried out, losing her grip on Markan's mouth, allowing him to use Sigiltech. Before he could throw her aside, she managed to sink her claws into his shoulder. They tumbled halfway across the workshop, slamming into a jutting rack of shelves before crashing to the deck and out of my sight behind a table stacked with machine parts.

I dove for the disabler, closing my fingers around it just as Izzak lunged for me. I barely managed to twist away before his claws could rake across my back. Gritting my teeth, I refused to relinquish our only hope for freedom from the Warden.

"Noah!" Ben shouted. He slammed into Izzak from the side, sending them both crashing into a workbench. Metal parts and circuitry flew in every direction. I staggered to my feet, shoving the disabler in my pocket as Archie climbed from his hiding place.

"Go!" Ben ordered, grappling with Izzak. "Get out of here!"

Before I could do anything, Archie leaped from my shoulder, its shape changing to a tiny maulvas as it landed beside the scuffling Ben and Izzak. Held in Izzak's head-lock, Ben's flailing legs nearly took Archie out before it could leap over them and lock its jaws on Izzak's throat. The reptilian screamed as he released Ben and reached to pull Archie off his already bloody throat.  Archie's flanks grew tendrils that stabbed through Izzak's mouth and eyes, sinking into his skull.

"Noah, go!" Ben shouted, pointing toward the door to the waiting room where the Stinking Badgers were fully engaged with Izzak's goons.

I bolted through the door, emerging in a chaos of armored bodies and flashing weapons, Ben right behind me. Tyler's rocket fist shot past us, slamming into a hulking brute and sending him flying. Ally called out her kill shot, dropping one of the mercs just five feet in front of me. Above it all, Ixy had taken to the overhead. Dropping her web line on a surprised merc, she pulled him up, deftly slicing through his armor with the powerful, sharp edge of a pedipalp. Shaq threw himself from Matt's shoulder, gliding across the room like a flying squirrel and landing on another guard. Scrambling down the goon's arm, he sank his teeth through the soft part of the brute's glove, venom instantly dropping the guard thirty times his size.

Ben bolted past me, disappearing into the melee just as a crash behind me jerked my attention back to Lavona. Still grappling with Markan, she struggled to hold him in the grasp of one clawed hand while shoving her other fist into his mouth to silence his use of Sigiltech.

"Lava!" I shouted, anguished. I couldn't just leave her.

"Run, you idiot!" she screamed back.

"Noah!" Matt called out, instantly pulling my attention back to the brawl in the outer sanctum. "Where's Lavona?"

"Still inside!" I replied, ducking a wild swing from one of Izzak's guards. I lashed out with an opportunistic kick, catching him in the knee. He stumbled and I followed up with a solid right cross to the chin that sent him crashing to the floor, down for the count.

A triumphant whoop from Tyler snapped my attention around. He, Matt, and Ally had finished off the last of the guards, standing among prone bodies and smashed furniture remnants.

"Hell yeah!" Tyler cried. "That's how we do it on Earth!"

"We can celebrate later," Ben growled, emerging from the melee. "We need to get out of here!"

"Wait!" I cried, heart in my throat. "We can't leave Lavona!"

I whirled back toward the doors just as Larev barreled past me and through the door closing on Markan's inner sanctum. with no regard for what awaited him on the other side.

"Damn it!" I swore. He was a bigger man than me in more ways than one. For a taut second before the door slid shut, I could only listen to the renewed sounds of struggle from within Markan's workshop.

"Ixy, get the elevator," Ben shouted.

"Yesss," she replied, scuttling along the ceiling and dropping down, wedging multiple appendages into the cab doors to force them apart.

"Let's go!" Matt roared.

I stood my ground. "Archie's still in there, and what about Lavona and Larev?"

"They made their choice to save our lives. Let's not waste it."

Before any of us could move, the door cracked open again. I tensed, bracing for Markan to come charging through, death raging in his eyes. Instead, Lavona, bloodied and barely conscious, lurched out and tumbled hard to the deck at my feet.

"Lava!" I started forward, but she held up a trembling hand to forestall me.

Braced on her hands, she looked up at me. "I said run, you idiot!" she managed through gritted teeth.

"I will," I replied, refusing to make the same mistake a

second time. I scooped her up into a fireman's carry, just as Archie slipped through the finishing last crack in the closing door before regaining its maulvas shape. "Now we can run."

"The elevator!" Ben shouted.

Tyler and Ally were already inside, frantically stabbing at the controls to close the doors. Matt waited just outside, throwing us in and squeezing in just before a deep, teeth-rattling boom shook the entire station. The sounds of tearing metal and popping rivets echoed around us as the elevator lights flickered and dimmed.

"What the hell was that?" Tyler asked, real fear in his voice.

He had barely finished speaking before a brilliant blue flame erupted outside the lift, engulfing the entire forward section of the robot's head in an apocalyptic fireball. In the split second before the doors finished closing, I caught a glimpse of the corridor collapsing, the bulkheads crumpling like tin foil.

"Geez, how did Larev do that?" Tyler asked.

"He didn't," Ben replied. "Markan did. He's not from here. Like us, he came through a rift, only he arrived a thousand years ago. He's a Gilded."

"What's a Gilded?" Ally asked.

"He has sigils carved into his flesh," Ben answered. "They're filled with a special metal that allows him to channel chaos energy through them."

"Like wizard tattoos?" Tee said. "That's so cool."

"Not when he's pissed at you, it isn't," Matt said.

"Why? Looks like he just blew himself up."

"No," Ben replied. "With the right sigils, he can survive an explosion and a vacuum. He was trying to catch us in the blast. Kill us all."

"Hah! He missed!"

The elevator reached the bottom level, and the doors

rolled open to a scene of barely controlled chaos. Klaxons blared as panicked crew members and civilians alike rushed in every direction. Meanwhile, Gargan's security forces charged toward us, opening fire the moment we came into view.

Matt took the brunt off his combat armor, the hard shell absorbing plenty of the firepower as he stepped out into the corridor, shooting back. Ixy followed behind him, quickly leaping and rolling over to clutch the overhead. She scrambled along it in a zig-zag pattern as confused and frightened guards tried to shoot her. Ally and Tee joined the fracas, firing back with Matt. Two guards went down before Ixy reached the others. Dropping into the middle of them, her appendages lashing out, she stabbed the sharp-clawed ends through the hard armor of three guards, pinning them against the bulkheads.

"Kill shot!" Ally cried, firing a single energy blast that angled perfectly through the last guard's helmet and into his skull. I glanced at her in time to see her face wrinkle with regret, but she recovered quickly.

"Cade," Ben called over the RFD as we raced through the passageways, retracing our steps back to the hangar bay. "Prep Head Case. We're coming in hot."

"Aye, Captain," Cade replied.

Reaching the corner, another unit of guards opened fire, peppering Matt and Tee with gunfire. They returned the assault while Shaq joined Ixy in rushing the group. Ixy kicked one of the guards into the bulkhead and webbed another beside him, leaving them for Shaq to climb onto and bite. Archie joined the melee, growling as it lunged at another guard, shapeshifting into its basic form in time to stab through the man's helmet and into his skull.

"Damn, they're good!" Tee said in admiration of our most alien crew members.

"This way!" Matt ordered, not slowing down. We

continued through the corridors, encountering two more units of guards along the way and dispatching them without breaking stride. Finally, the hangar loomed ahead, hopefully the last unit of guards we would need to dispatch trying to block our path.

Still a decent distance away, Matt opened fire, sending the first wave of guards diving for cover. The rest of us followed his lead, blasters spitting energy as we plunged into the fray.

The guards went down quickly, no match for our motley gang. The hangar doors opened ahead of us, revealing confused starship crews scrambling to evacuate the station while guards took up covered positions around the cavernous expanse.

"Get to Head Case!" Ben cried as an eruption of gunfire blasted in from all directions around us, one just missing Lavona's arm. Another clipped my shoulder, but I barely felt it through the surge of adrenaline.

"Almost there!" Tyler shouted, risking his life to save ours as he fell back to let his armor absorb the bolts and blasts coming at me and Lavona.

Before I knew it, Head Case's welcome bulk loomed before us, the ramp already lowering, Matt and Ally crouching at its base. I heard Ally's "kill shot" repeatedly, imagining another guard falling with each recitation.

They both filed in behind me as I carried Lavona up the ramp. "Ixy, take her to sick bay."

"Yesss," Ixy agreed, gently lifting her from my arms once I reached the hangar. The outer door was already closing. Matt shifted away from it as it clanged shut, the shields absorbing the guards' assault.

"She's still alive, isn't she?" I asked Ixy, voice trembling.

Ixy put a pedipalp to her neck to feel for a pulse. "Yesss."

Relief flooded through me, but only for a moment.

"Cade, get us out of here!" Ben ordered.

"Hold on tight!" Cade replied. Head Case lurched under my feet, nearly knocking me over before I remembered to activate my maglocks.

"Matt, Noah, you need to get up to the flight deck to help."

"Where are you going?" I asked.

"Sigibellum. I have a feeling Markan isn't done with us yet."

We hurried to the elevator with Shaq, Archie, and Ixy, crowding inside and taking it up to Two. Ixy carried Lavona out, and I hoped it wouldn't be the last time I saw her alive.

We exited on Four, sprinting to the flight deck. Cade had already guided Head Case out of the hangar and away from the station, rocketing toward the sea of asteroids. I quickly replaced Leo in the co-pilot seat, while Matt exchanged places with Cade.

My eyes snapped first to the rearview, getting a look at the wrecked mess that remained of Gargan's head. Instinct told me there was no way Markan could have survived the destruction he'd caused, but I knew he wouldn't have killed himself in the blast.

Which meant he was out here, somewhere, coming after us. With all the asteroids overwhelming the sensors, I wasn't sure if we could find him before it was too late.

Not that we needed to find him. All we had to do was get back out through the asteroid sphere, back to the wormhole, back through the wormhole station, and out into Warexian space—far, far away from here.

Easy peasy.

Head Case shot toward the asteroids at a reckless clip. I grabbed the stick, activating fire control and searching for targets. A quick visual showed none of the ships in the station were giving chase. If Gargan had gun batteries, they remained silent.

"Thirty seconds to the asteroids," Matt announced, eyes locked on his surround.

I kept my gaze pinned to the rear view, surprised by the lack of...my eyes narrowed as a shadow passed behind the station. Quickly zooming in, my blood ran cold, my hands suddenly shaking against the controls. "Matt," I squeaked. "We have company."

Reacting to my frightened tone, he quickly pulled up the same view on his surround.

"Ben," he said, activating his comms. "Markan has a sigilship."

"Yeah, he told us he did," Ben replied.

"It… it's glowing," I sputtered, staring at the huge, sleek, warship as it cleared the station and turned our way. Its entire hull was lit in an eerie red glow that emanated from extensive etchings along the hull.

I was so busy looking at it, I almost didn't notice the asteroids in our path suddenly  slamming into one another in rapid succession to create an impossible-to-breach wall.

"Matt!" I cried, returning his attention to what was in front of us.

He cursed as he quickly changed our vector, the G-force shoving me sideways in my seat. We shot horizontally along the sphere's edge, searching for a way out. The asteroids continued shifting, crashing into one another to create an impenetrable barrier, penning us in so that there was no escape.

"He's toying with us," Matt growled. "Bastard. How does he have access to chaos energy and we don't?"

"It's a long story," Ben replied. "I'll tell it to you if we don't die."

"Damn. I would have liked to have heard it."

They both laughed. I couldn't imagine how they found any of this amusing. "What do we do?" I asked.

"The only thing we can do," Matt replied. "Turn and fight."

"What?" I cried.

"Here we go," Matt announced, bringing Head Case around until we were facing directly toward the sigilship's bow.

"This is crazy," I said.

"Just handle the guns," Matt replied. He pushed the throttle open, sending us toward Markan's ship at increasing velocity.

Drawing closer, I noticed the front of the sigilship glowing a brighter, more intense crimson, like the Death Star preparing to fire.

"That can't be good," I said.

"No," Matt agreed.

"So why are we flying straight toward it?"

Matt didn't answer. The glow continued to intensify. We charged headlong directly at it. With a massive belch, the sigilship released its collected energy, sending it at us in a giant gout of celestial flame.

"Ben!" Matt cried.

The universe tore open in front of us, spacetime pulling apart with the power of chaos energy. The sigilship's fire spewed toward us, while we raced to make it into the rift before it arrived.

"It's going to be close," Matt muttered, face as tense as I had ever seen.

The edge of the star fire licked around the rift, beating us there. It slammed into the shields, flaring a blinding blue while struggling to absorb the intense energy. Head Case shuddered and shook. Sparks flew. Warning tones blared.

And then…
Silence.

————

Thank you for continuing Starship For Rent! For more information on the next book in the series, please visit mrforbes.com/starshipforrent4

# OTHER BOOKS BY M.R FORBES

**Want more M.R. Forbes? Of course you do!**
**View my complete catalog here**
mrforbes.com/books
Or on Amazon:
mrforbes.com/amazon

**Starship For Sale (Starship For Sale)**
mrforbes.com/starshipforsale

**When Ben Murdock receives a text message offering a fully operational starship for sale, he's certain it has to be a joke.**

Already trapped in the worst day of his life and desperate for a way out, he decides to play along. Except there is no joke. The starship is real. And Ben's life is going to change in ways he never dreamed possible.

**All he has to do is sign the contract.**

Joined by his streetwise best friend and a bizarre tenant with an unseverable lease, he'll soon discover that the universe is more volatile, treacherous, and awesome than he ever imagined.

**And the only thing harder than owning a starship is staying alive.**

### Forgotten (The Forgotten)
mrforbes.com/theforgotten
Complete series box set:
mrforbes.com/theforgottentrilogy

**Some things are better off FORGOTTEN.**

Sheriff Hayden Duke was born on the Pilgrim, and he expects to die on the Pilgrim, like his father, and his father before him.

That's the way things are on a generation starship centuries from home. He's never questioned it. Never thought about it. And why bother? Access points to the ship's controls are sealed, the systems that guide her automated and out of reach. It isn't perfect, but he has all he needs to be content.

Until a malfunction forces his wife to the edge of the habitable zone to inspect the damage.

Until she contacts him, breathless and terrified, to tell him she found a body, and it doesn't belong to anyone on board.

Until he arrives at the scene and discovers both his wife and the body are gone.

The only clue? A bloody handprint beneath a hatch that hasn't opened in hundreds of years.

Until now.

### Deliverance (Forgotten Colony)
mrforbes.com/deliverance
Complete series box set:

**The war is over. Earth is lost. Running is the only option.**

It may already be too late.

OTHER BOOKS BY M.R FORBES   **337**

Caleb is a former Marine Raider and commander of the Vultures, a search and rescue team that's spent the last two years pulling high-value targets out of alien-ravaged cities and shipping them off-world.

When his new orders call for him to join forty-thousand survivors aboard the last starship out, he thinks his days of fighting are over. The Deliverance represents a fresh start and a chance to leave the war behind for good.

Except the war won't be as easy to escape as he thought.

And the colony will need a man like Caleb more than he ever imagined...

### Man of War (Rebellion)
mrforbes.com / manofwar
Complete series box set:
mrforbes.com / rebellion-web

In the year 2280, an alien fleet attacked the Earth.

Their weapons were unstoppable, their defenses unbreakable.

Our technology was inferior, our militaries overwhelmed.

Only one starship escaped before civilization fell.

Earth was lost.

It was never forgotten.

Fifty-two years have passed.

A message from home has been received.

The time to fight for what is ours has come.

Welcome to the rebellion.

### Hell's Rejects (Chaos of the Covenant)
mrforbes.com / hellsrejects

The most powerful starships ever constructed are gone. Thousands are dead. A fleet is in ruins. The attackers are unknown. The orders are clear: *Recover the ships. Bury the bastards who stole them.*

Lieutenant Abigail Cage never expected to find herself in Hell. As a Highly Specialized Operational Combatant, she was one of the most respected Marines in the military. Now she's doing hard labor on the most miserable planet in the universe.

Not for long.

The Earth Republic is looking for the most dangerous individuals it can control. The best of the worst, and Abbey happens to be one of them. The deal is simple: *Bring back the starships, earn your freedom. Try to run, you die.* It's a suicide mission, but she has nothing to lose.

The only problem? There's a new threat in the galaxy. One with a power unlike anything anyone has ever seen. One that's been waiting for this moment for a very, very, long time. And they want Abbey, too.

Be careful what you wish for.

They say Hell hath no fury like a woman scorned. They have no idea.

# ABOUT THE AUTHOR

M.R. Forbes is the mind behind a growing number of Amazon best-selling science fiction series. Having spent his childhood trying to read every sci-fi novel he could find (and write his own too), play every sci-fi video game he could get his hands on, and see every sci-fi movie that made it into the theater, he has a true love of the genre across every medium. He works hard to bring that same energy to his own stories, with a continuing goal to entertain, delight, fascinate, and surprise.

He maintains a true appreciation for his readers and is always happy to hear from them.

To learn more about me or just say hello:

Visit my website:
mrforbes.com

Send me an e-mail:
michael@mrforbes.com

Check out my Facebook page:
facebook.com/mrforbes.author

Join my Facebook fan group:
facebook.com/groups/mrforbes

Follow me on Instagram:

instagram.com/mrforbes_author

Find me on Goodreads:
goodreads.com/mrforbes

Follow me on Bookbub:
bookbub.com/authors/m-r-forbes